"YOU MAY HAVE GONE TOO FAR," BRIGADIER GENERAL CLAYTON SAID

"What we don't need more of in Washington is investigations."

Senator Lawton leaned forward in his chair. "Call me paranoid, but I feel we should call off tomorrow's operation."

"That's absurd!" Admiral Addison shouted.

"I agree with Addison," Commander Sontag said. "Do you realize the months of planning that's gone into this operation? All we have to do is say the words 'kill one' into that telephone, then there'll be no further contact with our operatives. Even we couldn't stop it then."

"But the danger—" the senator said.

"The danger will be more imminent if we delay," Addison cut in. "If D-day goes ahead as scheduled, can't you imagine the chaos the country's going to be thrown into tomorrow? The entire world the day after?"

Senator Lawton, paling, gulped at his drink. Half a dozen military minds gone mad, he thought. He had meant it to be a political game. Now he was facing D-day and he was terrified. "We still must vote," he mumbled.

Admiral Addison smiled down at the senator. "And after we've voted, we'll place the 'kill one' call."

CONSPIRACY

PARLEY COOPER
CONSPIRACY

WORLDWIDE ®

TORONTO • NEW YORK • LONDON • PARIS
AMSTERDAM • STOCKHOLM • HAMBURG
ATHENS • MILAN • TOKYO • SYDNEY

To Alex Nebrensky, without whom
this book would not have been written;
and to Dr. Robert T. Webb, a friend who
fights the gallant battle

CONSPIRACY

A Worldwide Library Book/November 1988

ISBN 0-373-97088-9

CONSPIRACY

PROLOGUE

The Indian Ocean

CHAD BANNEN KNEW he was going to die.

They had chosen him as one of their elite. He had betrayed them and now, at twenty-three fucking years young, he was going to die.

He had rammed his fingers down his throat and puked on the deck, but the deadly dose Marshisky and Everett, his comrades until yesterday, had forced into him had already begun to take effect. He did not know what poison they were using to eliminate him, only that it was clear and tasted as sweet as molasses and was now burning the bejesus out of his insides as it surged into his bloodstream. Sudden stomach cramps caused him to double over, not that he could have stood straight anyway with the wind, saltwater and rain flattening him against the bulkhead.

Below decks, Marshisky and Everett were still searching for him. He had broken Everett's nose, shattering the bone and mashing the flesh to a bloody pulp. That gave him some slight satisfaction. Until yesterday he and Everett had been as close to being friends as was allowed by the military cabal controlling their lives. Damn Delta! Damn them all straight into hell!

For one brief moment he imagined himself beating the odds, surviving the poison and evading Marshisky and Everett. The thought of revenge tasted as sweet as the poison, but the fantasy was fleeting. Even if he reached a medic, how could he be given an antidote to the poison when he didn't know what it was? Marshisky and Everett had been trained to just as high a degree of efficiency as he himself had. They belonged to Delta's elite corps of assassins. He had been as good as dead the moment the order had been given to eliminate him.

Struggling against his pain, he edged his way along the bulkhead toward the denser darkness of the flight deck. He was determined to hide from them before unconsciousness overcame him; if he could conceal himself well enough, die alone, then his body wouldn't be discovered until tomorrow, would not be flung overboard into the stormy sea. He didn't want to be reported as another sailor lost at sea. That was all he could do to Delta in retaliation—embarrass them, raise momentary suspicions and pray that someone would investigate. It was not enough, but it was all he could manage.

The aircraft carrier USS *Alum Rock* was cruising somewhere in the Indian Ocean. The storm had hit them unexpectedly yesterday at sunset and was now at its peak. The metal groaned beneath Chad's feet; an occasional wave reached the deck, and the cold spray came at him out of the watery darkness. He was drenched and shivering, but more from the effects of the poison than from the cold.

Soon, he thought, all sensation would be extinguished. Dead at twenty-three, before he really knew what life was all about. He forced away the morbid thoughts, telling himself that self-pity was a luxury he couldn't allow himself if he was to succeed in hiding himself. Crouching, he crept along the bulkhead, grateful for the storm because it meant the sailors standing guard duty would be less likely to spot him. One sailor, maybe two, could be bribed or disposed of by Marshisky and Everett; in a severe storm, two or three sailors missing and presumed lost at sea would be readily accepted by those back home.

Chad stopped short as a flash of lightning revealed a dark figure moving in his direction. The surge of adrenaline increased his pain, shortening the time before he succumbed to the poison. His breath caught in his throat as the darkness closed around him again. He waited to be challenged, to be asked for his identity. If he was, he'd be unable to overcome the duty guard because of his waning strength.

Just then his outstretched fingers felt a sudden angling of the bulkhead. He lunged forward, unable to identify the space, but wedging his body into it anyway. A flashlight had been switched on, its beam thrown along the aft deck. Chad lowered his head against his chest so the light's glow would meet his dark hair and not his pale face. Unless the beam fell on him directly, it was unlikely he would be seen. He listened as the guard's footsteps approached, then began to fade. He let his breath out, then almost collapsed from the pain that stabbed at his abdomen and groin.

His head snapped up then as a sudden commotion made him forget his agony. His gaze was drawn aft as Marshisky and Everett bolted onto the deck and were caught in the beam of the guard's flashlight. He also recognized the sailor on duty as Seaman Ferguson, a farmer's son from Nebraska who suffered from a speech impediment and was easily conned by his shipmates into standing their watches.

"H-halt! Who goes th-there?" Ferguson shouted.

"Shit, Fergie, it's us!" Marshisky shouted back. "Get that goddamned light out of our faces!" The full beam of the flashlight was obediently lowered to their legs. "We're lookin' for Bannen. You seen the crazy bastard?"

"N-n-not seen anyone s-s-since I came on duty," Ferguson stammered. "Wh-what happened t-to you?" His question was directed at Everett, whose face must have resembled raw hamburger.

"Bannen did that!" Marshisky yelled. "The stupid prick took drugs and went wacko!" So they were already laying the groundwork, Chad thought. "We're tryin' to find the bastard before he hurts himself."

"W-well, he ain't b-back there," Ferguson said with authority. He turned and aimed the beam of the flashlight behind him, causing Chad to press even deeper into the recess in the bulkhead. "Y-you'd best s-see a corpsman," he told Everett. "You're b-bleedin' b-bad!"

Marshisky spoke again, but his words were lost in the howling of the wind.

When Chad dared to stick his head out again he saw the trio disappearing into the watery darkness. Gathering his strength through sheer determination, he pushed himself out onto the deck and half walked, half dragged himself toward the flight deck.

He had passed the shadowy forms of several aircraft when the worst spasm of pain yet brought him, gasping, to his knees. He vomited again, this time involuntarily. The vile taste remained in his mouth long after his stomach had been emptied onto the deck. His vision was blurring, and his heart was pounding so rapidly it threatened to tear through his rib cage. His head felt as if a pickax had been driven into the base of his skull. A cry of agony tore up through his throat, but the sound was immediately gobbled up by the wind and rain, and he had no fear of having been heard.

He clutched at the wheel of the nearest aircraft and pulled himself to his feet. Chad had always been proud of his body, six foot three and 185 pounds of sinew and muscle, but now his size became a handicap. His first attempt at hoisting himself onto the aircraft's wing failed, and he fell back onto the deck, winded and fighting to retain consciousness. He lay there for several moments, letting the cold rain wash over his face. Then, dragging himself to his feet, he psyched himself for an ordeal that under normal conditions he would have performed with thoughtless ease. He crouched, then heaved his body upward, his fingers clamping tightly against wet metal. Wiggling and twisting, he succeeded in pulling the upper half of his body onto the wing. He wanted to stop, to rest with his legs dangling, but even his diminishing reasoning told him he must not. He continued to struggle until he had gained the cockpit, opened it and crawled inside.

Slumped in the pilot's seat, eyes closed, he sat listening to the rain pounding relentlessly against the aircraft. He had left the hood slightly open, and the wind whistled against his left ear. Controlling his thoughts became difficult; his mind wandered, forming images so quickly that they appeared to have been stamped on the insides of his eyelids.

A little boy, himself, running through the spring fields of the Virginia farm, laughter on his lips and elation in his dark eyes as he ran to greet his parents. His father, tall and handsome and distinguished, wearing his naval uniform with obvious pride; except for a brief encounter at the airport in San Francisco, Chad had not seen his father in five years. How would he take the death of his only son? And his mother, beautiful and elegant, hiding her sensitivity behind a shield of aloofness.

Bile rose in Chad's throat. He coughed and wanted to spit but discovered that his throat muscles were too constricted to respond.

Then another image: Mona, lovely and insatiable with her soft, pliant body and her easy childlike laughter. He had left Mona in San Diego with a promise of marriage when he returned. "I'm not returning, Mona," he murmured thickly now. Mona would have no difficulty finding another sailor. She was not that discriminating; nor was she the type to grieve for long. He wondered if she would at least think of him on occasion. Where had he read that you continued to live as long as you were remembered?

Damn! Damn Delta! Damn Everett and Marshisky! Damn himself, too, for being idealistic in a world that only pretended to admire idealism!

A wavering beam of light appeared at the far edge of the flight deck. Marshisky and Everett had backtracked and were closing in on him. He wedged himself farther down in the cockpit. His long legs were folded up on themselves, and the muscles cried out in angry protest. The light swept closer, touched the cockpit briefly, then moved on. The rain was changing into mist, beading on the outside of the cockpit.

God, Chad thought, the pilot and the ground crew are in for one hell of a surprise in the morning. He tried to imagine the scene, but his thoughts wouldn't focus. Intense pain seized his stomach, drove all else from his mind. Clutching himself as if he could press away the pain, he drove his head back into the seat, and to keep from crying out he bit his lower lip until he tasted blood. The pain began to ebb, then struck again; there was a monster inside him, eating away at his organs.

Only moments now, he knew. Please make them go quickly.

Though I walk through . . . valley of the shadow . . .

His eyes rolled back in his head. His mouth drooped. Yellow spittle oozed from between his parched lips and down his chin.

Petty Officer Second Class Chadwick E. Bannen, U.S. Navy, was dead at age twenty-three.

PART ONE

1

THE TAXI PULLED to the side of the cemetery driveway and braked to a stop. Quinn Bannen climbed out and passed several bills back through the open window to the driver.

Like his late son Chad, Quinn was a tall man, six foot two, with broad shoulders, a narrow waist and a slim but muscular torso. Unlike Chad, he had blond hair, with streaks of gray at the temples that showed silver in the afternoon sunlight. Except for the gray strands and the deepening crow's-feet at the corners of his blue eyes, he had the appearance of a man much younger than his forty-five years. As he moved along the manicured border of lawn, his stride was youthful, determined. His face and hands were deeply tanned from many hours outdoors. He wore no jewelry, not even a wristwatch; when he had retired to his California farm he had sworn his only indicator of time would be the position of the sun in the sky, that he would not live his life ruled by a clock. His dress shoes were new, bought in San Francisco along with the dark suit he wore for the solemn occasion; the soles of the shoes, not yet scuffed enough for adequate traction, slipped threateningly on the wet grass as Quinn left the driveway and made his way among the tombstones toward the crowd already assembled to pay final respects to his son.

Due to an air traffic controllers' strike, his flight from San Francisco had been delayed. Then he had been forced to make an unscheduled stopover in Chicago. He had not only

missed the service at the church but was also late arriving at
the cemetery. Now he picked his way through the mourners
until he stood beside his ex-wife.

He realized with a sudden jolt that it was seven years since
he had last seen Dorothy. He'd always meant to call her, to
arrange to meet with her on one of his trips east, but he
never had. Fear, perhaps. Perhaps resentment, buried so
deep that he refused to recognize it.

Dorothy was dressed entirely in black. Her thick black veil
prevented him from viewing her face, but he sensed her gaze
on him. Her head turned momentarily in his direction, in
acknowledgment of his late arrival, then turned stiffly away.
Her shoulders were held back, and her body was rigid with
determination; no sound of weeping came from beneath her
veil. She clung tightly to her father's arm. Admiral Malcolm Burke, retired, who had taken his uniform and his
chestful of medals out of mothballs, stood with military
bearing, his expression vacant as he stared into space past
the flag-draped casket.

Quinn's gaze swept the faces of those gathered to pay final respects to his son. Two admirals besides Chad's grandfather, a captain, a commander and two commodores;
Quinn hadn't seen so much brass assembled since his retirement from the navy. He forced away the animosity that
threatened to flood over him.

There were half a dozen women present, all wearing
black, all his and Dorothy's age or older. It seemed strange
that there were no young people present, none of his son's
peers. Surely Chad had had friends. The sense of guilt
Quinn had been struggling with since he'd received the news
of his son's death swept over him. He closed his eyes and
brought his hand to his brow as if to smooth away the furrows the rush of guilt had etched there. He hadn't known his
son as a man, not beyond what he'd discerned from his
monthly letters.

Now it was too late.

He realized that, like Admiral Burke, he'd been avoiding looking at Chad's casket. As his gaze settled on the polished wood and brass, an unconscious groan of sorrow escaped his lips. Dorothy glanced at him again. Now there was a noticeable slump to her shoulders, as if his expression of grief had chipped away at her rigid reserve. Her father also turned stiffly to Quinn, his dark eyes cold and unrelenting.

Chad's casket was draped with one large spray of white chrysanthemums; apparently no one had remembered or had bothered to inform the funeral director that Chad had disliked chrysanthemums ever since his paternal grandparents died in an automobile accident and their caskets were similarly draped.

The clergyman was the youngest person present. He mumbled words in a singsong voice. The afternoon breeze kept catching his auburn hair and sweeping it into his eyes; he'd brush it away with veiled annoyance. He'd been reading from an index card in the palm of his hand, but Quinn hadn't been listening. Now the minister switched to the more familiar words of a passage of scripture and his voice took on more authority: "He leadeth me beside the still waters. He maketh me to lie down in green . . ."

Quinn stopped listening.

A rending sob came suddenly from behind Dorothy's veil.

Admiral Burke placed a bracing arm around his daughter's shoulders and spoke to her in whispered tones that didn't reach Quinn. Dorothy immediately straightened and made no further sound.

Quinn stole another glance at his ex-wife. The figure in black could have belonged to the eighteen-year-old girl he had married. He wondered if time and the past seven years had been equally kind to her face. He remembered piercing, deep-set brown eyes, naturally arched eyebrows, high cheekbones and a full, sensuous mouth.

Chad's casket was lowered into the grave, and the minister handed Dorothy the ritual trowel of earth. Her hand trembled as she dropped the earth onto the casket. The hollow sound as it struck the wood made her recoil. Quinn imagined he felt what she was feeling—the finality of their son's death, the loss, the utter waste. Instead of putting the trowel in her father's waiting hand, Dorothy turned and offered it to Quinn. He in turn passed it to the admiral, then abruptly turned from the grave and walked halfway to the drive before altering his quick stride. He took a cigarette from his coat pocket, lit it and stood smoking as he waited for the mourners to leave the graveside.

Dorothy and Admiral Burke headed the silent procession returning to the waiting limousines. When she saw Quinn waiting, she stiffened. The admiral tightened his grip on her arm and tried to force her past Quinn, but she stubbornly held back.

Across the distance that separated them wafted the familiar fragrance of her perfume—Shalimar, he remembered.

The procession of mourners stopped behind Admiral Burke and the grieving mother, curious about this confrontation with the stranger in their path.

Dorothy seemed oblivious to their presence.

"I'd like to talk to you for a moment," Quinn told her quietly.

Dorothy drew back as if she had been anticipating and dreading the request.

"My daughter has nothing to say to you, Quinn Bannen," Admiral Burke said curtly. "Leave us in peace."

"It's about Chad," Quinn said, ignoring him.

Dorothy reached for her father's hand and pried his fingers from her arm. "I'll meet you at the car," she told him.

Admiral Burke opened his mouth to voice an objection, but a glance from his daughter silenced him. Eyes downcast, he strode away toward the waiting limousines, the rest of the mourners at his heels.

Dorothy turned and gazed back toward Chad's grave. "He was very young," she said, more to herself than to Quinn. "He was everything to me. Now he's gone."

Quinn took a step closer to her and touched her arm. "Dorothy, I need to talk to you about—"

Dorothy shook his hand away and looked at him directly. Her veil gave her an advantage, he realized; he could not see the extent of her grief in her eyes, nor could he determine the effect on her of seeing him.

"You were late even for your son's funeral," she said evenly. "You'll never change, Quinn." She sighed and took a step away from him, as if his closeness disturbed her.

"I won't be put on the defensive," Quinn told her, "nor tolerate your tendency to make others feel guilty." His voice was stern. He had not intended to be abrupt with her, but if necessary he would even be cruel. "There are some questions I need to ask about Chad," he said. "About his death."

He fought the urge to reach out and draw the black veil away from her face. He knew the admiral was standing beside the limousine, watching them. If the old man witnessed the slightest adverse reaction from his daughter he would terminate the interview. Contacting her again would be difficult for Quinn, just as it had when he had tried to contact her seven years ago, after her attorney had notified him about the divorce.

Tread carefully, he warned himself.

"Of course you saw Chad's death certificate and the navy's autopsy report," he said. It was both a statement and a question.

Her answer was a stiff affirmative nod.

"The cause of death is listed as a drug overdose," he went on.

"I said I saw them," she murmured. She took several steps along the path, as if she were obeying a sudden urge to flee from him. Then she stopped and turned. "He's dead,

Quinn!'' she cried. "What difference does it make what he died of? He's gone! Forever!'' She extended a gloved hand toward the open grave, gesturing wildly. "I'm leaving my son here, and you come to me with questions! Why?''

Quinn understood that the grief she'd held so determinedly inside for appearance' sake was beginning to tear away at her. He had a compelling urge to go to her, to take her in his arms and comfort her. He needed comforting, too.

"Are you challenging me, Quinn?'' she demanded. "Are you questioning the way I raised him after you left us? I assure you I didn't ignore him. I loved him. I didn't know about drugs.'' She placed a hand against a tombstone to support herself. "Damn you!'' she cried. "Talk about inflicting guilt! Don't you think I've tormented myself enough without your coming to question me? I didn't know he took drugs, I swear. I never questioned him. I never felt it necessary. We were so open with one another. He was so levelheaded, so serious for his age—''

Quinn almost shouted, "Chad didn't take drugs, Dorothy!''

She pushed away from the tombstone and stared out at him through her veil.

"Chad was proud of the fact that he wasn't tempted by drugs,'' Quinn went on. "Most of his friends smoked marijuana, sniffed a little coke, but not Chad. He wouldn't touch anything stronger than an aspirin.'' He touched the breast pocket of his jacket. "I have a letter he wrote less than a week before his death. There's one whole page about his stand against drugs and how debilitating they're becoming to the military.''

Dorothy took a step toward him, then hesitated.

"There's something seriously wrong here,'' Quinn said. "I thought you might be able to shed some light on...''

He let the sentence trail off as Dorothy lifted her veil.

She was just as beautiful as he remembered her. Her eyes were red and swollen from crying, and there were dark circles beneath them, but they remained as piercing, as intelligent as ever. Her skin was pale, smooth and without wrinkles. She wore no makeup, and still she looked more like a woman of thirty than of forty-three. Who would have believed her to be a mother burying a twenty-three-year-old son?

She stretched out her right hand to him. Her composure had seemed to return the moment he had mentioned Chad's letter. "May I have his letter?" she asked. "Please, Quinn. I want to read it."

He disregarded her request. "I want to know what kind of a hoax the navy is perpetrating." And then he added, "This time!" in a voice that reverberated with anger.

Dorothy's hand fell to her side. "Then you have doubts, too," she murmured. "Oh, God, Quinn, the doubts are eating me alive!" From the corner of her eye she saw her father approaching. "There are more questions exploding inside my head than I can cope with. More than just the drugs, Quinn," she added hurriedly. "But we can't discuss it here. My father's taken Chad's death very hard. Chad was dearer to him than my mother, than me, than anyone or anything, including his beloved navy." She lowered the veil back into place. "Are you staying in D.C.?"

"At the Diplomat," he told her.

"Then I'll call you there," she promised. "We'll meet. Tonight."

Without waiting for Quinn to respond, she turned and hurried along the path to meet the admiral.

Quinn watched until all the limousines had driven out of the cemetery. Then he walked back to his son's open grave and stood quietly for a long time.

2

ADMIRAL ADDISON SAT stiffly at the head of the long mahogany conference table. His pudgy hands rested on the table's edge, the fingers splayed, and he stared between them at the graining of the wood.

Like a gypsy seeking answers to his problems in tea leaves, thought one of the other officers seated around the table.

The admiral's gray hair was cropped shorter than military regulations required. His eyes, too, were gray, and his complexion was ashen. He had shed his uniform on the flight from Washington, D.C., and was wearing a gray suit with a contrasting gray-striped tie.

If he had a visible aura, that, too, would be gray, the officer observing him reflected. He mentally nicknamed the admiral "The Gray Hawk" and knew he would never think of the man again without that phrase coming to mind.

Beyond the partially drawn venetian blinds the California sun was setting, streaks of magenta and scarlet cutting through the darkening blue. The air conditioner was whirring, spitting out cold air to combat the ninety-nine-degree temperature that would persist outside for an hour after sunset. A staircase ran directly outside one of the room's walls; in the silence they could hear the occasional heavy, hurried footsteps of naval and civilian personnel attached to the Moffett Field admiral's staff, located on the floor above.

The door to the outer office was closed and bolted. Yeoman Second Class Alex Mayfield had been instructed to hold all telephone calls and to see that they were not otherwise disturbed. The yeoman had been borrowed from the admiral's staff more to serve coffee and stand guard than for any clerical duties; no notes or written instructions would be carried away from this meeting.

Of the thirteen men in the conference room, all were seated except one. That man wore the uniform of a chief petty officer. The insignia on his sleeve designated him a boatswain, but the emblem above his chest medals, Neptune's scepter, also indicated that he was attached to UDT, the Underwater Demolition Team. He moved methodically around the room, examining lamps, the undersides of tables, window ledges, the wall behind pictures, the floor beneath the furniture, even the fixtures in the connecting head.

Admiral Addison began drumming his fingertips impatiently on the polished surface of the conference table. The crow's-feet at the corner of his eyes deepened, as did the furrows across his brow. The conference room had been made available to them as a courtesy, and the chief should have found time to examine it before now. What the hell was happening to their efficiency? First the Bannen boy, now this! His gray eyes cold and calculating, his gaze swept around the table, settling for a moment on each man's face. Then he turned his chair with an almost inaudible sigh and sat staring through the partially closed venetian blinds at the explosive colors of the sunset.

The chief emerged from the head and slipped awkwardly into his chair. "It's clean, sir," he announced. He stretched his beefy legs beneath the table and folded his massive hands in his lap.

Without turning to glance at those huddled around the table, Admiral Addison said, "I want to be apprised on the Bannen problem." His voice was deep and throaty and carried the hint of a threat.

"He's dead, sir." The commander who answered sat nearest the admiral. It was not by choice; it had been the only chair available when he arrived late.

"I know he's fucking dead!" Admiral Addison snapped. "I gave the order myself. Well?"

No one ventured to comment on the ambiguous "Well."

The admiral spun his chair back to the table and leaned forward on his elbows. "Why was the bastard's body allowed to be found? That is my question, gentlemen."

A middle-aged man seated at the opposite corner of the table looked up from the notepad on which he'd been doodling. Like the admiral, he wore civilian clothes, although his were less formal—an alpaca golf sweater, an open-necked print shirt and beige slacks. "Bannen was powerfully built," he said matter-of-factly, "strong and exceedingly clever. His profile shows him to have been one of our most qualified recruits."

"Then his profile is in error, Captain Musolf," Admiral Addison said pointedly. "He disregarded our first mandate. He talked. Do you gentlemen realize the damage Bannen could have done us? The young bastard could have destroyed us all. Everything we stand for and hope to achieve." He paused deliberately, allowing his silence to give emphasis to his words. "And you—" he let his gray eyes settle on the man who had spoken "—you, the psychologist, say he was one of our most qualified recruits! Damn! That makes me question *your* qualifications. It certainly gives me deep concern about the other fifty men on this project."

"We're in the process of updating their profiles, sir," the man said defensively, the authority gone from his voice. He picked up his pen and continued his doodling as he spoke. "We're adopting a method that proved successful within Hitler's SS. Each man—I mean each member of our team, sir, I don't want to sound sexist—is assigned another member to spy on. That, of course, requires that he know the identity of one other member, but we—" he indicated the other officers present with a sweeping gaze "—found that risk acceptable, considering the information we'll gather."

Admiral Addison's gray eyes narrowed as he considered the spying within the organization. Then, deciding not to comment on it at this time, he asked, "What's the explanation for allowing Bannen's body to be discovered?"

Chief Loomis, the man who had checked the conference room for bugging devices, sat forward in his chair. Unfolding his huge hands, he wiped their dampness onto his pant legs. "His body was found by a pilot and flight crew, so we couldn't dispose of it as planned, sir. But we did manage to have one of our men perform the autopsy. His report states Bannen's death was caused by a drug overdose." He sat back in his chair. "The body was returned to the family for burial."

"You are, are you not, Chief Loomis, aware of Bannen's background? Of who his family is?"

Chief Loomis nodded.

"The body should have been buried at sea."

"Since we were only one day from port, we thought that might seem suspicious, sir. I think our officer on board the *Alum Rock* made the right decision."

Admiral Addison's gray eyes indicated that he did not agree. "You don't anticipate any problems from the family?"

"No, none, sir." Glancing at the doodling Captain Musolf, he added, "Bannen, like the other recruits, was carefully screened for family closeness."

The admiral made a snorting sound through his pitted nose. "Apparently not carefully enough." He glared at Captain Musolf.

The psychologist laid his pen down again. The only visible sign of distress was the tightening of his jaw, but his stomach muscles were knotted and there was a nervous tingling in his groin. He silently cursed Loomis for casting the blame for recruiting Bannen back on him; he also refrained from blurting that Admiral Addison himself had first recommended the recruit. He was surprised at the evenness of his voice as he said, "Divorced parents. No close ties with his father. Questionable relationship with his mother since his enlistment. No close friends. He was, in short, a loner."

"What he was," Admiral Addison stated emphatically, "was a damned good actor. The CIA could have put the young bastard to good use. We can thank our lucky stars he was working as an individual, not for another agency. Still, we don't know who he's talked to, what he's said. We have to protect ourselves. What's been done about cleaning up behind him?''

The commander seated beside Chief Loomis flipped open a leather notebook. ''We've tied three names to Bannen as possible leaks, sir. We've located one already. A Mona Shriver, in San Diego. She's a part-time cocktail waitress, part-time model. An arrest record for prostitution—two counts. She's pretty much what we'd refer to as a navy camp follower. Likes her men in uniform. Bannen was involved with her for about six months.''

''And God only knows how many other whores,'' Admiral Addison said with disdain. ''Which operatives have you assigned to her?''

''That's not confirmed, sir.''

''Then assign the two bastards who bungled Bannen's execution,'' the admiral commanded. ''If they fuck up again, it'll be their own asses!''

YEOMAN ALEX MAYFIELD slid the directive he'd been reading into a desk drawer and snapped to attention.

The lock on the conference room had clicked open, the door swinging slightly ajar. He heard the officer identified as Admiral Addison saying, ''...because the agency's own covert capabilities have been dismantled, they're using outside forces to carry out...'' The door was pulled closed again, cutting off anything beyond a murmur.

Yeoman Second Class Alex Mayfield remained at attention, his broad shoulders pulled back, his intense brown eyes fixed on the conference room door, as he waited for those inside to emerge. He was of medium height, handsome, with dark hair and features that would have been sculpture-perfect had it not been for his once-broken nose. He had just turned twenty-eight and was beginning his tenth year of what he expected to be a twenty-year naval career. On the chest of his dress uniform Mayfield wore several ribbons, and commendations, among them the Legion of Merit, awarded for a brief but harrowing tour of duty in Vietnam. He was ambitious, with a need to excel at everything he undertook. The admiral to whose staff he was assigned had written in Mayfield's last evaluation: "An exemplary sailor, his uniform always immaculate and his performance of duties beyond reproach."

The only criticism of Mayfield the admiral had recorded was that he tended to be too diversified, excelling not only in his own duties but surpassing the other members of the staff at theirs. For example, Mayfield knew more about computers than the data processors. This tended to make him unpopular with other staff members, both military and civilian. The admiral had concluded his report by recommending Mayfield for the CAP advancement program.

Again the conference room door opened, and this time the officers began filtering out. Admiral Addison came first. Mayfield noted that the admiral was in his late fifties, with an easy-living paunch pressing tightly against the jacket of his gray suit. His eyes were gray and deeply set in a pallid face. From the man's carriage, the set of his square jaw and the bleak, calculating expression in his eyes, Mayfield decided the admiral was not an officer he would want to be assigned to. Looking neither left nor right, the admiral crossed the outer office briskly and vanished into the corridor.

There was an obvious gap between the admiral's departure and that of the other personnel, and not, Mayfield suspected, out of respect for the admiral's rank. Of the remaining twelve officers filing from the conference room, Mayfield was acquainted with two: Captain Musolf, a psychologist attached to Moffett Field's medical center, and Chief Loomis, a boatswain who had recently transferred in from San Diego to conduct some as-yet-unannounced training sessions. Mayfield had met the chief at the enlisted men's club. After several stiff rum and Cokes the bastard had bombarded him with questions of both a military and a personal nature, and he had decided to avoid the chief in future, having felt an uneasiness he'd been unable to explain.

"...christened him 'The Gray Hawk,'" one of the captains said as he passed Alex's desk.

"Don't let him hear you refer to him as that," a lieutenant warned. "He'll have your ass, and *it*'ll be gray when he finishes with you. You'll find yourself in some shit-duty station in the Antarctic."

The captain laughed. "I could use a change from this California heat."

None of the officers so much as glanced at the yeoman standing at attention behind his desk. Outside the office, they turned and dispersed in different directions.

Mayfield came from behind his desk, closed the outer door and then proceeded into the conference room. Despite the air conditioner the room smelled of stale tobacco smoke. All but two of the yellow notepads he had left on the conference table remained exactly as he had placed them.

It was part of his duty to remove and destroy any doodlings or notations left behind. He picked up the two notepads that had been used, but the pages had already been removed. He checked the wastebaskets beneath the table. In one he found a pile of still-smoldering cigarette ashes. Strange, he thought as he examined the ashes more closely; fragments of the notepads had also been burned. It was not uncommon for notes to be carried away from a meeting, but burned—very unusual.

He emptied the wastebaskets and ashtrays, ran a polishing cloth over the table's surface and carried the notepads back to the desk in the outer office. He was about to store them in the supply cabinet when he noticed indentations on the uppermost sheet of one pad. Because of his insatiable drive to know, to understand and to excel, he laid the pad on his desk, took a soft pencil from the drawer and began working the lead across the surface of the paper. The first words to become clear were *Mona Shriver*; then, *San Diego* and *Chad Bannen*. Beneath those, written at right angles to the first, was *Della* or *Delta*; the impression wasn't clear enough for him to be certain which. An officer scribbling the names of his whores, he thought. Nothing here to satisfy his curiosity.

Sighing, Mayfield leaned back in the swivel chair and sat staring at the impressions on the notepad.

Why would an admiral and twelve lesser officers lock themselves in a conference room at Moffett Field to discuss naval affairs with no yeoman present to take notes and no directives requested for reference sources?

It certainly was not standard procedure.

And anything out of the ordinary sparked Mayfield's curiosity.

3

Washington, D.C.

ADMIRAL MALCOM BURKE would turn seventy in another two months.

Naturally robust, until five years ago, when he had retired, he'd enjoyed excellent health. But retirement had changed him. His purpose in life seemed to have fled, and he'd retreated into himself. He'd been a widower for ten years. After his grandson, the light of his life, had joined the navy, he had seldom seen him, and his daughter's life was too active to include an old man with nothing but time on his hands.

First Burke had become susceptible to viruses and had seldom been without a head cold. Then he had suffered a stroke that left him partially paralyzed in his right arm and leg. His brain had not been affected, for which he heartily thanked God. He was as alert and mentally active as he had been at fifty, even at forty.

To keep his gray cells from deteriorating, the admiral had cast about for occupations that interested him. He had begun his autobiography, but had abandoned that after the first chapter proved dull and too much like the many military autobiographies that had preceded his attempt. Then, because Washington, D.C., where he lived, was a city of politicians, he had broken a cardinal rule from his years in military service and become involved in politics. He'd received a measure of fame for his outspoken views, especially his criticism of the present administration's handling of foreign affairs.

He'd been scheduled to speak at a Republican fund-raiser the night he'd heard of his grandson's death. His speech had been canceled, of course, as had all further political activities. He had retreated into himself again, struggling to retain a measure of zest for a life that now seemed emptier than ever.

His grandson Chad, he realized, was the only person in his life he'd loved unconditionally. Of course, he had loved his wife, but only when she hadn't been annoying him with her silly, socially oriented mentality. And he loved his daughter... but with reservations; her spirit was too independent, and that often put them at odds.

Dorothy frequently caught her father staring into space, oblivious to anyone or anything about him, his dark eyes unblinking, his expression vacant—just as he was sitting now in the back seat of the limousine. She reached across the space that separated them and gently laid her gloved hand over his.

Admiral Burke responded to the contact by blinking and shaking his head to dispel the thoughts that had been occupying him. Clutching the armrest, he pulled himself up in his seat and looked at her. "I take it Quinn believes as you do?" he said quietly. "That there's something mysterious and sinister about Chad's death?"

Dorothy removed her hat and veil. Her auburn hair was worn short, natural waves framing the sides of her face. Averting her gaze, she said, "Quinn has a letter proving Chad didn't take drugs, so naturally he doesn't believe Chad died from a drug overdose."

Admiral Burke sighed wearily. "Seventy percent of young enlisted personnel take drugs," he said authoritatively. "I've read the reports. Drugs are the curse of today's military. Of today's youth. In my day it was alcohol and loose women. Did you read this letter that so conclusively proves Chad was immune to the curse of his generation?"

Dorothy stared at the hat resting on her lap and said nothing.

"You'll eventually come to accept the fact that our Chad was no better or worse than his peers," the admiral murmured. "Knowing he died of a drug overdose doesn't make his memory less lovable. That he had a weakness—" his voice broke "—common to his age group doesn't surprise me. Nor does the fact that he hid it from us. You're probably feeling guilty. As his mother, you're thinking you could possibly have changed things, done things differently, and he'd still be alive. You must get that out of your mind, Dorothy. Whether Chad took drugs or not was entirely his decision. It had very little to do with you, or with Quinn." He raised his hand and flexed his fingers against the stiffening pain that often attacked the joints. "The navy says he died of an overdose. Accept it and your life will be easier."

"I can't," Dorothy said flatly. "Nor can you. You can't fool me. I can see the doubts behind your eyes."

"What you see behind my eyes is concern for my daughter," he told her. "I don't want you to get involved with that man again. Quinn is a troublemaker, always has been and always will be. The only good thing he ever did in his life was to sire Chad. Now Chad's gone. I can see no reason to even mention that man's name again."

"Quinn Bannen and I shared a good deal of our lives," Dorothy said. "I loved him once, very deeply. I won't have you forbidding his name be spoken, like some tyrannical father in a Victorian novel."

"If Quinn Bannen is allowed back into your life he'll only bring you additional pain," the admiral assured her. "He could use Chad's death as a means of doing just that. He caused a scandal before his retirement. He could easily do it again. For some perverse reason, he's probably planning to do it again. I want you to promise me you won't see Quinn Bannen, not as long as I'm alive."

"You're so unbending with everyone except...except Chad," Dorothy said. "You've never forgiven Quinn for the embarrassment he caused the navy."

"His conduct was inexcusable for an officer and a gentleman."

"As a military brat and then a military wife, I can tell you that Quinn Bannen was one of the most devoted naval officers I've know," Dorothy said firmly. "His devotion to the military once matched your own."

"I'd appreciate your not making any comparisons between me and your ex-husband. His actions were scandalous then, and will undoubtedly be so again unless he's convinced not to pursue this paranoid fantasy about Chad's death."

"Next you'll be accusing him of having a fixation about drugs," Dorothy replied, a sarcastic edge creeping into her voice. "Need I remind you that the scandal you speak of also involved drugs—the military's illegal use of them? You'll never forgive him for going public with the information he uncovered. As far as you're concerned, one mistake and he's a muckraker. You believe he should have overlooked his personal values and swept the dirt under the military rug, so to speak."

"He should have allowed the military to handle its own difficulties," the admiral stated with conviction. "All our lives would have been very different if he had."

"Would they, I wonder? I've never been able to determine how much of the blame for our failed marriage was Quinn's. Or how much to blame him for Chad's—"

"Let's not talk about Chad," the admiral said. "God knows why he took drugs, whether each of us failed him in our own way, but the fact is he did overdose. It cost him his life—and took the light out of mine. Stirring up controversy over that autopsy can do nothing except cast further aspersions on my grandson. I won't have that. I won't! The boy's dead. Let him rest in peace."

They rode in silence for some distance before the admiral turned once more to his daughter. "Promise me you'll not see Quinn Bannen again," he said.

Dorothy's gaze was fixed on the historical monuments on the Washington, D.C., skyline. Without looking at her father, she answered, "I can't do that. I'm meeting him tonight."

The admiral's disappointment was expressed in a deep groan. A muscle at the corner of his eye began to twitch. "You were supposed to be my hostess at dinner tonight," he reminded her. "Admiral Addison is flying in from some tour in California and is spending the night."

"You'll have to manage without me. I'm sorry."

The intonation in her voice told the admiral it was useless to pursue the subject.

4

THEY SCARCELY SPOKE during dinner.

The restaurant, Le Coq d'Or, was crowded. The service was slow, with the more experienced waiters assigned to the tables of known congressmen, who were the big spenders in Washington while Congress was in session. With the folks back home footing the bills, Quinn thought. If only people knew—no, if only they were less apathetic, and cared—how their tax dollars were squandered.

Quinn placed his knife and fork on the edge of his plate, his meal hardly touched; it was swordfish, too, his favorite. He looked appraisingly across the table at Dorothy. She looked especially beautiful that night. Her midnight-blue dress, which looked black in the restaurant candlelight, became her; it was conservatively styled and looked expensive. Around her slender throat hung a single mounted pearl on a thin gold chain. Memories flooded over him, and he felt an odd tugging of emotion in his chest.

"I remember giving you the pearl," he said quietly, "but I don't recall the occasion."

Dorothy smiled at him briefly, then turned her attention back to her dinner. "The day Chad was born," she said in a near-whisper. She laid down her knife and fork as he had done and leaned back in her chair and fixed him with her piercing brown eyes. "There," she said. "His name has been mentioned. We've been avoiding it all evening. We shouldn't have come to a restaurant. It's too noisy here, too difficult to talk. We should have stayed in your hotel room."

"Yes," he agreed, "but I thought— Never mind what I thought. Do you want to skip the pleasantries?"

A smile played over her lips, then vanished. "Not entirely," she answered. "Chad never mentioned you in his letters. I wasn't aware he corresponded with you regularly."

"It isn't easy to be the only child of divorced parents," Quinn said. "I remember that. Perhaps Chad understood the hostilities between us."

Dorothy flinched almost imperceptibly. "There are no hostilities, Quinn. Not anymore. They faded in the first two years after our divorce. Odd how that happens. The hostility I felt is as much past history as the scandal you were involved in before your retirement." Why, she asked herself, didn't she tell him the truth? The hostilities *were* still there; after the first two years they had simply turned into a dull numbness.

Quinn felt his stomach muscles tighten. "What you and your father refer to as 'the scandal' saved the futures, if not the lives, of several hundred servicemen," he said pointedly. "Those devious bastards were experimenting with hallucinogenic drugs. The men they were using as guinea pigs weren't even aware of what was being fed into their systems or what harm it could do to them physically or psychologically. If exposing that meant scandal, so be it."

"You made yourself their savior at the cost of your own career," she reminded him, and then added more quietly, "among other costs." Suddenly she leaned forward in her chair, her gaze unfaltering. "Is that what you think happened to Chad? That some madman forced drugs into him as retribution against you?"

"No. It occurred to me, but no," he said. "That's too bizarre. I only know they attribute his death to an overdose of drugs and that he was exceedingly proud of the fact that he didn't take drugs. I don't think he was lying in his letters to me. I may not have known my son well, but I'd have been aware if he'd been telling an out-and-out lie. I've thought it all through, and I don't believe there's any connection to what I did. My so-called scandal had become yesterday's news, a past embarrassment to the military, but one best forgotten." He reached into his coat pocket, withdrew a letter and passed it across the table to Dorothy.

She almost snatched it from his hand. Then she sat staring down at it for several moments before opening the envelope. She leaned into the candlelight to read. The noise of the crowded restaurant was forgotten as she read her son's familiar scrawl. When she refolded the letter and returned it to its envelope there were tears brimming her eyes.

"He closed with 'I love you,'" she said distantly. "He had stopped ending his letters to me that way." She put a trembling hand to her mouth to press back the threatening sobs. After a moment she regained her composure. "We fought, you see. Chad disapproved of a captain I was seeing. They met when Chad was home on leave, and it was hate at first sight. They argued about the extent of the power that should be given the military. I think the captain was goading Chad. Why, I don't know, but that's the feeling I got listening to them. Chad had only been in the navy a little over a year. He was fresh and eager and full of himself. There was a lot of his grandfather in him. A lot of you, too. He was proud to be coming up in the ranks, like you did, rather than attending the academy." She hesitated, then reached for her water glass and wet her lips. "When I told Chad I was considering marrying Captain Webb, he went berserk. All the things pent up inside him came spilling out. He even blamed me for what happened to you, your forced retirement and—"

"My retirement was requested," Quinn interjected. "By me. I explained as much to Chad."

"He never accepted your explanation," she told him. She handed back the letter, reluctantly, as if parting with it constituted losing yet another part of her son. "We made up before his leave ended, but things were never quite the same between us. He wrote, he telephoned dutifully, he came home on other leaves, but he had changed. He was withdrawn, secretive. The last time he was on leave he kept close to the house. He refused to visit his old friends, refused to allow me to invite them over. His room is—was—next to mine. He had nightmares that kept me awake. Of course, I questioned him, but his answers were evasive. He had developed the military need-to-know attitude with me, even with the admiral, I think, and Chad was closer to him than to either you or me."

Quinn found it difficult to accept that the son he remembered could ever have developed a close relationship with his maternal grandfather. Another reason to dislike my ex-father-in-law, Quinn thought. He found himself forcing away a twinge of jealousy.

The waiter appeared to remove their plates, his eyebrows lifting when he noticed they had scarcely touched their entrées. Before he could question them, Quinn ordered coffee and cognac for them both.

"Does the admiral still challenge you to cognac-drinking contests?" he asked, seeing how speaking of Chad was affecting Dorothy and wanting to draw her momentarily away from the subject of their son. "Has he ever succeeded in beating you at it? I see you still call him 'the admiral' rather than 'Father.'"

Dorothy managed a weak smile, aware that he was manipulating the conversation to allow her time to compose herself. "To answer your questions in sequence: no, the admiral doesn't drink since his stroke, and no, he has never managed to drink me under the table, which still baffles him. And yes, I'll always refer to him as 'the admiral.'" Her smile faded. "I do seriously need a drink now," she went on. "Just one. More would make me lose control. I mustn't do that, must I? I was a military daughter, a military wife and a military mother. Military women don't lose control. At least not in public."

"That sounds like the admiral speaking," Quinn murmured.

"Perhaps," she said with a sigh.

"Do you want to leave here? Go back to my hotel room, where you can lose control?"

Dorothy looked at him for a long moment before saying, "No, Quinn."

He shrugged. "It was only a suggestion." He was aware that she had read the desire in his eyes.

"I'm too vulnerable just now," Dorothy told him. "So are you. We could drift back into something that's better left as it is."

The waiter returned with the coffee and cognac. Quinn lifted his snifter in a salute, then downed the entire contents in one greedy gulp. He hadn't had a drink since he'd gotten the news of Chad's death. Perhaps, like Dorothy, he had feared losing control.

"'Drift back into something that's better left as it is,'" he repeated. "That, too, sounds like the admiral speaking. Did he warn you against seeing me?"

Dorothy nodded, then said, "But I'm here."

"You always were damned independent. Tell me, why didn't you marry your Captain Webb? Because of Chad's strong objections?"

"No. In the end I saw what a pompous ass he was. Besides, I'd made a promise to myself that if I ever married again it wouldn't be to a man in uniform."

"May I tell you that, despite the anger and the hurt, I've missed you like hell?" he blurted. "Looking at you now only makes me realize how deeply. I never stopped—"

"Let it go, Quinn, please," Dorothy said. "We met for an entirely different purpose. Let's not forget that."

"Yes, you're right, of course," he murmured. After a quiet moment, he continued. "At the cemetery you said there was more to question than just the drugs. Exactly what were you referring to? What is it about Chad's death that makes you doubt the navy's death certificate?"

Dorothy's dark eyes were fixed on him above the rim of her brandy snifter. She lowered the glass, and set it aside. Reaching down beside her chair, she lifted her purse onto her lap and snapped open the catch. Her hand was inside, clutching something, when she hesitated. When she brought her hand out it was empty. "The admiral feels we should let things be," she told him. "He says Chad is dead and no matter what we do we can't bring him back. We can only hurt ourselves."

"And possibly his precious naval image," Quinn said curtly.

"The navy isn't as important to him as it once was," Dorothy told him. "You never liked the admiral, Quinn. You never got to know him, not really."

"I'm not interested at this late date in knowing or loving your father, Dorothy," Quinn returned with a truthfulness he immediately regretted. "I'm sorry, but I'm interested in our son. No, I can't bring him back, but I can clear his name. I can discover why the goddamned navy insists his death is due to a drug overdose. I owe him that much. You owe him that much. We may be divorced, we may have been lousy parents, but we're not insensitive. Chad was proud of not being a drug user. The navy's taken that pride from him. Even dead, he deserves to be exonerated."

"Were we, Quinn? Were we lousy parents?" Her voice broke as she waited for his answer.

"I'm sorry. I should have spoken for myself only," he told her. "I certainly don't consider myself an attentive, caring father. Not after hiding myself away at a California ranch and scarcely seeing the boy. I guess uncovering the truth of his death is my way of . . . of trying to make it up to him."

Dorothy reached inside her purse again, and without hesitation this time she withdrew a crumpled envelope. "This in itself may mean nothing," she said as she handed it to Quinn.

Quinn opened the envelope and pulled out a torn piece of lined yellow notepaper. Typewritten across the middle of the sheet he read: They killed our Chad!

The fine hair on the back of his neck stood on end. "Do you have any idea who sent this?"

Dorothy told him she did not. "Only that it was postmarked San Jose, California," she pointed out. "It must be from a navy friend of Chad's who has the same doubts we do, but Chad never mentioned any of his friends to me. Or if he did, I don't remember."

Quinn continued to stare at the typewritten message until the words began to blur. "Most likely a girlfriend," he said, more to himself than to Dorothy. "Chad mentioned a particular girl and a couple of buddies in his letters. San Jose's near Mountain View. That's Moffett Field."

"Chad was stationed at Moffett Field for six months," Dorothy announced. "That was two years ago, right after our argument. If I remember correctly, it was for a special training program."

"Do you remember what training program?"

"No, I'm sorry."

"Did you show this to the admiral?"

"He said it was probably some crank. I believed him, then. That was before—" She hesitated, then said, "Before the results of the private autopsy."

Quinn was taken aback. "Private autopsy? Who ordered that?" he demanded. His voice had risen, and he was attracting attention from neighboring tables.

Dorothy noted that two men in dark business suits seated behind Quinn had caught something in their conversation that intrigued them. They made no attempt to disguise their interest.

"Quinn, perhaps we should go?" she suggested.

"No! Who authorized a private autopsy?"

Dorothy, who had started to rise, sank back into her chair. Her hand trembled as she lifted the snifter to her mouth and swallowed some cognac. "I did! I demanded it!"

"You? Why? Because of this note?"

"Actually, it was the day before I received the note," she answered.

"Then why?"

"Because of you," she said evenly. "I decided on a private autopsy the day I learned what the navy called the cause of death. The moment I heard the word *drugs* I thought of you and the scandal you caused by accusing the armed services of conducting illegal drug experiments on enlisted personnel. Perhaps it was intuitive, but I had visions of you repeating the same accusations because of Chad. You must understand, I had difficulty believing your accusation then, even after it was proved to be true, but this time my son was involved. If you cried 'drug experiment victim' in Chad's case, and I had failed to consider the possibility, I would never have been able to live with myself." She reached for the snifter again and found it empty. "That's when I demanded a private autopsy. I need another cognac."

Without taking his eyes from her, Quinn signaled the waiter to refill their glasses. "Did the private autopsy prove there were drugs in his system?"

"No." Tears began to brim in her eyes again. She impatiently wiped them away. "It couldn't have."

"I don't understand," he told her. "Why couldn't the autopsy—"

"The autopsy report, combined with this anonymous note, is why I've been so tormented with doubt," she said, the tears now spilling down her cheeks. "Chad's—" she shuddered, struggling visibly for control "—Chad's vital organs were not returned with his body!" She fumbled in her purse and brought out a handkerchief to dab at her eyes. Her head was lowered, and she didn't lift it until the waiter set the second round of cognac on the table. She drained her snifter before looking up at Quinn.

Quinn was staring at her but not seeing her, his blue eyes devoid of expression. His jaw had tightened, and the veins in his neck and forehead were protruding. Dorothy could almost read his thoughts, and they frightened her.

"I contacted the Navy Surgeon General's Office," she continued, trying to draw Quinn away from his thoughts. "They were as baffled about the missing organs as the private medical examiner. They said—" she felt a shiver along her spine "—it had long been their practice to retain samples of organs, but they never kept all of them. After that I hit a roadblock, I hounded the admiral to use his influence to learn what he could, but even he was unsuccessful. As incredible as it may seem, Chad's organs simply seem to have disappeared." She brought her hand to her face and covered her eyes. "Oh, God, Quinn! What I'm saying is that the body buried in Chad's grave is no more than an empty shell! If he did or didn't die of a drug overdose, we have no way of proving it either way. We have only this note and our doubts." She wiped her eyes again and willed herself to stop crying.

Quinn's eyes blinked, then refocused; the suspicion mirrored there was unmistakable. She had seen that expression in his eyes before—suspicion and determination and blinding anger.

"Where do we go from here?" she murmured.

Quinn straightened in his chair, shifting his weight as if suddenly incapable of remaining still. "First we get out of this restaurant," he said, and signaled for the check. "Then we're going back to my hotel room. We have to plan our strategy. I still have a few friends at the Pentagon. One of them will be willing to help us."

"Quinn, you're still considered a traitor and an agitator," she reminded him. "If the admiral failed to extract any information, how can you hope to succeed? You know Washington and you know the military. Memories die hard. Anyone who's caught even speaking to you will be suspect."

"I can only try," Quinn said. "It's for certain our doubts aren't going to go away." He held up the envelope she had given him. "This note isn't going to go away. It's not a figment of our imagination. Someone besides us believes there was a conspiracy involved in Chad's death. If I can get someone in authority to believe as we do..."

As Quinn paid the check, Dorothy noticed that the two men who had been openly listening to their conversation rose and hurriedly left the restaurant.

Outside, Quinn took her arm and led her away from the front of the restaurant. The parking lot had been too full when they had arrived, and they had been forced to park a block away. A cooling breeze had sprung up from nowhere and was lowering the Washington humidity.

Dorothy felt exhausted, drained, and she leaned into the protective curve of Quinn's body for support. He smelled of soap and after-shave; she hated to admit to the sense of pleasure it gave her to have his arm around her shoulders. Watch it, she warned herself. *I loved him once, very deeply,* she had told the admiral that afternoon in the limousine. Once? The admiral had known she was lying; he knew as well as she that she still loved Quinn Bannen, would always love Quinn Bannen. But sometimes love was not enough.

The squeal of automobile tires cut into Dorothy's thoughts; still, her mind didn't focus; she wasn't aware of the danger.

She screamed as Quinn flung her roughly to one side.

She landed against a low hedge that lined the darkened driveway of the parking lot. Her dress caught on a branch and ripped; something cut painfully into the soft flesh of her right thigh. She could feel the impact of the air from the speeding automobile as it passed within inches of her legs. The exhaust fumes filled her nostrils.

The black Lincoln Continental hit the low dip of the gutter. Metal scraped concrete, sparks flew, then the Lincoln sped away, turning at the nearby intersection and vanishing behind a darkened office building.

Screaming out Quinn's name, Dorothy pulled herself to her feet. Shaken, she cried out in relief when she saw him on the sidewalk, getting up.

"Are you hurt?" he shouted.

"No, I'm . . . fine," she assured him. "Shaken but fine." Her thigh was bleeding; she could feel the warm blood trickling down her leg. She decided not to tell Quinn about the cut until they reached his hotel; otherwise he might insist on taking her to a hospital emergency ward. Or, worse, taking her home and calling their family doctor. She didn't want to face the admiral and the visiting Admiral Addison. She had decided as she and Quinn had left the restaurant that regardless of her vulnerability, regardless of the pain and regret she might feel later, she wanted to spend the night with Quinn.

She fought against the pain in her thigh and tried not to limp as Quinn led her to his car, a white Nova with a Hertz sticker on the license plate.

As Quinn opened the door for her, he said, "I don't believe for a moment that was just some crazy driver who didn't see us."

Dorothy was convinced he was right.

As the Lincoln Continental had sped past her she had caught a fleeting glimpse of the driver's face in the harsh glare of the dashboard lights.

He had been one of the men who had been sitting behind Quinn in the restaurant, listening so intently to their conversation.

5

Washington, D.C.

ADMIRALS BURKE and Addison had once been close friends.

They had had more than their rank in common. Burning inside both men had been a fierce pride, and a malignant discontent with the declining power and strength of the military. Neither could tolerate weakness in any form; both were accustomed to being obeyed without question. Admiral Burke had been married, had a daughter and a grandson; Admiral Addison had remained a bachelor. Addison believed that gave him a decided advantage over the older Burke. He had no pulls on his emotions; he could forge directly ahead toward his goals without being hampered by emotional dependents. He had never regretted his aloneness, his single-mindedness, nor could he relate to Admiral Burke's suffering and sense of loss over his grandson. He pretended to understand, but it was obvious he didn't.

Until tonight, the two admirals had never argued.

Now, with their tempers finally cooled and the reason for their disagreement temporarily put aside, Admiral Burke rose from his chair and moved to the bar. Without glancing at his guest, he said, "Gin rocks?"

Admiral Addison fixed his gray eyes on the elder officer's back. His stare was cold and calculating. "I haven't touched alcohol since the launching of this project," he announced. "Nor coffee, nor cigars. My only stimulant has been the project itself." Rising from the wing chair he had occupied for the past hour, he began pacing the study, his hands clasped behind his back, his head slightly bowed. "Should you be drinking, in your condition?"

The question had been delivered like the concerned query of a close friend, but Admiral Burke had already discerned the truth. He understood that their friendship had ended, that one day they might even consider themselves enemies. He splashed gin into his own glass and raised it to his cracked lips. The alcohol burned his throat and instantly warmed his stomach. "My doctors forbid drinking, of course," he replied. "As far as Dorothy knows, I'm a teetotaler." He wiped his mouth on the back of his hand, returned to the matching wing chair and sat down, balancing the glass of gin on its padded arm. "I took my first drink in a decade the day I learned of my grandson's death," he said.

That was a lie; he'd drunk right up until the day of his stroke. But it didn't seem to matter anymore, lying to Addison—who was no longer his friend.

Admiral Addison's pacing came to a halt. He stood in front of the impressive carved mantel Dorothy had bought for her father's den. Taking his hands from behind his back, he laced his pudgy fingers together and stretched his arms wearily. Then his gray eyes settled on the seated man. "Apparently I must remind you I didn't want your grandson recruited," he said. "I was adamant against it when you suggested it. He didn't fit the requirements." He strode back to the chair and sat down with an air of impatience. "The fact that his father was a muckraker was against him, as was, indeed, that he had a father at all. All our other recruits are orphans or are permanently estranged from their families, as you well know, since you helped devise the requirements."

"Chad was more my son than Quinn Bannen's," Admiral Burke murmured, staring at his glass. "He was the son I wanted and never had. He was brilliant, Chad was. He had a brilliant future with the navy."

"Stop torturing yourself over futures that will never be," Admiral Addison said coldly.

"Chad would have been a credit to me. To the military. He was the last of my bloodline. After the trouble Dorothy had delivering him, she was terrified of becoming pregnant again. She made Bannen have an operation. He did it, too, without a complaint. I wouldn't have done that for any woman."

"I guess he loved her," Admiral Addison said, without understanding or interest.

"My grandson was the only good thing that came from that union," Admiral Burke stated with sudden vehemence. He raised his glass and drank until only the ice was left, clanking against the sides. He had an instinct to hurl the glass at the fireplace; instead, he clutched it tightly and hoped it would still his trembling hand. "All the same, you have to give Bannen his due," he said tensely.

"I'd like to give the son of a bitch the firing squad," Admiral Addison snarled.

"He wasn't a natural troublemaker," Admiral Burke returned. "He was a man who finally was forced to stand up for his ideals. He took a chance and lost, but he was true to himself. How many men can that be said about? The scandal ruined more than his own life. The destruction of his marriage was only one of the consequences he suffered. He lost his son, also. I became Chad's only link with stability. I stole the boy's affection and his respect."

Admiral Addison recognized the emotion creeping into the older officer's voice. "I suggest we don't continue this conversation," he said. "Neither talk nor the gin is go- ing—"

"How could I have anticipated his turning against the organization?" Admiral Burke asked him. He deliberately opened his hand and let the glass slip to the carpet. "I loved that boy with all my heart and soul. Do you understand that? No, of course not." He kicked the glass away from him with the toe of his shoe; the ice cubes scattered, twin- kling in the lamplight. "Why would Chad turn against Delta? It just doesn't make any sense."

Admiral Addison moved uncomfortably in his chair; one topic he didn't want to discuss was the admiral's grandson. "I don't believe he turned against the organization," he said with conviction. I might as well get it all out in the open, then decide how to proceed with Burke himself, he thought. "I don't believe your grandson ever believed in the organi- zation. It was all an act. He was out to expose us from the beginning. Possibly to top what his father had done by ex- posing the drug experiments."

Admiral Burke's eyes widened. "I can't believe that!" he cried vehemently.

"Then don't," Admiral Addison said flatly. "Believe what's easiest for you. We'll never know the answer any- way. If it'll keep you from torturing yourself, think of him as killed in the line of duty."

The sarcasm in his voice was not lost on Admiral Burke, but he chose to ignore it. He knew he was treading on un- sure ground. "You're right, of course. I have to separate the grandson I loved from the traitor he became, if only in my own mind." He turned suddenly and stared into Admiral

Addison's ashen face. "There's one thing I'd like to know," he said. "Then I'll put all of this behind me. Was it you who ordered his execution?"

Admiral Addison's answer was too quick; he had been anticipating the question. "It wasn't necessary for me to give the order. Each member is trained to execute anyone who becomes a threat."

The bastard's lying, and I can't even challenge him, Admiral Burke thought. He swallowed the bile that rose in his throat. "What do you plan to do about Bannen? He's here in Washington, you know. Neither he nor my daughter believe their son died of a drug overdose. That was a stupid decision. Chad was adamantly against drugs."

"We're following Bannen's movements," Admiral Addison said. His gray eyes narrowed, probed the face of his companion. "What about you, Malcolm? Are you going to be a problem?"

Ah, at last, the real reason for your visit, Admiral Burke thought.

He met the gray-eyed stare unfalteringly. After a moment of reflection, he said, "I'm as committed to the organization as you. The sacrifice was high, but so, too, will be the achievement of Delta."

Admiral Addison was obviously pleased with the answer. A smile of satisfaction flickered around the corners of his thin, colorless lips.

Admiral Burke rose, scooped up his glass and the ice cubes from the carpet and returned to the bar to pour himself another gin.

He had no doubt that Chad's execution had been ordered by the man he had once called his friend.

6

DOROTHY RAISED HERSELF to an elbow and looked toward the bedside table. The luminous dial of Quinn's travel clock read a quarter to four. She had not yet slept. Beside her, Quinn's breathing was heavy and even; she envied him his ability to sleep.

Slipping quietly from bed, she fumbled in the darkness for her clothes and dressed quickly. A turmoil of emotions boiled within her; she wanted to stay, yet felt she should go. She took a cigarette from her purse, sank into the chair beside the bed and collected her thoughts while she smoked the unwanted cigarette.

Always a restless sleeper, Quinn had kicked the top sheet away. His body was a dark shape against the white linen. After seventeen years of marriage, she knew his body almost as well as she knew her own. There was a strawberry birthmark on the cheek of his left buttock and another, smaller one just inside the hairline of his right temple. The scar on his right forearm that resembled a beetle came from a land mine fragment during evacuation of troops from Vietnam. The same close encounter with death had claimed the top of his right index finger. She remembered the erogenous zones he found most sensitive—she had proved her memory correct tonight—but she had forgotten, perhaps deliberately, how tender and loving he became after his passion had been satisfied. No man had ever pleased her as much as Quinn; no man had ever made her feel as secure or contented.

But now, her present was bleak, and the future looked bleaker. The prospect made her want to cry. Dorothy sighed deeply, and crushed out the cigarette just as her common sense crushed any glimmer of hope of a renewed relationship with Quinn. It was no use deluding herself, no use pretending she could have an affair with her ex-husband and not get hurt again. The admiral was right; if she allowed

Quinn back into her life, he would only bring more pain. Now that Chad was gone...

Memories of her son flooded over Dorothy and pushed thoughts of Quinn aside. Chad had to be exonerated. With Quinn's help, she would do what she could.

Something was dropped in the room next door. The cushioned thud snapped Dorothy out of her thoughts. Another insomniac? she wondered. She rose and looked down at Quinn's dark silhouette. From a navy commander to a horse rancher on the California-Oregon border; not even, according to him, a successful horse rancher. From Washington, D.C., society to small-town socials. That was what he'd wanted, expected of her, even before his retirement and their divorce. That was what he'd wanted for Chad. Sighing, she bent and kissed Quinn's cheek. He stirred, mumbled something incoherent, rolled over and returned to a deep sleep as she let herself out of his room.

The hallway was empty; so, too, was the elevator when the doors slid open. In the lobby a porter leaned against one of the columns, his arms folded across his chest, his eyes closed and his head nodding sleepily. The clerk behind the desk was bent over a ledger, making entries. Although neither man glanced at Dorothy as she made her way to the outer doors, she had an odd sensation of being watched. She glanced behind her, noting that neither the porter nor the desk clerk had altered his position. Pushing through the glass doors, she hurried along the sidewalk to the car she had left parked at the curb. Once inside, she locked the doors, and that made her feel more secure. Maybe I'm becoming paranoid, she thought as she started the engine and drove quickly away.

When she let herself into the house she was surprised to see a light on in the room the admiral referred to as his study, a room she had meticulously decorated for him with nautical collectables.

"Is that you, Dorothy?" the admiral called out.

Dorothy walked to the study and stopped in the doorway. The admiral sat behind his massive oak desk, a clutter of papers spread across the polished top so that the inkwell and the telephone were buried beneath. The collar of his navy-blue wool bathrobe was turned up around his scrawny neck.

"Admiral Addison just left," he told her. "An early flight to Florida, then back to California. He asked me to give you his best." He pushed his eyeglasses back on the bridge of his nose, and the lenses magnified his dark eyes. "You and Quinn?" he said. "You've started up the relationship again?"

When Dorothy didn't answer, he took her silence as affirmation.

"A pity," he murmured. "And a mistake. I suppose you're using Chad's death as an excuse?" He shook his head from side to side in an expression of angry resignation.

Dorothy moved to the chair in front of his desk and sat down. Her body ached from exhaustion. Quinn had washed and bandaged the wound on her thigh, but now it was throbbing painfully. She folded her hands in her lap and returned her father's stare. "I don't want to discuss my relationship with Quinn," she told him. "It's Chad I want to discuss. The navy's covering up the real reason for his death, I'm convinced of it."

"That's nonsense," the admiral said adamantly. "I knew no good would come of your meeting with Quinn. Granted, the navy may have committed a gross error in misplacing the boy's vital organs, but—"

"A gross error!" Dorothy cried. "Is that what you call it? I don't think it was an error at all. I think it was done deliberately, to conceal the truth—that there were no drugs in his system."

"Quinn has always seen treachery and conspiracy behind the most innocent mistakes," the admiral told her.

"Now he's managed to convince you, to drag you down to his own paranoid level. I never thought you were so gullible."

"You accused him of paranoid delusions once before," Dorothy reminded him. "Then his charges against the military were proved to be an embarrassing reality." Despite her efforts to prevent it, anger was creeping into her voice. "Court-martial proceedings against Quinn were already in progress when it was proved his accusations against the armed services were true. They were conducting illegal drug experiments on enlisted personnel. It was to my shame that I didn't stand behind him. I'm only grateful he was honorably retired."

"He ran away like an ostrich and hid his head in the sand," the admiral said angrily. "He aired our dirty linen for public criticism and then left us to clean up after his mess."

"*His* mess? Don't you mean the Defense Department's mess? Quinn didn't make the mess. He only uncovered it."

The admiral didn't appear to be listening to her, and was looking beyond her, as if into space. "Now the son he abandoned is dead of a drug overdose and Quinn pulls his head out of the sand to scream conspiracy once again. Unfortunately, his accusations were accurate the first time." He focused his gaze on his daughter again. "But not this time, Dorothy," he said with conviction. "Don't you believe if I thought there was anything suspicious in connection with my grandson's death I'd use every power at my command to expose it, navy or no navy? The boy was the continuation of my bloodline, and undoubtedly the end of it. I loved him more than life itself. I don't want to hear any more about this alleged conspiracy." He pulled some papers toward him and began jotting notes in the margins, motioning her away with a wave of his hand. "Now go to bed and pray Quinn Bannen goes out of your life again and leaves both of us in peace."

Obediently Dorothy rose and moved to the door, glancing back at him over her shoulder. She felt guilty for having brought up the subject of Chad's death again at a time when the admiral appeared to be as exhausted as she felt. He had aged noticeably since Chad's death; the loss had been more devastating to him than his stroke. "You should be in bed, too, Admiral," she told him. "You promised the doctors you'd get at least eight hours' sleep every night."

Without looking up, the admiral responded, "I had to wake Admiral Addison for his flight. When an old man's awakened he doesn't return to sleep so easily. I'll be along soon. Good night, Dorothy."

When he heard Dorothy's footsteps retreating down the hallway, the admiral pushed his papers aside and leaned back wearily in his leather chair. His watery dark eyes reflected worry and concern he could never express to his daughter.

Worry and concern that vied for a foothold with his consuming sense of guilt.

7

San Diego, California

IN CALIFORNIA it was three hours earlier than in Washington, D.C.

Inside the Interlude Club, located on a side street off busy Broadway, Mona Shriver glanced at her wristwatch and calculated bar time to be fifteen minutes before 2:00 a.m. Any minute, the bartender would shout "Last call." In fifteen minutes her shift as cocktail waitress would end and she could mercifully get off her aching feet.

It had been a hectic night. Two ships, the USS *Lexington* and the USS *Hancock*, had docked in the harbor that morning, and the bar had been crowded with sailors in a partying mood. Despite the carnival atmosphere, Mona's tips totaled less than forty dollars. The cheap bastards!

Whoever had invented the expression "spending like a drunken sailor" hadn't served cocktails at the Interlude.

Between hustling drinks and avoiding groping hands, Mona thought of Chad. She hoped there'd be a letter waiting for her when she got home. Chad wrote to her weekly; after his paydays he usually included two or three crisp twenty-dollar bills. She needed the money for her rent and utilities. The utility company had mailed her a final notice threatening disconnection, and the landlord had told her she'd have to vacate the apartment unless her rent was paid by Saturday.

Being poor was a bitch!

If it hadn't been for Chad, Mona would have considered another means of making money. Hell, she'd done it before—before Chad. She'd been good at it, sometimes making three hundred in a single night. But that was the old Mona, the Mona before Chad came into her life and gave her a reason to change.

Still, the temptation was strong. The money was easy and would get her out of the dilemma with the landlord and the utility company.

A man had approached her earlier, had offered to buy her a drink for a few moments of conversation. He'd been in civvies, but she had pegged him for military, a marine if not a sailor. She had told him politely that the management frowned on employees drinking with customers. Of course, that was a crock. Billy, the bartender, was the only management, and Billy didn't give a damn what the waitresses did as long as the drinks were hustled and he collected twenty percent of their tips at the end of the night. Maria Louise had balled two tricks in the storage room already that night and was eyeing a potential third to drag home with her. And her married to a handsome sailor who had shipped out only two weeks ago, Mona thought in disgust.

Mona glanced around the crowded bar with feigned disinterest. The man who had approached her was still there.

He'd chosen a stool near the curve in the bar, allowing him a perfect view of the cocktail waitress's station. From the way he watched her Mona guessed she was still his intended conquest for the evening; none of the other women seemed to have attracted his attention. He was good-looking, with sandy hair worn military-short and well-developed biceps that stretched the elastic in the sleeves of his polo shirt when he moved his arms. But there was something about him that disturbed Mona, although she couldn't pinpoint it. He was probably imagining her naked—the way Chad often told her he did—and was getting himself all worked up. But when she caught him watching her, there was more than sexual interest behind his cold blue eyes. A weirdo, she decided. Probably into S and M. Well, pound sand, buddy, she said to herself.

Mona had met her share of weirdos in the fifteen years since she'd run away from home in Wyoming. It hadn't been easy surviving as a cocktail waitress, hash slinger, telephone operator, boutique clerk and model—and sometimes masquerading as a model while she sold her body. A girl on her own met a lot of weirdos. This man was one of them, even if he was so damned handsome.

Chad was the first man Mona had ever been serious about.

As always when she thought of Chad, a warm, secure feeling edged into her chest. If that was love, she liked the feeling. Chad had promised to marry her when the USS *Alum Rock* returned to San Diego.

Goodbye Interlude, goodbye weirdos! She would be a married woman. An honest woman, whatever the hell that meant.

"Last call!" Billy bellowed. "Drink 'em up! Last call!"

Mona approached the service counter and slammed down her tray.

Many of the customers were aleady filtering out, leaving for prearranged parties, bathhouses or flophouses or for the openness of nearby Tijuana, the horny sailors' last resort.

The man who'd been cruising her remained on his stool—as if he'd paid rent until 2:00 a.m. and wasn't going to budge until his time expired, she thought. She noticed him exchange glances with another man, who was leaning against the back wall. They nodded at each other, and then the second man, in his early twenties with dark hair and eyes, set down his beer and walked out.

Maria Louise came up beside Mona. She smelled of cheap perfume. "If you're looking for a little company tonight, the man at the end of the bar is interested," she told Mona. "He asked your name and where you live."

Mona glanced at the man again. "I hope to hell you didn't tell him where I live. You know I've played it straight ever since Chad."

"Sure, honey," Marie Louise said in scarcely veiled disbelief. "Just thought I'd tell you in case you're getting lonely. Living with a sailor isn't easy, with them away so much of the time."

"Chad's worth waiting for," Mona said peevishly. She wiped her tray. Plucking out a maraschino cherry, she snapped the lid of the condiment tray closed. "It's been a bad night," she told Billy.

"Yeah, sure," Billy said. "About forty dollars bad. Drop eight of it on the bar and then help get the stragglers out of here so we can close."

It was uncanny the way that bastard could always judge her tips within two dollars, Mona thought. "You know, Billy, I'm going to miss your ugly face and nasty disposition when I become Mrs. Chad Bannen." She slammed eight singles onto the bar and went to hurry along the departure of the last few customers. When she glanced again at the bar, the sandy-haired man was gone.

Ten minutes later, Billy opened the door for her and let her out into the street. As she walked away, the red neon sign flashing Interlude was switched off and she was left in darkness.

There was a series of office buildings and a warehouse between the bar and Broadway. The single streetlight had burned out the week before, and the city's maintenance crews had not gotten around to fixing it. The moon, full and luminous, hung above the tall buildings like a gigantic balloon, but the light didn't penetrate into the deeper shadows.

Mona wasn't thinking about the darkness or the danger to a woman alone on the streets at night. The moment she had stepped out of the Interlude her thoughts had turned back to Chad. He was the best thing that had happened to her in her thirty years. She smiled, thinking that before they married, she must confess to Chad that she was thirty, not twenty-six. There was no sense starting her new life with a lie. Chad would be understanding. What did seven years' difference in age mean? Nothing, as long as the love was genuine.

Still, Chad was a man of contradictions. As much as she loved him, she didn't understand him. Sometimes she wasn't certain if he lived in a world of reality or fantasy. Before he'd gone away he'd told her some fantastic stories. He'd been drinking at the time, something he seldom did; perhaps that explained his whispering words like *secret*, *top secret*, and *navy intelligence clearance* between every other sentence. She had been tipsy herself and unable to concentrate fully on what he was telling her. Later she'd thought he'd seen too many spy movies and had incorporated them into his own experiences in his drunkenness—either that or he was a pathological liar. Whichever was the case, she'd tackle that problem after they were married. Chad did come from a wealthy military background—she had checked into

that. His father owned a horse ranch near the Oregon border, and his grandfather was a retired admiral.

Mona pulled the collar of her thin cloth coat closer
around her neck and quickened her steps toward Broadway
and the bus stop. After her marriage to Chad there would be
no more worrying about rent and utilities, about nights
when the tips were bad or the paychecks were delayed because of an overdraft at the bank. She'd be able to move out
of the dump of an apartment she'd lived in for the past year;
no more shabby apartments with peeling wallpaper and
roaches, no landlords spying on her comings and goings.
Chad had even promised to fly her to Washington, D.C., to
meet his mother. She imagined an open-armed welcome.
Mona Shriver would vanish from the face of the earth, and
Mona Bannen would be born—with an entirely different
and better life awaiting her. She began to hum beneath her
breath.

"Damn it!"

In the darkness she had stepped into a deep crack in the
sidewalk, and the right heel of her shoe had snapped.

"Fifty dollars!" she groaned aloud; that was what Chad
had paid for the shoes. Balancing herself on one foot and
then the other, she removed both shoes. The right heel was
gone. She fumbled in the clutter of her purse and brought
out a packet of matches. Crouching, she struck a match and
blinked at the sudden glare.

When her eyes adjusted, she spotted the detached heel,
but just as she was about to retrieve it there was movement
at the periphery of her vision. In the moment before the
match flickered and died, she saw a shiny pair of men's
boots. She cowered back, almost slipping to the sidewalk,
eyes probing the darkness.

The sandy-haired man from the bar...waiting to prop-
osition her, she thought.

A darker shadow disengaged itself from the doorway of
the warehouse and stepped toward her, the metal guards on

the heels of his boots resounding through the canyon of concrete and bricks.

There was just enough moonlight that she could recognize the familiar face. Her fright fled.

"Oh, it's you!" she said, her voice cracking with relief. Then a thought occurred to her that brought an excited smile to her lips. "But if you're back, then Chad must also—"

The words died in her throat when she saw the glint of moonlight on steel.

She opened her mouth to scream, but the scream turned into a gurgle as the knife was driven into her throat.

"A present from your boyfriend Chad!" the man murmured.

But Mona didn't hear.

She was dead before her body struck the sidewalk.

8

Washington, D.C.

IT HAD BEEN a frustrating Friday morning.

Of the half-dozen friends Quinn had at the Pentagon, two had been transferred, one was on leave somewhere in Florida and another had flatly refused to see him. He'd made appointments to see the remaining two, individually, although both were assigned to the same branch of operations.

Captain Simon McKay had been a buddy of Quinn at college, and was now an admiral's aide. He had been a jock, not overly bright but well connected, and his commission had raised many military eyebrows.

Their meeting had gone badly.

Captain McKay had risen behind his impressive desk with a smile and an outstretched hand. After a hurried hello, he'd launched immediately into reminiscing about "old times" at college; he had even referred to them as "the good old days." Quinn had played along, but only briefly. When he'd described the circumstances of his son's death, Captain McKay's face had paled. He'd mumbled insincere condolences; then, remembering a sudden appointment, he'd made excuses and left his office without so much as a promise to be in touch.

Now Quinn paced in Commander Blackmer's outer office.

Blackmer had been a friend of his and Dorothy's when he'd been stationed in Hawaii. He'd been a captain then. The lettering on his door now designated him Commander Nathan Blackmer, Department of the Navy, Vital Statistics. Judging from the stacks of papers, reports and letters behind which his yeoman third class, a blond woman in her early twenties, sat working, Blackmer was indeed a busy man.

Quinn glanced impatiently at his wristwatch. It was a quarter to twelve, already fifteen minutes past his appointment time. Blackmer would undoubtedly have a luncheon date and be too pressed for time to spare much for an old friend, especially an old friend who had left the service under questionable circumstances.

The yeoman caught Quinn checking his watch. She managed an encouraging smile. "Commander Blackmer's on the telephone, sir. He should be free any minute."

Quinn nodded his thanks.

The intercom sounded almost immediately. The yeoman answered, hung up and said, "You may go in now, Commander Bannen."

Quinn hadn't seen Nathan Blackmer in eleven years and wasn't prepared for the man who came from behind his desk, hand extended. In Hawaii, Blackmer had been youthful, robust, a storehouse of energy when others had been on the verge of collapsing. He had always been scuba diving, hang gliding, surfing; he had swum every morning before reporting for duty and every evening before retiring.

Quinn remembered a muscular man with golden-blond hair bleached almost white by the sun. The man who greeted him now was pale, his face heavily wrinkled, his blond hair thinning and gray. His uniform coat seemed too large for his frame, and he moved around the desk without zest, as if the mere effort of extending his hand in greeting drew from a dwindling reserve of strength.

"Bannen! I'll be damned! Good to see you, old friend." His handshake was weak, his palm moist. "How long has it been? Twelve years, at least. I heard you'd retired. How's Dorothy?" Motioning Quinn to be seated, he returned to his own chair behind the desk and sat down heavily. Although the intonation in his voice was one of surprise and delight, that was belied by his nervousness and the wariness in his pale eyes.

"Dorothy and I are divorced," Quinn said evenly. "And Melissa?"

"Divorced," Commander Blackmer echoed. "Eight years ago. She sent me a Dear John postcard while I was deployed to Alaska. Went back to Maine and eventually married her high school sweetheart."

"I'm sorry," Quinn told him.

"Yes, well, the statistics on military divorce are high, very high. That's how I've come to think of it, as a statistic."

Acutely aware of Blackmer's nervousness, Quinn began to formulate a suspicion that greatly distressed him. Settling back in his chair, he tried to appear more relaxed than he felt. "You'd be an expert on statistics, Nathan," he said, indicating the plaque on the desk that repeated the wording on the commander's door.

Commander Blackmer's laugh rang hollow. His smile faded. He leaned forward and laced his thin fingers together on the desktop. "Quinn, I'm short on time, only six months before my retirement." His pale eyes shifted down to his locked fingers. "I can't risk anything that will make waves, you understand?"

"It was obvious when I walked in that you knew about Chad's death," Quinn murmured. "You failed to inquire about his health. I remember you were always fond of Chad. You said he was the son you'd never have because of Melissa's sterility. In case you don't remember, you were his godfather."

"Of course I remember," the commander said. "If I hadn't been ill, I would have gone to Chad's funeral. But Quinn, you've been nosing around again. With your record, that means danger to a man like me, who's approaching retirement. I'm in poor health. The navy could force me to retire early. All they need is an excuse. I couldn't live on a reduced pension—I've remarried, we have a house in Virginia, a daughter six years old. There's a mortgage, home improvement loans, a college fund and—" He broke off, reading the disgust on Quinn's face, and turned his swivel chair to face the window.

"Who called you?" Quinn asked. "Simon McKay?"

Without turning, the commander nodded. "News of your visit to the Pentagon will spread faster than wildfire," he said. "A lot of conclusions will be drawn because of your past history. The question of illegally administered drugs will undoubtedly be brought up again. You can't escape a record like yours. You created the monster, old friend, and to the military you've become the monster you created."

"This has nothing to do with the past, Nathan," Quinn assured him.

"I know, I know! But your past won't be forgotten, not in your lifetime."

"I'm merely a father trying to get at the truth about his son's death."

"I read the reports," Commander Blackmer said. "A drug overdose. Statistically the highest cause of death in the peacetime military."

"I'm not talking about fucking statistics here!" Quinn blurted. "I'm talking about my son! Your godson! A boy you knew and claimed to love!" He struggled to hold back his anger, knowing it could only be detrimental to his cause. "Did you hear about the private autopsy Dorothy ordered?"

"There were...rumors," the commander said, still looking out of the window.

"And what conclusions do you draw from the missing vital organs?"

"A mistake," Blackmer answered quickly. "Some harried medical team disposed of them outside normal procedure."

Quinn slid forward to the edge of his chair. "When was the last time you saw Chad, Nathan?"

"Two years ago. My wife and I ran into him at a restaurant. A young woman was waiting for him at a table. I asked him if she was his wife. He said no, he'd never marry. He was adamant. I thought it an odd statement for a young man so handsome and virile, but I didn't question him then. I called later and spoke to Admiral Burke. The old man told me his grandson had returned to active duty. I never thought any more about it. Not until I read the report of his death."

Blackmer turned his chair back to his desk and faced Quinn. His wrinkled face was drawn, and his pale eyes were cold and determined. "We were once good friends, Quinn. I cherish that memory. We had great times in Hawaii, Melissa and I, you and Dorothy—and Chad. But that was the past. I have to think about myself, my future and my family. Just seeing you for a few minutes puts everything I hold dear in jeopardy. I'm sorry about Chad, I really am. But I can't help with your inquiries. You may be, just as you say, only a concerned father trying to learn the truth about his son's death, but you've been labeled a muckraker. Your name is synonymous with conspiracy. Chad's gone, Quinn. Let the dead be buried and the living get on with their—"

Quinn rose abruptly, his face flushed with outrage, and walked from Commander Blackmer's office.

As he descended the steps of the Pentagon a few minutes later, Quinn was so engrossed in his angry thoughts that he failed to hear his name spoken.

"Commander Bannen!" someone called again, louder this time.

Quinn turned to the man running toward him.

He was in his mid-thirties, with brown hair and blue eyes set close together. His nose was broad, the nostrils flared. His hair was worn long. There was a Cary Grant cleft in his chin, but unlike Grant's, it did nothing to enhance his appearance. He wore a gray business suit; the coat was wrinkled and looked as if it had been slept in. His blue-and-gray-striped tie was sloppily knotted and loose around his collar.

There was something familiar about the man, Quinn thought. Yes, it was his crooked eyeteeth. They were larger than the others, looked almost vampirish—

"Jonathan McKinney!" Quinn extended his hand in greeting.

"It's good to see you again, Commander." Jonathan McKinney had once been the youngest reporter on the *New York Daily News*. It had been he who, after several meetings with Quinn, had broken the story of the armed forces' illegal experiments with hallucinogenic drugs.

Jonathan was heftier now, his brown hair thinning on top; his once-impeccable sports clothes had given way to the business suits of success and middle age. He pumped Quinn's hand and repeated, "It's good to see you again, Commander."

"You're apparently the only person in Washington who thinks so," Quinn told him. He glanced back toward the Pentagon, anger still blazing in his eyes. "What newspaper are you with now, Jonathan?"

"I'm with one of the press services," came the answer. "What brings you back to Sin City, Commander? The last I heard, you were raising horses in the Northwest." His blue eyes narrowed. "If it's something I might use..." He shrugged, then smiled. "I owe my success to you. If you hadn't brought the drug experiments exposé to me..."

Although McKinney was a good writer, in speech he had the annoying habit of leaving his sentences dangling, Quinn remembered.

Quinn stared at the reporter for several seconds without speaking. Then he ran a hand thoughtfully through his blond hair and said, "I just might have something for you, Jonathan, but it won't be headline material. It's personal—human interest, I guess you'd call it." He looked again at the Pentagon. "Maybe even an inside-page column would shake those frightened, lethargic bastards into action!"

"I'm all ears," Jonathan said.

"Then come along, my friend," Quinn told him. "I'm going to buy you a cup of coffee and tell you a story."

"Just like old times, huh, Commander?" Jonathan said with a laugh. "Only make it Scotch and soda. Coffee gives me stomach cramps, remember?"

9

Washington, D.C.
CONGRESSMAN Duane Hackermann, a Democrat from North Dakota, was an outspoken critic of the military.

Congressman Hackermann was having a Friday as hectic as Quinn Bannen's was frustrating.

Recently he'd been appointed chairman of a defense subcommittee charged with the investigation of military spending. He was determined that his committee, unlike the 1984 committee charged with the same investigation, would uncover more than just three-hundred-dollar toilet seats and one defense contractor who'd cheated the government. There was an election only eleven months away, and he had every intention of being returned to his seat in Congress. The number of reports he'd read since his appointment had already passed one hundred; three times that number awaited his perusal. The subcommittee convened on Monday; he had planned to spend the weekend locked away in his study with the remaining reports. But his wife, Amanda, had made plans the month before to attend the opening of a play in New York, a revival of Tennessee Williams's *The Rose Tattoo*, in which her college roommate made her Broadway debut in a minor role.

He had tried to cancel the trip to New York, had discreetly suggested Amanda's sister in his stead, but his wife had been adamant. He had promised they would go, long before the chairmanship had been offered him; Amanda insisted he keep his promise, reports or no reports. She had sacrificed her career to be a congressman's wife; his sacrifice of one weekend was not an unreasonable request.

Congressman Hackermann barred his doors to his constituents that Friday, telling his secretary to inform all callers that he was out or involved in committee meetings; only those members of his staff working on the Defense Department reports were to be allowed to enter his office. The day before, he had discovered an irregularity in financial reports submitted by a New Jersey armaments contractor. In the preceding year the contractor had exceeded by $150,000 its budget for armaments delivered to a California naval base, by $54,000 to an army base in North Carolina and by $33,000 to an air force base in Arizona—a total overrun of $237,000—small potatoes compared to what Hackermann expected to discover, but a beginning, and one worth checking out. He had had a member of his staff accumulate all records relating to the contractor—budget, financial reports, per-item costs and bills of lading. All information had been fed into his computers, and comparisons had been made and cross-referenced. The computer readouts had been on his desk when he had arrived that morning.

It was late afternoon before he found time to study the information. He immediately put through a call to the president of the armaments company. They spoke for more than half an hour, during which the congressman made hasty notes. When he broke the connection he summoned the member of his staff who had handled the company's reports and gave him several sheets of notations.

"There's something definitely suspect here," he told the staff member. "The per-item cost of each weapon corresponds exactly to the budget, and so does the quantity shipped. Yet the billing exceeds the total cost estimate by $237,000. The president of the armaments company swears all related documents were submitted by his accounting department. He's even been paid and is submitting another bid on his next contract. Yet it doesn't wash. Look into it. Either the Defense Department has been overcharged or there's a hell of a lot of weapons floating around out there that are unaccounted for and unofficially authorized."

When the staff member scurried away, the congressman went back to reading his reports, determined to cram as much work as possible into the remaining hours before his wife picked him up on the way to the airport and their weekend in New York.

The diligent staff member made phone calls to the Defense Department. He was disconnected twice and shuffled from extension to extension until he was finally put in touch with a lieutenant commander responsible for approving payments to the armaments company.

The staff member identified himself and Congressman Hackermann and presented the congressman's inquiries into the irregularities he had uncovered.

The lieutenant commander said he would look into the matter over the weekend and return the congressman's call on Monday.

The staff member hung up, unaware that he had just put Congressman Hackermann and himself on the hit list of an organization that made the Mafia look like the equivalent of a neighborhood street gang.

10

QUINN BOUNDED UP the walkway and rang the doorbell.

Before the echo of the chimes had died away inside, the door was opened by a hefty black maid, who looked as if she had the ability to hold any man at bay. She eyed him suspiciously, arranging her bulk squarely in the middle of the door frame.

"I'd like to see Dorothy Bannen," Quinn told her. He had a copy of the late edition of the *Post* under his arm.

The maid glared at him threateningly. "Mrs. Bannen isn't seein' any reporters," she announced stiffly, and started to close the door in his face.

"Wait! I'm Quinn Bannen, her husband. Ex-husband," he corrected. "Tell Dorothy I'm here, please."

The woman nodded. Suspicion still evident in her eyes, she allowed Quinn into the entryway. "Wait here," she commanded. "I'll see if she's in, to you."

As the maid moved away, Quinn's gaze swept the familiar entryway: Italian marble floors, an Aubusson carpet, French crystal chandelier, an inlaid malachite table flanked by two authentic Louis XV armchairs upholstered in celadon silk brocade. Quinn had always felt intimidated by the admiral's wealth. Dorothy had settled for much less when she had married him—a modest home with modest furnishings and frequent upheavals when he was transferred from station to station. She had never complained, and he had admired her for it.

"Quinn." Dorothy emerged from a side room, closing the doors behind her. Her diaphanous white summer dress, waist snug and the skirt flowing, was reminiscent of late forties style, except for the length of the skirt. She had never been one to choose her clothes to fit the latest fashion trends. The dress was feminine and suited her, Quinn thought.

Dorothy tilted her head to receive his kiss on the cheek. When she looked up at him, her eyes were scolding. "You shouldn't have come here, Quinn," she told him. "The admiral is in a rage over the article in the *Post*."

"I thought he might be," Quinn confessed.

"The telephone hasn't stopped ringing. Nor the doorbell. We've turned away reporters from every major newspaper and news service. It's like—" She faltered. "Like before." The expression in her dark eyes told him she was remembering the past scandal with painful clarity. "The admiral is talking of leaving for Key West until this blows over," she went on.

"And you? Will you go with him?"

"Of course. He's not well, Quinn, and he refuses to hire a qualified nurse. You should have warned me you were going to the press. I could have prepared him, could have prepared myself."

Quinn took the edition of the *Post* from beneath his arm and opened it. A one-column photograph of Chad in uniform, smiling, stared back at him; he had taken it from his wallet and given it to Jonathan McKinney that morning. "I didn't expect the front page," he confessed.

The article was halfway down the page; the caption read: Parents Hit Naval Roadblock in Probe of Son's Death. The article was short and to the point, written in Jonathan's inimitable style. An ulterior motive for the navy's having failed to return Chad's internal organs was only hinted at. "I guess the human-interest aspect intrigued the editors," Quinn said as he refolded the newspaper.

Dorothy said nothing.

"I came to tell you I'm taking the red-eye special back to California tonight," Quinn told her. "I want to go through Chad's letters there. I know he mentioned names, places. I don't know where else to begin."

"I'd say you've already begun!" Admiral Burke's voice boomed from the doorway of his study.

Dorothy flinched.

"Come in, Bannen," the admiral said, his intonation making his words more a command than a request.

Dorothy followed Quinn into her father's study. When he seated himself in a chair across the desk from the admiral, she went to the window and stood with her back to the room. Her shoulders were stooped, and her head drooped forward as if the burden she carried had drained the strength from her neck.

The admiral had not shaved that morning. The gray stubble made his face appear even more haggard than usual. He wore a beige cardigan sweater that, since his stroke, was several sizes too large for him and sagged at the shoulders. "I won't ask if you know what the hell you're doing, Bannen," he said. "I know damned well you do not. Typical of your kind, you're seeing conspiracy where there is none."

"Exactly what is my 'kind,' Admiral?" Quinn challenged.

"You're a dinosaur, a throwback to the sixties," the admiral answered disparagingly. "You suspect treachery and intrigue behind everything connected with the establishment. While your peers have turned in their militant marching sneakers for hundred-dollar jogging suits, you've clung to the rebellious-college-student image, refusing to grow up. You're outdated, obsolete and, I suspect, a paranoid personality in need of a good psychiatrist."

The old man had been shuffling papers on his desk as he spoke. He suddenly flung them to one side, folded his liver-spotted hands on the desktop and glared at Quinn without bothering to veil his hatred. "You're the leper who'll infect us all unless we cut you out of our midst. Your type is well documented in history, Bannen."

"Not nearly as well as the Hitlers and Stalins, the Oswalds and the Sirhans are documented," Quinn retorted. "*Your* type, Admiral."

"I've always rued the day my daughter married you, Bannen. Except for Chad, your entire relationship was a fiasco. I believe you both realize that. For some obscure reason that's why you're so tenaciously pursuing this attempt to prove a conspiracy behind Chad's death. Neither of you can accept the fact that the boy was flawed, because that makes your relationship a *complete* failure. A less-than-perfect son leaves you no proud memories to cling to. Now, God forbid, the two of you are starting up again."

Dorothy turned her head and stared at them over her shoulder. "Father, don't!" she warned.

That she had called him "Father" instead of "Admiral" told both men the extent of her distress.

The admiral lowered his voice. "Do you realize the untenable position you've put my daughter and myself into, Bannen? You spread doubts about Chad's death to the press, doubts I don't share, and then you fly off to California and leave us to suffer the consequences. Again you threaten my family with scandal. Not to mention the irreparable damage you do the military at this crucial time in our history. Under this new president, the military is coming back into its own after decades of political repression. The Congress is about to approve an expanded military budget. The climate surrounding all branches of the armed forces is in a delicate balance until that approval is confirmed. Your accusations could tilt the scales of—"

"That's the crux of it, isn't it, Admiral?" Quinn cut in. "The delicate position of the military. You don't give a damn if your grandson's name is cleared! Not if it threatens your precious military!"

"Damn you, Bannen! Go back to California! Whisper your suspicions to your horses and leave the rest of us in peace." The admiral rose from behind his desk, his face flushed, his eyes bulging in their sockets. He was visibly fighting to control his anger. Then with forced calm, he said, "There's no place to take this, Bannen. There's no treachery or conspiracy involved, nothing malevolent to expose. Chad died of a drug overdose—that's it in a nutshell. Let the poor boy rest in peace. The interest of the press will fade when the next tragedy comes along and pushes Chad's to the back pages. I implore you to let this go, Bannen."

"I can't do that, Admiral. Not when there's a shadow of doubt."

Quinn got to his feet and turned toward Dorothy. She continued to stand with her back to the room, her hands clenched into fists at her sides.

"If there's anything I can do to prove my son didn't die of a drug overdose, I'll do it," Quinn said determinedly. "I owe him that. *We* owe him that." He waited for Dorothy to turn and support him. When she didn't, he spoke her name quietly; she stiffened but didn't turn. "Enjoy Key West," he said bitterly, and hurried for the door.

"Bannen, you're making the second biggest mistake of your life!" Admiral Burke called after him. "You challenged the power of the military establishment once and escaped unscathed. You won't be as fortunate a second time. They'll be prepared for you!" He heard the entryway door slam behind Quinn. Dropping back into his chair, he murmured, "The damn fool! The intractable goddamned fool!"

11

Moffett Field, California

IT WAS A MUGGY DAY in northern California.

Chief Loomis half reclined in his swivel chair, his feet propped on the corner of his desk, and stared from his second-story window at the summer storm clouds gathering over the distant San Francisco Bay. The storm was supposed to hit Mountain View before sunset.

Below the chief's window, a group of sailors were marching off punishment on the tarmac. The rhythmic thud of their feet was like music to his ears. In Loomis's opinion, the military was becoming too damned lax. He was an advocate of strict discipline and harsh punishment; the stricter the discipline and the harsher the punishment, the greater his satisfaction. The sailors under his command referred to him as the navy's Marquis de Sade, or simply as 'that sadistic son-of-a-bitchin' chief!' Instead of finding this offensive, Chief Loomis reveled in his reputation. It was, after all, his reputation as a "hardass" that had called him to the attention of Admiral Addison. Out of the numerous enlisted chiefs serving under the admiral, he alone had been picked for the special assignment of training the organization's new recruits.

The telephone rang, and Chief Loomis stretched to answer it without altering his comfortable position. As soon as he heard the voice on the other end of the line, however, he moved his feet from his desk to the floor and straightened in his chair as if his caller could have observed his relaxed stance. You never relaxed around Admiral Addison.

"Yes, sir. It's a secure line," he said in answer to the admiral's first question, chiding himself for not answering with his rank and name and whether the line was or wasn't secure. Sweat started to bead on his forehead. Nervousness like what he experienced before going into battle or sending a new recruit on his first mission began to tighten the muscles of his abdomen. Admiral Addison never called him unless there was a crucial assignment or a threat to the organization.

"What do you have to report on the San Diego exercise, chief?"

Bannen's whore, Chief Loomis thought quickly. "Terminated, sir."

"No complications?"

"None, sir." The chief had a mental image of the admiral sitting ramrod straight behind his desk in Norfolk, his gray eyes staring coldly out of his ashen face. One of the captains had christened the old boy "The Gray Hawk." It fit! It damn well fit!

"We have another dilemma now, Chief," the admiral informed him. "A much more delicate matter than reducing the whore population of San Diego."

Chief Loomis waited, saying nothing. He knew better than to question the admiral.

"We were all in error in failing to anticipate difficulties with Operative Bannen's family," the admiral said crisply. "Errors, Chief, cost lives. Promotions, at the very least. Do I make myself clear?"

"Yes, sir. Very clear." The chief wiped the sweat from his furrowed brow, then wiped his hand on his trouser leg. "Is it the grandfather, sir? Or the father?" he ventured.

"Commander Quinn Bannen, retired," the admiral answered. "The grandfather I can handle. He's all military, from his deteriorating gray cells to his shriveled balls."

Chief Loomis allowed himself a thin smile.

"Quinn Bannen is another story entirely," the admiral continued. "I thought the bastard was firmly entrenched at his goddamned horse ranch. Up to his neck in horseshit. But he's making waves in Washington. He managed to have a journalist buddy of his secure him a front-page write-up in the *Post*. Every other fucking paper in the country is likely to jump on the story like dogs on a bitch in heat. The stricken parents, the son's missing internal organs, the navy's lack of cooperation, that sort of crap. It's caught the fancy of the press. Those bastards are always looking for a reason to sling mud at the military establishment."

"Jesus! What do you want me to do, sir?"

"You? About the press? Nothing, Chief. Even you have your limitations." The admiral's sarcasm was not lost on Chief Loomis. "As long as the family doesn't grant further interviews—and I have Admiral Burke's assurances they will not—today's news will be, as they say, tomorrow's garbage-can liner. But Quinn Bannen needs watching. There's no predicting what that bastard will do next, or what damaging information he might stumble on. He leaves Washington tonight for California. His destination is that damned ranch of his. The address is, I presume, in his son's dossier?"

"Yes, sir. Along with a complete profile on the commander and the grandfather."

"I want you to assign our best surveillance man to Bannen," the admiral said. "I want him to become the son of a bitch's shadow, and I want him to report directly to you every eight hours. If Quinn Bannen takes a leak or farts, I want it in your report. Is that understood?"

"Yes, sir."

"Warn our operative not to underestimate Bannen," the admiral advised him. "The Defense Department did just that in the past, and they're still licking their wounds. Bannen is idealistic, moralistic, hotheaded, and he talks too much. Traits his son apparently inherited."

"Yes, sir," Chief Loomis said. He stood and looked out the window, leaning against the desk. He noticed that the rain had started to streak the windowpanes. "If the opportunity presents itself, sir, do you want Bannen taken out?"

"For Christ's sake, Chief! If I wanted Bannen taken out I'd give the order!"

"Yes, sir."

"What about the replacement for Chad Bannen? Have you located anyone who meets our stringent specifications?"

Chief Loomis turned quickly back to his desk and flipped open a file folder he had been studying earlier. He had decided to reject the sailor in question, but because the admiral seemed anxious about a replacement, he reconsidered. "There's someone whose record I'm scrutinizing now, sir," he said. "A yeoman second class named James A. Mayfield. He's assigned to the admiral's staff here at Moffett Field."

"Having a yeoman who's on the admiral's staff could prove a useful advantage," Admiral Addison said thoughtfully. "Just don't make the mistake you made with Chad Bannen."

"Uh, sir."

The admiral broke the connection without bothering with the customary farewell. Chief Loomis continued to hold the receiver for several moments, then slammed it down into its cradle.

The fucker! he thought. The buck-passing fucker!

It was the admiral himself who had chosen Chad Bannen. The chief had opposed recruiting Bannen because he didn't meet their specifications; he wasn't an orphan, and he was known to have influence in high places; he also came from a military family.

The chief had understood Admiral Addison's reasons for recruiting Bannen. The admiral had planned to use Chad Bannen in a manipulative power play with the youth's grandfather. Now, because recruiting Chad Bannen had proved to be a mistake, the admiral was making Chief Loomis the scapegoat.

One of the injustices of the military, Chief Loomis thought angrily. The officers made the decisions and took the credit for the successes, and the enlisted men took the blame for the failures.

A sudden, powerful clap of thunder rattled the window. A lightning flash streaked the sky, and then the rain began to sleet against the panes. Below Chief Loomis's window, the sailors continued to march off their punishment, their steps muffled now by the cushioning downpour.

12

California

BEHIND SCHEDULE because of head winds, Quinn's flight landed in Redding, California, at 2:15 a.m. By 2:30 he had claimed his luggage, located the eight-year-old Ford LTD he'd left in the parking lot and was driving north on Highway 5.

It had rained earlier, and the highway was wet and slippery. Traffic was light; there were the headlights of two automobiles behind him, and a semi with a double trailer kept passing in the fast lane on the level stretches and falling behind on the mountain grades. Occasionally he came to a section of highway that was not divided, and then the lights of the oncoming traffic stung Quinn's tired eyes. In another couple of hours logging trucks would be jamming the highway. He had lived among the loggers long enough to understand why they welcomed the rain. It reduced the threat of fire and kept the forestry service from limiting or canceling their seasonal work. Matt Wade, Quinn's nearest neighbor, was a logger. It was a hard life.

Quinn had slept only fitfully on the plane. Despite his exhaustion, he knew he wouldn't sleep when he reached the ranch. Whenever he closed his eyes either he was plagued by the image of Dorothy standing at the admiral's study window with her back meaningfully turned to him or he fretted over what to do next to uncover the truth about Chad's death.

An hour out of Redding, the sky cleared. When he reached Mount Shasta the moonlight had turned the snow-capped peak an eerie silver gray. No wonder, he thought, the Indians had worshiped the mountain and believed one of their gods resided there. His ranch was in sight of the mountain. Quinn began to relax, his body slowing shedding some of the tension of the past few days.

The reflected glare in the rearview mirror stung his eyes as one of the cars that had been following him picked up speed and passed. The second car changed to the fast lane but held its position behind him. Quinn glanced at his speedometer. He was doing seventy. The driver was probably pressing his automobile just to keep up with another car on the lonely highway.

Quinn slowed his speed when he began to see familiar turnoffs; so, too, did the car behind him. "Sorry, mister, but you're going to lose your traveling companion," he said aloud. He signaled, then turned off the highway. The other car sped on, its headlights lost around a curve.

Quinn's ranch was located at the near edge of a valley.

He switched off his headlights and pulled slowly into his driveway, hoping the crunch of tires on the loose gravel would not awaken his housekeeper. The sky was turning paler along the eastern horizon; it would be sunrise soon, and yet he knew he wouldn't be able to sleep. He left his luggage in the car and went quietly into the house.

He changed from what he called his "city clothes" into Levi's and a Pendleton shirt, and slipped out of the house again. He went into the stables, saddled the gelding he had meant to give Chad on his first visit to the ranch and rode away.

Sunrise found him on a high bluff overlooking the valley.

He went there often to be alone, to plan and to dream. Since his last visit he had lost two dreams: Chad would never share the ranch with him, and Dorothy had destroyed his hopes of reconciliation forever.

Although he'd been holding it off by force of will since receiving the telegram, suddenly now Chad's death struck him full force. His body shook with grief, but he refused to allow himself to cry. Tears were a luxury he would allow himself only after he learned the truth about his son's death. He had never felt so alone, so lonely; nor had his future ever looked so bleak. Then he chided himself for succumbing to self-pity. He took a cigarette from his pocket, lit it and sat smoking and gazing out across the awakening valley.

As much as it was possible to love a home, Quinn loved his ranch and the valley in which it was located. The ranch represented security and freedom and peace of mind; if his dreams had not died with Chad, it would eventually have offered total contentment. The valley was picture perfect, with unspoiled timberland circling the outer edges and knolls and patchwork fields comprising the center. To Quinn, the valley was an oasis of beauty hidden within the otherwise ugly terrain of that section of California. The residents of the valley were country people, weather-worn men who either farmed or worked in the lumber mills outside the valley and their down-to-earth, hardworking wives. Young people were at a minimum, most having sought what they believed to be the greener pastures and excitement of the cities as soon as they were old enough to take care of themselves. The parents clung to their belief that their children would eventually return when they realized what they had left behind.

In many ways, life in the valley was primitive. Many of the homes were heated by wood-burning stoves; meals were prepared on the same great cast-iron monsters, which made kitchens hell for the women in the summertime. Some of the poorer farms still had outhouses. Water was pumped from wells and heated in giant cauldrons for Saturday-night baths.

As he sat and felt the peaceful scene soothe his troubled mind, Quinn watched the smoke rise from several chimneys and hang in a blue haze in the still, clear morning air. Finally he crushed out his cigarette, mounted the gelding and rode down the mountainside to the ranch.

Esther Wade had seen his car in the driveway when she'd gotten up, and was preparing breakfast. She was a stout woman in her sixties, with gray hair worn pulled back se-

verely from her face and clipped into a chignon at the nape
of her neck. Despite her good nature, Esther Wade never
smiled because of her ill-fitting dentures, so people who
didn't know her often took her to be cantankerous. She always wore cotton print housedresses she ordered from
Montgomery Ward's sales catalogs and, regardless of the
weather, a hand-knitted cardigan sweater that she draped
over her shoulders. Although her hands were slightly
gnarled by arthritis, she never complained and never allowed the affliction to interfere with her duties. She'd been
a widow for the past ten years. Her son Matt and his wife
were Quinn's nearest neighbors.

Esther looked up from the stove as Quinn entered and
nodded a greeting. "Your breakfast will be ready in ten
minutes," she told him. "Two eggs enough?"

Quinn had no appetite, but he knew he would be lec-
tured if he didn't eat. "Two eggs are plenty," he assured her.
"Has Old Sammy been tending the horses properly?" The
man known only as Old Sammy was a retired logger who
acted as Quinn's handyman when he was not on one of his
frequent binges.

"Comes every morning, leaves every night," Esther said
dully. "He don't bother me in the house, I don't bother him
in the stables. It's fine that way, just fine." The old woman
had known Old Sammy since she'd been a girl and she didn't
approve of his excessive drinking.

"I'm going away again tomorrow," Quinn told her. "If
it's too lonely here for you by yourself, or if you're frightened stuck out here so far from the neighbors, I'll just close
up the house. I don't know how long I'll be gone this time."

Esther cracked two eggs into a pan of melted butter. "I'm
never lonely, Commander Bannen," she said, "and I'm too
old to be frightened by much. I've made peace with my
Maker. To tell you the truth, I feel better here than with
Matt and Joanna. Two women in one house never works.
I'd be glad to stay here and look after things as long as

you're away. Don't worry about me or the house. I'll even manage to keep Old Sammy sober if that's what you want. You go and do what you have to do. Your ranch and horses will be waitin' for you when you're ready to come home.'' Esther had been present during Quinn's phone calls concerning Chad's death and had discerned more than he had realized.

Quinn thanked her, accepted her offer to stay on and went to wash up. On his way back to the kitchen he stopped in the spare room he had converted into an office and gathered up Chad's letters from his desk drawer. In the kitchen, he laid them beside his plate.

Esther's coffee was good and strong. He had two cups, and because the old woman was watching he did his best with the bacon, eggs and homemade biscuits.

"Try some of them preserves, too," she urged him. "Made 'em from wild blackberries gathered up near Shasta Lake last summer."

Quinn spooned preserves onto a biscuit to please her; they tasted delicious. He was hungrier than he'd realized. While he ate, he stared at the letters Chad had written, and a dread of rereading them spread through him. In all honesty, he couldn't pretend he'd been a good father. While his son had been young he'd been busy with his career; then had come the divorce. The custody trial had given him only summers with his son, and of those many summers they had spent only the first two together before Quinn had retired and purchased the ranch and before Chad had followed his footsteps by enlisting in the navy. Quinn realized Chad had been virtually a stranger to him; during his important, formative years, Quinn had been an absentee father. He had always told himself he would eventually make things up to Chad. Now it was too late.

Before his determination could wane, Quinn pushed away his plate and began reading the letters, starting with the most recent.

Chad had written of his girlfriend, Mona Shriver:

I doubt you'd understand why a man like me would be attracted to a woman like Mona. She's what Mother would call "simple" or a "diamond in the rough." She's had a hard life and few lucky breaks, but she's retained a hopeful approach to life and her heart is pure. She's loving and understanding and has a remarkable talent for pleasing me. At this stage in my life, I feel she's good for me. I'm even considering marriage, although I have to admit that yours and Mom's breakup left me with a negative attitude to the state of matrimony. If you ever find yourself in San Diego at one of your horse shows while I'm deployed, I'd appreciate your looking up Mona and getting to know her. You're in for a shock, but I think your forty-plus heart can take it.

At the end of the letter, Chad had scribbled an address in San Diego.

Quinn found a notepad and jotted down the address. Then he went on reading the letters.

Sentences that had only slightly touched him when he had originally read them took on new meaning and reached him with greater impact now:

Sometimes I get lonely for you, Dad. I feel as if I've lost you forever, that you're not on a ranch in California, but that you've died and I'll never see you again. Funny, huh? How a guy needs his father sometimes, even after he's a grown man himself? I saw an old movie on television called *I Never Sang for My Father*, and the damned thing almost had me in tears. It's about this man who waits too long to tell his father he loves him, and I guess I related it to me and you. Before it's too late, Dad—I love you.

Quinn's throat tightened and his eyes began to brim as he fought for control of his emotions. He turned his head as Esther refilled his coffee cup and took away his plate.

When he could manage to continue, he read on:

The admiral tries to be a father figure. I know the two of you have had your differences, but he's basically a good man, even though he borders on being a fanatic when it comes to the military. He sees the armed services as misused and unappreciated, a pawn of the political powers of the nation, when they could be its savior. He considers you a traitor; my father—the Benedict Arnold. Myself, I'm proud of you, Dad. What you did took guts. I'd like to think of myself as a man of integrity who speaks out for what he believes regardless of the personal dangers, a man with an independent spirit. I'd like to make you as proud of me as I am of you. Maybe someday.

I was proud of you, Chad, Quinn thought. You didn't have to prove anything to me.

When I was a kid and saw you in your uniform I used to be impressed. Back then I never had any desire to follow you or Admiral Burke into the navy. I was proud of you, but it didn't seem like the life for me. If I didn't have an ulterior motive I wouldn't be here now, spit-shining my shoes and getting ready for an inspection. I'd be completing my law degree and planning to set out a shingle in good old Washington, D.C., where the attorney fees are the highest.

I'd never say this to the admiral, but the military is fifty percent horseshit and...got to run...inspection!

Love, Chad.

Ulterior motive. Quinn read the sentence over and over

again. What ulterior motive? Why hadn't he questioned that remark earlier? What possible ulterior motive could Chad have had for enlisting?

After spending an hour reading his son's letters, Quinn came up with three names besides Mona Shriver's. The one mentioned most frequently was that of Mae Aames, a corpsman at Moffett Field. No address, but she shouldn't be too difficult to locate, Quinn decided. The other two names were a Chief Loomis and a Raymond Everett. Chad had nothing but complaints about the chief: "A sadistic bastard who should get a special medal for being the most gung-ho prick in the modern navy." Everett, a boatswain second class, was mentioned as a drinking buddy and was the man who had introduced Chad to Mona.

Quinn bundled up the letters, then carried the notepad to the telephone and dialed San Diego Information. There was no telephone number listed for Mona Shriver. He'd have to surprise her with a visit; he didn't even know if she was aware of Chad's death. After San Diego he had intended to telephone Moffett Field's personnel locator to inquire about Corpsman Aames, but the heavy breakfast he had eaten intensified his exhaustion. He told Esther Wade he was going to take a nap, returned Chad's letters to his desk drawer and went into his room to stretch out across the bed. In less than three minutes he was sleeping soundly.

Esther turned down the radio in the living room so that it wouldn't disturb him. As she passed the window she heard the sound of an approaching automobile, always a curiosity, for there was little traffic on the country road. She peered through the sheer curtains and saw a red Mustang slow down at the ranch gate. Her eyesight had not been affected by age; she saw the young man behind the wheel distinctly. He was a stranger. She noted the close-cropped brown hair, unusual among the young people in the valley, who in her opinion wore their hair disgustingly long. She wondered if the stranger might be in the military, perhaps one of the retired commander's junior shipmates. But the Mustang paused only briefly, then drove on. Someone lost, Esther decided, and she went back to her duties in the kitchen.

The old woman had no way of knowing that the red Mustang was the same car that had driven north behind Quinn a few hours earlier, so she didn't mention it later, when Quinn got up and she was busy preparing his lunch.

13

DOROTHY LOOKED in the open doorway of her father's bedroom.

The admiral stood at the mirror, struggling with his necktie. Since his stroke he often found simple tasks too difficult to perform—neckties, shoelaces, tasks he had done before his illness without thinking about them. The fact that his body refused to obey the commands of his brain was a great source of frustration. His military rank had conditioned him to expect instant obedience, and now his own body was guilty of insubordination.

Dorothy saw his difficulty and entered his room to assist him with his tie. She was dressed for travel, ready to join the admiral for the limousine ride to the airport. She stood back and inspected the knot of her father's tie. "There are some reporters out front," she told him. "I think we'd best leave by the back way."

The admiral's eyebrows lifted disapprovingly. "I may be retired," he said sternly, "but I'm still an admiral in the United States Navy. I will not slip in and out of back doors like some blasted film or rock star. It's bad enough being driven away from Washington to Key West during off-season by that damned ex-husband of yours. I'll not steal away as if I've something to hide." He turned and scooped up his coat from the bed. "A rap on the head with my cane should send any reporter into retreat."

Dorothy accepted the uselessness of arguing with her father in his present mood. "As you wish, Admiral." She gave a mock salute and left him to finish dressing.

In the kitchen, Mati, their maid, was polishing silver and wrapping it in felt to be stored until their return. She had the portable television set tuned to her midday soap opera.

Dorothy poured herself a cup of coffee and glanced at the TV screen without interest. "The admiral refuses to leave by the back door," she told Mati, sighing wearily. It was not beyond the admiral to actually strike a persistent reporter; then he would find himself facing a lawsuit, not the first to result from his inability to control his temper.

Mati smiled. She was a fan of the admiral and his cantankerous nature. She wiped her hands on a towel and turned from the sink. She was a tall woman with a large-boned frame and a menacing disposition. "Leave the reporters to me," she said, and strode from the kitchen.

Dorothy was about to follow Mati as far as the entryway to watch the maid's success or failure with the reporters when the television caught her attention. A news flash had interrupted the soap opera; then the image of a bedraggled woman who seemed familiar came on screen. As Dorothy stepped forward to turn up the sound, the woman's identity came to her. "Amanda Hackermann," she murmured aloud. Dorothy and the wife of Congressman Hackermann of North Dakota had served as co-hostesses at a charity ball the year before, and the admiral had had the congressman and his wife to dinner the night before they'd received word of Chad's death.

Now Amanda Hackermann's hair was disheveled, her eyes glazed, her attitude suggesting she was heavily sedated. A microphone had been shoved into her face, obviously startling her. "They—they were young," she stammered. "I remembered thinking they were about our son's age. In their mid-twenties. They...were neatly dressed...with short, respectable-looking haircuts...." Tears formed in her eyes and ran unchecked over her cheeks. "They appeared more intent on killing my husband than on...on simply robbing us," she managed, and began to sob. "Even after they had my jewelry...and Duane's wallet and wristwatch...they kept hitting him with the pipe.... His head was— Oh, God! I can't—" She choked on a sob and leaned against a man who had been standing at her side.

"Enough!" the man shouted at the reporters. His arm protectively around Amanda Hackermann, he began pushing his way through the crowd of reporters to a waiting car. As the car sped away, the newscaster's image appeared on the small screen.

Dorothy heard the admiral entering the kitchen behind her and motioned for him to remain silent.

"Congressman Hackermann was pronounced dead on arrival at Bellevue Hospital in New York," the newscaster said solemnly. "The popular Democrat from North Dakota was an outspoken critic of the military and was recently appointed chairman of a defense subcommittee slated to begin investigations into military contractors on Monday. It was Congressman Hackermann who, during the past administration, accused United States intelligence agencies of illegal covert acts against private citizens who were opposed to the president's foreign policy." A photograph of the handsome congressman flashed on the screen. The newscaster's voice-over continued. "Congressman Duane Hackermann of North Dakota, dead at age fifty-five, the victim of apparent muggers on New York's fashionable East Side. Stay tuned for further details on the five-o'clock news."

Dorothy switched off the set. "How awful!" she murmured as she turned to the admiral. "We had dinner with Congressman and Mrs. Hackermann less than two weeks ago," she reminded him. "Amanda wrote me a letter of condolence when she heard about Chad. They were such nice people."

"The congressman was an idealist," the admiral stated flatly. "Like all idealists with a little power, he and his subcommittee were planning to enter waters best left undisturbed. He was against the military. He was even scheduled to attack our new policy on chemical warfare in front of the United Nations next month."

Dorothy was struck by the curious lack of feeling in the admiral's voice. He spoke not a word of regret at the sudden violent murder, just the bitter criticism of the congressman's stand on military issues. "All the same—" she began, but she stopped speaking as Mati came back into the kitchen.

"The reporters have been scattered," the formidable maid announced with satisfaction. "And your limousine's just pulled up."

Admiral Burke turned from his daughter with a laugh. "Mati, you should have been under my command," he said. "Or in a marine unit that specialized in hand-to-hand combat. You'd have been a wonder, yes, sir. I remember..."

Dorothy stopped listening to him as she followed him and the maid toward the front door. Still immersed in thoughts about Congressman Hackermann, she picked up a suitcase and followed her father from the house.

With the admiral settled in the back seat of the limousine and Mati having returned to her soap opera, Dorothy was supervising the loading of the luggage when a blue foreign economy car pulled up to the curb behind the limousine. When the driver climbed hurriedly from behind the wheel, she recognized him at once. Hoping to escape him, she made for the open door of the limousine.

"Mrs. Bannen? Please, Mrs. Bannen? Just a moment of your time?"

Dorothy hesitated briefly, then said firmly, "I'm not granting interviews."

The man continued his approach, not stopping until he was close enough for her to reach out and touch him.

"You do remember me?" he asked.

Dorothy's expression was cold as she stared at his wrinkled suit, his brown hair, with its cowlick at the crown, and his blue eyes, set too close together to be attractive. Memories flooded over her, memories of Quinn and this reporter locked in secret sessions in the family room of her home, of the scandal that had ensued when the armed forces' illegal drug experiments had been made public, of the disintegration of her marriage and the resulting hostility of her son.

"I remember you very well, Mr. McKinney," she said coolly. "I'm still not granting interviews." She turned to join the admiral in the limousine.

McKinney persisted. "It's about your son, Chad."

Dorothy stopped, her fingers on the door handle. She saw the admiral angrily motioning her inside, saw him fumbling threateningly for his cane.

"I've been investigating the disappearance of your son's organs," Jonathan continued hurriedly. "Mrs. Bannen, there's something mysterious about the navy's reluctance to answer questions. Call it a reporter's intuition, but I believe, as your ex-husband does, that there's evidence to be found of a conspiracy involving the death of your son. Everywhere I've turned I've run into a stone wall."

"What do you want from me?" Dorothy demanded.

"A follow-up interview with the boy's skeptical mother. Perhaps a subtle challenge to the navy to prove your son's alleged drug overdose. Quinn thinks publicity will ferret out answers. Perhaps friends or shipmates of your son's will come forward and divulge..."

Admiral Burke slid across the back seat and clasped Dorothy's arm in a viselike grip. "We do not dispute the navy's explanation of my grandson's death!" he shouted at the reporter. He pulled Dorothy into the car, then reached past her and closed the door, locking it. "Drive away quickly!" he commanded the chauffeur.

Dorothy watched Jonathan McKinney grow smaller as the limousine sped away. "Perhaps he was right," she said to her father. "About publicity bringing some of Chad's friends forward with information." The typewritten note she had received flashed through her mind: They killed our Chad!

"Nonsense!" the admiral said authoritatively.

"But if Quinn believes there's a possibility—"

"To hell with what Quinn Bannen believes!" the admiral snapped. "I told you I knew Chad was taking drugs. I'd known for some time and was trying to persuade him to seek professional help. Despite what you may believe, and despite the boy's letters to his father denying it, Chad fell into that large percentage of young servicemen who have gotten themselves addicted."

Seeing the tears in his daughter's eyes, the admiral reached for her hand to comfort her, but she withdrew it and turned to stare out the window, refusing comfort and struggling with her sense of failure as a mother.

14

Norfolk, Virginia

ADMIRAL ADDISON LEFT his hotel and instructed his driver to take him to another hotel near the waterfront. There he got out and, after ordering the driver to pick him up in thirty minutes, went inside.

The admiral knew this hotel well; he had used it many times in the past, both for meetings with other officers involved in the organization and as a place where he could satisfy his rapacious sexual appetite in complete anonymity. Luxurious when built in the 1920s, the hotel had fallen into a state of disrepair along with the neighborhood. Some of its old charm remained, however—the high domed ceilings, the frescoes and columns and the privacy the old structure afforded.

The admiral went directly to the private telephone booth, closed the door and extracted a handful of change from his pocket, which he laid on the narrow counter. The number he dialed had been committed to memory and was known to only seven other individuals: two more admirals, a brigadier general, a general, two majors and a senator. He deposited the exact amount of change and waited.

When the phone was answered, he said, "Addison here, sir."

The answer was curt. "One moment."

Though the mouthpiece at the other end was covered, the admiral heard someone, a secretary perhaps, being dismissed in muffled tones. He fixed his gray eyes on the graffiti-covered wall facing him.

"All right, Addison. We're clear. But make it brief. I have an appointment with the president in fifteen minutes."

"Our congressional problem has been eliminated, sir," the admiral reported with satisfaction.

"Yes, it was on the midday news. But that's only a temporary solution. Another chairman will be appointed. The investigation will go forward."

"But not until we've had time to cover our tracks, sir. The president of an armaments company in New Jersey had a fatal automobile accident this morning. A congressman's staffer was killed in a holdup at his neighborhood delicatessen. Certain records have disappeared from files and computers."

"That's all very well, but what about other loose ends? If one flaw in our planning was found, there'll be others."

"We're doing a sweep, sir. If other mistakes were made, we'll find them first."

"You'd damned well better be right, Addison. I've had news of a disturbing nature concerning a retired commander named Quinn Bannen. He's stirred up some press interest in his son's death."

"That situation is under control, sir." Perspiration beaded on the admiral's ashen face. Was it under control? he asked himself. Perhaps it would have been wiser to have Bannen handled in the same manner as Congressman Hackermann.

"I wish I felt assured. I've been informed that an NIS team has been assigned to look into the young man's death. What the father doesn't uncover, the team most certainly will, so there'd better be nothing to raise suspicions in either section. The withholding of those body parts was a blunder. Even if an operative is unable to identify me, I'd sleep easier knowing the organization is safe from exposure. Our main objective is less than a month away."

"Yes, sir. We're prepared."

"I hope so, Addison, I sincerely hope so. We've come too far to have the entire project blow up in our faces. Is there anything else?"

"No, sir. I'll check in with you on Wednesday as scheduled."

The phone went dead in Addison's ear.

15

Moffett Field, California

JAMES ANDREW MAYFIELD was known to everyone on the Moffett Field admiral's staff as Alex.

As a young man, he had developed a dislike for both of his Christian names and had adopted the name Alex from a biography of Alexander the Great. Only those few officers who had occasion to consult his military record were aware that the name by which he was known had never been legalized. Anyone attempting to investigate Alex Mayfield without knowing the yeoman's legal name would have come up against an Insufficient Data message from the computer's personnel program.

It was not unusual for Yeoman Mayfield to work late; indeed, it was usual. Although he was free to leave the base at five o'clock along with the other members of the admiral's staff, he often chose to remain behind and complete unimportant detail work that any other yeoman would have left in his In basket for the following day without a second thought. He prided himself on never beginning a new day with work left over from the day before. It offended his sense of efficiency; besides, he had practically no civilian social life.

Alex was career navy. He was beginning his seventh of twenty years and would retire at age thirty-eight, hopefully with enough money to buy a small farm in middle America where his retirement income would be sufficient for his meager needs. Although he liked children and wanted a family, he had no plans to marry, for he had great difficulty relating to women. If, when the time came to retire, he qualified for single-parent adoption, he planned to adopt two boys. He, himself, had been adopted. With the death of his adoptive mother, he had been moved from foster home to foster home until he had graduated from high school and gone directly into the navy.

The navy was the first real home he had known, the first place he had had a sense of belonging. After basic training, he had served a short stint in Vietnam, for which he had been awarded the Legion of Merit. Then he had been among the first Americans to return to Eniwetok in the Marshall Islands to clean up after the nuclear testing done there between 1948 and 1958. Moffett Field was Mayfield's fifth duty station. He liked it at Moffett, liked the status of being attached to the admiral's staff and the freedom and scope the position afforded him to satisfy his insatiably inquisitive nature. Because of his seriousness and his intensity he had few friends, and none at Moffett now that his last buddy had been transferred to Hawaii.

Alex had spent a restless night after serving as yeoman to the officers who had assembled in the conference room. He was unable to get the meeting out of his mind. Why would officers from an enlisted chief to an admiral lock themselves away for a meeting? Especially officers assigned to different divisions, who would normally have no contact with one another? Then there had been the ashes in the wastebasket. Standard procedure would have been to place all confidential material in a burn bag for the yeoman to dispose of routinely. Or, if the yeoman had not been cleared to handle secret material, it would have been shredded in the officers' presence. There had also been the names scrawled on the notepad: *Mona Shriver*, *San Diego*, *Della* or *Delta*— and *Chad Bannen*.

It had become customary most mornings for anyone arriving on duty in the admiral's office to find Alex already behind his desk and working. Because he was always well into his day's assignments when the other members of the staff started filtering in, jokes were often made about his having slept there.

When the flag secretary arrived on Friday morning, however, the day after the meeting, Alex wasn't working but just sitting quietly behind his desk, a newspaper open in front of him and his eyes fixed thoughtfully on the ceiling. He failed to greet the secretary, and she stopped to study him questioningly. His expression was troubled, his thoughts seemed to be far away, causing her to inquire if he was ill and wanted to make sick call.

Alex assured her he was in the best of health, folded the newspaper neatly and went to work. Still, he worked with half his usual interest, his thoughts returning again and again to the newspaper article that had caught his attention. He felt like an obsessed puzzle addict, the newspaper article teasing him with yet another fragment of what was becoming an intriguing mystery. A sailor's body had been returned to his parents for burial with the vital organs missing. The sailor's name was Chad Bannen—the name scribbled on one of the notepads at yesterday's meeting.

Although he attempted to concentrate on his duties, as the day progressed Alex realized it was futile for him to attempt to dismiss the mystery without endeavoring to solve it.

As quitting time approached, the other members of the admiral's staff began preparing to leave for the weekend. The admiral himself had already left for the day. The two female civilian employees had retired to the ladies' room to wait out the final minutes and thus avoid any last-minute assignments that might keep them late. One of the admiral's temporary secretaries, a civilian named Hadley, was involved in a heated conversation with a PN2 about personnel data reports the admiral wanted on his desk first thing Monday morning; if the personnel man didn't help out, Hadley would be forced to come in on Saturday, maybe even Sunday, and his plans for a weekend in Carmel with his girlfriend would be spoiled. The personnel man, PN2 Krebs, was not being cooperative. He hated the secretary, referring to him behind his back as that "fuckin' sand crab," a navy expression for civilian personnel that was equivalent to calling a black man a "nigger."

The office door had been left open by the civilian women when they had retreated to the ladies' room. Across the hallway, although a sign was posted reading Door Must Remain Closed, the door to the computer room also stood open. The data processing technician on duty was Chief Hargrave, a slow-talking Southerner from Louisiana who had helped satisfy Alex's curiosity about the computers by teaching him as much about their operation as he himself had learned. Unbeknownst to the chief, the yeoman had then gone one step beyond by taking an advanced course in computers at nearby De Anza College.

Alex watched as Chief Hargrave donned his uniform jacket and began switching off the machines for the weekend. Good, he thought. No last-minute requests for data from the computers was going to keep the chief late.

"You want me to do your work for you, you have the admiral give me the order," Krebs was telling Hadley. "Better still, talk to Mayfield. He feeds his ego by doing everyone else's work. How about it, Alex? You want to do the sand crab's work so he can spend the weekend in Carmel fuckin' himself silly?"

Alex lifted his intense brown eyes from the typewriter long enough to shake his head and dash Hadley's unasked request.

"Damned uncooperative bastards!" Hadley murmured hotly. He grabbed his briefcase and stormed out of the office, almost colliding with the two civilian women as they returned in time to cover their typewriters and depart for the weekend.

PN2 Krebs scowled across at Alex. "I've never known you to turn down an opportunity to nose through personnel records," he said pointedly. "Glad you did, though. Hadley deserves weekend duty. The prick!"

Without looking up, Alex said, "I've got my own work to do. I have to stay late as it is."

The directive he was typing was a sham; he had typed it earlier and marked it for distribution. He was retyping it merely to appear busy until the other personnel had cleared the office.

"Sometimes I wonder about you, Mayfield," Krebs said. "Don't you have a personal life?"

"The navy *is* my life," Alex answered without hesitation. Instead of turning to Krebs as he spoke, he let his gaze wander back to the open door.

Across the hallway, Chief Hargrave was leaving the computer room. He nodded and smiled at Alex, then secured the coded lock box on the door and vanished down the corridor.

PN2 Krebs cleared his desk and left in his customary manner, without saying good-night.

Alone, Alex ceased typing and sat listening intently to the familiar sounds of the building. He knew he had less than two hours before the maintenance crew came in to clean up. His hands were sweating. The muscles at the back of his neck were tight. Unlike a person, however, he thought, the computers would not be able to sense his tension. He rose and walked to the open doorway. The corridor was empty. Stepping back into the office, he closed and locked the door.

Security in the office, indeed in the entire command, had become lax. Usually when someone on the staff was transferred to another station all combinations to safes and lock boxes were changed immediately. In the admiral's office at Moffett Field there had been no personnel transfers in several months. Combinations were kept in a Combination Change Envelope in the admiral's wall safe. The safe was always kept secured when he was not present, but a similar envelope with the combination to his safe was kept in the vault. Since Alex was cleared to handle secret documents and always worked late, it had become his responsibility to secure the vault before leaving.

He went into the vault, opened the top file drawer and removed OPNAV FORM 5511-2, Combination Change Envelope. Admiral's Safe was typed above the label; below in the classification square was typed Secret. Before returning to his desk, Alex took an identical empty envelope from the stock.

His hand shook as he opened the envelope and removed the combination to the admiral's safe. He memorized the three digits and their sequence of turns, retyped the information from the original envelope onto the blank and re-sealed it. He returned the new envelope to the vault, and then went into the admiral's office, where he had no difficulty opening the wall safe.

The combination to the lock box of the computer room was in another combination envelope. He repeated the procedure of opening the envelope, memorizing the sequence of numbers and retyping and replacing the envelope. Since he was also borrowing the admiral's computer code book, he closed the safe without locking it. The entire operation took less than ten minutes.

The corridor was still empty when he stepped out of the office and crossed to the computer room. Quickly he pressed the coded numbers: 5, 3, 2, 4. The computer room door clicked open. He stepped swiftly inside. His breath was coming heavily, and his throat was constricted. He was risking a court-martial, and for what? To solve a goddamn puzzle. He wiped his hands on his trouser legs, then looked at the leather-bound computer code book. Across the face of the binding was stamped one word: CRYPTO, one of the military's highest secret classifications. It was rumored that even the president was not allowed access to CRYPTO data. It crossed Mayfield's mind that he could be shot for doing what he was doing now.

The computer room was always kept at a controlled temperature, but the chief's breaking of smoking regulations was evident from the odor of stale tobacco. The chief had also left a folder of computer readouts marked CLASSI-FIED on top of a machine instead of storing it in the locked cabinets. If any authorized staff member bucking for recognition entered the computer room during the weekend, the chief would be written up.

Alex smiled at the inconsistency of his concern for the chief when his own offense was so much more serious.

After making certain the door had closed, Alex fixed the interior lock in place—a foolish precaution, since anyone passing in the corridor would hear the hum of the machines. He stood with his index finger on the computer switch, listening a final time for sounds of personnel who had not yet left the building. When he heard nothing except automobile engines outside, he snapped the computer to On. Because his nervousness made his hearing acute, he thought the machines sounded unnaturally loud.

Despite his determination, Mayfield was shaking when he sat down and opened the computer code book.

First he punched in the code for naval personnel locator, followed by the name *Chadwick Bannen*, Bannen's rank and the location given in the newspaper article. The computer whined, pinpoints of light exploded on the dark screen, and then: *Bannen, Chadwick, NMN, 541-41-2864, RM2, USN.*

Alex waited, expecting that further information would follow the moment's hesitation while the computer searched for requested data. None came, so he repeated the coding procedure.

Again he read: *Bannen, Chadwick, NMN, 541-41-2864, RM2, USN.*

Alex flipped through the pages of the code book, then repeated the process, this time adding the admiral's security clearance code to the conclusion. He knew there were clearances above the admiral's, even above CRYPTO, but in his wildest imagination he had not suspected such codes would be needed for drawing out information on Bannen from the storage banks.

Chadwick Bannen's name appeared again, followed by NMN—no middle name—Bannen's social security number, rate and rank, and USN. Then the machine gave a rapid rat-tat-tat like the firing of a machine gun and a symbol appeared—a triangle bisected by a straight line running through it from its apex to the midpoint of its base.

Alex's curiosity was driven to new heights by a rush of adrenaline.

The symbol of the bisected triangle was obviously being used to block any information on Bannen that someone without higher rank and need-to-know status might attempt to draw from the computers.

To Alex Mayfield, the blocking symbol was like a red flag waved in the face of an enraged bull.

Now nothing would stop him from further investigation.

PART TWO

16

QUINN'S FLIGHT to San Diego ended during a summer storm.

The airport, considered by most of the country's airline pilots the most dangerous in the western United States, was a hive of activity. Carrying only a small valise, Quinn was able to avoid the crowd milling around the luggage claim area and make straight for the exit doors. As he was about to leave the terminal, he remembered he had smoked his last cigarette during the flight and turned back to buy another package; he'd been smoking more heavily in the past few days than he had for more than three years.

The young man he collided with was tall and muscular, with sandy hair and a bandage across the bridge of his nose. He wore tight-fitting jeans and a loose-fitting print shirt; his shoes were black regulation navy issue. In just as much of a hurry as Quinn, he'd been unable to avoid the collision when Quinn had turned so abruptly.

An apology began to form on Quinn's lips, but before he could make it vocal the young man said, "Sorry, Comman—" Color flooded his face then, and a shocked expression leaped into his dark eyes. He stepped quickly around Quinn and hurried through the glass doors into the crowd.

Quinn had reached the cigarette counter before it struck him that the young man had started to call him "Commander." He turned swiftly, his gaze sweeping the crowd of travelers outside the glass doors, but the youth had vanished. He was too young to have served under Quinn, yet he had started to refer to him as "Commander." Quinn knew that could only mean he was being followed. So he'd made greater waves than he had imagined!

He concentrated on the youth's face, stamping it on his memory for future reference. He cast his thoughts back to when he'd boarded the flight in San Francisco, but he had been preoccupied and couldn't remember having seen the young man then. Most likely he'd been picked up disembarking in San Diego on the instructions of another surveillance expert in San Francisco. *"Commander Quinn Bannen's on flight 409. He's your responsibility now!"* Then again, Quinn thought, perhaps his imagination was running away with him. He was damned tired, and maybe he was losing his sense of perspective. *A paranoid personality in need of a good psychiatrist*, Admiral Burke had called him; the old man's biting tone came back to Quinn with painful clarity.

He paid for his cigarettes, exited the terminal and stood in line for a taxi, a milling crowd of travelers all around him. He glanced fleetingly over the faces but saw no one else he would classify as suspicious. No one showed any interest in him. When his turn came for a taxi, he took the slip of paper with Mona Shriver's address on it from his pocket. When he was about to give the address to the driver, he hesitated, then said, "Somewhere on Broadway, near the center of town." He met the driver's eyes in the rearview mirror; their expression was dull. Paranoid or cautious, Quinn thought, if I'm being followed, I'm not going to make it easy for them.

On Broadway he left the taxi and walked for several blocks, and when he was sure he wasn't being followed he hailed another cab.

Mona Shriver's address on Columbia Boulevard was a run-down apartment building with a Spanish tile roof and faded stucco walls. The narrow strips of lawn on both sides

of the walkway were overgrown with weeds, and bougain-
villea choked the opening of the entryway. Upper windows
had been left open, evidence that the storm had been unexpected. Quite a few tenants would return in the evening to
find their apartments drenched.

As Quinn ran his index finger down the rows of names,
his finger froze suddenly, and he felt a quickening of his
pulse. *Shriver and Bannen, 4F.* His son had lived here with
this woman, been her lover, paid rent, bought groceries—
had been happy, Quinn hoped—and all Quinn knew of her
was what had been hastily written in one of Chad's letters:
*I doubt you'd understand why a man like me would be at-
tracted to a woman like Mona.... I'm even considering
marriage.... Looking up Mona and getting to know
her... her heart is pure.*

Quinn pressed the doorbell and waited.

A buzzer sounded almost immediately, and the outer door
clicked open.

The lobby had a tile floor with several squares missing,
and the walls were papered in an old-fashioned floral print
that had long since faded. As Quinn crossed to the elevator, he noticed that some tiles were loose beneath his feet.
An odor of decay permeated the entire lobby. A sign on the
elevator door read Out of Order. Beneath the sign someone
had written Isn't it always? And then in another hand:
Nothin' in this fuckin' place works!

Quinn paused to catch his breath when he reached the
fourth-floor landing. His heart was pounding against his rib
cage, and his breath was short. Not because he was out of
shape, he told himself, for the ranch kept him physically fit.
It was the tension of meeting Chad's girlfriend in this manner, perhaps being the first to bring her the tragic news of
Chad's death. As his gaze swept the dingy corridor, he noted
that the door to 4F stood open.

A burly man in faded blue coveralls stepped into the open
doorway. He wore a blue-and-white-checked handkerchief

tied around his forehead and was clutching the handle of a mop. His beard was scruffy, and his hair was long, below his collar. Despite the building's chill and the dampness left in the air by the storm, perspiration streaked the man's face. His eyes were heavily hooded, the corners etched deeply with wrinkles. He spotted Quinn and said, "Like I told the guy ahead of you, you walked them flights for nothing." With a grunt that was obviously meant to punctuate his statement, he reentered the apartment.

When Quinn stepped inside, the man was swinging his mop across a linoleum floor. The apartment consisted of one large room, with a makeshift kitchen in one corner and a sleeping alcove in another. The door to a small bathroom stood open. The furniture was heavy, wooden, in the style popular in the 1930s—a bureau, its drawers open and empty, a table and three chairs. The bed was stripped of its linen, the mattress folded back against the headboard. Several cardboard cartons and a battered suitcase were stacked at the foot of the bed. In the middle of the floor stood an overstuffed club chair with soiled, worn upholstery, its cushion missing; the cushion was on the tabletop, its stuffing protruding through a slash down its middle.

The man in the faded coveralls went on with his mopping without glancing up.

"I'm looking for Mona Shriver," Quinn said.

The man continued with his mopping, but his sweeps with the mop gradually slowed until he was cleaning only the linoleum in a small area around his feet. When he lifted his head, his dark eyes peered at Quinn from under his heavy lids. "You a relative?" he asked with sudden interest.

Quinn made a meaningless gesture with his hands. "No, I'm not a relative. She's a friend of my son's."

The man leaned on his mop handle. Pulling the handkerchief from his brow, he wiped his face. "She was a friend of a lot of men's sons," he said. "Was, that is, until she met that sailor named Bannen who put his name on the door but not on the lease.''

"Chad Bannen was my son," Quinn said.

"Was?"

"My son is dead."

The man's heavy eyelids lifted, then drooped back into place to shield his eyes. "So is Mona Shriver," he said without feeling.

Quinn was so shaken by the news that he failed to hear the door across the hall open or to see the woman who emerged and stood watching him.

"I'm the landlord," the man continued. "I own this building. I used to think that being a landlord was a symbol of success. Let me tell you, mister, it's nothing but trouble. You fight to collect your rent, you fight with the mortgage company. Then the damned tenants skip out on you in the middle of the goddamn night or they die or get themselves killed and you end up cleaning their goddamn messes." He let the mop fall to the floor, crossed to the stack of cardboard cartons and took a newspaper off the top. He carried the paper back to Quinn. "Doesn't say much," he said. "Just that she was found dead on the street near where she worked."

After Quinn took the newspaper from him, the man retrieved his mop and continued swiping at the worn linoleum. "I'm not goin' to rent to any more cocktail waitresses, bartenders, sailors or whores," he grumbled. "This apartment was a pigsty. Stuff thrown everywhere. Had to pick it all up. Pack it in cartons. Now I don't know what to do with it. No relatives have surfaced. Probably won't, either. Just more crap to jam up my basement."

Quinn stepped back into the hallway, as much to escape the landlord's droning complaints as to get away from the odor of disinfectant. Still shaken, he slumped against the wall and stared at the newspaper. *The body of a young woman later identified as Mona Shriver, a cocktail waitress*

at the Interlude Club, was found this morning by a watch-
man on his way to...

"Are you really Chad's father?"

Quinn's head snapped up.

The woman was in her mid-twenties, with ash-blond hair
too even in color to be natural. Her wide blue eyes were
heavily made up. She wore a dressing gown, the kind sailors brought home to their special girlfriends from tours of
duty in places like Japan or Hong Kong. It had a pink
background, with a blue-and-white dragon that entwined
itself around her body.

"You knew my son?" Quinn asked.

The woman nodded, staring at him blatantly. "Chad
never mentioned his father," she said in a tone that rang
with challenge.

"My name is Quinn Bannen. Would you like to see some
identification?"

"I heard you tell the landlord Chad was dead. I'm sorry.
Mona was my friend. She loved Chad very much. They were
planning to be married when his ship—" She lowered her
head, as if suddenly choked with emotion.

Quinn pushed himself away from the wall, folding the
newspaper and tucking it under his arm. "Miss...?"

"Mrs.," she murmured, and lifted her head. There was
moisture in her eyes, but she had succeeded in holding back
the threatening tears. "My husband's deployed." She extended a slender hand. "I'm Emily Everett," she said. "It's
good to meet you, Mr. Bannen. I'm sorry about Chad. It's
difficult to accept, both of them...it's..." She let the sentence remain incomplete.

"Could you spare a few minutes, Mrs. Everett? Pri-
vately?"

"I have nothing except time, Mr. Bannen," she answered.

She pushed the door of her apartment open and stepped
back for him to enter.

Emily Everett seated herself at the corner of a blue mohair sofa and drew the folds of her dressing gown around her legs. As soon as she closed the door behind Quinn it was obvious that she was nervous. He was aware of her musky scent and of the voluptuous body scarcely concealed by her silk dressing gown.

Emily motioned to Quinn to take the chair opposite the sofa.

"I didn't know Chad very well," she told him. "He was my husband's best man at our wedding in Tijuana. Mona was my maid of honor. Ray introduced them."

"Had your husband known my son very long?" Quinn asked.

"I don't know. You know how sailors are. Someone they've met the night before is called a friend and treated like a childhood buddy." She pushed her hair back from her face; a handsome face, Quinn decided, a face that would probably be beautiful without all the makeup. "Ships that pass in the night, that sort of cliché," she said, and sighed. "I honestly don't know how long Ray had known Chad. They both served on the USS *Alum Rock*." She had a curious habit of lowering her eyelids and staring at him through the lashes. "How did Chad die, Mr. Bannen?"

Something Emily Everett had said sparked a memory in Quinn.

"Mr. Bannen?"

"What? Oh, I am sorry. They say he died of a drug overdose."

As if his statement had jolted her, Emily leaned forward suddenly; then she immediately sank back into the worn sofa, her gaze averted. There was a nervous tic at the corner of her eye that did not escape Quinn's attention. He guessed that she regretted inviting him into her apartment.

"Why did that shock you, Mrs. Everett?" he pressed.

She looked at him closely, obviously studying him. Then she said, "Chad never mentioned his parents. Maybe to

Mona, but not to us. I just assumed he was an orphan, like Ray, like the other sailors Ray brought home."

"Perhaps I can explain later why my son might not have mentioned his parents," Quinn told her. "But first, would you mind telling me why you were shocked when I told you the navy attributed Chad's death to a drug overdose?"

Emily Everett reached for a glass cigarette box on the coffee table. Her hand shook as she lit a cigarette. "Chad wouldn't even smoke weed," she said. "He wouldn't let Mona smoke, either. She used to slip over here when Chad was away, and we'd share a joint."

Quinn rose, walked to the window and stood staring down at the ill-kept yard at the rear of the building. He decided that although Emily Everett appeared nice enough, open enough, she was obviously holding something back. From fear, he was pretty sure. Perched on the corner of the sofa, she reminded him of a frightened bird ready to take flight at the slightest provocation. "Are you positive about Chad's reaction to drugs?" he asked without turning.

"I certainly am," Emily responded. "Ray called Chad 'the prude.' Once when I baked cookies with grass in them Ray gave one to Chad without telling him what was in them. When Chad found out he hit the ceiling. I've never seen anyone so angry. He didn't speak to Ray for over a week. Poor Mona, she was beside herself. I was her only real friend, and she felt if Ray and Chad were feuding we'd lose our friendship, too." She fell silent, crossing and recrossing her shapely legs. Her eyelids lowered again, but her head turned to follow Quinn as he returned to the chair. Color flushed her cheeks. "You are really Chad's father, aren't you?" It was both a question and a plea for confirmation. "You wouldn't be from naval intelligence, anything like that?"

"I offered to show you my identification," Quinn reminded her. "Yes, I'm really Chad's father. Perhaps he didn't mention me because...well, we haven't been close in several years. Not since his mother and I divorced. Why would you suspect me of being from naval intelligence?''

"Oh, just things," she said evasively. "Would you like a cup of coffee?" Before he could say no, she rose, moved quickly to the makeshift kitchen in the corner and turned on the burner beneath a teakettle.

"What *things*?" Quinn probed.

"A combination of things," she replied. "Mona being killed. Someone searching her room. Now Chad. It's all very—"

Quinn interrupted her. "Searching her room?"

Emily Everett turned and leaned against the counter. Her dressing gown parted, and he had a clear view of her legs to the knees. "Mona was an immaculate housekeeper," she said, her voice suddenly lowered as if to impart a secret. "Because of Chad, she told me. Chad was fastidious, so she kept that dump—" she nodded toward the door to indicate the apartment across the hall "—as clean as if it was a mansion. You heard the landlord, about the apartment being a pigsty and having to pick things up. That couldn't be true unless someone else did the scattering. I heard someone moving around over there last night, but I just thought it was Mona coming home late and cleaning. She often did her housework at night. I was in one of my funks, or I'd have gone over and had coffee with her." She shuddered and folded her arms across her stomach as if to ward off a sudden chill. "Poor Mona." Her voice broke in a sob.

"What *other* things?" Quinn inquired cautiously.

She turned without answering and took two cups down from the cabinet, spooning in instant coffee.

"I assume the police have been here. Did you tell them about someone being in the apartment last night?" Quinn asked.

"Oh, they were here early this morning," she said. "I listened at the door while they questioned the landlord, but I didn't go out."

"Why was that? You said she was your friend."

"I have my reasons, Mr. Bannen." The spoon clanked against the sides of the cups as she stirred in tepid water.

"The same reasons you had for thinking I might be with naval intelligence?" Quinn ventured. "Look, Mrs. Everett, let me make myself perfectly clear. I'm not with naval intelligence, or the police, or any other government agency. I'm not concerned with whatever it is you feel you must hide from me—unless it involves my son. I'm a father who doesn't believe his son died of a drug overdose. What you've told me confirms that. For some obscure reason, the navy is covering up the real reason for Chad's death. I'm determined to discover the truth, if only to clear his name. I realize you don't know me from Adam, but you knew my son, you were his girlfriend's best friend. If there's any information that might help me, I'd appreciate your cooperation."

"Maybe I just have a suspicious nature," Emily said as she carried his coffee to him. "Cream or sugar?"

"Black, please." Quinn accepted the coffee, even though he didn't want it, and pretended to sip it as he watched her return to the corner of the sofa.

"Ray and I were married in Tijuana," she said when she was settled. "I told you that, about Chad and Mona standing up with us. I guess that's when I first got suspicious."

"I don't understand," Quinn said when she fell silent.

"I began to wonder if my marriage was legal," she explained. "If maybe we shouldn't have another ceremony on United States soil. Ray didn't get permission to marry me, something I understand he's supposed to have done. I don't get an allotment. Oh, he sends me money when he's deployed. I don't need for anything, I'm used to a simple life. But, well, I was expecting an allotment, my own money. When I questioned him he told me he was part of an elite naval group that doesn't allow its members to marry. That's why we had to keep our marriage a secret. I remember he said Chad was also a member.''

"Did he mention the name of the group?" Quinn asked, puzzled.

The silk dragon across Emily's chest moved its head as she shrugged her shoulders. "No. He told me I was never to mention it again, even to him. And I wasn't to answer questions if anyone came snooping around. For my own safety, as well as his, I was to pretend he was just one of my boyfriends. That's why I wanted to make certain you were really Chad's father and not with naval intelligence.''

"I understand," Quinn said. "Did you discuss this with your friend Mona?"

"I mentioned it when she told me she and Chad were planning to marry." There was a slight pause before she added, "She said she didn't know anything about an elite group, but you know, at the time I thought she was lying. Mona was a bad liar. You know how some people are when they have to tell a lie, even a small, innocent one? Their eyebrows lift unconsciously, or they avoid eye contact. Maybe there's a change in their voice. Mona was a very honest person. I was sure Chad had mentioned the group to her. They were what I call great communicators. When you passed their door at night you could hear them talking. I suppose Chad warned her not to mention the group, just as Ray warned me. Ray isn't much of a communicator. When he's home we mostly watch TV, eat and sleep and . . . well, I'm not complaining, you understand? Even though the navy doesn't recognize it, I'm still his wife.''

"Was there anything else that made you suspicious?"

Again there was a brief pause. Then: "Ray and Chad often got off by themselves and whispered. I used to watch them. Their faces would get serious and, well, several times I thought I saw fear in their eyes.''

"Fear?"

She nodded. "Once I asked Ray what they'd been talking about, was it something to do with the elite group they both belonged to." She touched her right cheek absently. "He slapped me, hard, told me he'd warned me not to mention the group, even to him. He was furious. But—" she looked thoughtful "—at the same time he looked frightened."

"Frightened of what? Retaliation from this group because you knew about it?"

"I don't know," she said.

"Do you remember ever seeing Chad look as if he were frightened in the same way your husband was?"

"Chad had what Ray called a poker face," she answered. "You could look at Chad, look right into the depth of his eyes, and you couldn't see what he didn't want you to see. If I didn't know how gentle he was with Mona, I'd have thought him a cold bastard. Oh, I'm sorry. Mr. Bannen. I didn't mean to speak badly of the—of your son."

"I take it your husband is more expressive, even if he isn't what you call a communicator?"

"Not verbally. Just in the eyes. His eyes are dark and very expressive. You can almost see what he's thinking. I once told him, 'Raymond Everett, with eyes like those you'd better never cheat on me or I'll know it.' What is it, Mr. Bannen?"

Quinn had stood suddenly, slopping the coffee from his cup onto the worn carpet. *Raymond Everett!* A name he had taken from Chad's letters. *A boatswain second class. A drinking buddy.* He had been slow in recognizing the name because Chad had a habit of never shorting a person's name. He had failed to connect Ray with the last name Everett until Emily had used her husband's full name in conversation.

Emily, who had begun to relax, again looked like a frightened bird about to take flight.

"It's just that your husband's name suddenly registered with me," Quinn explained. "Chad mentioned him in his letters." He set his coffee cup on the table and bent to examine the damage he had done to her carpet.

"Don't worry about that," she told him. "I bought it at the Goodwill for five dollars."

"I'd like very much to talk to your husband, Mrs. Everett," Quinn told her. "You said he was on the USS *Alum Rock* with Chad? Do you know when his ship is due back in San Diego?"

"Another six weeks, I'm sorry to say," Emily answered. "Another six weeks of being alone now that Mona's— God, the whole thing is so terrible! Who would have wanted to kill Mona? Especially since she'd gone straight? And then to search her room!"

Quinn had ceased listening to Emily. He made a mental note to find out what port the *Alum Rock* would dock in next. Perhaps Raymond Everett could tell him what he needed to know. Apparently both Chad and Everett had been involved in some clandestine group. The idea of such a group existing within the navy without the public being aware of it sounded preposterous. Yet...

Emily's voice broke into his thoughts. "I'm sorry you and Chad were estranged."

Quinn got up to leave. "Thank you for your time, Mrs. Everett."

Emily stood, clutching the dressing gown around her. "You're going to try to contact Ray, aren't you, Mr. Bannen?" she inquired.

Quinn said he was.

"Please don't tell him you spoke to me," she said in a quavering voice. She touched her cheek again, as if remembering her husband's slap. "If Ray thought I mentioned the group, even to Chad's father..."

"I won't mention we met," Quinn assured her.

As he was about to open the door, Quinn noticed the mirror above the bureau. Several snapshots had been stuck along the lower edge of the frame. He stepped up to the mirror, aware that Emily Everett had moved up behind him.

"There's one of Chad," she said, reading his thoughts. She reached around him and plucked a snapshot from the group. "Chad and Mona with Ray and me in Tijuana," she said, handing it to him. "It was taken the day of my wedding."

Quinn stared at the photograph.

"It wasn't the wedding I'd dreamed of," she murmured. "A ceremony conducted in broken English in Mexico. No flowers, no rice, no family. But at least I'm married to a man I love."

"You made a lovely bride," Quinn told her, his gaze fixed on the two men. Chad was smiling, his arm around a rather hard-looking brunette in a garish print dress unbuttoned to reveal deep cleavage.

"I tried to get them to dress up," Emily told him. "To wear their uniforms, at least, but they refused. It's the only picture I have of Ray. He hates to be photographed. He says women don't believe anything or anyone is real unless they have a picture to prove it, but I think he's just camera-shy."

When Quinn's attention switched to his son's drinking buddy, a sudden surge of current shot through his body. It was all he could do to prevent his hand from shaking as he passed the snapshot back to Emily Everett.

Thanking her again, he let himself out of her apartment.

He stopped at the top of the stairs before descending. He had to collect his thoughts, to reason and question. The mystery was becoming more complex than he had anticipated.

Raymond Everett, he decided, could supply the answers to many of his questions.

Quinn glanced back at Emily Everett's closed door. He wondered what her reaction would be if she learned her husband was not deployed, not aboard the USS *Alum Rock*.

Raymond Everett was the young man with the bandaged nose who had blown his surveillance cover at the airport less than two hours before by mistakenly starting to call Quinn "Commander."

17

San Diego, California

"ONE FINAL FAVOR . . ."

"I'm not into favors," Billy said pointedly. "I'm a bartender—or, as they're calling us these days, a mixologist." He snorted a humorless laugh. "That means tips. I can't make tips if I spend all afternoon answering questions." Billy grabbed a cloth and began wiping glasses. And leaving an even worse film on them, Quinn noticed. "I'm sorry about your son," Billy said. "Sorry about Mona, too. She turned the sailors on and made good tips. But like I said, I can't tell you much else."

"Did you meet my son?" Quinn pressed.

"Sure, I met him a couple of times," Billy told him. "He used to come in and pick Mona up when his ship was in port. She told me the kid was goin' to marry her, that right?"

"Yes, I think he planned to," Quinn said.

"It wouldn't have worked," Billy said. "They were from two different worlds. Your son had class. Mona, she had a heart of gold, as they say, but she was from nowhere and goin' nowhere. Poor bitch. She deserved better than a knife in the throat."

"Did you also know my son's friend Raymond Everett?"

"I met him, sure. A mean bastard when he was drinking."

"Have you seen him lately?"

"Lately? No. According to Mona, Everett and your son were stationed on the same ship. The *Alum Rock*, if my memory serves me right. The *Alum Rock*'s not due to return to port for another five, six weeks. Okay, man. No more questions. I've got my work to do, and I'm a waitress short. A carrier came in this morning, so it's going to be a hectic night."

Quinn reached into his pocket and placed a twenty-dollar bill on the bar; he might have more questions for the bartender and memory of the twenty might make him more talkative.

Quinn left the Interlude and took a taxi to his hotel.

There were several conventions in San Diego, and he had been lucky to get a hotel room without a reservation. His room was on the tenth floor and commanded a panoramic view of San Diego, the bay, Coronado Island and the Pacific Ocean beyond. There were several ships in port, including the aircraft carrier the bartender had mentioned.

Quinn showered and dressed. Before going out for dinner, he decided to call Esther Wade on the off chance that Dorothy had had a change of heart and telephoned from Key West.

The housekeeper answered on the second ring.

"Esther, it's Quinn Bannen."

"Oh, Mr. Bannen! I'm glad you called." Her voice was edged with excitement. "Something's happened here, Mr. Bannen," she said, then paused as if waiting to be questioned.

Quinn had visions of her having found old Sammy drunk in the barn. Patiently he asked, "What's happened, Esther?"

"Matt picked me up this morning and drove me into town to do some shopping," the old woman told him. "The house was empty for about an hour. No more than that, I swear. I didn't even notice anything out of the ordinary when we first returned. I fixed coffee for Matt and—''

"Esther, what happened?''

"Before Matt left, I went into your office, Mr. Bannen,'' the housekeeper went on. "It's the only room in the house with an ashtray, and Matt's gone back to smoking. Well, you know the photograph of you in your officer's uniform? The glass was broken, looked as if someone had driven a fist into the center of it. Then I noticed your desk. The drawers were half-open. Looked like someone had been through everything, Mr. Bannen. I know how neat and tidy you are.'' The old woman hesitated, taking a deep breath. "I don't know if anything's missing,'' she said. "I just don't want you blaming me if it is.''

Quinn felt his pulse quicken. "I won't blame you, Esther,'' he assured her.

"Matt says it was probably vandals from the city. We get them sometimes. But if it was vandals, they didn't take anything of value that I can see. The TV and the stereo and the silver are all still here.''

"Did you call the sheriff and report a break-in?'' Quinn asked.

"I certainly did! Sheriff Lockman says it might have been Old Sammy lookin' for liquor. He's disappeared, and they think maybe he got himself so drunk he went off his head. That man's a menace, always said he was, but I don't think Old Sammy would do such a thing to you 'cause he respects you, you takin' a chance on him and givin' him a job and all. It was a stranger, I can feel it.''

Quinn glanced at his travel clock. It was nearing eight o'clock. Darkness would be falling in the area of the ranch. "Listen, Esther. Are you alone there? Did your son stay with you?''

"Matt's gone,'' Esther replied. "Can't stay away from home after dark 'cause his wife's afraid to be alone after nightfall." She clucked her tongue disapprovingly against the roof of her mouth. "Why, Mr. Bannen?"

"I don't want you alone at the ranch," Quinn told her.

"You think whoever it was might come back?"

"They might."

"I'm not afraid, Mr. Bannen," Esther assured him after a moment's hesitation. "I have the shotgun, and I'm not afraid to use it if someone tries to break in."

Quinn understood her bravado, but he said, "I'd still feel better if you'd have your son come and pick you up for the night. I should be back tomorrow afternoon."

Ignoring him, Esther said, "They smashed some of your plaques and souvenirs, too, Mr. Bannen. Looks like they hate the military. That's another reason I don't think it was Old Sammy. He was a soldier in World War II, and he's mighty proud of the medal he won. It had to be some city kid. I'm sorry about your plaques and stuff."

"Those things don't matter to me any longer," Quinn told her, and he was surprised to realize that he meant it. "Have I had any telephone calls?"

"No, no one's called, Mr. Bannen."

Quinn buried his disappointment at not having heard from Dorothy. "If Old Sammy's not found by morning, I'll need someone to care for the horses. Will you ask your son if he can find someone?"

"Yes, Mr. Bannen, I'll do that."

"Ask him tonight when you call him to pick you up, Esther," Quinn said, emphasizing his desire to have her away from the ranch.

"I'll call and ask him," Esther said stubbornly. "And don't you worry. I'll take care of everything until you come home tomorrow."

Before Quinn could say anything further, she broke the connection.

Quinn returned the receiver to its cradle and began pacing the hotel room. It couldn't possibly be coincidence: the surveillance, the searching of Mona Shriver's room, her death, an intruder at the ranch, Raymond Everett—they all had to be connected. The waves he had made in Washington had caused the tenacles of the beast called cover-up to begin reaching out. But what were they covering up? And for whom? What had Chad gotten himself involved in? What was the elite group Emily Everett had mentioned?

Quinn left his hotel room and took a taxi back to the apartment building where Chad had lived with Mona Shriver. A few dollars in the hands of the disgruntled landlord and he was given permission to go through the belongings that were now stored in the dank basement. He reasoned that whoever had searched the dead woman's room might have overlooked something.

They hadn't.

The only item of interest Quinn found was a photograph of his son in uniform, which he slipped into his pocket.

When he climbed out of the basement he thought of paying another visit to Emily Everett but decided against it. She'd told him all she knew, and another visit would only frighten her more.

Discouraged, he returned to his hotel room without having dinner.

"HE'S BILLETED for the night, sir," Raymond Everett said into the telephone. His jaw was tight, giving his voice a clipped tone.

"Did he see anyone today? Talk to anyone?"

"The girlfriend's landlord," Everett reported, "and the bartender at the Interlude, where she worked."

"Would either of them have known anything?"

"No, sir."

"You sound damned definite, Everett."

"What would they know, sir? They were casual acquaintances. Chad may have been what you said, but he wasn't a fool. He wouldn't have talked about Delta to bartenders and landlords.'' He deliberately omitted a final *sir*.

''The bastard *was* a fool, Everett. Don't you doubt it for a moment. Only a fool would join our organization with the intention of exposing it.''

''Yes, sir,'' Everett said without conviction.

''If Quinn Bannen goes out again before morning, I want to know immediately. If not, report in in four hours, sailor. Understood?''

''Yes, sir, understood.''

Everett waited until his contact had broken the connection before angrily slamming the receiver back into its cradle and leaving the telephone booth across the street from Bannen's hotel. The summer storm had left the air heavy with humidity. The civilian shirt he wore clung wetly to his body. His nose ached; the clots of dried blood inside his nostrils made breathing difficult. He habitually checked the bandages as if to assess the damage. That bastard Chad had had a hell of a strong right hook.

Everett walked back across the street and peered through the plate-glass doors to the hotel lobby. Marshisky had settled himself in a chair with a magazine open on his lap. The prick stood out like a mismatched sock. He'd have to be replaced before the crowd of patrons thinned out; if not, the management might question his being there. It all seemed so nonsensical. Why not just take Quinn Bannen out? Like they had his son? Like they had Mona? Like they would have been ordered to do to Emily if he had told his contact about Commander Bannen's visiting her?

Everett leaned against the lamppost at the entrance to the hotel and lit a cigarette. When he exhaled through his nostrils, they stung. He threw down the cigarette and crushed it with his heel.

Damn! He should never have married Emily! That bitch was a threat to the organization—and to him!

Marrying her had been a mistake. He knew now that it was inevitable that he would be forced to rectify his own mistakes...unless he wanted to end up like Chad.

"SENATOR, do you know what time it is?"

"Yes, sir. But I didn't think this should wait until morning," Senator Lawton said into the telephone. "A replacement's been named for Congressman Hackermann. The defense subcommittee goes ahead on Monday as scheduled."

"Since when did any of those assholes in Congress start making quick decisions? We expected the subcommittee to be held up for at least a month while they decided on a new chairman."

"Someone suggested it would be a fitting tribute to Hackermann if his committee proceeded without interruption. It was unanimously agreed that Congressman Fedder take over as chairman."

"Well, we can't risk the death of a second chairman. Do we have a dossier on Fedder?"

"We have a dossier on everyone in Congress, thanks to you."

"Anything on Fedder we might use against him?"

"He's as clean as the proverbial driven snow."

"No man in Washington is that clean, senator."

"Fedder is."

"The son of a bitch!"

"Not even that. His mother's old Philadelphia society. His father's the chairman of a major steel company."

"His wife? Kids?"

"He's a widower. Married less than a year when his wife died of cancer. No children. That was fifteen years ago. He never remarried. He's completely devoted to his career. Word is he's a shoo-in for reelection."

"A bachelor congressman with no skeletons hiding in his closets? Impossible! He's dipping his wick somewhere, possibly outside Washington. If not with whores, then with boys. It's not natural for a man to mourn a dead wife for fifteen years, not unless women aren't his natural bent. Look into it. If you can't uncover something, plant it. We don't have time to be fucking around with subcommittees. D day is less than a month away."

"I'll do what I can."

"Senator, you'll do that and more! Do you remember reading about Hitler's 'Night of the Generals'? The night his generals tried to do him in and failed? Well, all of them were executed. If Delta fails, we'll all feel like execution would be a blessing!"

18

Key West, Florida

ADMIRAL BURKE LOOKED at his daughter over the top of his newspaper.

Dorothy sat opposite him in a wicker chair. She was perspiring, fanning herself with a bamboo fan, her gaze fixed unblinkingly on a darkened corner of the room.

There had been a power outage shortly after their arrival in Key West; that was nothing unusual for the island, but without the air conditioner the tropical air was like a heavy blanket on a hot night. A humid drizzle had fallen just after sundown and left an oppressive heat in its wake.

Because of their hasty departure from Washington, there had not been time to have the Florida house prepared for them; most of the furniture was still draped with sheets, and there was dust everywhere.

Ordinarily Dorothy would have pitched in immediately to clean things up, especially since she knew how the dust affected her father's sinus condition, but she had been strangely distant during the entire trip and had scarcely spoken to him since they arrived at the Key West retreat. She hadn't even warned him about damaging his eyesight by reading in the glare from the kerosene lantern.

The admiral had seen his daughter in this condition only once before—a week or so after her divorce from Quinn Bannen. With her, it seemed, shock had a delayed effect. He knew that now the full impact of Chad's death had hit her. He folded the newspaper noisily and dropped it on the floor beside his chair. "Hackermann's obituary is sanctimonious and filled with obsequious praise," he said. "When will the American public distinguish between its heroes and its enemies?"

He fully expected his statement to jar her out of her lethargy. Dorothy wasn't one to keep her thoughts or objections to herself. In that she resembled her ex-husband. He knew she had been fond of Congressman Hackermann and his wife.

The bamboo fan in Dorothy's hand slowed, then stopped moving. She blinked, focused her eyes on the admiral as if seeing him for the first time and said, "When indeed?" without any real interest. Rising from the wicker chair, she moved to the open doors of the veranda and stood looking out. The giant palm trees were swaying lazily in a hot wind. She slumped against the doorframe and held the fan at her side as if too weak to continue waving.

The admiral was disturbed by her attitude. His daughter was all that was left to him in the way of a family. Besides, if Dorothy didn't hold up under the strain, then she'd become yet another drain on his own reserves, and he had much to do.

"I hate this confounded island during the summer," he complained. He wiped the sweat from his brow with his hand. "It's paradise in the winter and hell in the summer."

Dorothy straightened and pushed herself away from the door frame. Distantly she said, "Chad loved it here."

"Yes, yes, he did," the admiral murmured.

"Do you remember the season he learned to scuba dive and found fragments of a Spanish galleon?"

"Yes, I remember it distinctly. He had a section mounted in plastic and gave it to me for a paperweight."

"He went back every day for the entire season because he was convinced there was treasure nearby. The following season, too. I wonder if he ever abandoned his dream of finding that treasure?"

"Dorothy, I don't think this a suitable topic of discussion at the present—"

"Once he got something into his mind, he never gave up," she went on.

The admiral put a wrinkled hand to his forehead and shielded his eyes from the glare of the kerosene lantern. Don't! he wanted to shout. Don't talk about the boy now! But he said nothing.

Dorothy returned to her chair and sat down heavily. Her face was less pale, her intelligent dark eyes more alert. She leaned forward, her elbows on her knees, and clasped her hands together in a nervous gesture. "Did you know I was very jealous of you and Chad? After the divorce he turned almost exclusively to you. You became his father, his mother, his friend. I felt excluded, as if he were punishing me for divorcing his father."

"That's absurd, and you know it," the admiral returned. "The boy wasn't punishing you." But there was no conviction in his voice, and he had to avert his eyes. "I think he may have felt abandoned by both you and Quinn," he said quietly. "It's not uncommon in divorce cases. Perhaps he was angry at both of you in the beginning. But I'm certain that passed as he matured. He turned to me because I represented stability."

"Did he join the navy because of you? Or because of Quinn?"

Some emotion she couldn't identify flickered in the admiral's eyes. Tension crept into his voice as he answered,

"Why should the boy emulate his father when his father disgraced the uniform he wore?"

"Did he never understand why Quinn did what he did?"

"Did you? Did I? We seldom discussed Quinn Bannen."

"I came to understand Quinn," Dorothy told him. "Quinn was a man caught between his values and his duty. I wish I had understood that then. But the scandal Quinn brought down on us was only the deciding factor in my decision to divorce him. You won't want to hear this, but even before the scandal I had had enough of being a military wife. It was the demands of the navy that destroyed my marriage."

"How can that be?" the admiral said incredulously. "Your mother raised you with the belief that you would one day marry a military man. As she had done, as her mother had before her. Saying the demands of the military destroyed your marriage is—is almost as disloyal as what Quinn Bannen did. You astound me, Dorothy!" In a gesture meant to conclude the unfavorable conversation, the admiral reached to the floor and retrieved his newspaper.

"I'm going to astound you further," Dorothy persisted. "Something struck me like a revelation on the flight from Washington. I loathe the military establishment. I guess I've always loathed it. As a child, because it took you away from me. And from Mother—she was alone most of the time, and lonely. Then later, because it took Quinn away. I knew then how terribly lonely Mother was. The military is as destructive of families as it would be to some threatening foreign power."

"That's nonsense!" the admiral blurted. "You're not yourself! You don't really believe what you're saying. You're just saying it to strike out at me because, as you said, you were jealous of me and Chad. I suggest you take a cold shower and get some sleep."

"Now the military has taken my son!" Dorothy cried. "It's left me nothing!"

"I refuse to listen to any more of this!" the admiral told her. He rose and moved out of the kerosene lantern's circle of light on his way to his study.

"And you!" Dorothy cried after him. "I don't understand you!" She stood, trembling, peering into the darkness of the hallway, where she saw his silhouette as he stood and watched her.

"Finish what you want to say, if you must," he told her.

"You accuse me of disloyalty. To the military, perhaps you're right. But I haven't been disloyal to you. Even when I knew you were lying about Chad I didn't challenge you. Even then!"

"Lying? Are you calling your father a liar?" His voice had taken on his "admiral" tone. "And what do you accuse me of lying about concerning Chad?"

"I know you," Dorothy said, undaunted. "If you had known Chad was taking drugs, as you said, you would have forced him into commitment for treatment. He would have been a threat not only to himself but also to your precious navy. Why did you lie to Quinn, to me, about the drugs? What do you know that you're not telling?"

Only silence came from the darkened hall.

"For Christ's sake, Chad loved you! You loved him! What are you hiding?"

At that moment the power flickered and died, then came on and stayed on to fill the house with a harsh glow. The air conditioner began to whir and rattle. The ceiling fan above Dorothy pushed hot air down on top of her head.

The admiral remained in the hall, blinking in the glare of the lights. His summer clothes, too large for him since his illness, hung loosely on his frame. The sagging flesh of his face was covered with perspiration. He lifted his head, and his eyes sought his daughter's. There was pain in his eyes, unmistakable and razor sharp.

"If it's any consolation to you and will put your jealousy to rest, Chad didn't love me in the end," he said in a near-whisper.

Turning, he stepped into his study and closed the door.

DOROTHY MOVED ALONG the narrow pathway to the swimming pool. The path hadn't been swept, and the grit cut into her bare feet. The caretaker had let the vegetation grow unchecked; it brushed against her bare legs, and she recoiled, remembering the scorpion she'd seen on their last visit. The pool was illuminated. She sat down at its edge and dangled her legs in the tepid water. It gave little relief from the heat. The breeze was growing stronger; the fronds of the giant palms were brushing together, their dried tips making a sound like a thousand insects.

Dorothy fussed with the halter of her bikini. She reminded herself to diet, then scolded herself for being so shallow as to worry about her weight when her entire world was crumbling around her. She glanced back toward the house. The light in the admiral's study was still on. She heard the sound of his typewriter and knew he had forgotten to close the window after the air conditioner had come back on. Poor Father, she thought, and wondered if he had gone back to writing his memoirs to occupy his thoughts. She regretted having lashed out at him. She had done it, of course, because of her jealousy and frustration. Because of the admiral she had lost Chad twice—first to him and then to death.

When she found her thoughts returning to Chad, Dorothy slipped quietly into the pool, scarcely disturbing the surface of the water, and began to swim. In her teens she had been a strong swimmer with a powerful stroke. Now her energy lagged, and she was soon exhausted. Still, she forced herself to continue, one lap after another, until she was almost too weak to hoist herself out of the water. She lay back, panting, feeling the heat from the tropical afternoon sun still caught in the concrete. Her eyes burned from the chlorine. She rubbed them, blinked and then lay quietly staring at the moonlit sky. Intermittent cotton-ball clouds were blowing across the island from the Gulf of Mexico. As she had done when she'd been a child, she searched the clouds for imaginary shapes of castles and dragons, or of knights and their steeds, but now her imagination would not turn to fantasy. She sat up and pushed her wet hair back from her face. She should have gone with Quinn instead of coming to Key West with the admiral. If Quinn was determined to clear their son's name, then she should be at his side doing her part.

The distant sound of the doorbell cut into her thoughts. She could hear the admiral's typewriter, its rhythm uninterrupted. Obviously he thought she was indoors and expected her to answer. She rose, her body aching from the exertion, and raced along the pathway to the house. She entered through her bedroom door and snatched a robe from the closet on her way to the door.

The bell was ringing a third time as she answered.

Her lips parted in a surprised gasp. She had failed to switch on the porch light, and the man standing on the porch was bathed only in moonlight. He wore the uniform of a commander. He was tall, like Quinn, with the same muscular, lithe build. The brim of his hat shaded his eyes, but the chin was the same, squared off and with a slight cleft. For one brief moment her mind deluded her into believing it actually was Quinn standing there. Time had lost perspective, and she felt as if she had been propelled backward into another decade. Quinn was coming home to her from another deployment to another foreign station; Chad was still a young boy; her life was happy. Then her hand tightened on the doorknob, and she shuddered and forced herself back to the present.

"Good evening, Mrs. Bannen." His voice was deep, resonant.

Dorothy reached for the light switch and snapped it on. "Good evening, Commander..."

"Commander Stevenson," he supplied, and removed his hat.

Now in the glare of the porch light, he looked nothing like Quinn. He was taller by several inches, and older, his dark hair streaked heavily with gray at the temples. His eyes were hazel and, although there was a thin smile on his lips, it was belied by the cold expression in his eyes.

"We met last season at the Lehmann party," he said to jog her memory. "The following day you went boating with my wife, Alice."

"Oh, yes," Dorothy recalled. The woman had almost killed them with her inexpert handling of the boat. "It's good to see you again, Commander. How is your wife?"

"She's in Southern California for the summer," the commander said. "She can't bear the Key West heat and humidity, she says. Actually, she's terrified of hurricanes. Is Admiral Burke still up, Mrs. Bannen?"

"Yes, he's up and typing," Dorothy said. She stepped back to let the commander enter. "Tell me, Commander, how did you know we had returned to Key West? We only arrived this afternoon, and the telephone hasn't been connected."

The commander's hazel eyes conducted a quick examination of her face; suspicion sparked in them, then faded abruptly. He was obviously a man who didn't take to being questioned. "Admiral Burke called and told me to expect him," he answered stiffly. "I'm late because of the power outage. I hope this isn't an intrusion."

"No, it's not an intrusion," Dorothy assured him. "The admiral must have forgotten to tell me he was expecting you."

The commander tucked his hat under his arm military-style and followed her into the house.

The admiral had ceased his rhythmic pecking on the typewriter.

"With the power having been out, it'll be another half hour before the rooms cool down," Dorothy said over her shoulder. "Would you like a drink, Commander? Something cool and refreshing? I make a mean piña colada."

"No, thank you. I don't drink, Mrs. Bannen." Something in the manner in which he said her name sounded almost rude. He must have recognized this, because he added more affably, "I mean I don't drink when I'm on duty."

"Oh, then this isn't a social call?" Dorothy stopped and turned to him with a quizzical expression.

The commander's lips parted in another thin smile, but he didn't answer.

"But it would have to be, wouldn't it?" she said. "The admiral is retired. This way, Commander." She led him down the hallway. "You know, when I opened the door to you I was startled. The military has such a low profile in Key West it's easy to forget they're here. Except, of course, that they still retain the island's best land, even the best beaches."

"Beaches that the military built," he reminded her.

"Whatever happened to the navy's plan to turn the land back to the community?"

"It's still in progress, Mrs. Bannen," he said with obvious impatience. "If I might see Admiral . . ."

The admiral's study door opened. "Commander Stevenson, good to see you," the admiral said, and extended his hand. "Come in, come in. Nice of you to pay a welcoming visit." He scarcely glanced at Dorothy as he admitted the commander to his study and closed the door.

Dorothy went back to the bar in the living room, and poured herself a weak gin and tonic. As she drank, she kept staring at the hall, wondering what the admiral was up to. *Nice of you to pay a welcoming visit*, he had told the commander. Yet the commander had said the admiral had called him and told him to expect their arrival. The admiral was definitely involved in something, but what?

She finished her drink and then refilled the glass with plain tonic water. It was still too early and the house too hot to allow sleep. She decided to return to the pool. If she swam again and completely exhausted herself, she would sleep without nightmares and without being haunted by dreams of Quinn and Chad.

She slipped onto the veranda and drew the sliding doors closed. To reach the path to the pool, she had to pass the admiral's windows. They still stood open, and she was stopped by the voices inside.

"Damn it, Stevenson!" the admiral said. "Are you telling me I no longer have the authority to call a special meeting of the committee?"

"No, sir, I didn't say that," the commander answered evenly. "I said if you give me the reason for your request I'll pass it along the chain of command to the controller."

"Might I remind you that I am the one who revitalized the organization?" the admiral said indignantly. "One of Johnson's first acts when he took office was to disband it. Too covert, they called it. Too masked in secrecy to control. Well, damn it, I gave it renewed life!"

"Yes, sir. I'm aware of that. Regardless—"

"Regardless, I'm still not allowed the simple privilege of calling a meeting without going through established procedures?"

"Might I remind *you*, Admiral Burke, that it was you who set the procedures for the organization? No single member, regardless of rank, may call a meeting of the committee without the approval of the controller. I'm here as a representative of the controller. Also, Admiral, you relinquished your active membership when you suffered your stroke. In addition, I might add, one of the dictates you insisted be included in our agreement, was that no member whose health had been seriously impaired be allowed to continue on active duty." The commander's voice was clipped, as cold as his hazel eyes.

"Yes, well, I wasn't thinking of myself, obviously," the admiral murmured.

"Unfortunate, sir. Our rules are unbendable."

"Don't 'sir' me, Stevenson!" the admiral said peevishly. "Let's forget rank and protocol. Speak to me as a fellow member of the organization. We both believe in its objective. It's the organization's survival that's important. At all costs. Do you agree?"

"I agree, *sir*."

"I'm not attempting to press the controller into an unwanted meeting," the admiral continued. "I know the importance of his anonymity. Aside from you, his aide, only seven other individuals are aware of his identity. As one of those seven, I now request a meeting of the full committee. What would you do, commander, if you believed there was a division of power or a misuse of power within the organization that threatened to split it asunder?"

"With all due respect, Admiral Burke, sir, the possibility of any member misusing his power is almost nil. We're too controlled."

"Are we indeed?" the admiral said doubtfully. "What if a defect in the character of one of our leaders began to surface, a defect no one suspected? What if the power he's been given began to go to his head and he began to make mistakes that threatened our security? Our very existence?"

Dorothy shifted her weight from one leg to the other and told herself she should creep away from the admiral's window, but the conversation intrigued her. All her father's military activities were supposed to have ceased with his retirement. She couldn't believe he was still involved in some operation, especially one that sounded so secretive.

"Are you saying you suspect we've such an individual in the organization?" the commander demanded, interest suddenly evident in his voice.

"That is my reason for requesting a meeting of the full committee," Admiral Burke told him. "I want this man destroyed before he does us irreparable damage."

"Then the man is a member of the inner committee himself?"

"He is."

"Will you trust me with the man's name, sir? The controller will want to know."

"He's become extremely dangerous," the admiral hedged. "He gives directives without clearance from the committee. He has, I fear, forgotten our purpose in his obsession with power."

"And his name, sir?" Commander Stevenson pressed.

"That bastard Admiral Addison!"

Shocked, Dorothy abruptly stepped back from the window. The two admirals had been the closest of friends for as long as she could remember. At her sudden movement, the ice in her drink clanked against the side of her glass. From inside the admiral's study, she heard a chair pushed back. A shadow loomed against the drawn shade and grew smaller as Commander Stevenson approached the window. Panicked, Dorothy stepped off the veranda and crouched in the overgrown foliage.

The commander lifted the shade. When he saw the open window he raised it even higher and leaned out. His gaze swept the veranda. When he peered toward the foliage where Dorothy crouched, she imagined his piercing hazel eyes boring into her. Closing her own eyes, she held her breath and was grateful her robe was a dark color that didn't reflect the moonlight.

After several moments she heard the window close, the latch click and the shade being drawn. She stepped quickly out of the shrubbery and hurried along the path to the pool.

What was the admiral involved in? Why, after decades of friendship, did he suddenly consider Admiral Addison his enemy?

And why had she experienced such an acute sense of fear when she had thought Commander Stevenson was going to catch her listening outside the admiral's window?

She sat down on the diving board, trembling and confused.

If the telephone had been connected, she would have called Quinn in California.

She felt a desperate need of him.

19

Key West, Florida

ADMIRAL BURKE CLOSED the door behind Commander Stevenson and returned to his study.

The house was now cold, chilled by the air conditioner, which had been running for a long time, but the admiral still felt overheated. Sweat glistened on his brow, and his palms were damp. The odor of stale cigar smoke stung his nostrils. Dorothy would be furious with him if she discovered he'd been smoking, but then, he reasoned, she had long since gone to sleep, and the odor would be gone by morning.

He emptied the commander's and his own ashtrays in the toilet in the connecting bathroom and flushed it, watching as the butts and ashes swirled around in the bowl. Then he flushed again because some ashes clung to the sides. He returned to his desk with the intention of working another hour or so. That, he thought, was one of the few advantages of old age; your body required less sleep.

The admiral had much to do—letters to write, plans to make. The task he had set for himself would not be an easy one; it was possible he would fail. If he did fail, it would cost him his life. He had considered that and had concluded that it would be no great loss. Death had been a close and constant companion since his stroke, and he had come to terms with it.

Perhaps he had already signed his death warrant by talking to Commander Stevenson. The commander was not an easy man to read; the bastard's eyes were the coldest, the most calculating he had ever encountered. Assuming the commander had bought his story and was not now reporting to Admiral Addison, he would have to prepare a detailed and believable brief for presentation to the committee, those seven officers, not counting Addison, whose decision would be final. Only the committee could destroy Addison without damaging the organization. The admiral knew he would have to obtain signed affidavits from those members he succeeded in convincing of Addison's misuse of power. That wouldn't be too difficult, for every man had his price, even those dedicated individuals who were leaders of the organization. Everything always boiled down to politics. What had Kennedy said? "Politics corrupts, poetry cleanses." Why had that particular statement occurred to him? He hadn't been one of Kennedy's fans.

The admiral began jotting down on a yellow notepad the names he felt were worth contacting. Brigadier General Simms would side with him against Addison; he and Addison had locked horns often in the past. The two men had an instinctive hatred of each other, perhaps because they were so alike. The reason for Simms's becoming his ally didn't matter to the admiral, so long as Simms sided with him.

A knock on the door interrupted the admiral before he had listed more than three possible allies. He covered the names on the pad quickly as the door opened and Dorothy stepped into his study.

She was wearing a bathing suit and a dark blue terry-cloth robe. There were puffy dark circles beneath her eyes, a telltale sign that she'd been crying. The chlorine in the pool had removed the curl from her auburn hair; it clung to her skull and made her eyes appear larger and more vulnerable. She fixed her gaze on him, and he realized that mingled with her vulnerability was determination. As she moved to the chair recently vacated by Commander Stevenson, he noted that his daughter's legs were long and shapely, like her late mother's. Without once taking her gaze from him, Dorothy sat down and folded her arms across her stomach.

The admiral told himself he should start making small talk to chip away at her determination, but he faltered under her direct gaze. *Once he got something into his mind, he never gave up*, she had said earlier of Chad. Like father, like mother, like son, the admiral thought. And like grandfather, too. He conceded he was a stubbornly persistent old bastard himself. He managed to return his daughter's gaze with a flintlike stare of his own.

Dorothy came directly to the point. "I want to know what you're up to, Admiral."

His first instinct was to shout at her, to tell her directly it was none of her business what he was involved in, but he knew that would only fan her persistence. Then he considered lying to her, but he recalled that she'd informed him she knew well enough when he was lying. The best solution, he decided, was to tell her half-truths.

Before he could speak, however, Dorothy said, "I heard some of your conversation with Commander Stevenson."

Admiral Burke's face drained of color. He suddenly remembered the open window and the noise that had prompted the commander to look outside and then close it, and his gaze turned in that direction. He fought for composure, his voice surprisingly even when he said, "Exactly what did you hear, Dorothy?"

"An old ploy of yours," she said, "answering a question with a question. You used to use that tactic with Mother."

Admiral Burke suddenly slammed his palms down on the desktop. "Don't play games with me, young woman!" he shouted, his composure gone. "It's imperative you tell me exactly what you heard in your spying! Tell me!"

His sudden, explosive anger frightened Dorothy. She uncrossed her arms and straightened her spine, leaning forward in the chair as if preparing to flee. Her dark eyes widened; she momentarily forgot that the man confronting her was her father.

But the fear ebbed quickly. "You're still involved in some military operation," she said accusingly. "I heard that much." She paused, giving him an opportunity to deny it; when he didn't, she shrank back in the chair and dropped her gaze helplessly. "You promised the doctors and me your retirement would be complete," she reminded him. "I stood by while you dabbled in politics because I knew a man like you couldn't be entirely inactive, but..."

"I'm not a man who can retire," the admiral told her gravely. "I deluded myself into believing it was possible, temporarily. It wasn't. It isn't." His voice became calmer, and the color returned to his face. "I know you love me. I know you're concerned about my health. Don't be, Dorothy. Every man must play out the role he's destined for. I understand my limitations. I won't overtax myself." He forced an encouraging smile, a fatherly smile—and if it appeared as false as it felt on his face, he hoped she would attribute it to his damaged facial muscles. "Now tell me exactly what you overheard," he prompted.

Dorothy studied him indecisively. Why was it so important that he know what she had overheard? she asked herself. She could sense his intensity, and it frightened her.

"All right," the admiral said quietly, "I'll tell you this much. I'm working with the military as a consultant."

"For what branch of the military?" she countered.

"We're not limited to one branch," he told her guardedly.

"Then this... organization is funded by the Defense Department independently of the navy or army or air force?"

"Independently," he echoed.

"And it's a secret organization?"

"Extremely," he answered. "The world is changing, Dorothy. Men of vision who are members of the military are limited by force regulations. Our country is facing dangers not only from foreign powers but from within. Men of experience and know-how have banded—been called together to devise new methods of defeating our enemies."

"Men like you?" she murmured.

"I'm afraid my contribution has been limited since my stroke, but yes, men like me."

"And like Admiral Addison? Your longtime friend?"

The admiral could no longer hold her gaze. "Oh, so you heard that part, did you? Sometimes men who appear beyond corruption find themselves with power they can't handle. Addison is such a man."

"You told the commander you wanted him destroyed," Dorothy said incredulously. "What possible action on Admiral Addison's part causes you to demand such vengeance?"

Admiral Burke sighed wearily. "I can't tell you," he said flatly.

"I've never seen this side of you," Dorothy told her father. "It frightens me. Commander Stevenson frightens me. When he leaned from the window and looked directly at me, my heart stopped."

Admiral Burke leaned forward over his desk. "Are you certain the commander didn't see you?" he demanded.

"No, he didn't see me," she assured him. "Why do you make it sound so menacing? What if he had? I'm not a little girl to be scolded for eavesdropping."

No, the admiral thought, you are a big girl who might be killed for spying, as Chad was killed. "What else did you hear?"

"Just military prattle," Dorothy answered. "Rhetoric about organizations and misuse of power and committees." She rose and pulled her robe tight around her slender body. "I keep remembering something Mother once said to me. You and some officers were meeting at the house in Washington on a Sunday afternoon. I asked Mother what you were talking about in such whispers, and she said, 'It's just games men play, darling. Games about power and might and who rules what and whom.' And I said, 'Oh, like king of the mountain?'" Dorothy moved to the door and stood with her hand on the knob. "Mother laughed and said, 'Yes, almost as ridiculous as that!' Good night, Admiral."

"Dorothy, I don't want you to mention my meeting with Commander Stevenson. Anything you might have heard is to be considered forgotten. It's imperative you obey me in this!"

"I want no part of your ridiculous games," Dorothy told him. "I'm tired. I can't think straight this evening. Good night."

"Wait! Promise me!" Admiral Burke insisted.

"All right, I promise," Dorothy said. "I saw nothing, heard nothing. I won't even tell your doctors you're working again as an consultant."

The admiral listened to her footsteps retreating down the passageway. When he heard her bedroom door open and close, he returned to his task.

20

California

IT WAS MIDAFTERNOON when Quinn returned to the ranch.

Esther Wade opened the door and stepped onto the porch when she heard the crunch of tires on the gravel driveway. A shotgun rested in the crook of her arm. "Welcome home, Mr. Bannen."

Quinn could tell by the tone of her voice that the housekeeper was still upset; she probably blamed herself for the break-in and for having been absent at the time.

"I see you spent the night here, Esther," Quinn remarked, indicating the shotgun. "Has Old Sammy returned?"

"No one's seen or heard from him," Esther told him. "Matt found a friend of Old Sammy's to care for the horses. His name's Pete Bostwick, one of Old Sammy's cronies." She leaned the shotgun against the living room wall and followed Quinn into his office. She hesitated in the doorway. "That's the photograph they smashed." She pointed to the far wall, where the photograph still hung.

Quinn glanced at the likeness of himself in his commander's uniform. The glass looked as if someone had smashed his fist into its center, the cracked fragments spreading out like a spiderweb to the edges of the frame. "The photograph doesn't matter," he told Esther. He pulled open the top drawers of his desk and immediately saw that the letters from Chad were missing.

"What did they take, Mr. Bannen?" the housekeeper inquired.

"Some letters," he answered absently. He opened the remaining drawers, then sank into his chair. "And my revolver," he added. The .45 had been his father's; he had fired it only once, for target practice—the day he had explained the dangers of firearms to a young Chad.

"What kind of thief would take only letters and a revolver?" the housekeeper asked, more of herself than of Quinn. "Then not touch the TV or anything of value?"

"Perhaps, as you suggested, some kid from the city," Quinn said to appease her curiosity. "A druggie, perhaps. Don't trouble yourself. They took nothing of importance." The letters from Chad had been important, but he couldn't explain that to her without raising further suspicions.

"Will you be going away again, Mr. Bannen?"

"Tomorrow," he told her. "To Moffett Field. It's south of San Francisco about forty miles. I can't say how long I'll be away."

"I'll look after things," Esther assured him. "If the intruder comes back, I'll be waiting for him. I'm not easily frightened, not like my daughter-in-law."

I doubt they'll be back, Quinn thought. They had what they wanted: Chad's letters. Now they knew every name on his list. Aloud, he said, "Thank you, Esther. Have there been any telephone calls for me?"

"Only Sheriff Lockman to see if you'd returned," the housekeeper answered. She read the disappointment on his face. "I'll get you some lunch, Mr. Bannen."

Before Quinn could protest that he wasn't hungry, she turned and shuffled away down the hallway.

Quinn leaned back in his chair and closed his eyes. He had clung to the hope that Dorothy would call. That night in his hotel room in Washington it had been as if the years had rolled away, all the hostilities and disappointments forgotten. Except that they had been brought together by the death of their son... No, he chided himself, he mustn't think about Dorothy now. He reached for the telephone and dialed.

"Bannen, I was about to call you," Jonathan McKinney said when he answered. "I don't know what kind of hornet's nest you've stirred up this time, but I believe it reaches into the heart of the Pentagon."

"Explain that remark, Jonathan."

"Call it intuition, if you like," Jonathan told him, "but my contacts at the Pentagon have suddenly developed severe cases of laryngitis. No one's talking to reporters, not to me or to any of the others who have tried to pick up on the story of your son. There's some kind of internal investigation going on, but it's classified. The mere mention of your name has the effect of crying 'Leper.' One thing I do know, your file's been pulled from Central Records along with Chad's and Admiral Burke's. The control clerk is a personal friend. A pretty little thing from Minnesota." Jonathan affected a Minnesota accent: "'The files have been taken without the customary request procedure, Mr. McKinney.' Why would that be, Quinn? Can you tell me?"

"I can't," Quinn said honestly.

"Well, it's very hush-hush," Jonathan concluded. "Just like in the old days, pal. Do you think we've stumbled onto a repetition of the drug experiments?"

"I—I just can't speculate at this point," Quinn answered. "Jonathan, there's something you can do for me. Have your girlfriend at Central Records see what she comes up with under the name Raymond Everett."

Jonathan told him he'd see what he could do.

"And another thing," Quinn added. "Apparently Chad was a member of some elite organization within the military. I say 'elite' because that's the word used in describing it to me. It's apparently a secret organization. It seems one of the requirements is that its members be orphaned or estranged from their families."

"You're kidding!"

"I'm deadly serious. I know it sounds strange. Maybe the fantasy of a recruit who was trying to impress his girl."

"Is this Raymond Everett a member of the organization?"

"Affirmative."

"Any other information on him?"

"U.S. Navy. Rank second class. Rate CT—communications technician. That automatically means a top-secret clearance, so he should have a file in Washington. He's supposed to be assigned to the USS *Alum Rock*, but I say 'supposed to be' because he's not at his duty station. The *Alum Rock*'s at Diego Garcia, in the Indian Ocean. Everett's not on board. That raises another interesting question—why not?"

Jonathan was mumbling to himself. "Anything else I should know? What's happening on your end?"

"My house has been searched," Quinn told him. "My son's girlfriend has been killed. And I'm under surveillance. Otherwise, there's little to report."

"Jesus!"

"Did you get an interview with my wife?"

"I tried," Jonathan told him, obviously disappointed. "It would have helped keep the story alive, but she refused. Maybe if the admiral hadn't been present..."

"Maybe," Quinn echoed. He heard the crunch of tires on the gravel driveway; a car door slammed, and then the doorbell rang. He heard Esther hurrying to the front door. "I'm leaving for Moffett Field in the morning, Jonathan, so you won't be able to reach me until I call and give you a number. If it's imperative you reach me, call my house. My housekeeper's name is Esther Wade. Leave a message. I'll be checking in with her every morning."

"Why Moffett Field?" Jonathan asked.

"Another lead," Quinn said. "Perhaps another blind alley, but it's the only way I know to continue. I pulled some names from Chad's letters. One is a corpsman named Mae Aames. She's stationed at Moffett, or was at the time of the letter. Another is a Chief Loomis." Quinn glanced up as the local sheriff filled the office doorway. He motioned to the sheriff to take a chair. "I have to go now, Jonathan."

"Well, good luck, Bannen," Jonathan said. "I'll see what information I can come up with on Raymond Everett." As was typical of the reporter, he broke the connection without the customary farewell.

Quinn returned the receiver to its cradle and turned his attention to the sheriff.

Sheriff Lockman was what the American public, through television, had come to think of as the typical country sheriff. He was fiftyish, with a receding hairline and a sizable paunch. His eyes, hidden behind slightly tinted gold-framed glasses, were dark and hinted at an intelligence that wasn't there. He had been elected to his post, and he had no fear of being ousted in future elections, because no one wanted his job. He spent hour after dull hour waiting for something to happen that required his attention, but little happened in the quiet community that the residents couldn't handle on their own. The break-in at the Bannen ranch was a godsend to the sheriff. Bannen, although he was still considered an out-sider because he had not been raised in the area, was a re-tired naval commander of considerable importance. Sheriff Lockman welcomed the chance to prove himself to one of the community's most prestigious citizens.

When Quinn hung up the telephone and looked across his desk at the sheriff, Lockman removed his glasses and wiped them with a dingy white handkerchief. His pupils narrowed in the sudden glare from the window behind Quinn's desk. "I understand there's been a robbery here," he said officiously.

"More an act of vandalism," Quinn said, indicating the photograph with the shattered glass. "But, yes, my re-volver was stolen. A .45."

"Registered?"

"Of course."

Esther Wade entered with a tray containing Quinn's lunch and set it down on the edge of the desk. "Coffee for you, Sheriff?" Quinn could tell from her voice and attitude that the housekeeper was not fond of the local sheriff.

"Maybe after the investigation," Sheriff Lockman said, without glancing in her direction. "Now, Commander Bannen, let's—"

"I'd prefer Mr. Bannen, or merely Quinn. I'm retired, Sheriff."

The sheriff fixed the stems of his glasses over his pro-truding ears. "As I understand it, Mr. Bannen, the house was empty when the robbery took place."

"I told you that," Esther said. "Get to the point, Sam Lockman. Mr. Bannen's a busy man. He has things to see to before he leaves on his next trip."

Sheriff Lockman glared at her. "You travel a lot, then, Mr. Bannen?"

"Lately," Quinn said without further explanation.

Esther, shaking her head in disapproval of the sheriff, made her exit.

The sheriff made a sweeping gesture with his hands meant to encompass the house. "Don't you think it unusual for someone to break into a place like this with all these valuables and steal nothing except a .45?"

"I can't say," Quinn answered. "Robbery in itself is unusual for me. I can't pretend to understand the criminal mind. Frankly, Sheriff, I'd just as soon chalk the entire incident up to experience and forget—" He broke off when he heard a loud noise from the direction of the kitchen—a door flung open, striking the wall, and then Esther's muffled cry.

Both Quinn and Sheriff Lockman were on their feet by the time the housekeeper charged through the office door. Her face was pale. "Pete's found Old Sammy," she said breathlessly. "You'd best come to the stables, the two of you."

Pete Bostwick, a gaunt-looking man in his early sixties with weatherworn skin stretched over an angular frame, had not ventured into the heart of the house. When Esther had fled the kitchen he had returned to the stables, and he stood waiting for them now at the open doors. Despite the cool air, he had been perspiring heavily; the T-shirt he wore was drenched. The legs of his dungarees were covered with dirt and grime and reeked of hay and horse manure. His dark eyes met Quinn's, and he motioned toward the interior of the stables. "In there," he said. "In the stall belonging to La Belle Bête." His pronunciation stumbled on the French name. "I took the mare out. She's spooked."

The stall gate had been left open.

Inside the stall, half covered with straw and matted with blood, lay Old Sammy.

Esther Wade cried out and turned away, crossing herself in the Catholic manner.

"He's dead," Pete announced as the sheriff bent beside the body. "Been dead for a while, too, by the looks of him."

"His head's bashed in," Sheriff Lockman said after a quick examination. His voice became tight as he fought the sickness that rose in his throat.

Quinn had seen enough. He turned and stepped out of the stall, placing an arm around the housekeeper and leading her toward the fresh air.

"That was Old Sammy's favorite horse," she mumbled. "He said her name meant 'The Beautiful Beast' and that's just what she was." She began to sob softly. "I never liked Old Sammy. We grew up together, you know. But what an awful way to die."

As the sheriff emerged from the stables, wiping his hands on his dingy handkerchief, Quinn nodded to Pete to see Esther back to the house.

Sheriff Lockman shoved his bloodied handkerchief back into his pocket. "Looks like he got drunk and crawled into the stall to sleep it off," he said. He held up an empty gin bottle. "Something spooked the mare, probably Old Sammy himself, and she popped his head like a watermelon. I doubt he ever knew what hit him. Probably woke up in drunk's heaven wondering how the hell he got there. Well, I've got to call this in, Mr. Bannen. I'll take care of everything."

Quinn leaned against the corral railing and watched the heavyset sheriff walk away. He was so lost in thought that he failed to hear Pete approaching until the gaunt man spoke to him.

"There's somethin' very wrong here, Mr. Bannen," Pete said. "Old Sammy was a boozer, there's no denyin' that, but he reeked of gin." The man stroked his chin with long, emaciated fingers. He cocked his head to one side and met Quinn's gaze. "I suppose the gin came from your house?"

"I suppose," Quinn said. "Why?"

"Mrs. Wade, she says you keep a fully stocked bar. Every kind of liquor she can name, and some she can't."

Quinn nodded. He kept plenty of liquor in the house, even though he drank very little himself, a holdover, he supposed, from the days when he and Dorothy had entertained so heavily. "What's your point?" he asked.

Pete stared down at the pointed toes of his worn boots. "Old Sammy had a passion for whiskey," he said. "I've never known him to take a swallow of gin. He hated gin as much as he loved whiskey. If he'd taken liquor from the house, it'd have been whiskey, not gin, no, sir, not gin!"

21

Mountain View, California

THE ENLISTED MEN'S CLUB was empty except for the female bartender and a lone sailor occupying an end stool. A country-and-western tune was playing on the jukebox, Willie Nelson moaning about a lost love. Though the lunch-crowd had long since left, candles still burned in the red glass holders on the tables, and the ashtrays were overflowing.

Alex took a stool at the opposite end of the bar from the sailor. He had no wish to be engaged in small talk. He ordered a glass of orange juice from the bartender, a bleached blonde in tight-fitting designer jeans and a nylon blouse unbuttoned to display her deep cleavage.

"You want that straight?" she asked sarcastically.

"No ice," Alex told her.

When she moved away to pour his orange juice, Alex opened the notepad he kept stuffed into the waistband of his uniform trousers. On the first page he had drawn the blocking symbol, a triangle bisected by a straight line. Below this he had made a large question mark followed by an exclamation point. On page two he had written thirteen numbers. Beside three of these he'd penciled in names: Admiral Addison, Captain Musolf and Chief Loomis, the men at the meeting in the conference room whose names he knew. Beside the remaining ten numbers he had written the other men's ranks as he remembered them: three commanders, four captains, two lieutenants and a master chief.

Since yesterday morning, when he had begun keeping notes, he'd spent as much time as possible wandering around the base checking faces his memory might attach to those present at the conference. So far he'd seen no one, identified none of the names missing from his list.

On page three he had written the name Chadwick Bannen, petty officer second class, with his serial number and all Bannen's duty stations since he'd enlisted in the navy. The only information he'd secured today was written on page three. He had gone to the computer room and told Chief Hargrave he was trying to locate an old friend he'd gone through boot camp with, requesting permission to punch into the personnel data program in an attempt to locate his friend's address of record. The chief had been less pressured than usual and had agreed. He had, in fact, taken the opportunity to go for coffee and had left Alex alone in the computer room.

The information about Bannen that Alex had drawn from the computer was jotted under his name: Born, Washington, D.C., June 8, 1962; Father, Quinn A. Bannen; Mother, Dorothy J. Bannen, née Burke. The current address for the father was a small town in northern California; beside his name had appeared *Commander, Retired*.

It was no help, none of it, and it wouldn't help even if Alex knew what he was looking for.

Chadwick Bannen's personnel data didn't explain his death, nor the bisected-triangle symbol that blocked all information sought by individuals without the need-to-know authorization.

"Your orange juice," the blond bartender announced, and set the glass in front of him. "Don't let it go to your head, sailor." She walked away with an exaggerated sway of her hips to join the friendlier sailor at the other end of the bar, the one who was drinking. She must have made a comment about Alex's choice of drink, because the two of them glanced in his direction and laughed.

Alex closed his notebook and returned it to the waistband of his trousers as another customer came in and took a stool close to his.

"A beer," the newcomer shouted at the bartender. "Make sure it's cold."

The voice was familiar. Alex's pulse quickened when he recognized Chief Loomis.

The chief looked directly at him and smiled, revealing uneven, nicotine-stained teeth. "You're Mayfield, aren't you? Yeoman with the admiral's staff?"

Alex nodded.

"I'm Chief Loomis. I've been wantin' to talk to you, Mayfield. Away from the office, that is. I saw you duck in here and thought this would be a perfect opportunity. Do you want another screwdriver?"

The blond bartender, bringing the chief's beer, glanced at Alex and smiled.

"I'm a teetotaler, Chief. It's only orange juice."

"A sailor who doesn't drink. That's unique." The chief slapped a dollar bill on the bar and eyed the bartender's figure as she moved away to the register. Then he said to Alex, "I've gone over your file, Mayfield. You're an exemplary sailor."

"My file? Why would you—"

The chief corrected himself. "Not your file, exactly. I've been hearing good things about you, your performance and dedication to duty. And here you are on a Sunday, putting in overtime. That's good, damned good. You like the navy, Mayfield?"

"Yes, sir."

The chief turned sideways to face him and leaned one arm on the bar. He raised his bushy brows above eyes that were cold and calculating, his expression belying the smile on his thin lips. He had cut himself shaving that morning, and there was a scar on his chin. "Why?" he asked. "Why do you like the navy?"

Alex felt perspiration forming in his armpits and groin. He wiped a hand casually across his brow and was glad the lighting in the club was dim. Was it possible, he wondered that someone, somehow, had discovered he'd been extracting information about Chadwick Bannen from the computers? Suddenly into his mind flashed the cliché one of his foster mothers had often used in regard to his inquisitive nature: "Curiosity killed the cat!"

Alex took a swallow of orange juice and fought to relax the constricted muscles of his throat. He was acutely aware that the chief's eyes were probing him, observing every detail of his expression and his body movements—almost, he thought, as if the bastard were reading his thoughts. "The navy's my home, chief," he said, surprised by the evenness of his voice. "I was an orphan, raised by several foster families that didn't give a damn about me. I never felt I really belonged anywhere until I joined the navy."

Chief Loomis studied the young sailor's face, handsome, he decided, too handsome, with intense dark eyes and well-defined lips. Only the once-broken nose saved his face from an effeminate appearance. Nervous, too. On edge. Hiding something, the chief thought. "Then you're career navy, right?" he asked.

Alex nodded affirmatively. "I'm in the third year of my second enlistment. I came in right out of high school, went to boot camp the day after graduation."

"No regrets?"

"None, chief. I expect to put in twenty, maybe thirty years."

"I suppose there's a wife in your near future? Kids?"

Alex wondered exactly what the chief was fishing for. "No wife or kids," he said. "My career keeps me busy. I'll retire young enough to begin a family then."

Chief Loomis smiled again. "No wife, no kids, no close family ties. You're a loner, Mayfield. Same as me. And so is every good military man." The chief tipped his beer bottle to his lips and wiped his mouth with the back of his hand. "Ever had any special assignments? Duty stations that were out of the ordinary?"

"I was among the first to go in for the Eniwetok cleanup."

"Must have been one hell of a sight, what those atomic blasts did. You volunteer?"

Alex nodded again. He was finding it more and more difficult to hold his questions in check.

"It must seem tame being on the admiral's staff after Eniwetok," Chief Loomis said. "Do you have the admiral's ear? Know a lot about what's going on in the command?"

"I'm his yeoman, Chief."

"Yeah, right. A good yeoman knows everything that's going on. Do you like the admiral, Mayfield?"

"He's okay," Alex said noncommittally.

"Too much of a dove, not enough of a hawk, that's my opinion," the chief confided. "What are you, Mayfield? A hawk or a dove?"

Alex said nothing.

"Do you believe the whole fucking world's going to be blown to kingdom come? I do. I don't just believe it, I'm damned well certain of it. Unless the powers that be stop playing their goddamned political games and get serious about the arms race, we're a doomed nation. The military needs more power and less interference from those bastards in Washington. What do they know about war? Eisenhower was a good president, knew what was going on, but his hands were tied. I think an additional requirement for a president should be written into the Constitution: that only a man with a strong military background should be allowed to run for office. What do you think, Mayfield?"

"I haven't really thought about it," Alex murmured. He drained the last of his orange juice and dropped some change on the bar for a tip. "I have to get back on duty, Chief." He slid off his stool. "Nice talking to you."

"Hold on, Mayfield." The chief took a final swallow of his beer and pushed the half-empty bottle away from him. "I'll walk back with you. There's something I'd like to talk to you about."

Outside, the afternoon sun was beating down on the tarmac, the heat rising in waves. Chief Loomis fell into step beside Alex, his hands shoved into his pockets. They'd walked only a short distance before the chief said, "It's my assignment to train a special group of navy men, Mayfield. All handpicked, with unique qualifications. The elite, you might call them. It's all hush-hush, top security. I wanted you to know you're being considered."

Alex's steps faltered. He fought to control his quickening pulse. "I have a level-six clearance, Chief, and I haven't heard of such a group. What's its designation?" Again he was struck by the evenness of his own voice.

Chief Loomis's stride was broken only slightly by the direct question. "Designation doesn't matter," he murmured. "Name's not important, not yet. You'd have to be carefully briefed. As I said, you're only being considered. We're selective, very selective. Before you're accepted we'll know you inside and out. I'm just feeling you out to determine if you're interested."

"Yes, Chief, I'm interested," Alex assured him. Too quick, he thought. He should have held back on his answer as if he were considering the offer.

"Good," Chief Loomis said. "I like a man who makes quick decisions."

A captain was approaching. Six paces before he passed, both men saluted. As he had done since yesterday, Alex carefully studied the officer's face. Recognition was instant; this was one of the captains who had been present at the conference meeting with Admiral Addison.

Alex glanced quickly at Chief Loomis as they walked on. "That captain's face is familiar, but I can't think of his name."

"Captain Ellison," the chief answered. "He's with WESTPAC. A real pain-in-the-ass prick."

They had reached the entrance to the building that housed the admiral's staff. The chief stopped, took a cigarette from his pocket and lit it. He drew the smoke deep into his lungs, the probing eyes beneath his bushy brows fixed on Alex. When he spoke he left the cigarette dangling between his lips. "We'll talk again soon, Mayfield. Until then I suggest you keep our little conversation to yourself."

"Certainly, Chief."

Loomis nodded stiffly and walked away.

Alex entered the building, but before climbing the stairs he took the notepad from his waistband and filled in one of the missing captains' names. *Captain Ellison*. Nine names of those attending the conference still unknown.

Alex didn't know exactly how to interpret his meeting with Chief Loomis, but obviously the chief was involved with some kind of security operation, and Alex had just passed an initial recruiting interview.

The symbol of the bisected triangle flashed through his mind.

Chad Bannen had been a topic of discussion at the meeting in Admiral Addison's office. Chances were Bannen had been a member of the handpicked, highly qualified group Chief Loomis had spoken of. *Had been*—Bannen was dead. The symbol that blocked information about Bannen on the computer could be a designation relating directly to the group.

As he climbed the stairs to his office, Alex wondered what would appear on the screen if he punched Chief Loomis's,

Admiral Addison's or Captains Musolf's or Ellison's names into the computer.

If the same symbol appeared, he would have succeeded in connecting those at the conference with Bannen—even if he couldn't identify the organization by name.

Where he'd take it from there, he wasn't sure.

"A GOOD AFTERNOON, you say, Loomis?" Admiral Addison shouted over the phone. "It is not a good afternoon. It has not been a good morning, and it will be an even worse evening if I don't get some proper answers from you!"

Christ almighty! Chief Loomis thought. Another ass-chewing! What for this time?

"Is this a secure line, Chief?"

"Yes, sir. Secure."

"Then suppose you explain to me why one of your operatives murdered a civilian."

Chief Loomis paled. He hadn't reported the incident to the admiral yet, and the old bastard already knew. "The operative acted on his own initiative, sir," the chief explained. Then he added, "As he was trained to do."

"It was necessary to murder a drunken stablehand?"

"Yes, sir. The operative was discovered while searching Commander Bannen's house. He had no choice."

"Is the operative a habitual bungler?" the admiral asked sarcastically. "Even a common burglar has the sense not to get caught. Your men are supposed to have been trained to a high degree of efficiency. If this is an example, then I worry about D day."

"The murder was made to look like an accident, sir."

"Ah, yes, an accident," the admiral said mockingly. "Has it occurred to you, Chief, that too many 'accidental' deaths around the commander might cause people to give credence to his accusations of something unusual in his son's death?"

"Yes, Admiral Addison, sir!"

"Yes, what?"

"Yes, it has occurred to me, sir," the chief said through clenched teeth.

"I think you need to reevaluate your operatives, Chief." The admiral's voice lost its biting edge. "They are our weakest link."

The operatives took all the risk, did all the dirty work, the chief thought, so of course they were the weakest goddamn link. "Yes, sir," he said.

"But I'm calling for a reason other than to reprimand you," the admiral went on. "I believe you served under Admiral Burke before the Vietnam pullout."

"I did, sir."

"The admiral's stroke and his grandson's death have affected him," Admiral Addison said. "I'm afraid Burke has become more enemy than ally. He's requested a meeting of the committee." Admiral Addison heaved a long, weary sigh, then added, "I don't want that meeting to take place, Chief. There's already dissension among our ranks, from those weaker members who put their personal welfare above their country's prosperity and safety."

Chief Loomis had always admired Admiral Burke—as much as he could admire any high-ranking officer. It was common knowledge within the organization that it was Admiral Burke who had revitalized Delta.

"Admiral Burke's in Key West now," Addison continued. "Fortunately, Commander Stevenson told me about a conversation he had with Burke before passing it on to the controller. I convinced him that the admiral was suffering from diminished capacity and that a special meeting of the committee was unnecessary and could be dangerous. Burke may drop the matter, but then again, he may persist. He's a stubborn old bastard. In any case, I want him watched. Do you have an operative who can perform his duty without getting caught and having to arrange another 'accident'?"

"Yes, sir. My best operative is named Raymond Everett. But he's in San Diego and isn't due back until—"

"Then pull him out of San Diego immediately," Addison cut in. "Get him on a civilian flight stopping off in Washington first. I'll be there tomorrow. I want to brief him myself."

"But, sir, that breaks the regulation of an operative knowing the identity of—"

"Just do as I say, Chief!"

"Yes, sir."

"Have you recruited the yeoman on the Moffett admiral's staff?"

"I approached him today, sir, but—" The chief hesitated. "There's something about the young man that doesn't sit right with me."

"Something? Can you articulate? Precisely what doesn't 'sit right' with you, Chief?"

"Nothing I can put my finger on, sir. But Mayfield's—"

"Don't tell me you use intuition to select operatives?" Admiral Addison demanded with renewed sarcasm. "Have our security check that yeoman out. Turn his fucking life inside out, and if he's cleared, get him into training immediately. An extra set of eyes and ears on the staff of the admiral at Moffett could be invaluable to us."

"Yes, sir." The bastard! Loomis thought. The operatives were his own responsibility. He saw to their selection, their training. It was he who sent them out on assignments; if they failed or made mistakes, it was his ass on the line. He didn't want an operative he didn't have complete confidence in, didn't want someone like Mayfield pushed on him merely because his position on the admiral's staff could be to their advantage. They might end up with another Chad Bannen. However, he reasoned, it was better to agree, then cover his ass by checking Mayfield out himself. "Yes, sir," he repeated.

"What about Commander Bannen?"

"He's still at the ranch, sir. The operative retrieved some letters written by Bannen's son. He's bringing them in now."

"Keep me informed."

Admiral Addison broke the connection.

22

Washington, D.C.

JONATHAN MCKINNEY LEFT his car parked illegally and rushed along the sidewalk to the entrance to Shannon's Restaurant.

As usual, he was late. He hadn't had time to return home for a quick shower and shave. The stubble on his jaw was thick and dark, and along with his sloppy mode of dress it gave him the appearance of a first-class bum. He caught his reflection in a shop window and cursed under his breath. Why would any woman, especially the sweet thing from Minnesota, give him a tumble?

The restaurant crowd had thinned out; only a few tables along the wall were still occupied by customers lingering over coffee. He spotted Ginny Devore as the maître d' approached him. Her face was etched with dreary resolution; she obviously thought she had been stood up. She glanced up, he waved, and her depression faded.

"We're closing in half an hour, sir," the maître d' called after him as he made for the table.

"Honey, you look like a million dollars." Jonathan slipped into the chair beside his date. "Sorry I'm late. I had to do some last-minute rewrites."

There was a pout on Ginny Devore's face, but Jonathan could tell she wasn't genuinely angry. "I've had two frozen daiquiris and a shrimp cocktail," she told him. "I don't think they'll serve us now. The waiter said the kitchen closes in fifteen minutes."

"Half an hour," Jonathan corrected, nodding at the maître d' who had given him that information. "Tell me, Ginny, did you manage to get—"

The waiter appeared at their table. "Sir, if I could take your orders? The kitchen closes in fifteen minutes."

"Half an hour," Jonathan repeated impatiently. "Yes, yes, take our orders. Have you decided, Ginny?"

"I've changed my mind three times," Ginny said with a laugh. "That's what happens when you give a woman too much time. I'll have the swordfish. No potatoes, no vegetables. And another frozen daiquiri."

Jonathan scanned the menu quickly. He was too impatient to decide. "The same," he said. "Only with potatoes and vegetables. In fact, bring her potatoes and vegetables, too, and I'll eat them." He closed the menu and passed it to the disapproving waiter. "Ginny, did you manage to get the information I requested?"

Ginny leaned forward and rested her elbows on the table. She was in her mid-twenties, with auburn hair worn stylishly short and wide, trusting brown eyes. She had bought a new dress for tonight's date, and was disappointed he hadn't specifically complimented her on it. She fixed her brown eyes on Jonathan and studied him. She'd been in Washington for only nine months, employed at Central Records in the Pentagon for seven. She and Jonathan had met at a charity bazaar. She'd gone with another date, but Jonathan had charmed her into excusing herself and leaving with him before the evening concluded. They'd had a delightful weekend, but then Jonathan hadn't called again until a few days ago. Her chin propped in cupped hands, Ginny asked, "What's this all about, Jonathan? I want to know."

"Nothing important, Ginny," he assured her. "It's just information I need for a follow-up on a story. Minor details. But to a good reporter..."

"Oh, yes." She laughed. "The night you met me you tried to convince me you were a reporter like Robert Redford and Dustin Hoffman played in that movie about exposing Watergate."

Jonathan smiled. "How quickly we forget the heroes of the American press," he said in an injured tone. "I wish I was as good a reporter as Woodward or Bernstein. I also wish I was as handsome as Redford or Hoffman."

"I shouldn't say it, but you *are* handsome," Ginny told him. "I know you were fishing for a compliment. Men and their egos! You haven't even mentioned the dress I bought for—"

"About the information, Ginny..."

"You know, Jonathan, I could lose my job for doing you these favors. The information you asked for is classified."

"I know, sweet thing, I know. But I'm not a spy. I don't ask for anything the Russians would pay to get hold of. I'm as American as Mom's apple pie, hot dogs and two cars in every garage. I only wanted information on a sailor named Raymond Everett."

"And before that, it was information on a Commander Bannen, a Chadwick Bannen and an admiral whose name I can't remember."

"Burke."

"What?"

"His name is Admiral Malcolm Burke."

"Well, whatever his name is, his records and those on the two Bannen men have been mysteriously pulled from the files." She leaned back in her chair. "I was afraid to tell my supervisor the files were missing, in case he asked me how I discovered it."

"Don't tell him. It doesn't matter."

"It matters to me. I take my job seriously."

"Of course you do. I didn't mean to imply otherwise."

"Jonathan, are you using me? Or are you really interested in me as a person?"

"Sweet thing, do you have to ask?"

"I've never been too smart where men are concerned. My sister tells me I'm a pushover. Be nice to me, take me to dinner, make love to me, and I become a man's slave. Christ, look at me with you! I'm already risking my job to steal information for you from Central Records. Not too smart? It's just damned stupid!"

"Ginny, don't get self-analytical on me. I like you as a person. I like you just as you are, I swear it."

"But would you like me if I refused to get information for you?"

"I would, of course I would. But—I can't pretend I don't want the information. It's important for my story. I'd have to go elsewhere, and I wouldn't have time to spend with you."

Ginny's brown eyes narrowed suspiciously while still managing to retain their trusting expression. "You're using me," she said uncertainly. Then, with more determination: "You are, you bastard!"

Damn it! Jonathan thought. He wasn't going to get anywhere this way. "Ginny, I—"

"And you're *not* handsome," she said. "I lied! You're a sloppy dresser. You don't bother to shave regularly, and those glasses make you look like some kind of egghead!"

Jonathan pushed his glasses back on the bridge of his nose. "A real pushover, huh?" he said. "You're tearing my ego to shreds." He made himself look offended, then hurt. "All right, Ginny. Don't give me the information. We'll have a quiet, sociable dinner. We won't discuss my profession or yours. In fact, we'll limit our conversation to the weather and the latest fashions. How's that?"

"Don't be angry with me, Jonathan. I can't bear to have people I like angry at me."

"I'm not angry," he said in a tone that he made ring false. "But it's offensive to be accused of using someone you're sincerely fond of. What kind of a cad do you think I am?"

"All right, damn you!" She reached for the purse on the floor beside her chair, opened it, then hesitated. "First, Jonathan, are you going to tell me what you're on to?"

"I told you, it's just follow-up details for a story I'm writing."

"Then why is it every time you give me a name to check on the file is missing?" Ginny demanded.

"Everett's file is missing?" he blurted.

Ginny nodded. "It's strange. We have very strict regulations and tight security, yet you've come up with four military personnel whose files have vanished. What's the subject of the story you're writing?"

"Nothing important."

"Oh? Your pupils dilate like someone who's just taken a hit of amyl nitrate, and it's nothing important. I'm not that stupid!" She started to snap her purse closed.

"All right, Ginny, I'll level with you. A friend of mine's son was killed recently. There was something peculiar about the circumstances of his death. When his body was returned for burial, a private autopsy was performed at the request of the mother, and the boy's vital organs were missing."

"How awful! Why— How could such a thing happen?"

"The boy's father is a retired commander with some notoriety attached to his record. He exposed the military drug experiments a number of years ago. You probably remember the scandal?"

Ginny nodded and leaned forward. "This is about Commander Bannen and his son?"

"When Commander Bannen first came to me I thought maybe he'd gone paranoid. He had retired, was divorced and had moved to a horse ranch in California where he's been living like a hermit. But I also reasoned that it was possible the military establishment still had it in for him and might have done in his son out of some macabre need for retribution. There's as many fanatics in the military as in civilian life, so why not? I thought. Some officer who'd been hurt by Bannen's exposé could have made himself a vigilante: kill the son and pay back the father.''

Jonathan stopped speaking while the waiter served their food.

Ginny sat patiently until the waiter had retreated, then said, "Maybe some crazy individual, but not the military. It's absurd. Kill a boy because of something his father did? No, that's absurd!''

"Just what millions said about Watergate," Jonathan said. "Just what people used to say about any scandal that broke in Washington. Not anymore, Ginny.'' He picked up his fork but only managed to push the fish around on his plate. "I'm not accusing the military. As I said, it could be some sick individual. Hell, it could have just been a mistake. The vital organs could have been misplaced, the kid could have taken drugs despite the evidence that he was clean...but I don't think so. There are too many other things.''

"Like the missing files?''

"Yes. That, and the closed-mouth attitude of the Pentagon. Then there's the strange reaction of the mother and the grandfather, Admiral Burke—suddenly leaving town, looking almost frightened, and refusing to say a word to the press. Call it a reporter's intuition, but to me it all reeks of cover-up.''

Ginny reached into her purse and removed a slip of yellow paper. "When I discovered that the file on the fourth name you gave me was also missing, I put all four names through the computer," she said. "There was nothing strange about Commander Bannen's readout, or Admiral Burke's. But the other two, Chadwick Bannen and Raymond Everett...''

"Yes, what about them?" Jonathan pressed when she hesitated.

"Jonathan, there was a blocking symbol.''

"A blocking symbol?"

"It signifies that information concerning those individuals can only be pulled from the computers by persons with specific clearances with a need-to-know authorization."

"I'm familiar with blocking symbols," Jonathan told her patiently. "I meant what type of symbol. Navy? FBI? CIA?"

"It's completely unknown to me," Ginny confessed. "I drew it to show you." Her fingers trembled as she unfolded the paper. "Jonathan, no one's going to find out about this, are they? You're not going to reveal your source? I like my job and I like Washington."

"I promise no one will know," Jonathan assured her.

Ginny unfolded the sheet of paper and laid it beside his plate.

Jonathan turned pale.

"You know what it is, don't you, Jonathan?" She felt a sudden chill that had nothing to do with the temperature in the restaurant.

His voice scarcely more than a whisper, Jonathan said, "Yes, I know. The bisected triangle. A symbol I haven't seen since... Damn! Ginny, are you sure?"

"I drew it several times until it was exact," Ginny said. "What is it, Jonathan? What does it mean?"

"It's a symbol for Delta!" Jonathan told her, and would say no more, no matter how much she prompted.

A few hours later Jonathan entered his apartment, flung his coat onto an already cluttered chair and went to the telephone.

The first time he dialed Quinn's California number the line was busy. He slammed down the receiver, went into the kitchen and took a can of diet soda from the refrigerator. Since he'd eaten only a few bites of his dinner, he was hungry. He settled for a sandwich of leftover meat loaf and some stale potato chips.

Back in the living room, he dialed Quinn's number again. Still busy. Damn it! he thought as he pulled off his loosened necktie and flung it over the discarded coat. The apartment was hot, the air fetid. He switched on the air conditioner and leaned over to let the cold air strike his face.

The telephone rang.

He reached the table with one long stride and snatched up the receiver. "Hello. Quinn? I've been trying to reach you...."

The line went dead.

Jonathan cursed aloud, then chided himself. Keep your cool, old man. You're a sophisticated reporter, you've been around, seen a lot, know too much. Don't let one of the hottest goddamn stories of your career make you lose control.

But it was imperative he reach Quinn Bannen, and the sooner the better—for Quinn. He picked up the receiver again; if the line was still busy he would ask the operator to cut in. He dialed and heard the connection made. The call was answered on the second ring.

"Bannen residence."

"May I speak to Quinn Bannen, please?"

"Mr. Bannen's not here," came the reply.

"What?"

"I said Mr. Bannen isn't here, sir."

"But I spoke to him earlier today," Jonathan said. "Where is he? Can you locate him for me? It's important I speak to him."

"I'm sorry, but Mr. Bannen left for Moffett Field shortly before dark," the woman on the other end informed him.

"He told me he wasn't leaving for Moffett until morning."

"He changed his mind, sir. May I take your name and number? When Mr. Bannen calls me I'll give him your message."

Jonathan recalled his earlier conversation with Quinn: *If it's imperative you reach me, call my house. My housekeeper's name is Esther Wade. Leave a message. I'll be checking in with her every morning.* Jonathan's throat went dry. Would Quinn call home early? Before he went to Moffett?

"May I ask who I'm speaking to?" Jonathan said.

Sounding surprised, the woman replied, "I'm Esther Wade, Commander Bannen's housekeeper."

"I'm a close friend of Quinn Bannen's. He told me he'd be checking in with you every morning."

"That's possible, sir. We've been having some difficulties here, and Mr. Bannen is concerned about my being alone with—"

"Listen, please, Mrs. Wade. I don't mean to be rude and interrupt, but the moment Quinn calls you, please tell him to try and reach me. My name's Jonathan McKinney. Tell him it's more serious than we imagined. Tell him he's in danger and not to barge into Moffett Field without consulting me and—"

"Mr. McKinney! Please! I can't get all this down. You're speaking too quickly!"

"Yes, yes, I'm sorry."

"I'm to tell Mr. Bannen to call you," Esther repeated. "That it's serious, that he's in danger. Mr. McKinney, you're frightening me." Then the housekeeper's voice changed its tone. "Is this some kind of practical joke? If it is, it's in poor taste. Mr. Bannen's been through a lot, with his son's death and—"

"It's no joke, Mrs. Wade," Jonathan cut in. "Tell him to call me immediately and not to go to Moffett Field before he speaks to me. That's important. *Not* to go to Moffett before speaking to me. I'm not easy to get hold of. He knows that. But tell him to keep trying."

"Yes, yes, I'll tell him," Esther said, sounding shaken.

"One more thing," Jonathan added hurriedly when he thought she was going to break the connection.

"Yes?" The one word was clipped, impatient, telling him the housekeeper wasn't convinced the call was not a macabre joke.

"Tell him *Delta*," Jonathan told her. "Please repeat that. Better still, write it down. *D-E-L-T-A!*"

"I'm not senile, Mr. McKinney," Esther snapped. "But I'll write it down. It doesn't make sense, but I'll tell Mr. Bannen. Delta."

She broke the connection before Jonathan could say any more.

His throat still dry, Jonathan returned to the refrigerator. There was no more soda, no beer—nothing except a bottle of ancient orange juice that had a suspicious-looking scum on it. There was instant coffee, of course, but he didn't drink coffee; it gave him an instant adverse reaction. He kept the instant variety on hand for his friends, his infrequent female guests.

The telephone rang again.

Jonathan dashed to it, hoping it was Quinn calling him by chance or because he had phoned his home immediately after Jonathan had talked to the housekeeper.

"Hello?"

Again the line went dead.

Son of a bitch! It was probably Ginny, deliberately annoying him. She'd been angry because he had hurried her through her meal and then dropped her off at her apartment without so much as a parting kiss. He'd had no time for Ginny, for lovemaking. In fact, he couldn't have screwed if he'd wanted to; the Delta symbol on Ginny's piece of paper had rendered him impotent as surely as a surgeon's scalpel would have.

Delta!

The organization had risen from the ashes to once again strike terror in his heart!

If Quinn Bannen stumbled across the wrong people at Moffett Field without knowing what he was up against, he just might not walk out.

23

Moffett Field, California

IT WAS NEARING MIDNIGHT.

Three hours earlier, Alex had parked his vintage Corvette in the lot opposite the office building used by Chief Loomis. The lights in the chief's second-story office had been on when Alex arrived, an occasional shadow passing behind the drawn venetian blinds; from the slumped shoulders of the shadow he had judged that the pacer was the chief. Then, after eleven o'clock, Alex had heard footsteps approaching from behind and had slid down in his seat just as Captain Musolf strode past and entered the building.

Within minutes of the captain's arrival, others began to emerge from the shadows of the buildings and the parking lot and go inside. If Alex's estimation was correct, seven men were gathered in Chief Loomis's office. He had recognized only Captain Musolf, but he'd seen reflections of the building lights shine off enough brass and braid to know that there were several officers present. Very peculiar—officers meeting with the chief in his office instead of in their own more elaborate accommodations.

Curiosity gnawed at Alex. It had been his intention merely to monitor Loomis's comings-and-goings, to see whether or not the chief would again attend a meeting with the men who had assembled with Admiral Addison in the conference room a few days ago. But now, knowing that several of those men were gathered so near and at this very moment, the passive waiting and watching in his car were inadequate to satisfy his nagging inquisitiveness.

When it appeared there would be no late arrivals, Alex eased soundlessly out of the Corvette, crossed the street and entered the building. A cleaning crew was working in the corridor, so the outer doors had been left unlocked. Mayfield waited until the man swabbing the floor tiles had put down his mop and disappeared into an office; then he let himself inside. Afraid to use the main staircase, he made hastily for the fire exit door, heaving a sigh of relief when he found it unlocked. His feet had made no sound on the tiles, but when he glanced over his shoulder he could see distinct footprints crossing the wet floor. He hoped the man with the mop would blame another member of the cleaning crew.

The staircase to the second floor was dark except for a tiny shaft of moonlight coming through a high window. Alex clung to the railing and climbed the stairs carefully. The fire door on the second floor had also been left unlocked. When he tested it the hinges creaked slightly, but not loud enough, he thought, to be heard at the far end of the building, where the chief's office was located. He opened the door wide enough to put his head through the crack and checked the corridor in both directions. The building, which had been empty since five o'clock, still smelled of stale tobacco. No light was visible except for that beneath the chief's door. He could hear muffled voices. After wedging himself through the narrowly opened door, he crept within three feet of the chief's office.

"...have to pull Everett from San Diego. That leaves only Marshisky." Alex recognized the chief's gruff, gravelly voice. "The bastard's an excellent exterminator, but beyond that his gray cells are mush. He's careless, needs a superior operative working with him."

"Wasn't it Marshisky who bungled the Bannen assignment?" someone asked. "We owe this mess to him."

"Gentry, we owe this mess to the man who recruited Bannen," Chief Loomis snapped. "And that's the old man himself, although I'm not going to remind him of that. Are you?"

There was a nervous laugh. "No, Chief. I'm only a lieutenant. Even though we're comrades outside military protocol, I'm not fool enough to confront an admiral with his mistakes."

Alex made a mental note to add the name Lieutenant Gentry to his list.

"If I recall, I didn't give Marshisky clearance." The voice was cultured and edged with a slight East Coast accent—Captain Musolf. "He's a borderline psychotic and should never have been admitted to the navy, let alone to our project."

"Shit! We all know the bastard's a mental case," Chief Loomis said. "Fifty percent of our operatives are. If they're not when we recruit them, they are when we've finished training them. If they weren't, how would we keep them? Why would we need them? We don't need a psychologist to tell us Marshisky or any of the others are mental defectives."

"I just thought I'd point it out. Especially in Marshisky's case," Captain Musolf said indignantly. "He's a more extreme case than the others."

"Your contribution is so noted," Chief Loomis said with a degree of sarcasm that Alex was astonished to hear directed at a captain by a chief. "The question is, what we should do with Marshisky in the meantime? You all know he's one of the key operatives in our plan for D day, but with Everett pulled for duty in Key West, we can't leave Marshisky floating around without supervision. There's no telling what that crazy son of a bitch'll get into. We need to slip him into a command where he'll scarcely be noticed."

"If I may make a suggestion?" Captain Musolf said, with a sarcasm that equaled the chief's. "Give him travel papers back to Moffett, then turn him over to me. I can keep him sedated, even in a padded cell if necessary, until we need his services."

"You want him to volunteer for a padded cell?"

"For the drugs you'll promise him," the captain said. "His craving for drugs matches his lust for killing. In fact, if I hadn't confiscated his last piss test he'd be behind bars now waiting for a court-martial."

"I'm becoming somewhat disturbed about the caliber of men we've been forced to consort with," someone complained.

"It's the objective that counts," another man said forcefully. "Delta wasn't revitalized for polite warfare. We can't expect the all-American boy to slit throats and bash in heads. What troubles me is what we're going to do with all these monsters we've created when we have no further need of them."

"We'll always have need of such men," Chief Loomis said with conviction. "Always have, always will."

Alex, moving closer to the door, stepped on a loose floor tile. The creak it made sounded to him like a siren. Conversation inside the chief's office stopped immediately. He heard a chair scrape back, then footsteps. Panicked, Alex fled back along the corridor. The fire door was too far away. The utility room was closer. He had just stepped inside and eased the door closed when he heard Chief Loomis's door open and several men emerge.

"Just the building settling," Captain Musolf said.

"Or one of the cleaning crew listening to our conversation," Chief Loomis said suspiciously.

"If it was one of the cleaning crew, don't worry. They don't speak English." It was the voice Alex identified as Lieutenant Gentry's. "Let's get on with the meeting. I promised my wife I'd be back in Atherton before two o'clock. Your call interrupted one of her rare passionate moods."

"I don't give a damn about your sex life, Gentry," Chief Loomis told him. "But there's no need to go on. We'll bring Marshisky back here and let Musolf keep him under control. As for Commander Bannen, I think we've covered all that ground. We know his next destination is Moffett Field. What we don't know is why, or who he expects to see here concerning his son's death. We may learn something when our operative brings in his son's letters. We have to stay one step ahead of the prick. We can't afford for him to learn more than he thinks he already knows."

Alex heard the men step back inside the office, but because of the volume of their voices he knew they had left the door ajar.

"If you think coming up against one blank wall after another is going to stop the commander," Captain Musolf said, "then you're wrong. Commander Bannen's profile is on my desk. I've studied it carefully. Have any of you gentlemen seen an authentic Scottish cairn terrier at work? They're bred for rooting out groundhogs, not to be the sweet little pets like Dorothy's Toto in *The Wizard of Oz*. They're trained for one objective—to reach and kill their prey. I watched one of those dogs at work in Scotland when I was a kid. He went right on rooting and tearing his way down a groundhog's hole even though the flesh had been torn from his snout and one eye had been ripped from its socket. That's what I'd compare Commander Bannen to. He's a man who'll go straight for his objective—in this case the truth about his son's death—and nothing short of killing him will stop him."

"Yeah, well, send your psychological evaluation to Admiral Addison," Chief Loomis said. "Maybe the old bastard'll give the order to eliminate him. Good night."

His ear pressed to the utility room door, Alex listened to the men leaving the chief's office, their footsteps fading as they moved down the staircase. He knew it would be foolish to attempt to leave his hiding place. The chief had remained in his office, perhaps with the door open and a clear view of the corridor. Alex cautiously lowered himself, folded his legs up under him and waited, hoping the cleaning crew would be slow in reaching the second floor. He heard the chief dialing the telephone and knew his door had been left open. If one of the cleaning crew opened the utility room door, Alex would be directly exposed to the chief's view.

"Everett, Chief Loomis. I want you on the first nonmilitary flight in the morning for Washington, D.C. Your final destination will be Key West, but you're to be briefed in Washington first." There was a short pause. "Yeah, well, I'm not so damned pleased about it myself. I don't like having my operatives pulled on such short notice. But be on that plane. I can't counter the order. You'll be contacted when you disembark at Dulles. What can I use to have your contact identify you?" After a moment's pause, the chief gave a deep-throated chuckle. "I forgot about your nose, Everett. I doubt there are many men traveling with bandaged noses. Follow the instructions from your Washington contact to the letter, understood? Otherwise, Everett, it'll be more than your nose that'll be bandaged."

The phone was slammed down.

Moments later, Alex heard footsteps, then the sound of the office light being switched off.

He held his breath as the chief strode past the utility room. Even after the footsteps had died away down the staircase, he remained in hiding. Half an hour passed before he heard the cleaning crew dragging their equipment to the second floor. He listened as they laughed and conversed in Spanish; then, when they went into one of the offices, he let himself out of the utility room and hurried down the stairs.

Outside, Alex breathed deeply of the night air. His legs ached from having been in a cramped position for so long and his neck muscles were knotted and sore from tension.

He had almost been caught. Almost!

If he wasn't more cautious, his foster mother's warning about the curious cat might come true.

24

San Diego, California

EMILY EVERETT LAID ASIDE the paperback romance novel she'd been reading and reached for a cigarette. The digital clock beside the sofa bed clicked as it turned to 3:00 a.m. She lit the cigarette and inhaled; she had smoked too much all day, and her throat was raw. It was her nerves, she thought, her damned nerves that drove her to excessive smoking, but what were her options—a nervous breakdown or throat cancer? The mere thought of the word *throat* reminded her of Mona—Mona with her throat cut—and she shuddered. She threw back the sheet, went to the cupboard and returned with a juice glass full of gin.

Sitting on the edge of the sofa bed, she stared at the clear liquor. When Raymond wasn't deployed she was forced to hide the gin, usually in the clothes hamper. He complained it made her mean and bitchy and loose-mouthed. And lousy in bed. That was amusing. She considered herself the least bitchy woman she knew. She was too damned frightened of life, of people, to risk their wrath by being unkind to them, even when she wanted to be. As for being lousy in bed, that was Raymond's problem, not hers. He didn't make love, he screwed, like an animal, with no regard for her satisfaction, ignoring her pleas for gentleness. Yet she loved him, and was tortured by loneliness when he was deployed. She hoped if he signed on again after this enlistment he'd be stationed somewhere nice, where they could rent a suitable house instead of this dingy apartment and begin to live like a properly married couple.

Her thoughts returned to the apartment across the hallway. Ever since Mona had been killed Emily had been unable to put her out of her mind for more than a few minutes at a time. She lifted the glass of gin and drained the contents in one greedy gulp. Mona had been her only close friend in San Diego. Poor Mona! Poor Chad! She returned to the cupboard and refilled her glass. Careful, she warned herself, or you'll give in to self-pity and depression. She returned to the sofa bed and picked up her paperback.

The words began to blur. She couldn't concentrate.

Outside, the wind had risen and was stirring the topmost fronds of the palm trees. She hated palm trees, especially when the wind blew and the fronds sounded like a huge swarm of insects, as they did right now.

As a matter of fact, she thought, she hated California. Always warm or hot. She'd been raised in the Midwest, and so in California she missed the changing seasons: winters with cold rains and snow that made you appreciate spring, hot summers that made you look forward to autumn. She liked having something to look forward to, even if it was only a change in weather.

Before Raymond had proposed to her she'd considered moving to New York or Boston. Bostonians had such class—those elegant accents and snooty mannerisms. She slid down in the bed and pulled the sheet up to her chin. Commander Bannen had class; she had liked him, had seen Chad in him. Why hadn't she held out for a man like the commander, a gentle man, with manners and charm, who wouldn't batter her as Raymond so often did?

After the last time, Raymond had promised never to beat her again, but she was a realist—she knew he would. Why did she love him? Why did she miss him so much? There was a wild, mean streak in him that frightened her. It angered her, too, that she was so meek and never fought back. Her mother had been like that, and it had sickened Emily; now, with Raymond, she was repeating her mother's long-suffering toleration of abuse.

Emily glanced at the clock again. 3:15. God, how slowly time passed when you were alone and afraid someone would come in the night and do to you what had been done to Mona. Poor Mona. She closed her eyes and fought to push away the image from the newspaper photograph of Mona lying dead on the sidewalk. Without realizing it, Emily drifted into a troubled sleep.

In her dream she was alone on a deserted, sandy beach. She was running; a man was chasing her. She was far ahead of him, but the faster she ran the closer he seemed to come to her. She didn't know why he was chasing her, only that he intended to kill her. As he ran after her, the sunlight glinted off a knife in his hand. The man had no face, but there was something familiar about him, something that convinced her she knew him. And knowing him only frightened her more, because he was faceless and she couldn't identify him. He was gaining on her. She heard him shout, "You're going to die like Mona!" She ran faster, though she knew he would soon catch her and slash out with the knife.

Emily woke with a start and sat bolt upright on the sofa bed. Her paperback novel slipped to the floor with a thud, and her hand shot out in alarm, knocking the half-empty glass of gin onto the floor, too.

"Damn it!" she cried.

She got out of bed to clean up the gin before it took the remaining color out of the carpet.

She was on her knees rubbing at the stain with a dishcloth when she heard the footsteps in the hallway. They weren't distinct, but the floorboards of the aged apartment building were worn and shrieked an alarm. She caught her breath and held it, hoping she'd been mistaken. But the footsteps came again, slow and deliberate. Someone was creeping cautiously down the hall toward her door. Her gaze turned to the door in panic. Thank God she'd not forgotten to turn the latch. Sometimes she forgot, because the door was seldom double-locked when Raymond wasn't deployed. Emily rose slowly to her feet, still clutching the dishcloth, her gaze fixed on the doorknob as if she were mesmerized by the expectation of seeing it suddenly turned from outside.

The floorboard directly outside her door creaked, and then silence settled in. The only sounds were the wind and the insectlike dirge of the palm fronds. The doorknob turned slowly. Emily clamped her hands across her mouth to stifle a scream. She turned her head and stared at the telephone; Raymond had sent her money to pay the bill, but she'd forgotten, and the telephone company had discontinued service.

Someone pushed against the door. It groaned but didn't give.

"Who's there?" she cried. "Go away! I have my husband's revolver! If you don't go away, I'll fire through the door! I'm warning you! Go away!"

Cautiously she edged toward the bathroom. The bathroom door had a new brass bolt. The old knob lock hadn't worked, and she'd installed the new bolt after Raymond had gone to sea. It was a ridiculously strong lock for a bathroom, but she'd bought it at a garage sale for three dollars. Her heart was pounding rapidly now against her rib cage. A vision of the dead Mona flashed through her mind again. If she locked herself in the bathroom, she could scream until one of the neighbors called the police.

"Go away!" she shouted again.

Then, softly: "Emily, it's me, baby!"

"Raymond?" Tears of relief streaked her cheeks. "Raymond, is it really you?" She rushed to the door and laid her cheek against the rough wooden surface.

"It's really me, honey. Your sailor home from the sea. Open the door. I forgot my key in my locker. Hurry, honey!"

"Yes, Raymond, I'm hurrying! Oh, I'm so glad you're home!" She twisted at the lock, but in her nervousness she turned it too far, and it made a complete circle. "Mona's dead, Raymond. Someone killed her. I thought someone was after me. I was terrified. Raymond, I don't want to live in this neighborhood any longer. I want— Oh, I'm having trouble with the lock. It seems to be jammed. I want to move to a better neighborhood, maybe even on the base, until—''

Raymond threw his weight against the door, and it burst open. It struck her and sent her reeling backward into the room. Her legs struck the side of the overstuffed chair, and she fell, bouncing from the chair arm to the floor. The force of the fall caused her to roll, and when she stopped, her lower body was wedged beneath the sofa bed. Dazed she saw Raymond standing just inside the room. He turned and slammed the door. There was something strange about his appearance.... Then she noticed the bandages across the bridge of his nose. She saw the fury in his eyes, and she trembled.

"Raymond, why?" she whimpered. Her fright seemed to be affecting her sight; she suddenly seemed to be looking at Raymond through the wrong end of a telescope. He was far away, yet he was coming closer quickly, like the man on the beach in her dream. "Why?"

"You talked to Chad's father!" he said sharply. "What did you tell him?"

Emily was afraid she was going to faint. She fought to quell her fear. "I—I only gave him my condolences," she cried. "Chad's dead!" But he'd know Chad was dead, she told herself, since they were both stationed on the *Alum Rock*. "His father had ... had Mona's address ... and came to see her. But Mona's dead, too, Raymond! Someone ... someone mutilated her ... They cut her throat and then ..."

Raymond crossed to the floor of the sofa bed. He flung up the bottom of the mattress, and the mechanism snapped it back into a closed position. "Shut up about Mona! I know she's dead!" He reached for her, grabbed her arm and hauled her to her feet. "I want to know every fucking word you and Chad's father said to each other."

Emily tried to struggle free of his grip. "You're hurting me, Raymond! Please don't hurt me!"

He flung her onto the cushionless sofa. "Tell me everything Commander Bannen said to you!" he shouted. "Everything you said to him! Did you lay him while you were telling him all our secrets? Tell me the truth, because if you lie to me—"

Emily was so frightened that her words came between terrified gasps for air. "He...told me...Chad was dead!" she managed. "He—he didn't believe...it was be-because of drugs like...the navy said." She stared up into her husband's eyes and saw the madness there. For the first time since their marriage, she realized she feared him more than she loved him. It was a sobering realization.

Raymond leaned down so that his face, with the bandaged nose and the madness blazing in the eyes, hovered close to hers. "What else?" he demanded. "Tell me everything! That's all that's going to save you!"

"Don't hurt me, Raymond! Please don't!"

His slap sent her halfway across the sofa. She instantly tasted blood in her mouth, felt the cut where he had driven her flesh into her teeth. He grabbed at her kimono, pulled at it, and she heard it rip. As the numbness of the initial shock wore off, she felt the pain of a broken tooth. She had always been so proud of her even white teeth, and he had broken one, maybe more. Damn him! Damn him to hell!

"Answer me, bitch! What did he ask you? What did you tell him?"

"Nothing! I told you, nothing!"

"Everything, you mean!" he snarled. "How much gin did you have while he was here? I should have known you couldn't keep your bitch mouth shut! Satisfy yourself only with whores, that's what they told us to do. And never the same one twice. But me, I thought I'd show them. A wife, a steady piece of ass. A nice little place of my own, no whore's bed for me. But I had to choose a bitch with a loose mouth!'' He drew back his hand to strike her again. "It'll be even looser when I finish with you. I warned you, you can't say I didn't warn you!"

Emily threw up her hands to intercept his second blow.

At the same moment she felt the pain in her arms, her fear turned to rage. She remembered her mother's meek acceptance of beatings, the cowering and whimpering that had sickened her, and something inside her cried out in rebellion.

Raymond appeared surprised at her sudden attempt to defend herself, probably because it wasn't the reaction he was accustomed to. He was leaning over her, legs splayed, raising his hand for another assault.

Emily kicked out with all her might, and her foot found its mark in his groin. Even before the cry of pain escaped his lips she was off the sofa and running for the bathroom. She had a fleeting glance at him charging after her before she slammed the door, shooting the new bolt into place.

Raymond struck the door, expecting the old lock to give and the door to burst inward. When it held, it threw him off balance. He staggered backward, fighting to stay on his feet. "You rotten whore! I'll kill you for this! I'll cut your goddamned throat just like Mona!"

Emily screamed.

He was at the door again, twisting the knob and slamming his shoulder against the brittle wood.

She knew the door wouldn't hold against his renewed attack. Fighting back panic, she climbed into the claw-footed bathtub, flung open the window and stared down into the garbage-strewn rear courtyard. There were no lights on in the other apartments. It was the sort of neighborhood where family fights occurred each and every night. No other tenants, if awakened by Emily's screams, had concerned themselves enough to switch on a lamp and look out their windows to investigate. Unless the fight disturbed their sleep for a long period of time, they would ignore it.

Raymond struck the door with such force that the entire bathroom vibrated. The door creaked and threatened to splinter. One or two more attempts, Emily knew, and the door would burst inward and she would be at Raymond's mercy.

Leaning out the window, she drew a deep breath into her lungs and shrieked, "Help! Help me! Please!"

Instead of causing Raymond to hesitate as she had expected, her call for help made him accelerate his attack against the door.

Across the courtyard, a light came on. A shade was raised, and a gray-haired, elderly woman peered out.

"Police! Call the police!" Emily screamed.

The old woman's gaze searched the building until she saw Emily in the bathroom window. She reacted as Emily had seen actors do in silent films, drawing back and bringing her hands to her face in an exaggerated gesture of alarm. The woman yanked down the shade.

Beyond the bathroom door, Raymond was cursing, cursing Emily and cursing himself for having to "clean up a loose end." The next time he threw himself against the weakening door, a crack appeared down the middle.

"Either I get her or Delta gets me!" she heard him cry.

Outside the bathroom window was a group of three palm trees. The tallest was slightly taller than the window and no more than four feet from the building. The other two reached the third and second floors and were only shadowy clumps in the darkness. As a young girl, Emily had been a tomboy who had climbed trees with her brothers—not palm trees, with their sharp, scaly trunks, but trees nevertheless. If she could somehow reach the tallest of the palms...

Hesitantly she climbed onto the inner edge of the bathtub and hoisted herself into the open window.

The window wasn't tall enough for her to stand, so she was forced to a crouch. The wind was cold enough against her face. Her torn dressing gown caught on the soap rack;

instead of pulling it free, she slipped it from her shoulders and let it fall away. Naked, she stared at the dark silhouette of the tallest palm tree and judged the force with which she had to fling herself.

Please, God, even though I've avoided you most of my life, please help me now!

Behind her, the door splintered and crashed inward.

With a final scream, Emily flung herself into the darkness.

But instead of throwing herself directly outward, Emily made the mistake of arching her body. The window frame caught her back. She felt the searing pain as her flesh was scraped away, felt the momentum of her lunge for freedom diminish, and knew she had failed.

Her grasping hands fell short of the palm tree. She was falling, falling faster and faster. Moments seemed to become an eternity, and then time lost all meaning.

She struck something, thought she felt her bones breaking, though strangely without pain, and then she continued her fall. Mercifully, blackness overcame her before she reached the courtyard.

25

Mountain View, California

MONDAY MORNING DAWNED sunny and clear on the San Francisco Peninsula.

Early the night before, Quinn had checked into a motel off Highway 101, less than ten miles from Moffett Field. It was a sleazy place, obviously patronized mainly by sailors and marines who used the X-rated closed-circuit television to boost sex drives dampened by alcohol and by the serviceman's female partners, whose interest lay mostly in the payment they would receive following a routine performance.

The drive had exhausted Quinn. He'd telephoned the ranch, but the line had been busy, and he'd fallen asleep across the bed with his clothes on and hadn't waked up until half past five in the morning.

When he opened the draperies a blazing sun was just peeking over the Fremont Hills. It was too early to call Esther Wade. He knew the woman's routine: up at six-thirty to shower and dress, breakfast on the table at seven-fifteen, dishes done and housekeeping chores underway by eight. He reasoned that there was no point in disturbing her so early; he'd call her after he had breakfast. After a leisurely shower, first with hot water and then cold, he shaved, dressed and left the motel with directions to a nearby Denny's. He ordered a Grand Slam and surprised himself by devouring everything on his plate. After four cups of coffee served by an amiable Australian waiter named Trevor, Quinn was ready to face the day.

He'd intended to return to the motel and telephone the ranch, but since he was on Highway 101 and the Moffett Field exit was in sight, he made the turn and soon pulled into the parking lot. He presented his identification to the duty officer and, as a retired commander, was given a temporary day pass.

Activity on the base was well underway. A group of marines were jogging on the tarmac, while sleepy-eyed civilians trudged doggedly from the parking lot into various buildings. Quinn had been at Moffett Field before, had been stationed there once for a four-month stint while his travel orders to Hawaii had been held up by red tape in Washington. Very little had changed. The gigantic metal hangar, built in the 1930s to house zeppelins, still dominated the surrounding buildings. He knew there was now a complete underground network of offices and tunnels beneath the hangar, safe ground for chosen individuals in the event of nuclear attack. Even fighter planes were stored there, lowered and raised by an enormous elevator that was so well disguised it was impossible to identify it from above.

The top floor of Building 17 housed the station admiral and his staff. Quinn parked as close to the building as possible without taking a reserved space; he intended to see the admiral later, especially if he failed to locate the two people mentioned in Chad's letters. The names were on a piece of paper in his jacket pocket: Chief Loomis and a corpsman named Mae Aames. He had no idea what he expected to learn from interviewing them, but he had nowhere else to turn. He locked the car and walked aimlessly until he spotted a sign that read Personnel Locator.

The office was manned by a PN2 and a civilian. The civilian, a woman in her late forties, possibly Spanish or Portuguese, approached the counter when Quinn entered. She had gray hair tinted blue and was clinging to a cup of coffee, evidently her first of the morning, with an attitude that said it would take an act of Congress to make her part with it.

Quinn identified himself as "Commander Quinn Bannen, retired." He showed her his ID and day pass and gave her the names of the two individuals he wished to locate.

The woman, who appeared bored, checked her files with precision. "Chief Loomis's office is in Building 12, but he doesn't report for duty until 0800," she told him. Corpsman Aames lived on the base. She gave him directions to the corpsman's building, then went back to her coffee without acknowledging Quinn's thank-you.

At Corpsman Aames's building, Quinn was told he had just missed her. "A tall blonde with shapely legs" was the description given him by a third-class petty officer he met in the lobby. "She's probably at the mess hall."

The mess hall was crowded and noisy. Quinn let his gaze sweep over the personnel breakfasting in the hall. He spotted a blond corpsman, but as far as shapely legs were concerned, hers were hidden beneath the table. She was not

particularly attractive, with a too-large nose and a high
forehead accentuated by short, straight hair combed back
from her face, which gave her a severe look. She sat with
two male corpsmen, punctuating each statement she made
with a forkful of scrambled eggs.

Quinn approached the table and waited until she had acknowledged him, then asked, "Petty Officer Aames?"

"Over there against the window." The woman pointed
with her fork. "The Greta Garbo type. She always sits
alone." She and her companions laughed as Quinn turned
away.

Mae Aames was a second-class petty officer. She was attractive, almost beautiful, and, although her legs were hidden beneath the table, Quinn had no doubt they were
shapely. Her wavy, naturally blond hair was worn regulation length. Her uniform was immaculate. She had only
toast and coffee on her breakfast tray.

"Petty Officer Aames?" Quinn was forced to raise his
voice above the din.

Mae Aames wore no makeup, had no need of it, for her
beauty was as natural as her blond hair. When she saw
Quinn, something sparked behind her startlingly blue and
intelligent eyes. "Yes, I'm Petty Officer Aames." Her me-
lodious voice was pitched low.

"May I sit down? My name is—"

"I know who you are, Commander," she told him.
"There's much of Chad in your face, in your stance and
overall appearance. Besides, I've seen photographs of you.
You haven't aged." She indicated that he could take the
chair opposite her, and she studied him closely as he sat
down and pulled his chair up to the table. "I've been
expecting you," she said quietly, her voice scarcely audible
above the noise. "I've been dreading this moment."

"Dreading seeing me?" Quinn said. "I don't understand." He judged her to be about Chad's age, perhaps a

year older or younger. He wondered exactly what her relationship with his son had been.

As if she'd read his thoughts, she said, "Chad and I were very close at one time, Commander. Actually, I was in love with him." Her lips parted in what Quinn took for an expression of irony. "There!" she murmured. "I've said it. It's out at last." She nervously averted her eyes and reached for her coffee cup. "It's not true that confession is good for the soul."

"I take it you never confessed your love to my son?" Quinn said.

"I didn't. It wouldn't have mattered."

"But surely..." He let the thought remain unexpressed. Mae Aames was so beautiful, he thought; in appearance, at least, she was the ideal young woman, whom any parent would be pleased to have his son bring home, the type of woman welcomed as a daughter-in-law without hesitation, with pride.

"Chad transferred suddenly to the USS *Alum Rock*," Mae Aames said. "While he was in San Diego, he met another woman. A Mona Shriver. I never met her, but Chad wrote me about her."

The image of Mona Shriver as he'd seen her in Emily Everett's photograph flashed through Quinn's mind, and he wondered how Chad could have chosen her over a woman like Mae Aames.

"What have you learned about Chad's death, Commander?"

The directness of the question was unexpected, and Quinn's reaction must have been visible in the tightening of his features.

The woman's eyes were fixed on him again. "I wrote a note to your wife," she said. "'They killed our Chad.' No doubt she showed it to you. I felt foolish after I mailed it."

"What did you mean? Who are the 'they' you accuse?"

"I can't really answer that question," the corpsman confessed. "I know Chad was involved with some organization that was confidential. He was very secretive. He could be very closemouthed. You didn't know your son very well, did you, Commander?"

No sense in denying it, Quinn thought. Chad had probably told her about his parents. "Regrettably, no," he said.

"You're wondering why he chose a woman like Mona Shriver instead of me. I've seen her photograph, you see. Chad continued to write to me after his transfer. His letters were no more than quick notes, conscience-easers. He felt guilty about me and tried to keep our friendship alive. If he couldn't love me, the next best thing he could offer was friendship. He was perceptive; he knew how I felt from the beginning." Her voice cracked, and Quinn realized the effort it cost her to remain outwardly calm and collected.

Quinn told himself to avoid discussing the love triangle of his son and the two women in his life; that sort of discussion would get him nowhere.

Mae Aames stared down at the toast on her plate. "God, I loved your son, Commander," she said. "If only he'd been capable of a commitment to a woman."

Her statement rattled Quinn. "Are you trying to tell me my son was a—a homosexual?"

"Chad, a homosexual!" She appeared shocked at the idea. "No, Commander."

Quinn felt himself relax.

"Maybe it would have been better for Chad if he had been gay," Mae Aames said. "He was as near to being asexual as any man I've known."

"I find that difficult to accept," Quinn said incredulously.

"Whether you can accept it or not, it's true," the young woman maintained. "Your divorce affected Chad more than you or his mother understood. Chad felt abandoned, frightened, maybe a little responsible. If the two of you—

whom he considered so perfectly suited for each other—couldn't make a lasting commitment, how could he? If he couldn't make a commitment, why get involved sexually when it wouldn't lead anywhere?''

Quinn felt a rush of guilt, then anger. ''That sounds like a purely vindictive remark, Petty Officer Aames. Made, perhaps, to shift the blame to me because my son chose another woman over you.'' As soon as the words were out of his mouth, he regretted them.

''Have you met the other woman, Commander? She was a prostitute. She felt Chad's lack of sexual demands was refreshing. I guess so many men had taken advantage of her body she convinced herself the first man who didn't was in love with her. As far as I know, she didn't realize Chad was using her. I don't know why he took up with her, but I think it had something to do with that organization he got involved with. Oh, he became fond of her. Judging from his letters, he even managed to have sex with her. I don't know how deep his feelings for her went, or how much he was deluding himself to keep from facing the fact he was using her. It doesn't really matter now, does it?''

''You've obviously been deeply hurt, Miss Aames. I'm sorry,'' Quinn told her sincerely. ''I never met Mona Shriver, but I've been to her apartment, seen her photograph, talked to her best friend. Mona Shriver's dead, Miss Aames. Brutally murdered on the street outside the club where she worked.''

The corpsman's head shot up. The blue eyes that had held tears were suddenly filled with fear. ''Did they catch her murderer?''

Quinn shook his head. ''Can you tell me anything more about this organization Chad became involved with?''

''No, nothing,'' she answered quickly.

''You can't, or you've decided not to?''

Mae Aames stared at him for several moments without speaking. Her eyes were as expressive as they were intelligent; he knew she was trying to decide whether she should say any more to him.

"I want to clear Chad's name," Quinn said to encourage her. "I want justice for my son."

"Justice for Chad? Or to appease your own conscience, Commander?" she asked.

"Both," Quinn answered truthfully.

After another few moments of studying him, Mae said, "I can't tell you anything about the organization, Commander. Chad only referred to it twice—once when he was drinking and once in his sleep." She noted his reaction and added, "Yes, commander. Chad talked in his sleep. He had nightmares. I'd wake him up and hold him until the terror passed."

"He didn't mention the organization by name?"

"No, but I assumed from what he said that it was a military group. He kept repeating an admiral's name."

"His grandfather? Admiral Burke?"

"No, he spoke openly of Admiral Burke," she said. "He admired his grandfather—at least he did in the beginning. Later, he refused to even mention his name. He talked a lot about you, Commander. He was determined to make you proud of him. It was almost an obsession. He told me he was going to emulate you, that he was putting his life on the line to expose a scandal more explosive than the one his father uncovered."

"Through the organization?"

"I suppose so. I don't know for sure."

"But the 'they' you referred to in the note to my ex-wife—you actually meant the organization?"

She nodded. "But I have no proof. I shouldn't have written the note. Chad's dead. Perhaps it would be best for all of us to let him be buried."

"You don't believe that. You want his name cleared as much as his mother and I."

A yeoman approached and took the table next to theirs. He was a second-class petty officer, handsome, with dark hair and an intense expression in his dark eyes.

Quinn, irritated by the intrusion, lowered his voice as he asked, "Do you still have the letters my son wrote you?"

"Yes, commander."

"You're luckier than me. Mine were stolen. May I read your letters?" He saw her flinch and added, "You see, Petty Officer Aames, I'm not only looking to clear my son's name. I've become as obsessed with knowing him as you say he was with making me proud of him. It's something I must do for myself."

"You may read them," she said. Her voice was suddenly pitched lower, but there was also a tremor in it that caused Quinn to look up.

Mae Aames was staring at the yeoman who had seated himself at the next table. Quinn followed her gaze. The yeoman appeared to be ignoring them, drinking his coffee and staring off into space. Yet his obliviousness to them and their conversation seemed to be too deliberate to be natural.

Quinn hadn't seen the slip of paper being shoved quickly under the ashtray beside his arm, but Mae Aames had. That was why she was staring at the yeoman. She indicated the note with a nod of her head, then a look at the yeoman who'd put it there.

Quinn glanced around the crowded mess hall before slipping the note from beneath the edge of the ashtray. No one appeared to be paying the slightest attention to their table. The yeoman had turned in his chair and was facing away from them, affecting an attitude of boredom. Quinn brought the note down under the edge of the table and opened it. "They know you're here, Commander. You're endangering everyone you talk with! YN2 Mayfield."

Beneath the name was a telephone number.

When Quinn looked up, the yeoman was gone. His half-empty coffee cup was still steaming.

"What is it?" Mae Aames demanded in a whisper.

Quinn reread the message. *You're endangering everyone you talk with!* In all fairness, he couldn't keep the note from the corpsman. He tore off the name and telephone number and casually passed the paper across to her.

She displayed no discernible emotion when she read the message. Still, her hand trembled as she crumpled up the paper and dropped it in the ashtray. "What do we do?" she asked dully.

"I suggest you take an unauthorized leave immediately until we know what's behind this," Quinn told her. "Do you have a place to go? Somewhere not listed on your records?"

She answered thoughtfully, "Yes, but don't you feel you're overreacting, Commander? I haven't told you anything of consequence. I don't know anything, and that's the honest truth."

"Mona Shriver didn't have the opportunity to tell me anything at all," Quinn said pointedly.

"Don't frighten me, Commander. I don't handle fear well."

"Do you have a car on the base?"

Mae Aames nodded. "It passes for a car. It's a 1968 Chevy Chad found for me."

Quinn pushed back his chair. "I'm going to see you to your car," he told her. "I want you to give me a number where you can be reached. Then I want you to go there and stay put until you hear from me. Will you do that?"

"Yes, but if I lose a stripe because of this—"

"Better a stripe than your life," Quinn murmured.

26

Mountain View, California

QUINN RETURNED to the motel and immediately dialed the telephone number slipped to him by the yeoman.

The woman who answered the telephone had such a heavy accent and spoke so rapidly that he was unable to identify the office he had reached. He asked for "Petty Officer Mayfield, please."

Presently a man's voice came on the line, "Petty Officer Mayfield. May I help you?"

"This is Quinn Bannen. I'd like an explanation of—"

"This is not a secure line, sir."

"Then when can we talk? Where can we meet?" Quinn asked.

"I'm off duty at 1800, sir. If you'll give me a telephone number where I can reach you?"

Quinn read out the telephone number from the instrument he was using.

"I'll call you at 1800, sir." Then, in a low voice: "I repeat, Commander, you're being watched."

"I understand," Quinn said. "Thank you. If you agree to meet with me, I'll make certain we're alone and unobserved."

"Goodbye, sir."

Quinn hung up, rose and began pacing the motel room. It had occurred to him that Mayfield might be part of a setup. Yet that was a risk he had to take. He returned to the telephone and dialed the ranch.

Esther Wade must have been sitting beside the phone, because she answered on the first ring. "I'm glad you got through, Mr. Bannen. We've been having trouble with the phone." As if to substantiate her statement, the phone buzzed, then clicked. "Are you still there, Mr. Bannen?"

"Yes, Esther. I'm still here. When did the trouble with the phone start?"

"Yesterday, right after you left," Esther answered.

"Would you call the telephone company and ask them to check out the line?"

"I was going to do just that, Mr. Bannen, but they sent out a nice young man before I called. He's here now."

A thought struck Quinn like a bolt of lightning. "Esther, do you know the man?"

"No, Mr. Bannen. He's from the Redding office. He told me the local office couldn't fix problems like ours."

"Is he in the room with you now, Esther?"

"No. He's outside. I can see...yes, I can see him through the window. He's climbing a telephone pole. Like a squirrel, he is."

"Esther, were there any messages?"

"A Jonathan McKinney called last night," the housekeeper told him. "He's a strange one, Mr. Bannen, if I may say so. Most of what he told me didn't make any sense. I thought he was some kind of practical joker. Said to tell you it was more serious than you imagined. For you to call him immediately. You'd be in danger if you went to Moffett Field without talking to him first."

Damn it! Quinn thought. He should have broken Esther's routine and called her before leaving his motel room that morning.

"Mr. McKinney said he's not easy to get ahold of," Esther continued. "Then he gave me a word to pass on to you. He insisted I repeat it, even write it down. I told him I wasn't senile. I've kept my wits about me. The word is—"

"Esther, don't give me the word now!" Quinn said sharply. "Now, listen to me carefully. I don't want to frighten you, and I can't explain why I'm going to say what I am. Do you trust me, Esther?"

"With my life, Mr. Bannen," the old woman assured him.

"Will you promise me to do just what I tell you?"

"Well, yes, Mr. Bannen." Hesitantly she added, "You're beginning to sound as strange as that Jonathan McKinney."

"Do you still have the shotgun handy, Esther?"

"Right against the wall by the front door."

"Esther, exactly what does the young man from the telephone company look like?"

"Young," she answered, as if the word described him completely.

"Is there anything unusual about him?" Quinn pressed.

"Like what, Mr. Bannen?"

"Is there anything about him that strikes you as different than most of the young men you know?"

"Well," Esther said thoughtfully, "he's cleaner, and he's a gentleman. He wears his hair nice and short, and he's neat."

"A military regulation haircut," Quinn murmured.

"What's that, Mr. Bannen?"

"Esther, I want you to lay down the phone. Don't hang up, just lay it on the table. Go get the shotgun. Please do that now, Esther."

"All right, Mr. Bannen, but I don't—"

"Please do it, Esther."

"Yes, I'm going." Her voice shook; he had obviously frightened her. But it was necessary. She had told him she trusted him with her life, and it might be her life he was saving. "I'm back, Mr. Bannen. I've got the shotgun."

"Esther, what I'm going to tell you to do might upset you," Quinn said, as gently as he could. "You told me you knew how to use the shotgun, isn't that right?"

"Yes, Mr. Bannen. I'm a country woman. We all learned how to use firearms when we were kids. My dad taught us. We hunted for a good deal of our food." Pride had crept into her voice to replace her fear. "What do you want me to do, Mr. Bannen?"

"I want you to lay down the phone again. Then I want you to step out on the porch. I want you to point the gun directly at the man on the telephone pole, and I want you to tell him to get the hell away from the ranch and not come back. If he's reluctant, I want you to fire a warning shot."

"Mr. Bannen!"

"Esther, I'm reasonably certain he's not from the telephone company," Quinn explained. Then, to make her understand, he added, "He's the man who broke into the house. Possibly the man who killed Old Sammy."

"Killed Old Sammy? But the mare—"

"Esther, trust me!"

"Yes, Mr. Bannen. I'll do it. But it don't seem right. He's such a nice, polite young man."

"Is he driving a telephone company truck?"

"Well...no, Mr. Bannen. He told me he used his own car 'cause it was cheaper than driving the truck all the way from Redding." Suspicion had crept into the old woman's voice. "All right, Mr. Bannen, I'll do as you say." There was a thud as she laid down the receiver.

Quinn pressed the phone tighter to his ear, covering his other ear to block out the traffic noise from Highway 101. He heard the screen door open and slam closed. Then he heard Esther's faraway voice: "You there on that pole! Get your ass down from there! Now! You think you can pull the wool over my eyes? You ain't going to rob this house again! You ain't no telephone man! You're a robber, maybe even a killer!"

Quinn broke into a sweat when he heard the report of the shotgun.

"The next one goes right through you, you young bastard!" Esther cried.

Despite the situation, Quinn couldn't help smiling. He'd never heard Esther Wade use so much as a "damn" or even "darn." She was from pioneer stock, as she frequently reminded him, and she was a religious woman; until now, only

Old Sammy and his drinking had been able to raise her hackles.

Moments passed in silence. Then, very faintly, Quinn heard a car engine turn over, heard tires squeal. The screen door opened and slammed again, and Esther came back on the line. "He's gone, Mr. Bannen," she said with a quiet laugh. "I don't think he'll be back."

"He might, Esther, he might," Quinn murmured. "I want you to call your son Matt. Ask him and his entire family to stay at the ranch tonight. Tell him it's an emergency and I'll owe him one. He'll understand." The phone began to make a worse sputtering sound. "And, Esther, if Jonathan McKinney calls again and he hasn't heard from me yet, tell him his warning boomeranged. Tell him it's possible my phone was bugged. Did you hear all of that, Esther?"

"Yes, Mr. Bannen." Her voice was beginning to fade.

"Call your son now before the phone goes dead," Quinn instructed her. "I'll check in with you later."

Quinn hung up, then continued his pacing, trying to piece things together before calling Jonathan McKinney. The more he considered all he had learned, the more confused he became. Sighing in frustration, he looked up Jonathan's Washington number and dialed the operator.

The phone rang a dozen times before he accepted that Jonathan wasn't home.

27

Key West, Florida

DOROTHY SLEPT LATE.

She awakened to find the air conditioner whirring softly, but the air stirred gently by the ceiling fan was still too warm for comfort. The admiral was right, she conceded. Key West was miserable during the summer months. She rose, tied her hair back from her face and showered in cold water. She dressed in white cotton slacks and a loose-fitting blouse and went to awaken the admiral.

His room was empty, and his bed had not been slept in. Concerned, she rushed to his study. That room was also empty. His desk was strewn with papers—that was not like the admiral at all—and the ashtray was overflowing with cigarette butts. The sight filled her with anger; she would scold him, remind him of the doctor's orders about smoking, but of course it would be to no avail. Her father was a man of stubborn will. Why were all the men she knew stubborn and unbending?—the admiral, Quinn—even Chad had been like that.

In the kitchen she found a note in the admiral's familiar scrawl propped against the toaster. Gone for a stroll, it read. See you for lunch.

"A stroll in this heat!" she said aloud, her anger growing. Damn him, what was he trying to do, deliberately bring on another stroke? The admiral was not a man who took strolls, so she knew the note was a lie. Damn him! She crumpled the note and dropped it in the trash can. She knew he was involved in something more serious than he had let on last night. I'm working with the military as a consultant, he had told her. Nonsense! She knew the admiral, and she knew he was involved in more than that. She was determined she would damned well discover what he had gotten himself embroiled in.

The only person she could think of to talk to was Commander Stevenson.

The commander might not tell her everything, but she had enough womanly wiles to get some information from him. But she had promised the admiral she would put everything about last night from her mind. The idea of betraying a promise made her pause for a moment's reflection. She finally decided she would speak to Commander Stevenson; she wouldn't mention last night's conversation with the admiral, but she'd still pump him for information.

On her way to the closet for a straw hat to protect her from the tropical sun, she passed the telephone, lifted the receiver and found it working. The admiral must have called the phone company early this morning. She thought again of calling Quinn, then decided against it.

The shed where the bicycles were kept was unlocked. She opened the door, and a musty odor rushed out to sting her nostrils. There were three bikes: the admiral's, hers and Chad's. The three of them had once ridden all over the island together. As she pulled her bicycle out into the sunlight, she noticed the garden tools, all nearly arranged against the wall, their blades rusted. Later she might tackle some gardening, she thought, to keep her mind occupied.

She pedaled down Catherine Street and turned onto Watson, heading for the Gulf side of the island. With the Gulf of Mexico on one side and the Atlantic Ocean on the other, Key West was the southernmost tip of the United States. The island had remained under control of the North during the Civil War. It had at one time been the richest per-capita location in the country, then the poorest. Now, with the tourist trade booming, it rivaled Fire Island and Provincetown as a popular resort, but during the opposite season.

When she reached Simonton Street, Dorothy stopped and pushed her bicycle up against a wall that lined the sidewalk, deciding there was no sense pedaling to the navy base without first checking at Commander Stevenson's house. The navy presence in Key West was very small, only a skeleton force most of the time, unless there were threats from nearby Cuba. The commander might still be at home, escaping the heat in front of his air conditioner.

Pushing open the iron gate, she stepped into the courtyard.

The rambling three-story house looked like something conceived by a Hollywood set designer of the 1930s. Great white columns in the tradition of the antebellum South rose from the ground to the peak of a sloped roof. Topmost were a cupola and a widow's walk, where sea captains' wives had supposedly paced while searching the horizon for the sight of their husbands' ships returning. Rococo carvings decorated the eaves, carved, it was said, by the sea captains between voyages, no two designs alike. All the windows of the house were fixed with shutters, the paint peeling. A transom window in the shape of an open fan had been set above the front door, the small panes beveled and cut from the finest crystal.

As she looked at the house, something Commander Stevenson had said last night suddenly came into Dorothy's mind. He'd told her his wife was in Southern California for the season, that she couldn't bear the heat and humidity and was terrified of hurricanes. It hadn't occurred to Dorothy then, but now she remembered that Alice Stevenson was a Conch, a term applied to those whose families had been residents of Key West for generations. Why would a Conch be frightened of hurricanes and not accustomed to heat and humidity? If she remembered correctly, Alice had told her the day they had gone boating together that she'd persuaded her husband to request Key West as a duty station so that she could remain on the island in her family home. Why, then, would she have run away to Southern California to escape the familiar? And if she hadn't, why had the commander lied?

Dorothy closed the iron gate behind her. As she was about to proceed up the walkway, her gaze was drawn upward by a movement. There, in a second-story window, stood Alice Stevenson, in a white nightgown. The curtain fluttered closed, but not before Dorothy acknowledged Alice's presence with a wave. She moved to the door, feeling the aged floorboards of the porch give beneath her weight, and rang the bell. Several minutes passed as she waited for someone to come to the door. When no one did, she rang the bell again, listening to its echo die away within the massive house.

The door was finally opened by a Cuban maid. "No one home," she announced before Dorothy spoke.

"But I just saw Mrs. Stevenson in an upstairs window," Dorothy protested.

"No one home," the maid repeated, and started to close the door.

Dorothy put up her hand to keep the door from being closed in her face. "I know Mrs. Stevenson's at home," she said firmly, "and I intend to see her."

The maid's dark eyes registered surprise; apparently no one else had had the audacity to challenge her lie. "No one at—"

From behind the maid, Alice Stevenson said, "It's all right. I'll see Mrs. Bannen."

"But Commander Stevenson, he said no one—"

"I said I'd see Mrs. Bannen!" she snapped at the maid.

Dorothy pushed past the maid into the entryway.

Alice was standing halfway down the staircase. She was as white as the gown she wore, her eyes dark hollows sunken into her head, giving her a skeletal appearance. Her hair had been allowed to go completely gray. She looked a good two decades older than when Dorothy had last seen her.

As the initial shock passed, Dorothy noted that Alice was extremely tense. Her jaw was firmly set, rigid, the muscles in her neck tightened so that the veins protruded. It seemed to require a great deal of effort for her to continue descending the stairs. She motioned Dorothy into a large room off the entryway.

The maid made clucking sounds of disapproval, but Alice dismissed her with a flutter of her hand. "I don't normally see visitors," she told Dorothy as she chose a wicker chair with a butterfly back and seated herself. "I haven't been well, you see." She turned to the maid, who was standing just outside the door, watching them. "Go away, Maria!

Away!" Again she made a fluttering motion of dismissal with her hands.

"I had no idea you were ill," Dorothy said. "Your husband told me you were spending the season in Southern California." She noticed the maid moving reluctantly out of sight. Although she hadn't been invited to sit, she took a chair opposite Alice Stevenson.

"Key West is very social," Alice said. She leaned forward in her chair and peered through the open door as if looking for the maid. "By pretending to be away I avoid invitations and visits by friends who feel obligated to come and see me." Apparently relieved that the maid had at last gone about her business and was no longer listening to them, she leaned wearily back in her chair. "I heard about your son, Dorothy. I'm so sorry." Again she turned her sunken eyes toward the open door.

"Shall I close it?" Dorothy inquired.

"No!" The response was almost a shriek. Then, more calmly, she added, "If it's closed, she listens. Would you like coffee? Tea? A drink? That woman might as well do something besides spy on me."

Dorothy noted Alice's dilated pupils. Her illness must require that she take strong medication. Perhaps the drugs explained her unusual behavior. "Nothing, thank you, Alice. I won't stay long. Actually, I came to see your husband."

"He's away," Alice said in a clipped voice, her Southern accent becoming more pronounced. "Some admiral's flying in at noon. Robert went to the airport to meet him. No doubt they'll go directly to the base." Her large eyes were fixed on Dorothy. "I thought it was me you came to see. I thought you were my friend!"

"Alice, of course I'm your friend," Dorothy assured her, shaken by the sudden flare of fury in the woman's voice. "I wanted to see the commander about something involving my father."

"Admiral Burke's in Key West, also?"

Dorothy told her they had arrived the night before.

"We seldom see high-ranking officers in Key West anymore, then suddenly we have two admirals at once. It makes one think the military may be going to build up rather than diminish their installations."

"My father's retired," Dorothy reminded her. "We're here strictly to...to rest." She had almost said "to escape the news media in Washington." "Who's the admiral the commander is meeting? I might know him. He might be a friend of my father's." She felt extremely uneasy about the way Alice was staring at her with her strangely probing, dilated eyes.

"It isn't a wife's place to pry into her husband's business," Alice said, the intonation and spacing of her words making her sound as if she were parroting an often-heard statement.

"Oh" was all Dorothy could think to murmur.

The women sat in awkward silence for several moments. Then Dorothy asked, "Didn't your husband tell you last night that we'd arrived?"

Alice looked at her blankly. "Last night," she echoed. "I...I can't remember." She brought a trembling hand to her brow and pressed at the furrows above her eyes. "I often...lose time...confuse time," she murmured indistinctly. "My illness, I suspect, and the drugs I take. I don't remember talking to Robert last night. I've been moved into a separate room, you see. Robert can't bear sickness and sick people. Sometimes, when I'm in a morbid frame of mind, I think he'd be happier if I succumbed to my illness, I really do."

"Alice, I'm certain the commander is very concerned about your health," Dorothy assured her. "Many men are uncomfortable around sickness, but that doesn't mean he doesn't want you to get well."

"My husband's concerned with one thing only," Alice stated flatly, "and that's his precious career." She leaned forward, her frail body dwarfed by the wicker chair. "My father warned me about marrying a military man," she said in a near whisper. "I thought it was just part of the old prejudice—the military was never very popular in Key West. The Conch thought all their daughters would be defiled if they went out with servicemen. It was considered a disgrace to marry a military man. My father died thinking I'd shamed the family name." Pulling a lace handkerchief from the pocket of her gown, Alice wiped at her eyes. "What Daddy died without knowing was that he was right about Robert Stevenson." She began to twist the handkerchief between her hands.

"Alice, perhaps we should get you back to bed and call—"

"Maybe it would have been different if I'd been a stronger woman," Alice continued, as if she were unaware that Dorothy had spoken. "I always came second to Robert's career, always. I hated all those times he went away on duty and left me alone. I'm a true Conch, you know. My ancestors were salvagers, then sponge fishermen, and God knows what else. Pirates, no doubt. But after several generations, we became Key West's elite. Why, when I was a girl here, oh, what a social life we had! All those young men, all from proper Conch families...and then I had to go and fall in love with a sailor. Daddy was so angry.... I never told him he was right about Robert Stevenson. I did admit I wasn't suited to being a military wife." She hesitated, blinking and trying to focus her eyes. "What was I saying? I forget sometimes.... I can't seem to retain...my thoughts." She looked helplessly at Dorothy.

"You were talking about the difficulties of being married to a military man," Dorothy said, wishing she knew what to say to ease the woman's distress.

"Well, I don't have to explain that to you, do I? You'd know better than anyone. Grandfather, father, husband, son—all navy men. Did I tell you I was sorry about Chad?"

"Yes, you told me. Thank you." As always, condolences affected Dorothy badly; they always seemed to drive the pain of loss deeper into her heart.

"He was such a handsome young man. So like your husband," Alice said.

"My former husband," Dorothy murmured.

As if she hadn't heard her, Alice continued, "Maybe you became more conditioned to marriage to a military man because of your background. I'm not a very intelligent woman, I never pretended to be. I was brought up in the old Southern tradition, to be a lady. I guess Robert's right...I'm shallow, really. Do you know this house was built before the Civil War? Daddy said Robert had no grasp of what it meant to be a Conch. Oh, my head's killing me. I don't know if it's my illness or the drugs. They run the tourist trams pass our house now, you know? The historical society put a plaque on the door. Are you an inquisitive person?"

"No, not really," Dorothy replied. As Alice's ramblings became more disjointed, Dorothy's concern grew.

"I didn't mean to read those papers!" Alice's voice had risen to a shout.

Startled, Dorothy slipped forward in her chair, almost got to her feet in alarm.

A wildness came into Alice's eyes then it dissipated almost immediately. With a whimper in her voice, sounding like a little girl, she said, "I wanted Robert to be proud of me. I wanted to be able to speak intelligently to all those officers he invited to our home."

"I'm sure you are a splendid hostess, Alice," Dorothy managed. "Your charm and Southern hospitality, and—"

"It was only to make Robert proud of me that I finally started paying attention to what all those officers and enlisted men were talking about at my dinner parties. Before that...well, I'd been trained that a hostess should keep everything in a lighter vein and be amusing." She shrugged her shoulders and began to pick at the fabric of her gown. "Shallow, shallow, shallow! Just a dumb Southern broad Robert kept around as a decoration and for screwing."

"Alice, I—"

"All because of my money," Alice went on. "We mustn't forget all that Conch money, all those lovely dollars accumulated by salvagers and sponge fishermen and pirates. Only I got tired of being a dumb broad. I got tired of not knowing what people were talking about when they were discussing things in front of me as if I weren't even there."

Dorothy realized suddenly that Alice had even forgotten *she* was there. It struck her with a jolt that the woman was close to madness, that she was babbling to herself. Dorothy considered getting up, making a quick farewell and escaping, but she was afraid that she might upset Alice even more.

"I started reading the papers Robert brought home in his briefcase. I only wanted to know what was going on, to understand so I could talk to our guests and sound intelligent." She shuddered, and her eyes focused on Dorothy again. "They'd lock me up for that, wouldn't they? If they learned I had all that information classified as top secret stored away in my silly head?"

"No, no one's going to lock you up," Dorothy said reassuringly. "Perhaps I should go now, Alice. You need your rest, and I've a million things to do. We've just arrived, and the house had been closed up since—"

"Please don't go!" The cry was plaintive, ending almost in a sob. "You're my friend, aren't you? I have to talk to someone who'll listen and understand. The only people I see are the maid and the doctor. She speaks hardly any English and does nothing but spy on me, and the doctor comes from the base, and he's so closemouthed." She began to weep quietly. "A woman like me wasn't meant to know the things

I read in Robert's reports. So horrible...so... Oh, God, I wish I could forget! Daddy always protected me from things that weren't suitable for a lady...but now...I just can't forget!''

"Perhaps you misunderstood whatever it was you read," Dorothy suggested. "Anyway, those couldn't have been top secret reports in the commander's briefcase. He couldn't take top secret documents from the base."

"But they were!" Alice insisted vehemently. "The papers were stamped Top Secret, and there was some kind of symbol on them!"

Dorothy was at a loss as to what approach to take with the obviously confused woman. Finally she said, "If the commander brought such papers home he'd have been breaking security regulations. I doubt he'd do such a—"

Suddenly Alice cowered back in her chair, her eyes with their large pupils, widening even more. "You won't tell anyone, will you? He'll kill me! Promise me you won't tell on Robert, or me."

"I promise," Dorothy assured her.

In the few seconds of silence that followed, Dorothy could hear a jangling sound coming from the telephone at her elbow, as if someone on an extension in another part of the house were dialing a number. Perhaps the maid was calling the doctor or Commander Stevenson, she thought, to report Alice's upset state. She knew the maid must have heard some of Alice's louder cries, even down the long hallway; if she hadn't understood the words, she would have recognized from the tone that her employer's state had been worsened by her visitor.

"I never took an interest in politics," Alice whispered, her head bowed, as she continued to pick absently at the fabric of her gown. " 'So boring, not for a lady to trouble herself with,' Daddy always said. I liked President Kennedy, but he was the only one. He was so handsome and looked like such a gentleman. Did you like President Kennedy?"

"Well, yes, I thought he—"

Alice's head shot up. Her pupils were now fully dilated, and her expression was that of a woman bordering on dementia. "It's a conspiracy, you know! They're going to kill him! They'll get away with it, too, you'll see!"

Dorothy decided her best course was to continue to placate the disturbed woman, to keep her talking, until the doctor or Commander Stevenson arrived to take charge. Quietly she asked, "Kill who, Alice?"

"The president, of course! Only by killing him will they achieve their purpose!"

Oh, President Kennedy, Dorothy thought. Alice was lost in a world with no concept of time; her mind failed to distinguish between past, present and an imagined future. "In Dallas, you mean?" she prompted.

"No, no! In New York!" Alice cried in obvious exasperation. "Oh, I should have listened to Daddy! 'He'll be the death of you, Alice,' he told me. The only time I ever saw Daddy angry at me was when I told him I was going to marry Robert. Daddy was such a gentleman, a truly gentle man. Robert wants them to stop running the trams past the house. He says the loudspeakers are an intrusion on our privacy. I don't know.... It kind of fills in the loneliness."

Alice continued to ramble on, moving apparently at random from one topic to another. As her moods changed from sorrow to amusement to fear, she wept, giggled and moaned. Sometimes she seemed unaware of Dorothy's presence; then she would reach out and grip Dorothy's arm with her icy fingers.

Dorothy saw movement out of the corner of her eye and looked toward the door. The maid was standing in the entryway, her face creased with worry. Dorothy glanced back at Alice, who was staring through the sheer curtains into the yard and continuing her incoherent prattle. Quietly Dorothy rose and tiptoed from the room, closing the door behind her.

"How long has she been like this?" she asked the maid.

The woman stared at her, struggling, it seemed, to comprehend the English words. Then she mumbled, "Not well. Mrs. Stevenson not well. Husband say let no one see her."

"Yes, well, I think the commander has some explaining to do," Dorothy said. "His wife obviously needs trained medical professionals."

The servant continued to stare, as if she failed to comprehend. Yet Dorothy felt the woman understood more than she let on.

"Have you called her doctor?" Dorothy demanded.

"Doctor, *sí*!"

"A military doctor?"

"*Sí*, doctor in uniform. He give shot." She made a gesture, stabbing her finger against her arm. "She sleep then. Doctor come. You go."

"Yes, I'm going," Dorothy said peevishly. She stopped, her hand gripping the doorknob. "Please ask Commander Stevenson to call me. Do you understand? I'm Dorothy Bannen, Admiral Burke's daughter."

The woman nodded.

From inside the closed room, Alice Stevenson suddenly shouted. "They're going to kill him, the president! Oh, God, Daddy, don't let them do it!"

The maid took a step toward Dorothy. "Doctor come soon. You go, *por favor*."

Dorothy stepped onto the porch. When the door closed behind her, she heard the lock click into place. She remained on the porch for several minutes, listening to Alice Stevenson's periodic outbursts, then her weeping. Finally, there was silence.

Feeling guilty about having left the sick woman before her doctor arrived, Dorothy walked down the path and let herself out through the iron gate.

"Damn it!" she cried.

Her bicycle had been stolen.

28

Key West, Florida

"IF I REMEMBER the woman accurately, she never had a firm grip on reality," Admiral Burke told his daughter. "Tall, rather thin, with deep-set eyes and nervous gestures and a very pale complexion. A Southern-belle type, isn't she?"

Dorothy had arrived home, drenched with perspiration from her long walk, to find her father had returned. She'd dropped into the chair facing his desk to tell him about her visit to Alice Stevenson. "You always said you liked Alice," she reminded him. "Now you act as if you scarcely remember her. I don't understand you, I really don't. I think you're taking news of the commander's wife's illness very casually, not to mention the commander's conduct. Lying about his wife being in California while he keeps her drugged and locked away in that crumbling old mansion."

"I believe there's a higher rate of madness among Southern women," the admiral commented without looking up from his desk. "It may be the earlier inbreeding. Or this damnable weather."

"Oh! You're exasperating!" Dorothy told him irritably. "Since Commander Stevenson is a member of your precious military cabal, I should think you'd take the responsibility for seeing he obtained professional help for his wife."

"His handling of his wife's illness is the commander's own personal responsibility," Admiral Burke answered. "I can't involve myself in his personal life. And neither should you." He was staring at her over the top of a manila folder. "Now, if you wouldn't mind, I have a lot of work to do."

"In your position as consultant?" Dorothy asked irritably.

"Precisely."

"Where did you go this morning?"

"What?"

"Where did you stroll to? I believe that's how you put it. 'Gone for a stroll.' You were never the strolling type, Admiral."

Ignoring the sarcasm in her voice, Admiral Burke replied, "I walked as far as the beach. There's a new restaurant on the Atlantic side. Outdoor tables with brightly colored umbrellas. I had coffee and watched the sun worshipers, then I came home."

"You've always hated the beach," she said. "You'd only go to please Chad, and then only grudgingly."

"Old age is changing me," the admiral explained. "Watching the waves roll in and out is calming. They seem so permanent in comparison to human beings and their concerns."

"Do you really think you can make me believe old age is changing you?" Dorothy said. "For that matter, do you think I believe you strolled to the beach without some other, hidden, purpose?"

"Since when am I expected to give an accounting of my movements to my daughter?"

"Since you started disobeying doctors' orders," Dorothy answered. "If you don't stop smoking, stop driving yourself and stop strolling in this heat and humidity, your status is going to be more temporary than you anticipate."

"Your warning is duly noted," the admiral said dryly.

Dorothy rose. "What would you like for lunch?"

"Anything, whatever's here," he answered without interest.

"Since I have to go shopping anyway, I thought I'd ask," she told him. "If Alice Stevenson wasn't totally out of touch with reality, we may be having a guest this evening, so I'd best replenish our supply of liquor."

The admiral looked up. "What do you mean, a guest?"

"Alice said the commander had gone to the airport to meet an admiral. She couldn't remember his name, but you'll undoubtedly know each other, and he may well drop by to pay his respects."

"An admiral? Here?" For the first time since she had returned home, interest sparked behind his eyes. "You're sure she didn't mention his name?"

"As I told you, she'd lost all sense of time. She was babbling about the visiting admiral, about being a Conch, about her mistake in marrying a navy man, even about the assassination of President Kennedy. Only she thought it was in New York instead of Dallas. The poor woman! Why don't you call Commander Stevenson and ask him the admiral's name? And be a dear... while you're talking to him, mention that his wife needs professional care, the kind of care she can't get from a navy doctor."

"Yes, yes, I'll do that," Admiral Burke assured her.

When the door closed behind his daughter, Admiral Burke tossed the papers he had been holding to one side. He hadn't strolled to the beach as he had told Dorothy. He had, in fact, walked to the navy base, to repeat again his demand that Commander Stevenson arrange a meeting of Delta's committee. The commander had mentioned nothing to him about a visiting admiral.

He reasoned that the commander's reluctance to tell him of the visit could mean only one thing: the admiral arriving in Key West was his old friend and new enemy, Admiral Addison.

Commander Stevenson had betrayed him.

ADMIRAL ADDISON SETTLED in the back seat of the limousine and waited for his luggage to be stored in the trunk. Glancing over his shoulder, he noted the young operative with the bandaged nose climbing into a taxi.

More automaton than human, he thought. The young man was certainly well-conditioned and trained. If he ever had reason to compliment Chief Loomis, it would be for operatives like Everett.

Commander Stevenson climbed into the car beside the admiral and signaled the driver, then cranked up the dividing glass. "As you requested, I've arranged a private bungalow under the name of Jack LaSalle, sir." The commander had never seen the admiral out of uniform; the gray suit he wore emphasized his pallor, his ashen face. The lines around the admiral's eyes and mouth seemed to be etched deeper than when he had last seen him.

The road the limousine followed bordered the Atlantic Ocean. Admiral Addison stared thoughtfully at the waves and shafts of sunlight piercing the cloud cover and feeding a brightness onto the water. His hands lay quietly in his lap. He nodded his head to acknowledge his gratitude for the secured bungalow; he knew bungalows were not easy to rent in Key West, even during the off-season. He had not looked forward to this trip, had only decided it was necessary after Commander Stevenson had called him late last night.

Stevenson stretched out his long legs and adjusted his uniform trousers. He wanted to smoke but decided against requesting permission unless the admiral himself took out a cigarette.

"It's damned hot here," the admiral said. "I'll need some sports clothes if I'm to pass for a tourist. You shouldn't have worn your uniform, Commander."

"It's all right, sir. I've listed you as a civilian, a businessman selling supplies to the island navy station. In fact, your bungalow is navy property. It's on the Gulf side, near the street, with a private entrance. You won't need to see service personnel, but if you want to avail yourself of any station facilities, you have civilian clearance." From his pocket he took a temporary pass and privilege card made out in the name of Jack LaSalle and handed it to the admiral.

The admiral stuffed it into his coat pocket without comment. Then he asked, "What about accommodations for our operative?"

"A garage apartment two blocks from Admiral Burke's," the commander told him. "I didn't know how long we'd require it, so I rented it for a month."

"That'll be more than adequate," the admiral said.

"Admiral Burke came to see me again this morning, sir. He insisted that as the controller's aide I make contact immediately and arrange a committee meeting. He even suggested that the controller himself be asked to attend."

The admiral remained silent for a long moment, then turned his gray eyes to the commander. "I've decided you should suggest a committee meeting to the controller," he said. "As per Burke's requests."

"But Admiral Burke plans to denounce you! To accuse you of being a threat to the organization!" the commander blurted in disbelief.

"I said you were to suggest the meeting at the admiral's request," Admiral Addison said. "I didn't say Admiral Burke would attend."

"If the admiral did attend such a committee meeting, sir, he'd be a formidable opponent. He is, after all, the one who revitalized Delta. The seed of the entire plan for D day is his."

"But in this case the plan has outgrown its designer." Something resembling a smile played over the admiral's colorless lips. "Of course, I'll try to reason with my old friend first—that's why I'm here—but knowing Malcolm Burke as I do, I believe he's gone beyond reason. He can't be allowed to create dissension in the organization at this crucial time." Glancing over his shoulder again at the taxi behind the limousine, he said, "And he won't."

29

Mountain View, California

YEOMAN MAYFIELD had arranged to meet Quinn at a sleazy bar on El Camino Real.

The building was constructed to resemble a country barn, the outside made of naked planks with knotholes and high double barn doors with a normal-size door cut in one side. Its neon sign flashed Country Dan's; a billboard promised Western Dancing Friday and Saturday Nights to the Music of Big Bill Barton and His Country Boys. To one side of the entrance was posted an Off Limits notice. Must be one hell of a place, Quinn thought. He hoped it wasn't representative of the yeoman he was to meet there.

Quinn opened the door and stepped inside.

A bluegrass number blared on the jukebox. Sawdust was scattered on a concrete floor. A half-dozen electrical signs advertising beer illuminated the bar, and a hula-girl lamp with a dim bulb illuminated the cash register. The stage where Big Bill Barton and His Country Boys performed was in a corner and was dark. The candles on the tables had not yet been lit; coming in from the sunlight as he had, Quinn thought the bar was like a dark pit.

He stepped to one side of the door until his eyes adjusted to the dimness. The air was heavy and repugnant; the smells of cleaning solutions, stale cigarette smoke and alcohol blending with the unmistakable odor from the toilets. Quinn made out two silhouettes sitting on bar stools. As his vision cleared, he saw that both were men. Neither had glanced up as he'd entered. They sat slumped over beer bottles, cigarettes burning in an overflowing ashtray in front of them. The bartender was middle-aged, with a beer belly and dark, unkempt hair protruding from under a cowboy hat with a plume. He wore a Western shirt with the snaps unfastened to reveal a hairy chest.

Quinn stepped to the bar and ordered. "A beer, no glass." He wasn't about to drink from one of the spotted glasses arranged along the bar.

The bartender served him without speaking, then moved back to the far end of the bar, where he was peeling and cutting lemons.

Quinn glanced at the two customers. Both were middle-aged and as scruffy as the bartender; one wore a striped flannel shirt, the other a brightly patterned pullover. Neither had shaved in a couple of days. Convinced they weren't military, he dismissed them from his mind.

A handlettered sign behind the bar read Happy Hour 5–6 Weekdays, Drinks Half Price! It was just turning six o'clock. Mayfield had arranged to meet Quinn at 6:15. Precise, he thought. A man who would say 6:15 would arrive at exactly 6:15, not a moment before or after.

The jukebox stopped playing, and the bar became silent except for the whir of the cooling unit and the click of the bartender's knife on the Formica counter as he cut through the lemon peels. Quinn let his gaze sweep the interior. Country Dan's was definitely a dump, but the military didn't place Off Limits signs on bars simply because they failed health inspections; he wondered if the place was a hangout for prostitutes, homosexuals or drug traffickers. A back room was curtained off with dirty beige drapery, a sign above the door reading Private.

The man in the striped flannel shirt belched, laughed for no apparent reason and took a greedy gulp of his beer. "Got any red tokens, Hank? I ain't payin' for music if you've got tokens!"

The bartender abandoned his lemons long enough to dig into a glass beside the cash register and pass two red-flagged disks to the customer. The man walked unsteadily to the jukebox; moments later, the same bluegrass tune blared again. One of the speakers was above Quinn's head. He took his beer, slipped off his stool and moved to a table in a dark corner.

At exactly 6:15, the door opened and a young man stepped into the bar. As Quinn had done, he stood just inside the door, waiting for his eyes to become accustomed to the dim lighting. Quinn studied him. He was in his mid-twenties, of medium height, with dark hair. His clothes were immaculate and looked new—designer jeans and a wool sweater, the sleeves pushed up around strong forearms, regulation navy shoes. His hair, too, was regulation. Among current hairstyles, a regulation cut made a man stand out like a sore thumb. Quinn saw the young man's eyes scan the bar.

Quinn shifted his position, deliberately scraping the legs of his chair across the floor. The man turned his head in Quinn's direction, hesitated, then walked across the room to Quinn's corner.

"Commander Bannen, I'm Petty Officer Mayfield, sir." He was standing almost at attention.

"For Christ's sake, sit down, Mayfield," Quinn told him. "And let's forget the military bullshit. My name's Quinn, not commander or sir. And you?"

"Alex, sir—I mean Quinn." He pulled out a chair and sat down facing Quinn.

"Would you like a drink, Alex?"

"No, sir. I don't drink."

"Well, I'll order you something. We don't want to appear suspicious. What'll it be? A Coke?"

"Orange juice, please."

Quinn went to the bar and returned with an orange juice and another beer. When he sat down he noticed Alex glancing nervously toward the door. He wondered if the young man's eyes were always so intense. Or was his expression attributable to his nervousness? "Were you a friend of my son's, Alex?"

"No, sir. I never knew your son."

"Quinn, please, not sir. You said I was endangering everyone I spoke to at Moffett Field. Your note said, 'They know you're here.' Who are 'they'?"

"I don't know who all of them are, sir—Quinn. Not yet."

"But you know some of them?"

"I have five names. There were thirteen present at the meeting where I first stumbled onto the mystery. I guess that's a proper way to describe it, a mystery. I'm a puzzle addict," Alex explained, "and I'm addicted to mystery novels." He started to lift his orange juice to his lips, noticed the spotted glass and set it aside.

"I wouldn't drink out of that glass, either," Quinn told him with a smile. "Why did you choose this place to meet?"

"Because it's listed off-limits. I thought if either of us were followed we'd easily spot military personnel."

"And they'd easily spot you," Quinn suggested. "Tell me what you know, Alex. Perhaps together we can fill in some of the missing pieces and solve this mystery."

Alex gave Quinn a detailed account of how the meeting of officers and enlisted personnel at Moffett Field had sparked his curiosity. He then related how he had entered Chadwick Bannen's name into the computer and run into a blocking symbol. "The symbol used was a bisected triangle," he said. "Does that mean anything to you?"

"Nothing specific," Quinn said. "The triangle itself represents the increment of a variable. A deltaic. That brings us to *delta*, the fourth letter of the Greek alphabet. Also a communications code word for the letter *D*. As for the bisecting line, that would be a specific code symbol given an organization or project."

"I believe I'm being recruited for the organization," Alex went on. He told Quinn of his meeting with Chief Loomis.

"Loomis—that's one of the names mentioned in my son's letter," Quinn said. "I have him on my list of persons to contact."

Alex repeated the conversation he had overheard between Chief Loomis and the other men meeting in the chief's office.

"So this Captain Musolf compares me to a groundhog dog, does he?" Quinn smiled humorlessly. "The man may be right. One thing is certain: they're correct in thinking nothing short of killing me will stop my investigation. You say they expect an admiral to give the okay to eliminate me?"

Alex nodded.

"You didn't hear the admiral's name mentioned?"

"No, sir, but I assumed it was the admiral present at the first meeting. He's one of my five names. Admiral Addison."

"Addison! Are you sure? Christ, I know that bastard! He's a friend of Admiral Burke's, my ex-father-in-law." More to himself than to Alex, he added, "I was sure Addison was involved with the illegal drug experiments, but I could never prove it. He was clever—"

Both Quinn and Alex's heads turned sharply as the door of the bar was thrown open.

Even before Quinn could focus on the newcomer, Alex said, "It's the lieutenant who was at the meeting. Lieutenant Gentry. He must have followed me!"

"Or me," Quinn murmured. "He hasn't seen you yet. Quickly, Alex! Leave through the back! That curtained doorway! There must be a back door! Go!"

Instantly Alex was on his feet.

"Contact me at the motel," Quinn instructed him. "We'll meet again later tonight."

Without acknowledging Quinn's parting words, Alex hurried across the bar before the lieutenant's vision could adjust to the darkened interior. He vanished through the curtained doorway marked Private seconds before the lieutenant trusted his eyesight enough to advance to the bar and order a Scotch and soda.

Quinn remained at the table in the dark corner. The lieutenant stood with one foot on the bar rail, his back to Quinn. Without being observed Quinn rose, walked quietly to the telephone and dialed Moffett Field's shore patrol. "I'd like to report an infraction in an off-limits establishment by military personnel attached to your command," he said. He gave the name and address of Country Dan's, refused to identify himself when asked and hung up.

He returned to his table, still unseen by the lieutenant, and sat sipping his beer.

The lieutenant turned to face the room, leaning his elbows on the bar behind him. At that moment the doors opened again and two women entered; both were dressed in low-cut blouses and tight-fitting jeans. The lieutenant, his eyes accustomed now to the lighting, not only took in the details of the two women, but spotted Quinn at the same time. Recognition sparked behind Gentry's eyes, and his gaze dismissed the women entirely.

It was now apparent that his assignment was Quinn, not Alex Mayfield. The lieutenant pulled his elbows from the bar and straightened. He seemed suddenly undecided whether to remain at the bar or take a table nearer Quinn. In the end he remained where he was; his assignment was apparently to tail, not to engage.

The lieutenant was still standing at the bar when the door opened to admit the shore patrol.

As the two uniformed military policemen approached Gentry, Quinn rose and slipped out through the curtained door as Alex had done minutes before and returned to his motel room to wait for Alex's telephone call.

As he paced the floor, it crossed his mind that Alex Mayfield might have been telling him half-truths. Perhaps Alex, instead of being recruited for the secret organization, was already a member. Contacting Quinn and telling him a fabricated story could have been a perfect way for the group to learn what Quinn had already uncovered. While his instincts told him to trust the yeoman, the events of the past few days had made him suspicious, even, as Admiral Burke had said, paranoid. His thoughts turned to his ex-father-in-law and then to Admiral Addison. If Addison was involved in a secret organization, it stood to reason that Admiral Burke was also connected with it, or at least aware of its existence.

Sitting at the desk, Quinn took paper and pen from the drawer and drew a triangle, the blocking symbol the yeoman had told him about. The triangle itself was a common enough symbol, but the bisecting line was the key. His thoughts drifted back to when he had been on active duty; there had been many such symbols—squares, rectangles, octagons—but none he could recall with a bisecting line.

Rising from the desk, he resumed his pacing.

Nine o'clock, then ten, and Mayfield did not call.

Quinn telephoned the desk, asked them to cut into his line if any calls came for him and then dialed the ranch. Esther Wade answered on the first ring. There was no static on the line.

"No, Mr. McKinney hasn't called again, Mr. Bannen," the housekeeper informed him. "There was only one call. That was from a Mrs. Anna Stanyon in San Diego." She carefully repeated the telephone number. "Matt and his family are here with me. I called the telephone company, and you were right, Mr. Bannen. They hadn't sent out a repairman. I gave the young man's description to the sheriff."

After they had chatted for a few more minutes, Quinn told her he would call again tomorrow and said goodbye. It was after 1:00 a.m. in Washington, but he dialed Jonathan's number anyway. The phone rang several times, and he was about to break the connection when it was finally answered.

"Quinn, thank God! Did you receive my message before you barged into Moffett Field?"

Quinn told him he had received part of his message, then explained that the ranch telephone was undoubtedly tapped, that he hadn't dared let his housekeeper repeat the word Jonathan apparently thought so important.

"The word is *Delta*," Jonathan said. There was a moment's hesitation, and then he added, "Doesn't that mean anything to you?"

Quinn said it didn't, except that he had heard it used earlier that evening.

"From whom?" Jonathan asked.

"A yeoman from Moffett," Quinn said. "Suppose you explain."

"Where were you in the 1960s?"

"Australia and Vietnam," Quinn said shortly. "Why?"

"Because that's when Delta made headlines here," the reporter told him. "In the early sixties the media had already begun to zero in on the CIA. Reporters were ferreting out details of their covert activities, some of them questionable, legally and morally. There were great cries of outrage from the American public. Foreign powers used the exposure of the agency to place blame for their own political upheavals. It was all part of the cold-war game." Jonathan was speaking quickly; his words were clipped and he sounded breathless. "Hold on while I get comfortable," he said. "I was just coming in as the phone rang."

Quinn waited patiently, listening to Jonathan as he apparently switched on lamps, the air conditioner. Then he heard a woman's voice. "Mix yourself a drink," Jonathan told her. "No, nothing for me. Quinn? I'm back. I'm not alone. Ginny's here. She's the beauty I told you about from Central Records. An exceptional woman. The type I'd ask to marry me if I was the marrying kind." All this, Quinn realized, was being said for the woman's benefit.

"Is her presence going to limit what you can tell me?" Quinn asked.

"No, Ginny's the one who told me about the symbol of the bisected triangle," Jonathan answered.

Quinn's pulse rate quickened as adrenaline surged through him. He stared down at the crude drawing he had made of a bisected triangle. "Did she get it from a computer?" he asked.

"That's right! How did you know?"

"It doesn't matter." This meant that Quinn could trust Alex Mayfield; the yeoman had been telling him the truth. "Then the symbol is a designation of an organization called Delta?"

"That's what I've been telling you," Jonathan rushed on. "Because the CIA could no longer operate with as low a profile as required, another organization was created and shrouded with secrecy. Although the military wasn't directly involved with the new organization, all members were recruited from the different branches of the armed services, leaders, as well as subordinates. The operatives were mostly taken from brigs and guardhouses, the worst assortment of criminals and misfits imaginable. They were trained in private camps. Most of them already had a natural bent toward killing, but they were trained to perfect it. There was also a sizable group of civilians recruited, both men and women, handpicked and carefully trained, physically and psychologically. Those that were eventually exposed had some common denominators; they were either orphaned or estranged from their families, and they had to be subversives. Aside from killing techniques, they were taught languages, code communications, skill with firearms and explosives, even theatrical makeup for disguises. It was said that some even had their fingerprints removed à la Chicago mobsters. They were sent out on assignments and told to expect no support from the organization if they failed. After all, the organization didn't exist. If caught they could either rot in prisons, be executed or commit suicide, preferably the latter. Are you still with me?"

"I'm still with you," Quinn said tightly.

"But Delta soon overstepped itself," Jonathan continued. "Each leader had independent charge of a group of operatives. Assignments were to be agreed upon by a committee and coordinated by the highest-ranking member, who was called the controller. There was a power struggle between the individual leaders, and the controller lost control of operations. The individual groups of operatives were running amok for the good of God and country as determined by a single man, their group leader. The CIA was suspected of intervention in the politics of several foreign powers, while in fact it was Delta that was responsible.

"Then one of our own politicians was murdered, supposedly during a robbery of his home, but in the ensuing investigation the name Delta surfaced. Delta apparently attempted its own cover-up, each independent leader and his operatives turning against the other. Before the organization could be exposed and proved an embarrassment, Delta was disbanded and all records destroyed. The name Delta and the symbol of the bisected triangle became a myth. Reporters who were trying to prove the existence of the organization and expose its activities were persuaded to destroy any information they had gathered. A few continued chasing the myth, but nothing ever came of it. Only the name, the symbol and a few unprovable whispers remained of the Delta organization."

Jonathan broke off, breathless. Quinn remembered that same excitement in the reporter's voice when they had worked together during the exposure of the drug experiments.

"Seeing that symbol," Jonathan said, "was like showing an artifact from some lost civilization to an archaeologist."

"So you think Delta was never dissolved?" Quinn said.

"If it was dissolved, then, as incredible as it seems, it's been reestablished," Jonathan said. "Everett, the man whose name you gave me—Ginny ran it through the computers. There was a Delta block. No access without proper code. But here's the kicker, Quinn. Chad's data was also blocked by a Delta symbol."

Quinn said nothing. A shiver had run along his spine and settled in his chest and groin.

"Quinn? You still there?"

"I'm still here, Jonathan. I have some other names for your girlfriend. Can she run them through the computer as quickly as possible?"

"First thing in the morning," Jonathan said without hesitation. "I've got a pen, so give me the names."

"Admiral Addison, Chief—"

"Admiral Addison?" Jonathan echoed. "Are you sure?"

"Admiral Addison," Quinn repeated. "Chief Loomis and a Captain Musolf. The last two are stationed at Moffett. There's a lieutenant, but I can't remember his name. Also a yeoman second class named Alex Mayfield." No reason not to be cautious, Quinn told himself.

"Okay, I have the names," Jonathan confirmed. "Listen, Quinn. If Delta's what it was rumored to be, you're in extreme danger, my friend."

"If I'm to believe Petty Officer Mayfield, I'm endangering everyone I speak to," Quinn murmured. "Apparently my elimination is only waiting an order from an admiral, possibly Admiral Addison."

"Christ!"

"And since my telephone was probably bugged and you mentioned the name Delta to my housekeeper, your well-intended warning may have boomeranged, Jonathan. You're not treading safe water yourself."

"A good reporter never does," Jonathan said. "But I'll manage to avoid the jaws of Delta. If the organization is in existence again, I'm determined to discover who reformed it and why."

"And if Chad was an operative, I must know why," Quinn said quietly. He shook the disturbing thought from his mind. "I'll call you daily, Jonathan."

"Wait, Quinn! There's something I'd like to clear with you. I think Chad's mother knows more than she's admitting. Her father, too. I'm considering taking a jaunt to Key West and trying for an interview again, but of course I won't do it without your approval."

A memory of the last time he'd seen Dorothy flashed through Quinn's thoughts—in Admiral Burke's study, with her back to him in silent rejection. Then there was Admiral Addison, her father's longtime crony. "You have my approval," Quinn said flatly.

When he hung up after talking to Jonathan, Quinn called the motel office to verify that Mayfield hadn't called while the line had been engaged. The clerk assured him that there had been no calls for his room. He then dialed the San Diego number Esther Wade had given him.

The woman who answered was obviously elderly, her voice weak and quavering. "Yes, Mr. Bannen, I did call you. Are you related to Mrs. Emily Everett?"

Quinn concealed his surprise. "We're not related," he said, "but I'm a friend. Why, Mrs. Stanyon?"

"I'm a neighbor across the courtyard," the woman explained. "I'm the one who called the police when I heard Mrs. Everett's screams."

"Screams?"

"Mrs. Everett threw herself out her fourth-floor window," the old woman told him. "She'd have succeeded in killing herself if two palm trees and some cardboard boxes hadn't broken her fall."

Quinn visualized the cluttered courtyard behind Emily Everett's apartment building; he also visualized the young women as he had last seen her, in her silk kimono.

"She's still in a bad way," Mrs. Stanyon continued. "Only conscious for short periods at a time. I'm the only one who visits her. I don't know why, but I feel sorry for the young woman. I never understood why someone would take their own life. Life is so precious, a gift from God. I guess Mrs. Everett doesn't have any family. She kept repeating your name, Mr. Bannen, so I asked the landlord to let me into her apartment, and I found your telephone number."

"What hospital is she in, Mrs. Stanyon?"

"The one near Balboa Park. It's the closest, and—"

"I'll be there in the morning," Quinn told her.

30

Key West, Florida

ADMIRAL BURKE looked up from his desk when he heard his name spoken softly.

Admiral Addison stood in the study doorway.

His face registering no surprise, Admiral Burke said, "It's customary in polite circles to knock, Admiral. I've been expecting you."

A flicker of dismay crossed Admiral Addison's face. "No one knew I was coming to Key West," he said.

"We all have our spies," Admiral Burke told him. "I believe Commander Stevenson picked you up at the airport around noon. It only surprises me that you waited so long before visiting me. You never were a patient man. Sorry, I hope you didn't consider that one of your virtues."

"At my age, virtues no longer come easily, Malcolm." Admiral Addison stepped into the room and closed the door behind him. He had noted that Admiral Burke flinched at the use of his Christian name. "I thought you'd forgive me for letting myself in, Malcolm, us being old comrades. I came in through the patio doors. I saw your light on, and I didn't want to disturb your daughter. Dorothy is here, isn't she?"

"You know damned well she's here," Admiral Burke said peevishly. "Do you think I didn't notice the man you've had watching my house all afternoon?"

"I should have known you wouldn't be outsmarted," Admiral Addison said with a humorless laugh. "These young operatives think they're so infallible. If this were the old days, they'd be picked off in an instant. However, the man was assigned to you for your protection, Malcolm, not to spy on you. Key West isn't the tropical paradise it once was. There are drug addicts, dealers, all sorts of desperate characters here now. You've been through a lot. Your stroke, the loss of your grandson, those damned reporters in Washington. The man outside is a bodyguard. He'll see that you're not unduly bothered."

"Your sudden concern for my welfare is touching, Admiral. Since you're here, do sit down." He watched his unwelcome guest closely as he moved to the leather wing chair and sat down. He had a sudden impulse to tell Addison how ridiculous he looked in his white linen slacks and brightly colored sport shirt. Instead he said, "I'll tell you straight off, Admiral, I'm not going to continue pretending we're still friends, old comrades and all that bullshit! If we're to have a discussion, it's going to be hard facts and truths."

"You offend me, Malcolm, by suggesting I'd be anything but truthful with you," Admiral Addison said, affecting an injured tone.

"I assume Commander Stevenson informed you that I requested a meeting of the committee?"

"Of course. That's why I'm here."

"He also told you why I requested this meeting?"

"I believe the commander said you intend to question my character and accuse me of misusing my power. That's a damning accusation, Malcolm. You know what my fate would be if the committee believed your accusations?"

Admiral Burke's eyes held his visitor's unfalteringly as he said, "The same as Chad's."

"Oh, I see," Addison said thoughtfully. "You're also going to tell the committee I personally ordered your grandson's execution? I don't believe you've thought this through, Malcolm. The committee's going to consider you a grandfather gone mad with grief and guilt. Why else would you endanger the organization by accusing your old comrade of having your only heir killed unjustly? You will say *unjustly*, won't you, Malcolm?" Admiral Addison rested his elbows on the arms of the chair and made a pyramid of his wrinkled fingers. "You can't substantiate the charges. Again, I can prove without a shadow of a doubt that Chad was planning to expose Delta. No, old friend, it's an error in judgment to think the committee would be swayed in your favor."

"There's more than just Chad," Admiral Burke said. "Not that you'd ever allow a committee meeting."

"That's why I've come all this way, Malcolm. To assure you I'll tell Commander Stevenson to proceed with your request if I can't persuade you otherwise. It is your inalienable right to request a committee meeting. I've made it my mission to convince you to hold off. The committee meets again soon, anyway. The night before D day. It could be dangerous to call them together beforehand. The members are a bit nervous. Your ex-son-in-law is running around making waves. Although his meddling is only an undercurrent now, he could be problematic." Collapsing the pyramid of his hands, Admiral Addison eased himself to the edge of his chair. "Regardless of your hatred of me, Malcolm, I know you wouldn't want the organization to fail. After all, it's rebirth was your doing."

"Don't remind me," Admiral Burke said angrily. "It cost me my grandson! Because of you, damn you!"

"I suggest you keep your voice down, Malcolm. We wouldn't want to wake Dorothy. There's no need for her to learn something that would make the organization consider her expendable."

Admiral Burke paled.

"Your daughter knows nothing, does she, Malcolm?"

"Of course she knows nothing! I lost my grandson! Do you think I'd risk losing my daughter?"

"It's unfortunate her ex-husband doesn't feel as protective of her," Admiral Addison murmured. "They met in Washington, had dinner at Le Coq d'Or, then spent most of the night together in Bannen's hotel room. According to the man we had stationed in the room next door, they did much more than chat about old times."

"Damn you, Addison! You had no right to spy on my daughter! Dorothy's no threat to Delta! She's accepted that Chad's death was due to an overdose. It was difficult for her, especially since she had a private autopsy performed without my knowledge and found out about the missing organs, but she has accepted it. Incidentally, it was damn stupid on the part of your operatives, blaming drugs, when the boy had never taken drugs in his life."

"The circumstances were unusual. There was no time for planning and not much could be arranged because of the way he was found." Admiral Addison rose suddenly, and as he did he noticed that Admiral Burke reached instinctively toward a mound of papers at his elbow. "Of course, you read the operatives' reports," he said hesitantly. "You know the details."

"Yes, I know the details," Admiral Burke said painfully. He knew his sudden movement toward the pile of papers had been noted. "As I said, Admiral, I was expecting you." He lifted the papers to expose the revolver hidden beneath. A wave of pleasure passed over him when he saw perspiration bead on Addison's ashen face. "We're both old men," he said. "We tend to be careless. I heard your footsteps in the passageway. I could have killed you the moment you stepped through the door." He picked up the revolver and pointed it threateningly at Addison's head. "Even now, Admiral, I could shoot you between the eyes and have only one regret. You'd die too quickly. You wouldn't suffer as Chad must have suffered. My revenge would be hollow."

"Revenge, indeed, Malcolm," Admiral Addison said with mock amusement. "I've told you repeatedly I did not order Chad's execution. The operatives who knew your grandson acted independently—and, I might add, correctly—"

"You recruited him!" Admiral Burke snapped. "To use against me! Even after my stroke, when my power was transferred to you, you feared I'd recover enough to reclaim a portion of it. I knew then you wanted absolute control. You thought if you had Chad under your control I wouldn't dare try to reclaim power. Only the boy proved more of a man than you bargained for, Addison. I could have told you he wouldn't accept the concept of Delta. You recruited him to use against me, and he proved an even greater threat than I could ever be. I'm not the senile, gullible old bastard you take me to be. I wasn't blinded by our friendship. I knew what you were doing, and I was trying to get Chad out. Then, when you told him I was the reorganizer of Delta, you destroyed my control over the boy." The revolver waved in the admiral's hand as his emotions grew stronger. "You're the one who put Delta in jeopardy, Addison! You!"

His gray eyes never leaving the barrel of the revolver, Admiral Addison said, "And this is what you intend to present to the committee, Malcolm?"

"It is. You said Quinn Bannen was creating an undercurrent that made the committee nervous. Well, you're the one responsible. How do you think the committee is going to react when they learn the truth?"

Admiral Addison raised his bushy eyebrows, but he said nothing.

"You're repeating the same mistake made by the original leaders of Delta," Admiral Burke said. "Independent action without clearance from the controller. It was the power struggles within the organization that destroyed it before. With men like you in positions of leadership, the same thing will happen."

"You've seriously misjudged me, Malcolm," Admiral Addison said evenly. "I guess there's no alternative except to inform Commander Stevenson to go ahead with your request for a committee meeting. We'll both present our cases. For now, may I request you put your revolver away? As you said, we're both old men. We tend to be careless. A trembling finger on the trigger..."

Admiral Burke shrugged his stooped shoulders and lowered the revolver. "I already told you a bullet was too quick for you." He placed the revolver at his elbow.

Admiral Addison removed a handkerchief from a pocket of his white linen trousers and mopped his brow. "I regret things have happened as they have between us, Malcolm. I never imagined we'd one day be adversaries. We're two of a kind, you and I. We both recognize what has to be done, and we're both brave enough to do it. We're the backbone of a country that's gone soft and contents itself with negotiating while our enemies continue stockpiling nuclear weapons. If Delta succeeds, we'll have no glory. If it fails, we'll be branded as traitors, and it will cost us our lives. You're wrong about me, you know. Dead wrong. I haven't misused my power. If you were physically capable, I'd gladly hand it back to you with my blessing. You're wrong about the reason I recruited Chad, also, but I can see it's hopeless to try to convince you otherwise." Admiral Addison stopped speaking and wet his cracked lips with his tongue. "Would you offer me a cognac, Malcolm?"

"I think not," Admiral Burke said. "We've nothing more to discuss. Your visit has ended, Admiral." His hand moved back toward the revolver.

"You do still believe in the concept of Delta, don't you?"

Admiral Burke's eyes narrowed. "The concept, yes," he said. "But perhaps it's a concept that's destined not to succeed because men such as you are as they are." His hand hovered above the revolver; both men noted its trembling. "You'll go now, please, Admiral."

"Yes, I'll go, Malcolm," Admiral Addison said, "but not without one last attempt to implore you to forsake this folly of requesting a committee meeting, at least until after D day. Why endanger Delta for a personal vendetta? Even if I'm the evil son of a bitch you think I am, why can't you let it wait until we have our objective behind us? I'll square off with you then. I'll prove to you and the committee that I'm innocent of your charges." Sighing wearily, Admiral Addison turned and, eyes downcast, moved to the door. "The decision is yours, of course, but I implore you, as a military man who supports Delta's cause, to delay your request."

"I'll inform Commander Stevenson of my decision tomorrow," Admiral Burke said. "Good night, Admiral."

After Addison had gone, Burke slumped in his chair and gave in to the exhaustion he felt. Addison had known how to reach him; aside from Chad, the dearest thing in his life was Delta. The admiral stroked his brow thoughtfully; there was a painful aching between his eyes, and an even worse ache in his heart. Of the two things he had loved most in life, one had caused the death of the other.

Perhaps, he reasoned, Addison had been justified in imploring him to hold off on his request for a committee meeting. He wanted Delta to achieve its purpose.

Opening his desk drawer, he placed his revolver under a notepad, so that Dorothy, if she should be looking for paper or pen, wouldn't discover it. Then, rising wearily, he went to the liquor cabinet and poured himself a snifter of cognac. Despite his exhaustion, he knew he wouldn't sleep for hours. He wanted to complete the brief he was working on, then hide it.

ADMIRAL ADDISON EMERGED from the shrubbery of the yard, his white linen trousers and sport shirt given an eerie, ghostlike quality by the moonlight.

He walked to the streetlight, stopped and lit a cigarette. Then, looking up and down the deserted street, he crossed to the compact car parked in the deep shadows of a monkeypod tree and bent down to the window.

Raymond Everett, who had been slumped in the front seat, straightened as the admiral approached. Except for the muted whiteness of the bandages across the bridge of his nose, his face was a blur in the darkness.

"Kill the son of a bitch!" Admiral Addison blurted. "Commander Stevenson will supply you with the medication and a syringe. It has to appear to be another stroke. There can't be any mistakes."

"I understand, sir," Everett said evenly.

"It'll have to be tomorrow evening, no later. His daughter's living here with him, so I'll have to get her out of the house. I'll have Commander Stevenson invite her out, keep her away from the house for at least an hour." The admiral tossed his cigarette to the pavement and ground it out with his heel. "The old fool keeps a revolver. Don't underestimate him. He may be old and ill, but he's cunning."

"Yes, sir."

"I don't think he suspects he's marked for elimination, but I can't guarantee that. I think I persuaded him to bury the hatchet until after D day. Do you have any questions?"

"No, sir. It's just another assignment."

"After you've injected him with the syringe, I want you to search his study. Do it discreetly. Leave no mess that might arouse suspicion. If you find any papers that refer to Delta, take them away with you. Turn them over to Commander Stevenson, since I'm taking the first flight out in the morning. When your duty's been completed, get out of Key West immediately. The commander will supply you with air tickets back to California. I know you're one of the key operatives for D day, Everett. If we don't meet again, good luck, sailor."

"Thank you, sir. Good luck to you, too, sir."

Admiral Addison straightened and looked back toward Admiral Burke's house.

Before he walked away, he said quietly, "It'll be good to see that old bastard in hell with his grandson!"

31

Mountain View, California

QUINN WAS SITTING beside the telephone, unable to sleep. When it rang, he answered immediately.

"Alex here, Commander," the yeoman said. "I'm sorry I couldn't call earlier, but when I returned to my apartment Chief Loomis was waiting for me."

"Any problems?" Quinn asked.

"The bastard stepped out of the shadows and scared the hell out of me," Alex told him. "Real cloak-and-dagger. I thought they were on to me because of the lieutenant in the bar and—"

"The lieutenant was tailing me," Quinn said. "What prompted the chief's visit?"

"He put me through four hours of grueling interrogation," the yeoman said. "Questions about my personal relationships, political views, reactions to the arms race, even my opinion of our president. Would you believe the bastard even asked me how often I masturbated?"

Quinn laughed. "Did he explain why he was giving you the third degree?"

"He aluded to what he calls his elite group again, even referred to it as the savior of our country. I tried to get the name of the organization from him—discreetly, of course—but I failed. He wanted to know my specific duties on the admiral's staff, what directives and codes I had access to."

"Did you tell him the truth?"

"Yes, I thought it best, since I didn't know what he could or couldn't verify. It's unknown to what extent they've infiltrated the staff already."

"True," Quinn agreed. "I've managed to learn a little more since our meeting. The name of the organization is Delta, which explains the symbol of the triangle with the bisecting line. With what status did you and Chief Loomis part company?"

"He's not that easy to read, Commander, but I guess I passed his preliminary examination. I've got an appointment tomorrow with Captain Musolf. He's the psychologist I told you compared you to a dog trained for groundhog hunting. It wasn't made clear to me, but there's apparently a time element involved. The group must be powerful, Commander. The chief told me there'd be no difficulty having me transferred from my present duty station if I was needed elsewhere."

Quinn had listened carefully to all Alex had told him. He had one further concern. "Do you think you can pull this off, Alex? You'll be infiltrating an organization I've been warned is highly dangerous. If anything makes them suspect you, there's no question but you'll end up like my son."

"I couldn't back down now even if I wanted to, Commander," Alex said. "I guess it's my insatiable curiosity. One of my foster mothers was fond of telling me it'd be the death of me. I intend to prove her wrong. Besides, if the organization is as dangerous as you say, it's already too late to back down. I'd be a loose end."

"And you have no inkling why there's a time element involved?" Quinn pressed. "What they've planned for the near future?"

"No, but I'll make a point of finding out," Alex assured him.

"Be careful," Quinn warned him. Then he added, "I'll be leaving the motel now that I've heard from you. I'm flying to San Diego in the morning. I'll contact you as soon as I return. We can't risk using your home telephone. Even your staff phones may be tapped. Can you give me a friend's number where I can leave messages?"

There was a pause before Alex said, "I'm a loner, Commander. I have no close friends." Another longer pause, then, "I suggest you call the personnel locator's office at Moffett. The PN there is an acquaintance. His name is Robinson. Tell him you're my uncle Dester and leave a number where I can reach you."

"Agreed," Quinn said.

"Until next time, Commander."

"Alex?"

"Yes, Commander?"

"Take care of yourself, son. Remember, you want to prove that foster mother wrong."

"I sure do, Commander," Alex told him, and broke the connection.

Quinn had a queasy feeling in the pit of his stomach as he placed the receiver back in its cradle. The yeoman was so young, so inexperienced, and if Jonathan was correct, Delta would know more about Alex Mayfield before he finished the psychological interview than the youth knew about himself.

Quinn had already packed his suitcase. Now he carried his luggage down to the car and stored it in the trunk before walking to the office to check out.

The motel manager was a scruffy little man in his late forties. He was watching the final moments of *The Tonight Show*, and he grumbled at being disturbed. "You could have just left the key in the room," he complained. "You already paid the bill." He snatched the key from the counter and hung it on a peg.

Quinn forced a polite smile. "I've missed an important business contact," he explained. "Should anyone call me, I'd like you to refer them to this number." He jotted down the number at the ranch and pushed it across the counter, along with a twenty-dollar bill. "For your trouble," he said, still smiling.

The manager's attitude changed as he pocketed the money. "Sure, sure, anything to oblige," he said. "Come back and stay with us on your next trip. Good motels are hard to find in Silicon Valley."

Quinn nodded and walked out of the office. If anyone checked with the motel manager, for a while at least, they'd think he'd returned to the ranch. Undoubtedly the lieutenant at Country Dan's had managed to talk himself out of his difficulties with the shore patrol and was back on duty, possibly watching him at this very moment. Quinn's gaze swept the parking lot, but he saw only empty cars.

When he drove away he kept his speed below the limit, his eyes constantly checking the rearview mirror, but no other car pulled out of the motel behind him. To be on the safe side, he took the freeway entrance going north, drove for five miles, then swung over to an exit, crossed the overpass and merged back onto the freeway going south. No other car followed his erratic pattern.

As he drove past Moffett Field, he had the intuitive feeling that the answers he sought were to be found there. The return trip to San Diego would probably prove futile, but he felt a sense of guilt where Emily Everett was concerned. Now, in hindsight, he knew he should have informed her that her husband wasn't on USS *Alum Rock* as she'd believed. Quinn was certain Emily Everett hadn't flung herself from her fourth-floor window as her neighbor believed. The young woman had been raised in the school of hard knocks; she was a survivor, definitely not the suicidal type. The only thing he wasn't sure of was whether her husband had pushed her himself or had relied on another Delta operative to do his dirty work for him. He recalled the cold and humorless eyes above the bandaged nose of the man who had been following him at the airport and decided Raymond Everett looked like a man who would relish killing, even if the victim was his own wife.

Quinn took the freeway exit for the San Jose airport, parked the rented car in the rental company's parking stall and switched off the headlights. The airport lounges had just closed, and the employees were filtering out onto the sidewalk. The interior lights were dimmed. He had checked the schedules and knew his flight didn't depart for four and a half hours.

Adjusting the driver's seat to a reclining position, he folded his arms across his chest, closed his eyes and prepared to wait until flight time.

He failed to observe the motorcycle with its headlight doused that had pulled into the parking lot behind him, or that the rider had killed its engine.

Lieutenant Gentry removed his helmet and walked to the bank of telephones outside the terminal. When his number answered, he said, "Commander Bannen's at the San Jose airport. He's sleeping in his car, apparently waiting for a morning flight."

"Flight to where?" Chief Loomis grumbled.

"How the hell should I know, Chief?" the lieutenant snapped.

"Well, find out as soon as he buys a ticket. We've got to keep one step ahead of that bastard until Addison gives elimination approval. And, Gentry, watch your tone of voice with me, boy. We're operating outside regular military. Your piss-piddly rank doesn't mean shit with me!"

32

San Diego, California

EMILY EVERETT STARED at Quinn with the one eye visible in her bandaged head.

The fall had broken both her legs, her right arm and her collarbone. In addition, her left eye had been pierced by some unidentified object, and she had received a concussion.

Quinn had stopped to buy her flowers. She watched silently as he handed them to a nurse, then as the nurse left the ward in search of a vase.

Quinn approached the side of her bed. "I'm sorry about what's happened to you," he said sincerely.

Emily lowered the lid of her one eye. "They say I might lose sight in my eye," she said quietly, "and I'm having plastic surgery on my cheek."

"I know. I spoke to the doctors," Quinn told her. "I'm sorry."

"You already said that, Commander," she murmured, and lifted her gaze to stare at him. "Do you know what ward they have me in?"

Quinn nodded. The front desk had directed him to the psychiatric ward when he'd given her name. To be admitted to the ward, he'd had to tell them he was her uncle.

"The woman in the bed by the window believes she's an alien from a planet called Altra," Emily said. "She tells the nurse if they touch her they'll be infected by a virus unknown on earth. The seventy-year-old woman next to her is convinced she's pregnant. An immaculate conception, she's calling it." A tear formed in her eye, and her voice cracked. "I don't belong here, Commander. I didn't try to commit suicide."

"I never believed you did," Quinn assured her. "Was it your husband?"

Emily turned her face away, hiding her good eye against the pillow. "It's Raymond who belongs in a psychiatric ward, not me. Oh, God, Commander, he's insane!" She wept for a minute, then recovered a tenuous control. "I guess I always suspected the violence festering inside him, but I never thought he'd turn against me like that."

"Have you talked to the police, Emily? Explained what happened?"

"*They* talked to *me*," she answered between sobs. "I had nothing to say to them. When I regained consciousness they were hovering over me like vultures, asking questions and telling me I'd broken the law by attempting to take my own life. Christ, I didn't even know it was illegal to kill yourself. How utterly stupid! If someone wants to kill themselves, what good does it do to make it illegal? Do they think someone's going to stop and consider they're breaking a law?"

"You should have told them the truth," Quinn told her. "You could have spared yourself that ordeal."

"And be thrown into another one!" Emily said, moving her head away from the pillow so she could confront him. "What was I supposed to tell them, Commander? That I fell trying to escape a husband who wanted to kill me? My husband, who's aboard the USS *Alum Rock* somewhere in the Indian Ocean, burst into our apartment and tried to murder me? I can't even prove he's my husband. He kept the licence they gave us in Tijuana. Telling them the truth would just have confirmed what they thought, that I was crazy. Maybe I am! I wish I was! It would be easier to accept madness than accepting that Raymond wanted me dead!" Tears flowed freely from the visible eye onto the bandages covering her high cheekbone.

The nurse returned with the bouquet of flowers in a cheap vase. She looked at her patient as she set the vase on the bedside table. Then she turned to Quinn. "Please make your visit short, sir. We want to keep Mrs. Everett as calm as possible. She goes back into surgery this afternoon." She raised her voice and spoke to Emily. "Dr. Schmidt's going to save that eye of yours, you can bet on it."

When the nurse had moved away and Emily had quieted, Quinn asked, "Why did your husband want to kill you, Emily?"

"Because I talked to you," she answered without hesitation. "I don't know how he knew I had, but he knew. He also knew Mona was dead—and Chad."

Did Raymond Everett know because he was the operative who killed both Chad and Mona? Quinn wondered.

"Why did it matter so much that I talked to you?" Emily murmured. "I told him I was only expressing my condolences over Chad. He didn't believe me. He even accused me of sleeping with you, Commander. He wouldn't listen to reason.... He was—he was totally insane!"

"Emily, did you ever hear your husband or Chad mention the word *Delta*?"

"I told you they were very secretive, Raymond and Chad, always whispering among themselves," she said. "No, I never heard— Oh, yes! Raymond did mention the word *Delta*! When he was trying to break down the bathroom door to get at me, he said, 'Either I get her or Delta gets me!' I heard him distinctly. What did he mean, Commander?"

Quinn had no wish to frighten her further, but he felt it necessary to say, "It means, Emily, that you must talk with the police. You must tell them everything, and you must make them believe you. They can check the records in Tijuana and prove you married Raymond Everett. They can also verify that he isn't presently on the USS *Alum Rock*."

"I won't! I can't!" she cried. In her excitement she moved carelessly, and he could see by her expression that her body was racked with pain. She collapsed back against the pillows. "Raymond would never forgive me," she said breathlessly.

"Forgive you?" Quinn said incredulously. "You're still concerned how he feels toward you after—"

"Raymond's ill!" Emily cried weakly. "I—I might have overreacted. He wouldn't have actually hurt me seriously. He just loses control. There's a lot of anger and hostility bottled up inside him, more than he can handle sometimes. If I could convince him to seek professional help, then—''

"And is there no anger in you?" Quinn demanded. "Do you love that madman so much it's blinding you? You're right, he is ill, but it goes beyond what you realize."

"He's my husband! It's my duty to stand by him!"

"At what cost?" Quinn asked, indicating her broken and bandaged body with a sweep of his hand. "Your life's in peril and you worry about a man who'd finish what he started if given a second chance. That's incredible, absolutely incredible! You were lucky this time. Next time it may be different."

"There won't be a next time, Commander," she said firmly. "Despite what happened, Raymond loves me!"

"What can I say to convince you?" Quinn said helplessly.

"Nothing. I wish you hadn't come," she told him.

"Your husband's involved with a very secret, very illegal organization called Delta," Quinn persisted. "If he even knew you'd heard the name it would be enough to cost you your life. The only way you can protect yourself is to tell the police everything you know."

Moving her head painfully back and forth against her pillow, Emily cried, "No, no! You're as mad as that old woman who thinks she's an alien! I think you'd better go, Commander."

In a final attempt to convince her of the danger she was in, Quinn said, "There's a possibility your husband was involved in the murder of both my son and your friend Mona. He's an operative trained to—"

"I don't believe you!" Emily shrieked. "You're lying! I don't know why, but you hate Raymond! You can't blame him for Mona or Chad! I won't believe you! Get out, Commander! Just get out and leave me alone!"

The nurse who had brought the vase for the flowers appeared in the doorway. The remaining patients in the ward were watching Quinn with blatant curiosity; one old lady had begun to cry out, babbling with fear. The nurse started forward.

Lowering his voice to a mere whisper, Quinn said, "When your husband learns that fall didn't kill you, Emily, he'll be back to finish the job. Think about it. Talk to the police. He can't afford to have his name linked with Delta. It would be signing his own death warrant."

"Liar! Nurse, get this madman away from me!"

"It's your life or his," Quinn finished. "I thought you were a survivor. Maybe I was mistaken. If you don't do anything about this, you *will* be committing suicide."

"Sir, I think you'd better leave!" the nurse said, and reached for his elbow to escort him from the ward.

Knowing there was nothing more he could say to Emily Everett, Quinn turned on his heel and strode from the room.

33

Key West, Florida

JONATHAN CHOSE A TABLE with an umbrella to keep off the tropical sun and ordered a piña colada from a shapely waitress in a tight-fitting T-shirt and white culottes. From the table he had chosen he had an unbroken view of the row of benches facing the beach.

Admiral Burke was seated on a bench, staring quietly out at the bathers and the water-skiers. To Jonathan, the admiral looked like a mere shadow of the man he had been a decade ago, when his stature alone had commanded attention. Now he might have been any old man sitting on any beach from Key West to the Cape. Nothing about him hinted at the power he had once wielded or the military strength he had once commanded. His white hair had thinned so that the pale pink of his scalp showed through. His neck and gaunt face were heavily wrinkled, his broad shoulders stooped. He sat with his hands folded in his lap, large hands that were skeletal now, discolored by dark liver spots. The oversize sport shirt he wore hung on his frame and made him appear even more emaciated. The young muscular bodies of the sunbathers all around him accentuated his frailness and vulnerability. A fading dinosaur, Jonathan thought.

The waitress returned with Jonathan's piña colada and gave him an inviting smile. He sipped the too-sweet drink and tried to ignore his discomfort; he'd left Washington in such haste that he hadn't packed hot-weather clothing, and he was drenched with perspiration. In his dark suit slacks and a dress shirt open at the neck, he imagined he must stand out in contrast to the vacationers as blatantly as Admiral Burke did.

When he'd arrived in Key West he'd taken a taxi directly to Admiral Burke's address on Catherine Street. Just as the taxi had pulled up he'd seen the admiral emerge from his house and walk away. He had followed the old man on foot, wondering why he didn't simply approach him and make another demand for an interview. The truth was, he was still in awe of the old bastard.

Chiding himself now, Jonathan got up, walked over to the bench and sat down beside the admiral. He waited for the man to glance in his direction, but without doing so, Admiral Burke said, "You're a long way from Washington, aren't you, Mr. McKinney?" Still without turning, the old man smiled at the expression of surprise he knew was on the reporter's face. "Don't ever go into surveillance work, McKinney. You're no good at it. I knew you were following me from the moment you climbed out of that cab."

Admiral Burke turned then and met Jonathan's stare. Although his body was frail and showed the ravages of age and illness, his eyes were still alert and intelligent, his stare unfaltering. "The same with the other one," he said, and indicated a muscular young man in jeans and a polo shirt with bandages across the bridge of his nose leaning against the low wall dividing the beach from the restaurant patio. "He's here for my protection," the admiral said, "or so I've been told. I wonder if I called him over now and told him you were threatening me—"

"Please don't do that, Admiral," Jonathan said. "I'm not the physical type."

"No, McKinney, I can see that. You've let your body go to seed," the admiral said bluntly. "That's what comes of exercising the gray cells and ignoring the body. I'd bet even at my age I could give you a run for your money."

"As I said, Admiral, I'm not the physical type," Jonathan murmured.

"Not very intelligent, either, if you think coming to Key West is going to gain you an interview with either my daughter or myself. My grandson has been buried, McKinney. I won't have his name dragged through the media as the alleged victim of an alleged conspiracy. His father may be paranoid and imagine conspiracies behind every incident in life, but not me, not his mother. My advice to you is to let it go. Ferret out a story elsewhere. Or invent one. You media people are good at fiction."

Jonathan noted that everything the old man said was spoken in a quiet, even tone of voice, which was unusual, for he was known for his quick rages and his sharp-tongued attacks. Perhaps, the reporter reasoned, the admiral was even more ill than he appeared.

"I don't invent stories, Admiral," Jonathan said patiently. "Any more than you invent wars. They're there and I go for them. The American public has a right to know—"

"Ah, yes, the apathetic American public," the admiral cut in. "A scandal tickles their fancy for a day, maybe two, then they go back to their humdrum lives without concern while the protagonists of these media scandals find their lives destroyed. All for amusement, just amusement. Take the drug experiments you and my ex-son-in-law uncovered.

The military suffered, but what else was accomplished? How long did the public's interest last?"

"The experiments were stopped, Admiral," Jonathan said. "The victims were spared, future victims saved."

"You—or Quinn especially—could have called the experiments to the attention of the Defense Department," the admiral suggested. "They would have been stopped, but without publicity. We'd have cleaned our own dirty laundry."

"I doubt that, Admiral. The whole incident would have been tied up in bureaucratic red tape and eventually added to the dung heap hidden behind the secrecy acts. Commander Bannen and I didn't invent the drug experiments scandal, just as we haven't invented the strange and questionable circumstances surrounding his son's death."

"Strange and questionable? What is so strange and questionable about a young sailor dying of a drug overdose? It happens more frequently than you'd imagine. Drugs are a serious problem to the military. That's why we've devised surprise piss tests, any number of other tests. Still, we can't catch every drug user in uniform. If we could, my grandson would be alive."

"What about the missing vital organs?" Jonathan demanded.

"A mistake on the part of some young corpsman," the admiral answered without hesitation.

"What about the fact his letters to his father expressed his pride in refusing drugs despite the pressure of his peers?"

"He didn't want to hurt his father by admitting the truth," the admiral replied.

"What about the note received by his mother? 'They killed our Chad'?"

"A crank. The world's full of them, McKinney."

"What about the murder of your grandson's fiancée? Mona Shriver?"

The admiral's bushy eyebrows arched slightly, and color flooded his face. "My grandson had no fiancée. Not to my knowledge. Not to his mother's." He made a visible effort to calm himself, but the tension remained.

"What about the attempt on Commander Bannen's life?"

"Oh, I haven't heard this paranoid fantasy, McKinney. Suppose you tell me about it."

"I would have thought your daughter would tell you, Admiral. She was with him at the time in Washington. Someone tried to run them down as they were leaving a restaurant."

The admiral couldn't conceal the effect of news concerning an attempt on his daughter's life. The color returned to his face, the cords in his scrawny neck protruded, a nerve at the corner of his mouth ticked out of control.

Jonathan pressed his advantage. "What about Delta, Admiral?"

The admiral's entire countenance seemed to crumple before Jonathan's eyes. The question had struck him with the effect of a physical blow; his mouth fell open, and his head turned sharply in the reporter's direction. Struggling for control, he brought up a skeletal hand and wiped the spittle from his chin. His eyes suddenly blazed with fury. "I don't know what the hell you're talking about, McKinney, and I dare say you don't, either!"

"You can't deny you never heard the name Delta, Admiral," Jonathan said. "I've spent hours in congressional libraries and computer rooms in the past twenty-four hours. There's very little remaining evidence to substantiate the existence of an organization called Delta, but a few precious documents remain that weren't destroyed, erased or locked away in top-security vaults. One of the documents I managed to locate listed the officers charged by the president with investigating the scuttlebutt that such an illegal organization existed. You were one of those officers."

"Damn you, McKinney! Damn your infernal meddling! That was two decades ago, ancient history."

"But you don't deny it did exist?" Jonathan pressed.

Admiral Burke turned his attention back to the sunbathers, but it was apparent he was rattled. He said nothing.

"The mere name Delta has the same effect on a reporter that the Lost Dutchman Mine would on a prospector," Jonathan said. "Or a man on foot to a bull raised for the—"

"Spare me your stupid metaphors, damn you!" The old man rose, and Jonathan, too, came to his feet; though stooped by age, the admiral was as tall as the reporter. "I'll tell you this much, McKinney. Yes, I investigated rumors of an unauthorized agency existing within our military, but the investigation proved no such agency as Delta existed. It was only myth."

"Excuse me, Admiral, but I must call you a liar," Jonathan said evenly. "Delta existed then. It exists now. I'm convinced of it, and I'll prove it."

"You ignorant, ill-informed son of a bitch!" the old man shouted. "I tell you no such organization existed then or exists now. I should know since, as you said, I was in charge of the investigation."

Undaunted, Jonathan said, "Your grandson was a member of Delta, Admiral."

"Quinn Bannen put you up to this! That bastard! Is there no end to the harm he'll cause me and my daughter?" Turning abruptly, the admiral signaled to the young man with the bandaged nose. "Come here, damn you!" he shouted when the young man hesitated.

Jonathan backed off reluctantly as the formidable young man approached, confusion mirrored in his cold eyes.

"According to your superior, you are supposed to be protecting me," Admiral Burke told the young man sarcastically. He pointed at Jonathan McKinney. "This man has threatened me," he said. "Not only me but the reputation

of the United States military. Do whatever it is you're supposed to do!''

"Now wait a minute, Admiral—" Jonathan stammered.

"Only if, in that minute, I see your ass running away,
McKinney!" Admiral Burke said.

Knowing when to retreat, Jonathan turned and hurried
quickly to safety.

34

DOROTHY WAS on the telephone when the door opened and
Admiral Burke came in. She recognized immediately that he
was agitated; he crossed the room without glancing at her,
entered his study and slammed his door.

She had covered the mouthpiece; she now pulled her hand
away. "I'm sorry, Commander Stevenson." Rather than
explain the admiral's dramatic entrance, she said, "We have
a bad connection. I missed what you were saying."

"I asked you to dinner this evening," the commander repeated.

"Oh, I'm sorry. I don't think—"

"I understand you visited my wife, Dorothy," the commander interjected. "Alice's condition is . . . well, a delicate
situation. I'd like the opportunity to explain—"

"Commander, it's really not my affair," Dorothy said. "I
find it peculiar you haven't committed your wife to a hospital where she'd receive proper care, but I'm sure you have
your reasons."

The commander's voice hinted at desperation as he said,
"I'm really at my wit's end. I need to discuss this with
someone understanding."

"But your wife's a Conch, Commander," Dorothy said.
"She must have family in Key West."

"A maiden aunt. That's all the family she has living,"
Commander Stevenson told her. "The aunt's even less sta-
ble than Alice. Something has to be done, that's apparent,

but just what will be right for Alice, I can't decide. I've talked to doctors, of course. All of them have recommended commitment, but I've looked into some of those institutions and frankly... Dorothy, I'm pleading with you to have dinner with me, to act as a sounding board, if nothing else."

"Commander, I don't like leaving the admiral alone. You know he's not well, and—"

"A quick dinner wouldn't take you away from the admiral for more than an hour," he assured her. "It would mean so much to me. And to Alice, if she wasn't beyond comprehending her condition."

"Very well, Commander," Dorothy conceded.

She jotted down the name of a restaurant on Simonton Street, near the commander's home, and agreed to meet him there at seven o'clock. The gratitude in the officer's voice when he thanked her sounded insincere to Dorothy, but she dismissed that thought as she hung up the phone and went to check on the admiral.

She tapped on his study door and entered without waiting to be invited. He had removed the books from the third shelf of the bookcase, those that concealed the wall safe, and was opening the heavy metal door.

"Must I be denied privacy?" he barked. "First that goddamned reporter! Now my own daughter!"

"What reporter?" Dorothy managed evenly.

"McKinney!" the admiral cried. "The bastard flew down from Washington to harass me with his suspicions." He removed a file from the safe and moved back to his desk. "That ex-husband of yours is behind it! He's pushing me beyond my limits!"

Dorothy moved behind the admiral's chair and began to massage the tightened muscles of his neck. "Calm down, Admiral," she said quietly. "The doctors warned you about overexciting yourself."

"You're right. I mustn't let them drive me into another stroke. That would please the bastards, all of them. Bannen and McKinney and Addison." His voice showed he was calming down. "I'm sorry I shouted at you," he said apologetically, still struggling to control his agitation. "Be a dear, and bring me a cognac. A small one won't hurt me. Strictly medicinal."

Dorothy laughed. "One," she agreed. "And a very small one." She crossed to the cabinet and covered the bottom of a snifter with cognac.

"And a cigarette," the admiral said after she had placed the cognac in front of him.

"You're pressing your luck!"

"Then you light one. Let me smell the smoke, at least. What is life without vices, I ask you."

Again Dorothy acquiesced, chiding herself for her weakness. She lit a cigarette and handed it to him. "Only a few puffs," she warned.

As the admiral inhaled greedily, she moved to the wing chair and sat down, watching him enjoy the cognac and the cigarette. His coloring worried her. The tic at the corner of his mouth hadn't gone away yet. His hands were trembling. Finally, after he had taken several puffs on the cigarette, his nerves seemed to settle. She rose, removed the cigarette from his fingers and crushed it out. "No more concessions," she told him.

"You should have been a nurse, my dear. One of those hefty dykes in white who love pushing men around." He swallowed the cognac in one greedy gulp, as if afraid it, too, would be taken from him. Sighing, he leaned his head against the chair back and closed his eyes. "I feel much better." The nerve at the corner of his mouth had stopped twitching. "You should have seen McKinney run when I threatened him with my bodyguard," he said, laughing.

"Bodyguard? What bodyguard?" Dorothy asked.

"An unnecessary, unwanted six-foot-two tower of brawn that Adm—that the military has assigned to protect me," the admiral answered.

"Protect you from what?"

"From reporters such as McKinney, I suppose. You should see the young man. A mean-looking individual who must love to fight, judging from the bandages across his nose."

"But, Admiral—"

"Don't alarm yourself, Dorothy. He didn't touch the reporter. There'll be no lawsuits. Not unless McKinney can sue for wounded pride. It was amusing to watch that bastard run." The humor vanished from his face. "It would have been more amusing if it had been Quinn Bannen running away," he said without opening his eyes.

Dorothy refrained from saying that Quinn would never have run from a fight. "Did Jonathan McKinney question you about Chad's death?" she asked.

"He did," the admiral told her. "I gave him the same answers. Neither you nor I question the navy's findings. We're convinced there was no conspiracy." He opened his eyes and let his chair snap back to the floor. "Now, Dorothy, if you don't mind, I need to be alone. There are some papers I need to finish...."

"Why don't you join me for a swim instead?" Dorothy suggested. "The water's refreshing. You'll forget about McKinney."

"You know I hate swimming pools," the admiral said. "I haven't been in that one since the day you had it put in. You run along. Enjoy yourself. I'll join you later for something cool."

"Something cool and nonalcoholic," she told him. "Not too much later. I have a date at seven."

"Oh? With a man, I hope?" Interest sparked behind his eyes.

"Yes, with a man," she said. She didn't tell him that the man was Commander Stevenson and the date was to discuss the commander's wife, because she knew he would disapprove. Let him hope she had turned to other men and was no longer plagued by thoughts of Quinn.

A little later, after swimming several laps, Dorothy pulled herself out of the pool, exhausted, and stretched out on a lounge chair. The sun was so hot that she knew she couldn't lie there for long without getting a sunburn. She had exposed her back for five minutes and was turning over when a shadow fell across the lounge. Her eyes fluttering open, she cried out at the sight of a man's silhouette outlined by the sun.

"It's only me, Mrs. Bannen. Jonathan McKinney. I managed to avoid the admiral and his henchman. I'd like a few moments of your time."

"I have nothing to say to you," Dorothy said crisply. "Go away, Mr. McKinney."

"But I have something to tell you," the reporter persisted.

Dorothy sat up, reached for her towel and pulled it around her shoulders to protect them from the sun's burning rays. "You're an irritating man, Mr. McKinney. You were irritating when you had all those plotting sessions with my husband, and you're even more irritating now. You upset the admiral, though you're aware of his condition. I repeat, go away!"

"I spoke to your husband last night, Mrs. Bannen."

"My former husband," Dorothy said, but the anger was gone from her voice.

Jonathan lowered himself to the foot of her lounge chair.

"Tell me what you want, then please leave," she told him.

Jonathan hesitated, and didn't speak until she lifted her eyes to confront him. "Quinn is in grave danger, Mrs. Bannen," he said. "So, for that matter, am I. Possibly even you." The reporter removed his glasses, wiped the perspiration from around his eyes and then fixed the sidepieces over his ears again.

"Are you always so cryptic, Mr. McKinney?" Dorothy demanded. "Or do you wish me to engage in a guessing game? All right, I'll play along, since that appears to be the only way to get rid of you. Why are the three of us in danger?"

"Because we've managed to uncover some surprising information in our search to learn the truth about your son's death."

Dorothy bolted off the lounge. "I'm suddenly not amused by your game. What surprising information?"

"Your son was involved with an illegal organization existing within the military," the reporter told her. "My guess is that he was trying to emulate his father and expose the organization as Quinn exposed the drug experiments."

Dorothy stared at Jonathan, wide-eyed, as if she couldn't comprehend what he was saying.

"They're no more than assassins, Mrs. Bannen. Their exact activities are shrouded in secrecy. They hide themselves in the branches of the military and blindly obey the orders of their leaders. It's rumored they have created bloodbaths all over the world, assassinated political figures, manipulated governments."

"And Chad was part of this? I don't believe you!"

"Believe me, Mrs. Bannen," Jonathan said firmly. "It's the truth, I swear to you. We haven't any proof yet, but we'll get it. This organization makes the activities of other intelligence agencies pale by comparison. I won't tell you more, for your own safety. I've only told you what I have to convince you to open up about your son. I know there's more you're not telling. I know the admiral knows more. I've planted seeds in Washington. Quinn's in California trying to uncover—"

"Stop!" Dorothy cried. "It's like before! Only worse! You and Quinn, acting like adolescents playing spies! Is that what you think my son was emulating? What he died for? The admiral was right. Quinn is paranoid. And you! Get out of here, McKinney, or I'll call the admiral's bodyguard!''

Jonathan rose from the lounge. "Mrs. Bannen, you can't ignore this. I'm imploring you to help. Give me an interview to keep the public's interest in your son alive. A human-interest story would build the momentum in the press. People in high places would be forced to take notice. The power of the press is remarkable. We could reach into the Pentagon, even the White House. Accusations of an illegal organization would be investigated."

"Your accusations. And Quinn's. I can't believe my son died trying to expose some mythical organization."

"Not mythical," Jonathan said sharply, losing patience. "Ask your father, the admiral. Ask him about an organization called Delta." He saw that Dorothy's anger was about to explode, and he held up his hands in a gesture of surrender. "All right, Mrs. Bannen, I'm going. I tried. I'll tell Quinn I tried. We'll succeed without your help. An organization like Delta can't be allowed to exist. Not two decades ago, not now, not ever. Your son must have realized the danger. I hope he didn't give his life in vain."

Jonathan left Dorothy beside the swimming pool and let himself out of the yard through a gap in the hedge of hyacinths.

35

Alameda, California

ALEX LEANED FORWARD as if to rise, then hesitated on the edge of his chair, his gaze fixed on the door to the adjoining office.

Following Chief Loomis's instructions, he had taken the base shuttle bus to Alameda, and once on the island had reported to Captain Musolf. Until then he hadn't known that

the captain divided his time between Alameda and Moffett
Field.

He'd spent more than an hour with the psychologist. The
interview wasn't what he'd expected, although exactly what
he'd expected was uncertain. The captain had given him a
test similar to a Rorschach, but the remainder of the hour
had been spent merely talking. They had gone over his
childhood, the moves from foster home to foster home, the
foster parents and his reactions to them, the hostility the
captain said he must have felt. He had refrained from telling the captain that loneliness, not hostility, had been his
worst enemy. Then, just as the captain had broached the
subject of politics, they had been interrupted by a corpsman, a first-class, who had informed the psychologist that
a patient named Marshisky was reporting and would speak
only to him.

Alex had noticed the spark of recognition behind the
captain's dark eyes. As he'd said, "Put the patient in the
next office. I'll be with him directly," Alex had also de-
tected a nervousness that hadn't been in the captain's attitude before. His jaw had tightened, and his smooth brow
had furrowed. "Excuse me, Mayfield, I won't be long,"
he'd said, and had gone into the adjoining office and closed
the door.

Even from his chair across the office Alex could hear
muffled voices, but the words were not audible. Rising, he
moved stealthily closer to the door.

"...claustrophobic, doc! I can't be locked in any fuckin'
small room! This was supposed to be R and R, that's what
they told me when they pulled me out of San Diego."

"It will be R and R, Marshisky. I assure you it'll be the
greatest R and R you've ever known," Captain Musolf said.

"In a fuckin' padded cell?" The voice was young and
angry. "I became a member of Delta to escape the fuckin'
brig. Now you want to stick me in a padded cell! Hell, no!"

The mention of Delta caused adrenaline to surge through Alex. He stepped even closer to the door, not wanting to miss any of Captain Musolf's quieter reply.

"It's only for a few days," the psychologist said quietly. "It isn't our intention to punish you. Far from it, Marshisky. You're our most important operative. Wasn't it you we selected for D day? Out of seventy-five operatives, you are the most highly qualified to—"

"Knock off the shit, captain! So I'm to pull the trigger on the son of a bitch! So what? For that I'm rewarded with a padded cell and I'm expected to think of it as R and R?"

"I guarantee you'll not even know you're there, Marshisky. You won't care where you are." There was a noise that sounded to Alex like a cabinet being opened. "You see, we're going to take excellent care of you, sailor. Nothing but the best. Roll up your sleeve. Ah, I thought this would make you more cooperative."

"As often as I want it?" the young voice asked suspiciously.

"As often as you want it, yes," Captain Musolf said reassuringly.

There were several moments of silence, making Alex consider returning to his chair before the captain suddenly opened the door and discovered him listening.

As he was about to turn away, he heard: "And when it's over? After I've killed him?"

"We take care of our own," Captain Musolf answered. "You'll be well cared for, my young assassin."

There was a sound of something being discarded in a metal waste can.

"When? Has the date been set?"

"You mean how long till you get to live in drug paradise?" the captain murmured, so softly Alex could scarcely hear him. "The schedule's not been confirmed yet, but soon. Within two weeks. We'll know in plenty of time for final preparations. Now I'm going to call the corpsman and have him take you to your—your room. I'll drop by and see you later. With another of these."

Alex fled back to his chair. He fought to wipe the excitement from his expression. Reaching for a magazine, he opened it on his lap just as the door opened and Captain Musolf entered.

The captain resumed his position behind his desk. "Now, Mayfield, where were we? Oh, yes, we were about to discuss your political views."

36

Key West, Florida

ADMIRAL BURKE TOOK the papers from his wall safe and spread them out on his desk. The brief he was preparing was almost complete; he had only to make a final check of the details, correct his grammar and polish his style.

Then the brief would go to the committee.

The decision had been agonizing for him, but Admiral Addison would be charged, Chad's death would be avenged.

A sound from the terrace caused the admiral to glance toward the windows. Magenta streaked the sky above the garden. Half the population of Key West, he knew, would be gathering at the southern tip of the island for the ritual known as Sunset. The locals and tourists would mingle, drink, chat, ooh and aah over the colors of the sky and then wander away to restaurants and parties.

The admiral wondered if Dorothy's date had taken her to Sunset. Leaning back in his chair, he closed his eyes. It was time for Dorothy to get over Quinn, he thought, to find another man and remarry. Because of his physical condition and the recent strain he had been under, Burke drifted into a fitful sleep in the middle of his thoughts.

Moments later he awakened abruptly and sat up straight. He listened for a repetition of the sound that had brought

him from his nap. When it came again he recognized it as
the creaking of the floorboards in another room.

"Dorothy, is that you?" he called as he covered the brief
at his elbow with a newspaper. No answer.

"Dorothy?" he repeated.

He got up and walked to the study door. The living room
was cast in a dull glow, its draperies drawn. The air conditioner hummed quietly. Perhaps that was what he had
heard, he reasoned, some mechanism of the air conditioner
creaking as its thermostat adjusted the force of the motor.
He'd noticed a slight breeze stirring in the garden, reducing
the heat and lightening the load on the air conditioner.

So that Dorothy wouldn't have to return to a dark house,
the admiral switched on a lamp in the living room. Then he
returned to his study and poured a cognac, replacing the
liquid with water from the pitcher in case his daughter had
noted the level in the bottle. He resented being forced into
sneaky practices, but he wanted to avoid an argument.

As he turned from the liquor cabinet, snifter firmly in
hand, a movement drew his attention to the open door. The
snifter slipped from his hand and shattered on the floor at
his feet.

In the doorway stood the bodyguard Admiral Addison
had assigned him, the one who had helped send McKinney
on his way.

Anger swept over the admiral, at the intruder for startling him, and at himself for having dropped the glass. Now
Dorothy would smell the cognac and be furious with him.
"What the hell are you doing in here?" he demanded.
"Look what you've made me do!" He took a handkerchief
from his pocket and bent to wipe up the spilled cognac and
glass. While he was crouched, he saw the bodyguard's feet
move forward. A glance at the young man's face told him
immediately it had not been for his protection that Admiral
Addison had assigned him the bodyguard. Burke read in the
youth's eyes, made to look even crueler by the bandages

across his nose, that he was a killer. He told himself he should have realized Addison would never allow himself to be attacked before the committee.

"Make it easy on yourself, Pop," the man said as he stepped closer. He held a syringe in his left hand; his right was doubled into a fist.

Continuing to stare into the "bodyguard's" eyes, Admiral Burke straightened and backed against the liquor cabinet. This man was the instrument of his death, he thought, fascinated to the point of being mesmerized. Death itself didn't frighten him. Since his stroke he'd accustomed himself to the idea that sometime soon his heart would cease to beat and he would cease to exist. His heart was racing now. It struck him that because of this man he would fail to avenge his grandson's murder. Addison would be the victor! Anger boiled inside him. His instinct for survival surfaced, and his mind began to function rapidly, clearly. He knew it would be impossible to overpower the young assassin. If he could reach his revolver . . . but the revolver was in the desk drawer, and the killer stood in his way.

"Make it easy on yourself," the young man repeated. "A tiny prick of the needle, that's all you'll feel." He bent forward slightly at the waist, extending his arms away from his sides as if he read the admiral's intention to try to rush past him to the desk. "Digitalis, old man. That's what they said I'd be giving you. Your worn-out old ticker will burst. Seconds is all it takes!" His lips set in a cruel, thin line. His right fist opened, and he motioned the admiral toward him, to his death.

Go for the bastard's nose, Admiral Burke told himself, his most vulnerable spot because it wasn't yet healed! Then the groin! Avoid the syringe. You only need a moment to reach the desk drawer and the revolver.

As the admiral had backed against the cabinet his hands had been behind him. He felt for the cognac bottle. Not letting his locked gaze with the assassin falter, he closed his fingers around the bottle's neck, felt the stickiness of the liquid that had dripped down the neck. He swallowed to speak and found his throat constricted, his voice a croak as he said, "What you're doing is against Delta. Admiral Addison hasn't the authority to order my execution."

A flicker of doubt sparked in the assassin's cold eyes.

Play on it, Admiral Burke told himself. "You don't know it, young man, but I'm the officer responsible for Delta's rebirth. Admiral Addison is the traitor! He's an egomaniac. Power has gone to his head. Only a committee can order my execution, not Addison."

The operative was so close that Admiral Burke could smell his body odor, his breath, and could see the specks of dirt on the bandages covering his nose. "Think, man!" he pressed. "By obeying Admiral Addison and killing me, you'll be signing your own death warrant!"

Again the admiral saw the young man's hesitation, but he knew it was only momentary. The operatives of Delta were not trained to reason, only to fulfill their assignments—in this case, to perform an execution. Quickly the admiral stepped to one side and brought the cognac bottle forward with all the force he possessed.

The bottle found its mark.

Crying out in agony, the young man staggered backward, clutching at his face with his right hand. He stumbled and fell but stubbornly clung to the syringe, holding it away from him protectively as his back struck the floor. With remarkable agility, he sprang back to his feet before Admiral Burke reached the desk.

The blow caught the admiral in the small of the back, driving the air from his lungs and hurtling him forward. He crashed into the leather desk chair and sent it teetering across the floor to smash into a side table. The admiral landed facedown behind his desk. Gasping for breath, he lifted his upper body and lunged for the desk drawer. He managed to get it open and was fumbling inside when the killer slammed the drawer and crushed the old man's brittle fingers.

Raymond Everett knelt on the admiral's back and pulled his shirt collar away from his scrawny neck. Everett's nose was bleeding heavily, the blood spattering the admiral's clothes and white hair. "You old son of a bitch!" he snarled. "Both you and your fucking grandson went for my nose! Both of you are going to die for it!"

Admiral Burke cried out in protest as he felt the prick of the needle in the wrinkled flesh of his neck.

"YOU SAID YOU WANTED to discuss your wife, Commander," Dorothy said. "Yet every time I raise the subject of her illness, you manage to change the subject."

They had dined lightly on fruit salad on the terrace of the restaurant and were now drinking coffee. The commander was out of uniform, in sport clothes. Dorothy realized he'd been charming, but also evasive when it came to the reason for their meeting.

The commander took her accusation with a smile. "It's true," he said. "I somehow don't want to discuss Alice." He changed his position, and his knee touched hers under the table. "It somehow doesn't seem appropriate," he said when she moved to avoid contact.

"Appropriate? That was my only reason for having dinner with you!"

"Yes, of course. It's just that . . . well, to be perfectly truthful, I deliberately pushed thoughts of Alice aside the moment I saw you. Don't judge me harshly," he added when she opened her mouth to speak. "I've been under the pressure of my wife's illness for months. I saw a chance to escape it temporarily, and I took it. A beautiful woman, a pleasant evening, a good meal— Can you blame me for avoiding the issue of a mentally ill wife?"

Dorothy stared at him thoughtfully for several moments before saying, "Commander, I can appreciate the strain you've been under. I can understand your wish to escape reality for an evening. Still, the fact remains that Alice is seriously ill, and something has to be done about seeking professional help. You're not helping her situation or yours by keeping her locked up in your home."

"I know. I've just been reluctant to commit her," Commander Stevenson said.

"Commander, this isn't the dark ages, the days of *The Snake Pit* or *One Flew over the Cuckoo's Nest*," Dorothy told him warily. "There are perfectly good hospitals where Alice can receive proper treatment and be cured. You do want her cured, don't you, Commander?"

"Naturally." He shifted uncomfortably in his chair. The smile was gone from his face, and his expression had become inscrutable.

A handsome face, Dorothy decided. In the dim light since sunset, he had reminded her again of Quinn. She pushed the thought from her mind. The fact that the commander had used her as a way of escaping the reality of his wife's condition angered her. "Without treatment she can only get worse, Commander. You're an intelligent man. I can't imagine how you failed to recognize any warning signs in her behavior long before her illness evolved to the degree it has." I might as well be totally truthful, she told herself. "In fact," she said, "I find it criminal."

The commander's expression ceased to be inscrutable as his facial muscles tightened with indignation. "I admit she's ill," he said defensively, "but I think you're exaggerating the severity of her illness." His eyes narrowed. "Exactly what did she tell you?"

"What she told me isn't important," Dorothy said. "What *is* important is that she's lost her grip on reality. In her confused mind she's imagined some sort of sinister plot—against President Kennedy, I believe. She can't relate to a time frame. She believes he's going to be killed—in New

York, not Dallas. She doesn't realize it happened in the past, but thinks it's going to happen in the near future."

The commander had turned pale. "She actually said President Kennedy was to be assassinated in New York?"

"I don't remember her exact words," Dorothy said. "I was so disturbed by her condition I was only partially listening. Surely, Commander, she's made similar statements to you, enough for you to realize the seriousness of her illness."

"I—I'm away much of the time," Commander Stevenson said. "I divide my time between here and Washington. Of course, I know Alice needs better care than local military doctors can provide, but—" He reached for his coffee cup, casually glancing at his wristwatch as he did so. "I'll look into it," he said with finality.

Dorothy stared at him incredulously. "I take it from your attitude, Commander, that you wish to carry the discussion of Alice's illness no further?"

"I see no need for further discussion," he answered flatly. "You've convinced me her condition is more serious than I realized. I'll locate a proper facility for her as quickly as possible."

Dorothy opened her purse and removed a slip of paper. "Here's a list of military hospitals I looked up where Alice could receive competent treatment. I'm sure you could get her in anywhere if you pulled the proper strings."

The commander took the list of hospitals she had compiled and stuffed it into his pocket without glancing at it. "Now may we finish our coffee and discuss something more pleasant?" he said dryly.

Dorothy returned home an hour later to find the house dark. It was unlike the admiral to retire so early, she thought.

She switched on a lamp and tiptoed down the hall to the admiral's bedroom door. The door stood open, and she could see by the moonlight filtering through the sheer curtains that his bed hadn't been slept in. She came back down the hallway to the other branch of the house's L shape and checked his study. That door was also open, and the room was dark. The open door was particularly puzzling, because the admiral was so adamant about the door being kept closed when he wasn't there.

There was a strong odor in the study that she failed to identify at first as she stepped inside. Then it struck her—cognac. She threw open the doors of the liquor cabinet. The bottle of cognac was gone. When she turned she saw the stain on the floor. She bent, touched a spot where the wax had been lifted from the wood and brought her fingers to her nose—cognac. Damn! He'd been helping himself to cognac despite his promise, and had managed to drop the bottle. She went to his desk to check the ashtray for evidence of the other forbidden excess. The admiral was always precise about where objects were placed on his desk—the ashtray to his right, pushed up against the paperweight Chad had given him with a piece of the sunken galleon encased in plastic. The ashtray was now on the left. A copy of yesterday's edition of the *New York Times* had been placed neatly in the center of the blotter, the corner of a file folder protruding from beneath. The middle desk drawer was slightly ajar—unusual, too, because the admiral, a creature of habit, always locked the drawer when he left the house.

Dorothy pulled the drawer open. Unfamiliar with the contents, she couldn't tell if they had been disturbed by someone other than the admiral. There were notepads, pens, paper clips, his revolver, passport and international driver's license and a framed photograph of the admiral with Chad, possibly put away because the admiral found it too painful to look at while he worked at his desk.

Dorothy closed the drawer and sat down in her father's chair. Uneasiness had begun to spread through her. It occurred to her that the admiral wouldn't have gone out without leaving a lamp burning for her, without leaving her a note. She walked quickly through the house. There was no note in the kitchen, nor was there one propped against the living room telephone or in her room. Her uneasiness began to turn to panic.

Then she chided herself, told herself her father must have gone for a walk, perhaps for a drink with some military acquaintance who had dropped by unexpectedly. But even as these thoughts crossed her mind, she dismissed them; she knew he would have left a note of explanation. The man might be cantankerous, but he was thoughtful.

She opened the terrace doors and stepped outside. The breeze was becoming stronger, cooler, and there was the smell of a storm in the air. The two neighboring houses were dark, the owners being "snowbirds," northerners who used their houses in Key West to escape the snow of winter months. She was about to return inside when she noticed that the pool light was on; the silhouettes of the palms and ferns were outlined against the rectangular shape. Perhaps, she thought, the admiral had gone out to welcome the cooling breeze and had fallen asleep in a lounge chair.

"Admiral?"

The moon was full and moving behind lacy clouds. Dorothy had the eerie sensation of being watched, and she shuddered.

"Father," she called again. Then, "Daddy?" She hadn't called the admiral that since she was an adolescent.

Somewhere in the neighborhood, a dog barked, and then another. A car horn blared in the distance. A woman's laughter floated on the breeze, coming from nearby Duval Street. Then Dorothy heard the distinct sound of footsteps running on pavement.

Crossing the terrace, she hurried along the wooden walkway to the swimming pool, her heels clicking hollowly on the planks.

She found the admiral floating facedown in the pool, the shimmering light playing over his emaciated body. His swim trunks, bought when he had been a heavier man, had slipped down to reveal his shriveled buttocks. She gave a piercing scream, then managed to get control of herself and leaped into the pool. But even before she hooked her hands beneath her father's arm and started dragging him toward the pool step she knew he was dead.

She sat with his head cradled in her arms, and kissed his lifeless eyes as she rocked back and forth. "Daddy," she cried. "Oh, Daddy!"

AFTER THEY HAD ZIPPED the admiral's body into a plastic bag and carried it away, Dorothy went back into the house, scarcely aware of those milling about her: two policemen, Jonathan McKinney and another reporter from the local newspaper, Commander Stevenson and a captain who wore medical insignia, and a woman neighbor who had responded to her scream.

"I'm sorry, I'm so sorry," the woman kept repeating, as if she had known the admiral well; her voice was a droning irritant to Dorothy, like a buzzing mosquito that would not be discouraged.

Inside the house, Commander Stevenson took Dorothy's arm and directed her to the wing chair in the admiral's study. Echoing the woman, he said, "I'm sorry, Dorothy. The admiral was a good friend."

Her hands folded quietly in her lap, Dorothy stared at the group assembled in her father's study. Commander Stevenson had pulled up a chair and was sitting beside her; Jonathan McKinney was watching her from the far corner, his expression sympathetic; the neighbor had disappeared briefly and now returned with a tray of coffee and cookies. The atmosphere was social, as if she and the woman whose name she didn't even know were entertaining invited guests—and her father was dead, zipped up in a plastic body bag and carried away. He wouldn't have liked them here, she thought; he had jealously guarded his privacy. With her emotions in turmoil inside her, she willed herself to be calm, though she wasn't sure why that seemed so important.

For a moment she seemed to lose touch with reality, to drift outside herself. The people milling around in the admiral's study seemed to be characters in a television play, but with their movements and voices not properly synchronized. There was a ringing in her ears, and then the voices faded entirely while the lips of the policemen and the reporters continued to move soundlessly. There were tiny explosions of light in front of her eyes. I'm going to faint, she thought, clutching at the arms of the chair.

"She needs a sedative," Commander Stevenson said. "Captain?"

No, no sedative, she thought. Her eyes had closed, but she opened them again as strong hands gripped her shoulders and gently shook her.

The captain, who had arrived with Commander Stevenson, was hovering above her. She saw by the emblem on his sleeve that he was a doctor. He pressed two tablets into her hand. "Take these," he said. His voice was detached, and his blue-gray eyes lacked sensitivity. "Will someone get her a glass of water?"

While Commander Stevenson went to the wet bar beside the liquor cabinet for water, Dorothy stared up at the captain. She wondered vaguely if he was the navy doctor who had been caring for Alice Stevenson. He had a young face, unlined, but his eyes hinted at age beyond his years. She didn't know why, but she disliked him, even feared him. The expression of sympathy he affected seemed blatantly false.

When the commander returned with a glass of water, Dorothy put the pills under her tongue and pretended to swallow them, then spit them into her hand as she wiped water from her chin. No one noticed her stuff the pills between the cushion and the arm of the chair.

"It'll be a few minutes before they take effect," the captain told her, an encouraging smile on his thin lips.

Commander Stevenson moved behind the admiral's desk and sat down. He touched the edge of the blotter, absently fingering the paperweight Chad had given his grandfather. Dorothy thought he appeared to be taking possession of the admiral's things, as if by right. She refrained from voicing her objections.

Her head began to clear; the room and its occupants came back into perspective. Clutching the chair arms, she forced herself to her feet. Dizziness swept over her, but she quickly pushed it away.

"There, there, dear," the neighbor said. She came forward and tried to ease Dorothy back into the chair. "It's tragic, my dear. I'm so sorry. Just sit down, relax until the doctor's pills take effect and then—"

Dorothy pushed the woman's hands away and stared at her as if seeing her for the first time. The woman was in her late fifties, with hennaed hair and fleshy eyelids that dropped over colorless eyes. "Who are you?" Dorothy said dully.

"Just a friend, my dear," the woman answered. "I heard your scream and called the police. Such a horrible thing for you, finding your father like that. My late husband, God rest his soul, died in his—"

"Thank you for calling the police," Dorothy cut in, "but I'd appreciate it if you'd go now." Her voice was calm. She watched as the woman, confused by her dismissal, backed to the door. "Again, thank you," Dorothy told her.

The woman vanished out the door.

Dorothy spun to face the commander. "I'd also appreciate your getting up from my father's desk," she told him in the same even tone of voice.

Commander Stevenson rose, his face pale. He opened his mouth to speak, but evidently decided against it. He moved from behind the desk.

Jonathan McKinney, who had remained in the corner, recognized the anger veiled by Dorothy's forced composure. The lenses of his glasses magnified the hope that sparked behind his eyes.

"Perhaps you should sit down, Mrs. Bannen," the navy doctor said. "The medication I gave you is strong. You may need—"

"I'm not going to sit down, Captain," Dorothy said crisply. She moved to the desk chair the commander had vacated and sat. Pulling the chair up behind the desk, she fixed her attention on the two policemen. "I'm quite capable of answering your questions," she said. "My father had a bad heart and was recuperating from a recent stroke. No doubt the autopsy will confirm death by heart attack or stroke." Her gaze left the policemen and sought Jonathan. "Through recent experience I've learned that autopsies are not always accurate," she stated pointedly. "You requested an interview, Mr. McKinney. Do you work with notes? A tape recorder? I don't remember the method used with my former husband."

"A tape recorder," Jonathan replied spiritedly. He removed the small device from his pocket, switched it on and came forward to place it in the center of the desk.

Dorothy's gaze turned to the local reporter, a young man in his mid-twenties. To Jonathan she said, "I regret this can't be the exclusive interview, Mr. McKinney, but I think the time for exclusivity is past."

"Anything you say can be on the press wires in less than an hour," Jonathan told her. He moved back to the corner and stood watching expectantly.

"A human-interest story—I believe that's how you phrased it," Dorothy said. "The plight of a mother trying to unravel the mystery surrounding her son's death."

Jonathan nodded.

Dorothy turned to Commander Stevenson. "Mr. McKinney feels the Pentagon is too involved with infighting and power struggles to devote full attention to questions that have been raised concerning my son's death," she said.

"You told me you divided your time between Key West and
Washington, Commander. Have you ever been stationed at
the Pentagon?"

Commander Stevenson's jaw was firmly set, but his eyes
revealed nervousness. "No, I haven't had the honor," he
said tensely. "Mrs. Bannen, I don't feel this is the proper
time to grant an interview. You've had a severe shock. Even
though the admiral's condition made another attack inevitable, his death has been devastating for you. Perhaps if you
postponed this until tomorrow—"

"No!" Dorothy cried, emotion creeping into her voice for
the first time since she'd come inside. She saw the navy
doctor glance at his wristwatch and exchange a puzzled
glance with the commander. "I didn't take your medication, Captain," she told him. "So don't expect me to suddenly crumple into a tranquilized heap."

Commander Stevenson's defeated expression caused her
to laugh. "We're a stubborn family, Commander," she said.
"The late admiral, my late son and myself. Genetic, I suspect. Another thing we've had in common is an aversion to
drugs—because of my mother. She lived her last years in
great agony, incurably ill and relying on drugs to get her
from day to day. She developed an immunity to every drug
the doctors prescribed, but she continued to take them anyway. Her mind was eventually affected. You may have an
inkling of what it's like living with someone who doesn't
have full control of their mental faculties, because of your
wife, Commander. Can you imagine the effect it would have
on a *loving* husband and daughter? On a small boy?"

Commander Stevenson averted his gaze and said nothing.

"The admiral balked at taking the medication prescribed
for him after his stroke," Dorothy continued. "And I seldom even take an aspirin. As for Chad, even as a small boy
it was a major struggle to get him to take his medicine when
he was ill." Her eyes brimmed with tears as she recalled her

son suffering typical childhood illnesses. "I used to slip medicine into his orange juice and his cereal until he got wise to me. I remember when he had measles and—"

"Mrs. Bannen, I really feel this can wait until tomorrow," the commander said, looking to the others for confirmation. "These gentlemen, myself included, sympathize with your grief, but nothing can be gained while you're so distraught." He picked up his hat where he'd left it on the liquor cabinet and tucked it under his arm, causing Dorothy to realize for the first time that he'd changed from his civilian clothes into his uniform in the short time after he had driven her home from the restaurant.

"If you want to leave, Commander, go," McKinney said firmly. "I, for one, would like to hear what Mrs. Bannen has to say." Ignoring the commander's angry glare, Jonathan turned to Dorothy. "Is this aversion of Chad's to medication the reason why you had difficulty believing your son died of a drug overdose, as reported by the navy?" he asked.

"That's part of it," Dorothy replied. "But then the admiral swore he was aware Chad had been taking drugs. I never knew my father to lie unless it was for a very important reason. He seemed so determined for me to accept the fact that Chad used drugs that I pretended to believe it. I knew he would eventually tell me why he was lying, why he supported the navy's explanation of Chad's death when he knew it was untrue."

"Now we'll never know if the admiral was actually lying," Commander Stevenson said with thinly veiled satisfaction. "But I strongly doubt it. The admiral was an honorable man. Honorable men do not lie."

"Chad's father has letters from our son that substantiate his rejection of drugs, even though most of his peers indulged," Dorothy said.

"What son would admit drug addiction to his father?" the commander demanded.

The captain leaned forward in his chair. "Especially a father who gained notoriety by exposing—" A warning glance from the commander silenced the captain.

Jonathan spoke up quickly. "It seems you're familiar with Commander Bannen's exposure of illegal military drug experiments, Captain."

Reluctantly the captain said, "Yes, of course. It's common knowledge."

Jonathan smiled. "It was some time ago, Captain. You're a young man for such memories. From your appearance I'd say you were in your late teens when the Commander broke the scandal. Even though it was common knowledge then, why would you so easily recall the incident and relate it to Commander Bannen and to a son who allegedly died of a drug overdose?" Jonathan walked to the desk, picked up the tape recorder and extended it toward the captain. "Well, Captain?" he prompted when the officer hesitated.

The captain's thin lips drew even tighter. "I suppose someone mentioned it recently," he murmured evasively.

"Who might that have been, Captain?" Jonathan prodded.

The captain turned away from the recorder. "I have nothing more to say."

"Then shall we let Mrs. Bannen continue?" Jonathan returned the tape recorder to the middle of the desk.

"What I'd like to stress," Dorothy said, "is that although I was convinced my son didn't die of a drug overdose, I wasn't persuaded that there was a conspiracy involved, even when his vital organs were not returned with his body. Perhaps a navy doctor made a mistake during his autopsy. Perhaps my son's organs were misplaced. Perhaps the report on Chad had been mislabeled and belonged to another sailor. Perhaps some other parents were spared the additional agony of learning their son died of a drug overdose. Perhaps, perhaps, perhaps! So many possibilities occurred to me, tortured me!" She knew her control of her

emotions was slipping, was aware that the others could see
her hands trembling. She placed her hands in her lap with
her fingers laced together and took a few deep breaths in an
effort to calm herself.

After a moment she said, "I no longer have any doubts
about my son's death. And I have very few about my father's. As I said, the admiral's autopsy will undoubtedly
show he died of a heart attack or stroke. However, as I did
with Chad, I want an independent autopsy performed on my
father, in Washington, and by doctors of my own choos-
ing. I particularly want an identification of any drugs present in his body at the time of death."

"What are you saying?" Commander Stevenson shouted.
"Admiral Burke was a respected officer in the United States
Navy! Are you going to turn his death into a public specta-
cle? There's no reason for this. I absolutely forbid it!"

"There's nothing you can do about it, Commander,"
Jonathan said.

Dorothy's eyes were blazing when she turned them on
Commander Stevenson. "The admiral had a particular
loathing for swimming pools," she said. "He had ours installed for Chad and me. He never swam in it—never! The
fact that he was found dead in the pool leaves no doubt in
my mind that he was murdered!"

The two policemen had stood quietly by, listening to all
that was being said, though they obviously didn't understand much of it. At the word "murdered" they suddenly
became alert and began to look at everyone present with renewed interest.

Before they could interrupt, however, Dorothy said, "I
know the admiral was involved in something secret within
the military, Commander." She remembered her promise to
the admiral not to mention his meeting with Commander
Stevenson, but with the admiral dead, she believed she was
released from the promise. "I overheard enough of your
meeting with my father to know you're involved in the same

project, Commander. Could there be a connection between the project and the admiral's death?''

"Definitely not," Commander Stevenson said. He dropped into the wing chair as if his legs were suddenly too weak to support him.

"And Admiral Addison?" Dorothy asked. "Why would my father suddenly turn on a fellow officer who had been a friend most of his life?''

Commander Stevenson stared at her without answering. There was anger in his eyes, anger mingled with fear.

"I intend to have the answers!" Dorothy said firmly. "About my father's death, and about my son's!" As her hands came back to the desktop they brushed against the newspaper that had been left on the blotter. She suddenly recalled the file folder she had seen protruding from beneath the paper. She lifted the paper, then fluttered its pages. She lifted her gaze to meet Jonathan's. "It's gone," she said. "There was a file folder here earlier. I saw it before I found the admiral."

Commander Stevenson pushed himself out of the chair. "Now there's a missing file folder," he said sarcastically. "Gentlemen, Mrs. Bannen has obviously been more affected by her experience tonight than was first evident. Conspiracies, murder, secret military involvement by a retired admiral, stolen file folders! I suggest we all forget what we've heard here tonight." He looked at Dorothy, a pitying expression on his face. "After a good night's sleep I'm convinced you'll forget these insane accusations. Please understand, we all sympathize with your loss. First your son, followed so closely by your father. It's enough to affect the strongest of women." He turned from Dorothy to the two policemen and the local reporter. "It would be inhumane to question Mrs. Bannen further tonight," he said. He seemed to be deliberately avoiding eye contact with Jonathan McKinney. "Shall we say good-night and—"

The commander's words were cut off by the ringing of the telephone.

Jonathan stepped forward and answered. After handing the receiver to the commander, he reached across the desk and snapped off the tape recorder. He looked steadily at Dorothy, trying to convey his thoughts without words. *We don't need them. It doesn't matter if they believe you.*

But Dorothy could only think that she had lost, and the commander had won. She knew that if she pressed the issue she would only make herself less believable; she could tell by the policemen's expressions that they considered her an unstable woman driven to the edge of sanity by grief. Even the local reporter was obviously giving no credence to what she had said.

Commander Stevenson hung up the phone. "It appears to be a night of tragedy," he said quietly. "I must go, Mrs. Bannen, gentlemen. My wife's had an accident."

"Alice," Dorothy murmured as the commander and the captain hurried from the room.

The policemen and the reporter left shortly afterward with assurances that they would contact her in the morning. After they had gone, Jonathan said, "We don't need the local police or press, Mrs. Bannen. With your permission, I'll write a story as explosive as my editor will allow. I'll fill it with implications that can't be ignored." He slipped the tape recorder back into his pocket. "Now I want you to pack a bag quickly."

Dorothy shook herself from her thoughts. "I don't understand. Why?"

"We're leaving Key West immediately," Jonathan told her. "I have no wish for either of us to end up like the admiral or your son or any other victims of Delta. We'll drive to Miami tonight and take the first morning flight to Washington."

"But we can't leave now!" Dorothy cried. "The admiral was a fanatic about writing things down. We must go through his papers. There might be some proof, some explanation of—"

"Like the file folder you swore was on his desk?" Jonathan asked pointedly. "We have to leave immediately. I'm not letting you out of my sight for the next few days. If anything happened to you, I wouldn't want to face Quinn Bannen. That prospect is almost as frightening as Delta itself!"

37

Washington, D.C.

"THE SCHEDULE'S NOW FIRM," the controller said quietly into the telephone. "The president capitulated because the First Lady wishes to attend a summer auction at Parke-Bernet. You have seven days, Addison."

"Yes, sir. Seven days until D day," Admiral Addison repeated.

"Will you be ready?"

"We'll be ready, sir."

"Goodbye, then. And good luck," the controller said, and broke the connection.

PART THREE

38

EVEN BEFORE CHIEF LOOMIS spoke into the telephone he knew the caller was Admiral Addison by the sound of the officer's labored breathing.

"Have you seen the morning papers, Chief?" the admiral shouted.

Chief Loomis held the receiver slightly away from his ear. He had been awakened from a sound sleep, and the admiral's loud voice made his head ring. "No, sir. It's 5:00 a.m. in California. I won't get my paper for another half hour. What is it, sir?"

"The Bannens again!" Admiral Addison barked. "This time it's the wife—Admiral Burke's daughter, my goddaughter. She's given an interview to that goddamned investigative reporter, McKinney, and it's made the front page here in Washington. The bitch is now claiming conspiracy in both her son's death and the admiral's. With only seven days left, we can't afford this! What about Commander Bannen? Is he still under surveillance?"

"Yes, sir," the chief answered. "The commander's in a motel less than a mile from the base."

"Did you discover why he made another trip to San Diego?"

The chief hesitated before saying, "He visited someone in the hospital."

"Someone? Who?"

"We don't have that information yet, sir."

"I don't like this, Chief! I don't like it one fucking bit! Out of the six divisions of Delta we were chosen for this operation. Do you realize the ass-licking I had to do to get this assignment? Now it all threatens to blow up in our faces because of some goddamned sailor who decides to play amateur detective."

Chief Loomis sat up in bed, reached for a cigarette and lit it. He had left the air conditioner running all night, and the bedroom was cold, but still he was perspiring. He didn't know what to say to the admiral except "Yes, sir."

"Dorothy Bannen can be dealt with. So can McKinney," Admiral Addison said. "The question is, how much damage have they already done? If they're disposed of, will their deaths delay or confuse the investigation? Absolutely nothing can be allowed to happen in the next seven days that will call attention to us. Nothing! That includes anything from that bastard Quinn Bannen. If he so much as looks like he's going to the press, take him out. Is that understood?"

"Yes, sir," Chief Loomis said with satisfaction.

"Get the operative Everett back to me on a morning flight," the admiral continued. "He has to be in New York in six days anyway. I can use him here along with my local operatives."

"Yes, sir."

"What about Marshisky?"

"Captain Musolf is keeping him under wraps, sir. We'll dry him out twenty-four hours before D day."

"His final day. And the president's," Admiral Addison said with a hollow laugh. "Keep in touch, Chief."

After the line went dead, Chief Loomis climbed out of bed and opened the bottom drawer of his bureau. He moved a pile of uniform shirts from the drawer to the bed and stared down at the collection of weapons he had accumulated over his years in the military.

Take him out, take him out! kept repeating itself inside his skull. *If he so much as looks like he's going to the press* was forgotten.

ALEX HAD BEEN SUMMONED to Chief Loomis's office at 7:00 a.m. and then left cooling his heels in the outer room. Although the door between the rooms was closed, he could hear the muffled voice of the chief as he spoke on the telephone. The door had a semiopaque glass panel, so he dared not approach to listen as he had in Captain Musolf's office. He was forced to content himself with grasping a single word or phrase here and there:

"...New York..." he heard distinctly. "...the thirteenth, right... What?... Parke-Bernet auction...Everett and Sloane are backups.... No...Marshisky's the lead...."

The name Marshisky was strangely familiar, but Alex couldn't remember where he had heard it.

Then the chief lowered his voice, and Alex heard nothing above a muffled droning.

He looked around the outer office. It was austere even by navy standards. No pictures on the walls, nothing personal on the tables, no plants, no magazines. Just two bare metal tables and two straight-backed chairs with torn Naugahyde cushions, one of which he was sitting on. There had once been lettering on the glass panel of the dividing door, but that had been scraped away, leaving an unreadable imprint on the frosted glass. Alex decided the best word to describe the chief's office was *temporary*. He wondered what Chief Loomis's station had been prior to Moffett, for what purpose he had been transferred in, and with what future destination, since it didn't look as if he expected to remain there for long. The computers might be able to answer the first of these questions. He made a mental note to try it at his earliest opportunity.

After his interview with Captain Musolf at Alameda the day before, Alex had been told to report back to the admi-

ral's staff and await instruction. He had felt he was being
watched, at the office and at his apartment. Yesterday afternoon he had caught Chief Hargrave watching him
through the open door of the computer room. The chief had
had a strange expression on his face, and it struck Alex that
Chief Hargrave might be a member of Delta. The slow-
talking Southern chief, he had reasoned, would be an important asset to any organization, because with the man
came the knowledge buried inside the computers; no information was immune to computer probing if the operator
was supplied the proper access codes. Indeed, Alex had begun to look at everyone around him with suspicion, wondering if they had been considered or approached, or were
already members of the secret organization he now knew as
Delta.

Finally, an hour after he had arrived at Chief Loomis's
office, Alex was summoned into the inner room.

Motioning Alex into a chair, the chief paced back and
forth across the narrow room, his hands clasped behind his
back and his great bulldoglike neck lowered over his barrel
chest.

Alex watched him, hoping he was managing to conceal his
nervousness.

"The navy's too goddamned soft nowadays!" the chief
suddenly said, his voice sounding explosive because it broke
the silence unexpectedly. "Do you agree, Mayfield?"

"Discipline could be stricter, Chief," Alex answered.

"Everything could be stricter, but, yes, discipline in particular is lax. And it's not just the navy. It's all branches.
They're trying to make the military more appealing to the
sand crabs. They no longer want us to take the little boys in
and make men of them. That's become obsolete. Now we
have to see that the enlisted men are kept happy. If they're
not happy, they don't reenlist when their first enlistment's
up, and that costs the government money. It costs a hell of
a lot to train one sailor. If he breezes through a single en-

listment and then goes back to civilian life, the investment goes down the shitter. Get enough men who refuse to reenlist and you've cut away a sizable chunk of the military budget. That's what it all boils down to nowadays, budgets and statistics."

The chief suddenly stopped pacing and stood at the window, staring down at the tarmac with his back to the room and Alex. "Getting a decent military budget is half the battle. The public screams 'cut tax,' Congress goes at it with a machete, and the first thing to be chopped is the military budget. They cut the fucking guts right out of it, the stupid assholes! Why don't they go after the bureaucratic agencies that really waste tax dollars? Welfare, food stamps, housing, the whole goddamned mishmash? Every male from seventeen to thirty-five who's on the welfare rolls should be put into the military. Blacks, Chicanos, even the goddamned boat people and Cubans. Then add their relief checks to the military budget. That'd be a start. If we don't have the tax dollars, we can't defend our country." The chief glanced at Alex over his shoulder, his bushy eyebrows raised. "Do you agree, Mayfield?"

"It makes sense, chief," Alex said stiffly.

"When there's another war—I said when, not if—the voters and the Congress will understand the importance of a powerful peacetime military, but by then it'll be too late." Again the piercing eyes beneath their bushy brows were turned on Alex.

Alex nodded in agreement. He wondered if he'd been summoned to the chief's office merely to listen to him expound on the injustices Congress committed against the new military.

"We now have the most hawkish administration we've had in decades," the chief continued. "The president's fighting for us, demanding a higher defense budget, but the goddamned pussies in Congress keep beating him down. It doesn't matter to them that we're second in the armaments race. They don't believe the threat of Communism is actually going to reach us here at home. The president has good intentions, but they've cut off his balls." Turning from the window, the chief moved back to his desk and sat down. "There are too many doves in Congress. They have too much control. But there are those of us who are fighting the imbalance. We can't fight openly or the pricks would have us out of uniform—dishonor us, even though we're the backbone of the country."

Alex noted that the chief's eyes had become glazed over as he spoke. Almost like a madman's, he thought. He shifted uncomfortably in his chair, still wondering why he had been summoned.

A shudder suddenly passed through the chief. His eyes focused. "How did your interview with Captain Musolf go, Mayfield?"

"Fine, Chief," Alex said, though he was far from certain. "The captain just asked me questions, gave me an inkblot test, that sort of thing."

"More horseshit!" the chief exploded. "We have to put up with horseshit even in our own ranks!" Then more calmly, he went on, "You judge a man by what's in his eyes, his handshake, maybe a gut feeling. Not by what he sees in a bunch of goddamned inkblots. Who cares what a man sees in inkblots so long as he does his duty? I think you're a man who'd do his duty to his country, Mayfield."

Because he knew an answer was expected, Alex said, "My duty to my country is important to me, Chief."

"Of course," the chief said, his lips forming a smile that revealed his nicotine-stained teeth. "Did you see all those John Wayne movies when you were a kid, Mayfield?"

Alex struggled to hold back laughter at the expression on the chief's face. "His war movies, Chief?"

"Yes, his war movies. Do you know young people laugh at those movies now? Call them propaganda films? The other night I was watching one of those movies in the rec room. When the hero, John Wayne, died for his country, the fucking sailors howled with laughter. Do you see anything funny in dying for your country, Mayfield?''

"No, Chief. Some of those movies were badly made by today's standards, but—"

"Would *you* die for your country, Mayfield?"

It seemed to Alex that Chief Loomis was egging him on, trying to trap him with his simplistic prattle into revealing himself as unworthy for inclusion in Delta. As for laughing at John Wayne movies, sometimes the dialogue made Alex laugh, but death and dying were not laughing matters. As for sacrificing himself for his country, he could say sincerely, "Yes, Chief." To make his answer sound more thoughtful, he added, "I'd give my life for a cause I believed in, and I believe in my country."

"Would you do something slightly illegal for your country?"

"Like what, Chief?"

"I've been told you're a stickler for regulations," the chief told him. "Would you bend regulations if you knew it would help your country?"

"I suppose I would, Chief. What are you asking me to do?"

Chief Loomis laughed. "I like that in you, Mayfield. You get right to the point." Opening his desk drawer, the chief removed several sheets of paper and placed them on his desk.

Alex recognized them as rough drafts of leave papers, travel orders and vouchers for disbursements.

"Our group," Chief Loomis said with an emphasis on *our*, "has to move some men around very discreetly within the next few days. Five from Moffett to New York over a period of six days. But that's not the problem I need your help with. There's a certain officer I need to get out day after tomorrow. He's a commander, but the captain he's assigned to is a real prick. He doesn't have any use for the commander, so the commander is certain he won't sign his leave papers." The chief's eyes narrowed to mere slits and he appeared reluctant to continue.

"So you want to know the procedure to get the leave papers through over the captain's head?" Alex asked. "A way of ensuring the commander won't be denied leave?"

"I thought perhaps if the admiral signed the leave papers himself..."

Alex was used to officers asking him to have the admiral sign inconsequential papers. It was common knowledge that sometimes the admiral signed papers his trusted yeoman put before him without reading them. Alex had always refused such requests, regardless of the remuneration promised. "I'm afraid the admiral wouldn't sign such papers," he told the chief. "Besides, when he saw his signature overriding the captain's he would be suspicious." He read the disappointment on the chief's face. "However, there is a way, Chief," he went on. "Have someone call in and say they're from the Red Cross, then put someone on the line who says they're the commander's wife or mother and that there's an emergency in the family. Regardless of how the captain feels about the commander, he won't be able to deny him emergency leave. If he does, the admiral might challenge his refusal and override the objection."

"Can you arrange the whole thing, Mayfield?"

Not "Will you?" but "Can you?"

Alex's curiosity was sparked. What commander at Moffett Field was important enough for Delta to be fighting the system to get him to New York by the day after tomorrow? And for what purpose? "Just give me the particulars," he said. He watched as the chief removed one of the rough drafts. When it was handed to him, he took it without glancing at the name, folded it and stuffed it into the waistband of his trousers. "I'll do it this afternoon," he said.

Chief Loomis smiled with satisfaction. "You're going to be invaluable to—to us," he said. "Welcome aboard, Mayfield."

"Thank you, Chief."

But as Alex left Chief Loomis's office he felt more threatened than welcomed by Delta.

Back at his own desk, he examined the rough draft. The commander's name was Sontag, Samuel T., and he was with Intelligence. Alex entered Commander Sontag on his list of officers connected with Delta.

Within an hour the first call came in, from a man who said he was with the Red Cross in the Swan Lake area of New York State. Commander Sontag's father had died suddenly of a coronary, and the commander was needed by the surviving members of the family. The personnel man who worked at the desk across from Alex's took the message. Alex heard him repeating some of the information as he jotted it down on a notepad.

"Damn it!" the PN said when he hung up. "As if I don't have enough to do!"

"Emergency leave papers?" Alex asked casually.

The PN nodded, his brow furrowed with anger. "And me with this damned report to get out before 1700."

"My work load's light today," Alex said. "Do you want me to handle it for you?"

PN2 Krebs, the personnel man's supervisor, looked up from his desk and laughed. "Mayfield likes to nose into everything," he said. "Let him do your work and finish your report."

Alex took the notepad and examined the name as if he hadn't seen it before. Because he had the chief's rough draft, there was no need for him to call the personnel locator, but he did anyway, in case either of the personnel men was listening. He identified himself as the admiral's yeoman and requested an extension for Commander Samuel Sontag. Although it was a civilian who answered the telephone and took the request, it was Alex's acquaintance, Robinson, who came back on the line.

Robinson gave him the requested extension for Commander Sontag, then added, "You had a personal call, Mayfield. Your Uncle Dester called, said he was in town and left a number where you can reach him. I told him to call your office, but he didn't have any more coins."

Alex jotted down the number, deciding he would wait until he could get to a pay phone before calling Quinn Bannen. In the meantime he completed the necessary forms to send Commander Sontag on emergency leave. Later he went personally to the intelligence building to inform the commander of the death of his father and to present him with his leave papers.

Commander Sontag was in his late forties, his face pinched, his features birdlike. His eyes were dark and small and set deeply into his skull. As Alex suspected, he had seen the commander before, at Admiral Addison's meeting in the conference room.

"Good to see you again, Petty Officer Mayfield," the commander said, indicating he remembered the yeoman from the meeting.

The commander was no actor. His expression of grief over the death of his father left much to be desired. He murmured, "Oh, no," without any discernible emotion and eagerly took the emergency leave papers from Alex's hand before they were offered.

The captain, who according to Chief Loomis had no use for the commander, had been watching through his open door, and had heard most of the conversation. Coming from behind his desk, he stepped into the inner office and confronted the commander. He appeared about to take the papers for examination; then, apparently changing his mind, he said, "Sorry about your father, Commander. Go on and make your arrangements."

Commander Sontag made a hasty exit, clutching his leave papers in a tight grip.

"He's a fucking flake," the captain said as he went back into his office. "It stretches the imagination to think he even had a father."

39

Mountain View, California

QUINN LAID THE NEWSPAPER on the bed and continued to stare at the dark-lettered heading: Mother Blames Conspiracy in Son and Father's Deaths. There was no byline, but the style was unquestionably Jonathan McKinney's. The reporter had raised suspicion without making any direct accusations; he appealed to the human-interest aspect by detailing a woman's anguish at losing both her son and father, then capped the story with the complications Dorothy had met in her attempt to discover the truth. No direct mention was made of the navy, the Pentagon or the Defense Department.

Quinn reached for the telephone and dialed Admiral Burke's number in Washington. The maid answered and quickly called Dorothy.

"Quinn, we were trying to locate you," Dorothy said. "Where are you?"

"In California. I'm sorry about the admiral. We had our differences, but I'm genuinely sorry."

"Thank you for that, Quinn," Dorothy said quietly.

"According to Jonathan's article, you think the admiral was murdered?"

"I'm certain of it," Dorothy said with conviction. She explained the circumstances surrounding her father's death, then concluded by relating the coversation she had overheard between the admiral and Commander Stevenson. "Of course, the admiral admitted nothing to me," she concluded, "except that he was working as a consultant for some branch of the military. Quinn, I'm certain that's not true. The navy wouldn't use him as a consultant since his stroke. It was common knowledge that his condition was deteriorating."

"You mention his attack on Admiral Addison," Quinn said. "Think carefully. Is there anything he said in reference to Addison you haven't told me?"

"No. Only that he was demanding a meeting of some committee, a meeting where he intended to bring Admiral Addison up on some kind of charges. I don't understand what could have happened between them. They were so close. Admiral Addison is even my godfather. He treated Chad like a grandson. I always suspected my father was jealous of Chad and Admiral Addison when he thought they were getting too close." Her voice broke, evidence to Quinn that she was still under a great deal of strain and had not come to terms with her father's death—or Chad's. "What does it all mean, Quinn? What is this organization Jonathan mentioned to me? Delta?"

"I can't give you details," Quinn said. "Especially not over the phone. Besides, Jonathan probably knows more than I. I think Jonathan made a mistake in writing that article. I'm afraid he's put you in extreme danger. Are you alone in the house?"

"Except for Mati," Dorothy said. "Quinn, I'm perfectly safe here. The admiral had the house wired with an elaborate alarm system. If anyone so much as rattles a window, the alarm goes off here and at the security company."

"I'd still feel better if you were safely away from the house," Quinn insisted.

"I told you, I'm safe," she said stubbornly. "Besides, Jonathan is coming by in the evening and plans to stay with me until bedtime. His attentiveness makes me feel guilty for the opinion I once had of him. I'm going through the admiral's private papers. You know how meticulous he was, how fanatical he was about keeping records of everything.

The basement and attic are filled with his logs and journals. If he was involved with a secret organization called Delta, I intend to find the evidence.''

"I wish I were with you," Quinn said. "To help you go through the admiral's papers, I mean."

Dorothy took a quick gulp of breath, then said, "I wish you were with me, too, Quinn. I made a mistake divorcing you. I knew it right after you were served with the papers, but then my pride wouldn't let me back down and confess the truth. I love you, Quinn. I always have, I always will."

"Dorothy, you mustn't—"

"Don't stop me now," she said. "It's too difficult as it is. If I don't say it now, I never will. What's even more painful, Quinn, is that I not only destroyed our lives, but I put Chad through an emotional hell. I can see that now. It's no wonder he turned against me in the last few years. Do you think our son hated me, Quinn?"

"No, Dorothy. I'm certain Chad didn't hate you."

"But I'll never know for certain, will I?" she said quietly. "I'll never know if he died resenting me because—" She began to weep.

Quinn steadied himself. "Dorothy, I'd like to be there to comfort you," he said, "but you realize I can't be."

"I've always had men around to comfort me," she said, composing herself. "The admiral, you, even Chad. Especially, the admiral, in spite of his stiff, unemotional ways. I never realized how much strength I drew from him until the night I watched them zipping his body into a plastic bag. Oh, God, Quinn! I feel so lost, so insignificant."

"Stop dwelling on what you've lost, Dorothy," Quinn told her firmly but sympathetically. "You have strength of your own, now, when you need it. Don't let your grief get the best of you. Don't give in to it until we've accomplished what we must."

"You're right, of course. I shouldn't. I won't. It's just so easy to fall into a pattern that's..." She didn't complete the thought, but went on to say, "Jonathan's told me a little about Delta. It's hard to believe such an organization could have existed twenty, thirty years ago, let alone today. Then, for my father to be connected in any way...that's why I'm going through his papers, looking for the name Delta written anywhere in his notes. I have to know, if only for my own peace of mind."

"Going through his papers is certainly a good idea," Quinn told her. Even if she found nothing connecting the admiral to Delta, he hoped the search would keep her mind off her grief. "You might also make a list of the admiral's close friends and officers who met with him often just prior to his stroke. Try to recall any conversation that may not have made sense to you then but would now in reference to Delta."

"Yes, I'll try," she assured him. "My father was an honorable man, Quinn. That he could be a party to anything illegal, especially anything attached to the navy, is almost inconceivable. His life was lived by the book. He would have died rather than dishonor the navy or his country. He was so—"

A knock on Quinn's door forced him to interrupt. "Hold on, Dorothy. There's someone at the door."

He crossed quickly to the door and admitted Alex. "I'm on the phone," he told the yeoman, and motioned to the bottle of vodka and a bucket of ice. "Help yourself."

"Thank you, Commander. I don't drink." Alex took a chair as far away from the telephone as the room permitted.

"I'm sorry, I forgot. No orange juice." Quinn picked up the receiver. "Dorothy, did you say Jonathan is going to visit you tonight?"

"Yes, but later," she answered. "He's going to Central Records first."

"At night?"

"His girlfriend, Ginny, is going to get him inside," Dorothy said. "Jonathan said they were going to check out some computer data on names you gave him. Jonathan's incredible, Quinn. He's breathing and sleeping nothing but Delta. Ginny says he's demented."

"Jonathan's eagerness sometimes makes him careless," Quinn said. "That worries me, because of you, as well as Jonathan. When he arrives will you ask him to call me?"

"Yes, Quinn. Do you have to hang up now?"

"I'm afraid so, but I'll talk to you again when Jonathan calls." Quinn hesitated, then said, "Dorothy, do you have a gun in the house?"

"A military house without a gun?" Dorothy said with a weak laugh. "The admiral has a cabinet full of guns in his study. I also slipped the revolver from his desk in Key West into my suitcase before we left."

Since he couldn't remember, Quinn asked, "And you know how to use it?"

"Of course I know how to use it. The admiral taught me when we had the ranch in Maryland. Even you took me for target practice once, remember? I hit the bull's-eye six times running, and you said to remind you never to get me angry at you. I ... Oh, Quinn, why is it that for the past twenty-four hours things have kept on coming back to me, past memories, incidents that happened when I was no more than a child, memories of you and of Chad? Things that happened before my life turned into a nightmare? Is that what they mean when they say a drowning person's entire life passes before their eyes in the moments before unconsciousness? I'm frightened, Quinn. If only I could be with you."

"You must call forth all that training as a military daughter and wife, Dorothy. When this is over we'll get the pieces of our lives back together."

"Is that a promise?"

"It's a promise." In a lowered voice, he said, "I love you, Dorothy. Goodbye, darling."

"Say it again, Quinn, please."

"I love you," he whispered, and broke the connection.

Alex was looking uncomfortable. "If I'd known, Commander, I could have waited outside."

"It's all right," Quinn assured him. He went to the bureau and poured himself a stiff vodka without ice. "You said on the phone you had a meeting with Chief Loomis."

Alex told him about the arrangements he had made to get a commander to New York, arrangements made outside normal channels and at the chief's request. "Five people are to be routed to New York within the next few days," he said. "The commander didn't impress me as the sort of man who'd be an asset to an organization like Delta. His captain even referred to him as a flake."

"What's his classification?" Quinn asked.

"Intelligence."

"And his name?"

"Commander Sontag."

Quinn's eyebrows shot up. "Samuel Sontag?"

"Yes, Commander. You know him?"

Quinn nodded gravely. "If Sam Sontag is known as a flake, it's because he's playing the role for some ulterior motive. Sontag has a mind like a computer. He's a natural-born strategist, one of the best. He has an IQ above 160, and a diseased mind to go with it. I'm not surprised Sontag's part of Delta." Quinn took a healthy swallow of vodka and felt it burn its way down his throat. "Sontag was involved in illegal drug experiments several years ago. You're probably too young to remember the scandal, but I—"

"I know about the drug experiments, Commander," Alex cut in. "I also knew you were acquainted with Commander Sontag. I ran a computer check on both you and Sontag this afternoon. Commander Sontag was busted from captain because of his involvement in the scandal."

"It was a slap on the wrist," Quinn said angrily. Then his anger faded, and he smiled. "You're thorough, Alex. I like that. What else did your computer check turn up?"

"Very little on you, Commander, because you're retired. I hope it doesn't offend you that I ran the check, but it...well, it occurred to me that maybe you, yourself, were—"

"A member of Delta?" Quinn finished. "I assure you, Alex, I am not now nor have I ever been a member of any secret organization."

"I believe you, Commander. But as you said, I'm thorough." The yeoman took a notepad from his pocket and flipped open the cover. "I've made notes of everything I've learned since our last meeting. I had a session with Captain Musolf in Alameda. That was interesting." He related the conversation with the sailor the captain had referred to as his "young assassin." He read aloud the hasty notes he had made after leaving the captain's office: " 'Kill him!' Who? Within two weeks. Seventy-five operatives. Sailor's name, Marshisky." Alex's expression suddenly became thoughtful. He thumbed through the sheets of the notepad until he came to his meeting with Chief Loomis. "I knew I'd heard that name before," he said.

"What name?" Quinn pressed.

"Marshisky, the sailor Captain Musolf was talking to," Alex said. "Later I overheard Chief Loomis mention it on the phone when I was waiting in his outer office." He glanced back at his notepad and read, "New York, Parke-Bernet auction, Everett, Sloane and Marshisky. Those were the names I heard the chief use. Also the thirteenth. He said there would be five men needing travel orders from Moffett to New York and—" Alex stopped speaking when he saw the expression on Quinn's face. "What is it, Commander?"

"You said Everett. Would that be Raymond Everett?"

"I don't know, Commander. The chief just used the name Everett. Who's Raymond Everett?"

"An operative who tried to kill his wife," Quinn answered. "Who possibly murdered my son and his fiancée." He glanced down at the notes on Alex's pad, his gaze riveted to the name Everett.

"Commander?"

Quinn straightened, tore his eyes from the notepad and moved back to the bureau. He started to reach for the vodka bottle, then slammed his fist down on the top of the bureau. "We've got to find out what those bastards are up to! One thing for sure, if Everett's going to be in New York on the thirteenth, so am I!"

40

Mountain View, California

CHIEF LOOMIS BACKED his car into a parking space at the far end of the motel parking lot and turned off the engine. The car windows were down, and he could smell rain in the air. The weatherman had predicted another summer storm for that night; for once the bastard was going to be correct. The chief shifted his position and settled in for a long wait.

The motel was busy. As he had turned into the parking lot the No Vacancy sign had flashed on above the office door. The building was a two-story structure. Quinn Bannen's room was on the second floor—Room 220, according to Gentry, who had followed Bannen from the airport to the motel. The chief bent his head and peered through the windshield. He had a perfect view of room 220. The lights were on, and the shadow of a man occasionally moved behind the drawn draperies.

Before replacing Gentry, Chief Loomis had called the motel and requested Commander Bannen's room number just to verify that he was registered. He had been told he wasn't registered, so he knew the commander was using an assumed name. That meant Bannen had learned enough to become cautious; caution made him an even more dangerous threat. The commander obviously had contacts in the area, possibly even on the base, and the chief was determined to learn their identities. Of the names he had extracted from the son's letters, only Mae Aames might prove a liability—he had no idea what Chad Bannen had told her—but Corpsman Aames was listed as AWOL. Chad had also mentioned Everett and the chief in his letters. The chief wondered why the commander hadn't yet contacted him. Very strange.

The chief believed Quinn Bannen should have been taken out the moment problems had come up. As soon as it had been learned that the wife had ordered a private autopsy for her son, Delta should have been pressed into action to eliminate any possibility of questions arising from the Bannen boy's bungled death. There had been too many loose ends, too many mistakes. The operatives were to blame, of course; they were young, not well enough trained, most of them bloodthirsty young bastards without the capacity to think beyond their assignments. If he had been allowed to train them in the old tradition, there would have been no mistakes and Delta wouldn't now be in danger of exposure.

Addison hadn't been too clever, either, ordering the elimination of his old buddy Admiral Burke without first verifying the details of the man's life-style. A heart attack in the swimming pool when the old bastard never swam— careless, very careless. It wasn't surprising that the daughter had gone to the press. No doubt the bitch's interview would attract the attention of the Pentagon. Hell, the whole project was in jeopardy. If D day had been planned any farther into the future it would have had to be scrapped. Unless the current schedule was changed, they just might be able to hold Bannen, the press and even a Pentagon investigation at bay—silence Bannen, appease the press, embroil the Pentagon in red tape. After D day everyone would be too involved to care about an illegal secret organization called Delta. When the truth was eventually known, the members of Delta might be touted as heroes. To the chief, that was what they were—heroes. But failure, exposure, that would cost them their careers, perhaps even their lives. Commander Bannen, along with everyone he had managed to elicit help from, had to be stopped. And immediately. Why had Addison put a restriction on his order? *If he so much as looks like he's going to the press, take him out!* Well, that order was ambiguous enough. Chief Loomis imagined himself saying to Addison, "Yes, sir, it was my opinion he was going to the press."

The chief lit a cigarette, cupping the match in his hands to hide the flame. He had also brought a bottle of the best bourbon so that his vigil wouldn't be totally unpleasant. He uncapped the bourbon and took a healthy swallow. The bottle was still at his lips when he saw the door to the commander's room open. He snapped the lid back on the bottle and huddled down in the seat for a better view of the second-floor balcony. He had expected the commander to emerge, but despite his failing eyesight he knew that the figure that suddenly appeared was not the commander. The man was shorter, younger. The chief leaned forward, squinting, but the lights in the room were creating a silhouette of the man and blurring his features. The commander appeared in the open doorway. The two men spoke briefly and shook hands; then the commander stepped back into the room and closed the door. The younger man moved along the railing to the stairwell and started to descend.

Chief Loomis quietly opened the door of his car and climbed out. If the young man moved off in the opposite direction, he would never learn his identity. The lights in the parking lot were dim. He would have to get within a few feet of the man to see him clearly. Crouching, the chief moved hurriedly forward behind the parked cars. Halfway to the stairwell he stopped, stepped between two cars, and waited.

A car turned into the lot, braked, then began to back out, the driver apparently having seen the No Vacancy sign. The headlights caught the young man just as he reached the bottom steps. Chief Loomis's breath caught in his throat. He cursed silently, raging.

Mayfield!

The fucking bastard was the commander's contact.

The chief crouched lower as the yeoman turned in his direction. Kill the bastard here and now, he told himself. It'll be easy. Catch him from behind by surprise, and snap his neck before he even has time to cry out. Adrenaline pumped through the chief's blood vessels, and he felt perspiration bead on his forehead. Just like Nam, he thought. He raised himself carefully and peered through the car windows. Mayfield was headed for the Corvette parked one car over. So easy, the chief thought again. He'd wait until the yeoman had unlocked his car and was bending to get inside. That was when he'd be most vulnerable. He'd grab him around the throat and by the hair, pull his head back, give one quick, powerful twist. Then he'd dump the prick's body in front of the commander's door.

Mayfield inserted his key in the lock in the car door. Then, as if alerted by some sound, he straightened and glanced right and left, then over his shoulder.

The chief trembled with impatience. The word *kill* kept repeating itself inside his skull. He perspired heavily, sweat rolling into the crevices around his eyes, then into the eyes themselves with a burning sensation. Not daring to move, he blinked rapidly, trying to clear his vision. His stomach turned over, and the taste of bourbon rose up in his throat. The yeoman was obviously suspicious, yet Loomis knew he hadn't made a sound. The young bastard probably had an intuitive sense of danger. He continued to stand beside his car, peering around the parking lot.

There was a sudden clap of thunder in the distance. The chief saw Mayfield's head turn toward the mountains that divided the valley from the coast. A flash of lightning illuminated his handsome face. He appeared to be savoring the feel of the rain-laden wind on his skin. The last thing you'll feel except the cracking of your neck bones, the chief thought, and he prepared to spring forward as the yeoman inserted his key in the door lock.

Then the chief hesitated. His mind was crowded with a myriad of thoughts and considerations.

Mayfield climbed into his Corvette, and the door slammed. There was a click as the lock was pushed into place. The engine started with a roar, and the yeoman drove quickly from the parking lot.

Chief Loomis straightened, his face a mask of confusion. He had done what he warned every operative to avoid. He had hesitated. The perfect opportunity for the kill had passed while he had debated with himself.

The sky exploded with thunder once again, this time closer. The first rain started to pelt the parking lot.

The chief hurried back to his car and climbed inside. His hands trembled as he uncorked the bourbon and took another swallow. Then he lit a cigarette and inhaled deeply. The perspiration continued to pour off his forehead and into his deeply etched crow's-feet, which channeled it into his eyes. His heart pounded against his rib cage. He felt the muscles in his chest constrict, felt his breathing becoming labored and painful, an old man's wheezing. The rain was now drumming on the car roof. The chief brought the bottle to his lips again, spilling bourbon on his chin and his shirtfront. He rolled up the windows and sat staring at the rain-sheeted windshield. A thought forced itself into his mind, and despite his efforts to push it away, it persisted.

You hesitated because you were afraid!

No, impossible! He had never feared physical conflict; he had thrived on it. He was a fighter, a killer—the best on the UDT.

Face it, Loomis. You're not the man you once were. You're old, just an old man that kid might have bested if you'd tried to snap his spine. You're no longer good for anything except training young operatives. And how long will you last as a trainer if they suspect you're used up? They won't call you a sadistic son of a bitch then. They'll laugh at you behind your back. You should be put out to pasture, Loomis. Along with those other impotent old bastards, like Addison.

"No, it's not true!" the chief cried aloud. The tremor in his voice made him tremble all the more.

He wasn't used up. He wasn't an old dinosaur.

He'd prove it.

It had been wise not to take Mayfield out in a public place. He'd do it somewhere private. Commander Bannen, too. There were plenty of places to conceal their bodies until after D day. He'd prove that age hadn't dulled his nerve. He'd prove it to himself and to the other officers of Delta.

41

Washington, D.C.

"JONATHAN, IT'S HOPELESS," Ginny said warily. "We can't stay here any longer. If the night supervisor comes back and—"

"Only a few more attempts," Jonathan pleaded.

They stood side by side in front of a computer in Central Records. Ginny had been feeding in requests for information involving Delta, but each request had ended with the appearance of a bisected triangle blocking the data.

"Jonathan, it's no use," Ginny said when the symbol appeared again. "To get the information you want from the computer banks we need the Delta access code." She glanced nervously around the large computer room. The night staff was kept to a minimum, only a few operators in the event of emergency requests; she knew most of the operators, having started on the night shift before being transferred to days. Because she was known by the operators, Jonathan's presence had not been questioned.

The badge he wore on his lapel had been stolen. She had arranged to have after-work drinks with a fellow employee, then had stolen the badge from his pocket like a common thief. The identification photo that stared back at her from the badge Jonathan wore looked nothing like the reporter.

"Jonathan, if the night supervisor comes back and finds you here, he's going to call Security," Ginny warned. "I could lose my job, and you—hell, both of us would probably end up in jail. And for what? It's futile without the access code."

Undaunted, Jonathan said, "Try Admiral Addison's name again."

Ginny sighed in exasperation. "All right, Jonathan, I'll put the admiral's name in again, but the results aren't going to change." She fed the request quickly into the computer. Moments later, Admiral Addison's name appeared, followed by information relating to his career.

"Still no bisected triangle," Jonathan murmured, disappointed. "But why? If Dorothy's suspicions are correct, the admiral's up to his ass in the mire of Delta. Why wouldn't it show in the computers? Why nothing out of the ordinary?"

"Perhaps only the operatives are coded," Ginny suggested. "The leaders would be a small, elite group who would be well aware of one another. There would be no need to risk their identities by coding their profiles. The operatives would be a larger group, perhaps more mobile. If one of the leaders needed an operative in any location, he would need only to reach a computer and punch in the access code to discover which operatives were in his vicinity."

"Perhaps you're right," Jonathan conceded. "Then again, perhaps the operatives are coded for easy elimination in case of a threat of exposure." The reporter's brow furrowed as he pushed his glasses back on the bridge of his nose. "If they're coded by the bisected triangle symbol for easy access for the leaders, then why can't we use the same method to get a complete readout of operatives?"

"We could if we had their code," Ginny said. She cleared the computer screen and turned to Jonathan. "A favor in the name of love is one thing, Jonathan, but staying here any longer is asking more than I'm willing to sacrifice. Even if I didn't end up in prison, I don't want to be fired and end up back in Minnesota in a keypunch pool." She gave Jonathan a gentle push toward the exit. "Go!" she ordered. She turned to the other operatives. "Good night, Dave. Harry." She gave them a casual wave as she propelled Jonathan ahead of her to the door.

Outside, the humidity struck them. After the air-conditioned coolness of the computer room, the heat was oppressive. Jonathan loosened his tie and removed his jacket. "There must be something we've overlooked," he grumbled. "I'll talk to a computer expert I know. Perhaps he'll know how we can bypass the access code and pull the names of the operatives."

"It's possible, of course," Ginny told him. "There's reverse entry, but even then you'd have to unravel more technology than I'm capable of. Perhaps your friend can help, though," she said doubtfully. "Where are we going now, Jonathan?"

"To Dorothy's," he said. "We must go over everything again and—"

"Again?" she said, not veiling her disappointment.

"Again and again, if necessary," Jonathan said. He unlocked the car door and held it open for her. "Maybe Dorothy has come up with something useful from her father's papers."

Ginny looked up at him before he closed the car door. "Is it always going to be like this, Jonathan?"

"Like what?"

"If I agree to make our arrangement permanent, are there always going to be sleepless nights while you probe for information on your articles?"

"Always," he said with a laugh. "You'll learn to love it as much as I do. It's second nature to me, and will be to you, too." He winked at her. "If I agree to making our arrangement permanent." He closed her door, walked around the car and climbed behind the wheel. Removing the security badge from his jacket, he handed it to her. "You'd better take this before I forget. Leave it lying somewhere inconspicuous so it looks like the guy merely misplaced it and— What is it, Ginny?"

Ginny was watching a man who came rushing along the sidewalk in their direction. When he had passed the car, she said, "That was Ross, the night supervisor. If we'd stayed in there only a few minutes more..." She turned frightened eyes on Jonathan. "Why couldn't you have been an accountant or a salesman? I never thought a reporter's life was so dangerous."

Jonathan laughed. "I can tell you love it already," he said. "The excitement of almost being caught by the night supervisor, you find that exhilarating, don't you?"

"All right, I admit it," she said. "I do find it exhilarating, but I wouldn't want a steady diet of it. Don't ask me to risk my job again, Jonathan."

"I promise," he assured her.

"Look at me." Ginny held up her hands to show him they were trembling. "I can't stop shaking."

Jonathan leaned toward her and brushed her cheek with his lips. "At Dorothy's you can take a hot bath, have a cognac, relax. Maybe she'll offer us a guest room for the night." He touched her thigh and kissed her again.

"I only want to sleep," she said teasingly. "You've exhilarated me into a state of exhaustion."

THE BOOKSHELVES of Admiral Burke's study were laden with his journals and military textbooks. Some of his journals dated back to before Dorothy's birth. Most were devoted exclusively to the military, but some had personal notes jotted hastily in the margins.

My wife has disregarded doctors' warnings and is pregnant. Her constitution is too weak to bear children, and I know she has allowed herself to become pregnant only because she knows how badly I want a son. I've tried to tell her an abortion can be obtained in Europe, but she refuses to have one. I am burdened with guilt. Still, I want this child.

Poor father, Dorothy thought when she read the entry. He wanted a son so badly his wife sacrificed her health, and then she bore him a girl instead. Thumbing through the pages and reading the personal notes made Dorothy feel she was stepping back into the past.

Finally recognizing she was wasting her time with the older journals, she sorted them by date, ignoring those more than ten years old. The most recent journal in the study was two years old; this surprised her, for she knew the admiral had continued with his journals even after his stroke. She distinctly remembered visiting him in the hospital while he'd been recuperating and seeing him impatiently close a leather-bound journal because of her visit. She checked the closet, the desk drawers, the file cabinets, but found no more recent journals. She knew he had not taken them to Key West. The island house was empty too much of the time, and robberies had become commonplace during the off-season.

Dorothy reasoned that if the admiral had made entries of a secret nature he would have hidden his journals. She went upstairs and searched his bedroom. Nothing. She conducted a thorough search of his closet, removing every item from the footlockers where he had kept mementos of his years overseas. Nothing. She checked the basement. Only more old journals. Then she looked in the attic, and found only love letters her mother had saved, written when the admiral was courting her and when he was in England during the final months of World War II, and a few journals, all more than a decade old.

After she had searched every place the admiral might have hidden his later journals, Dorothy returned to his study in defeat. She sat at his desk, eyes closed, battling her disappointment, knowing, too, that Quinn's and Jonathan's hopes of her uncovering important information would also be dashed. She wondered if the admiral might have kept his journals in a safe-deposit box, then decided he wouldn't have; his parents had lost almost everything during the depression of the 1930s, and he had never trusted banks, using only checking accounts and keeping only important legal documents like his will in his safe-deposit box.

She remembered with a smile how the admiral had been prone to hiding things around the house, even money. When she was a young girl, the admiral's fondness for hiding things had become a game between them. When he returned from a trip or a deployment he always brought her presents, hid them and challenged her to find them in a given period of time. To help her along, he would give her hints. She remembered some of his favorite hiding places: the long case of the grandfather clock in the entryway, the tall Chinese vases on the dining room mantel, the hidden drawer in the old armoire that had once stood in his study.

A surge of current passed through Dorothy's body when she recalled the armoire. The admiral had always been fond of the piece, a Louis XV original inherited from his grandmother, but she had relegated it to the attic when she had redecorated his study. "Oh, well," the admiral had concluded when she had convinced him the armoire would not blend with the new decor, "I can always visit it in the attic. I suppose all old things, including admirals, must one day be hidden away." Now, with his words echoing inside her head, Dorothy hurried from behind his desk and into the hallway. *I can always visit it in the attic.* Could this mean, she asked herself, that the admiral had continued using the hidden drawer in the armoire as a hiding place?

There was no staircase to the attic. When the house had been remodeled, the designer had eliminated the stairs to allow larger closets for the bedrooms. A panel had been placed in the ceiling as a replacement for the stairs, with a switch beside one of the overhead lights that, when pressed, opened the panel. Then a cord had to be pulled to unfold the ladderlike steps.

Dorothy pressed the switch, then lowered the steps.

Just as it had when she had checked the attic earlier, a stale odor assailed her nostrils when she stuck her head through the opening. At that moment Mati appeared on the landing. "What are you doing, Mrs. Bannen?" she asked. "If you want something up there, I'll get it for you."

Mati had been badly shaken by the admiral's death. She had idolized him, despite his constant teasing about her size and lack of femininity. When Dorothy had returned with the tragic news, the maid had fled to her room to shed tears in private and had not emerged for several hours. Since then she had moped around the house, turning all the attention she had focused on the admiral onto Dorothy.

"I'm looking for something special, Mati," Dorothy called down to her. "I have to do it myself. What you can do is prepare a late supper for Mr. McKinney and Ginny. They should be arriving soon."

"Oh, all right." The maid moved away, grumbling.

The heat and humidity had made an oven of the attic, and Dorothy was soon soaked with perspiration. She thought briefly of returning below and waiting until the air-conditioning had sent cool air through the open panel, but in her impatience she dismissed the idea, moving farther into the large room, until she spotted the armoire, as double mirrored doors reflecting her image in the harsh light.

The armoire shelves, installed by the admiral himself during one of his infrequent do-it-yourself periods, were laden with newspapers and magazines, each carefully flagged for some article that had held his interest. Dorothy focused her attention on the bottom shelf, which didn't hold nearly as many newspapers as the others. She slid them onto the floor; then, remembering what she had done as a child, she turned the metal clips at both ends until the shelf swung out to reveal the space beneath.

Her heart skipped a beat, and she wanted to cry out in triumph.

The missing journals were there, three of them. The absence of dust told her the admiral had hidden them there shortly before the trip to Key West. Her hands trembled as she carried the journals to where the light was better, sat down and began reading pages at random.

I firmly believe it will take a serious threat of war to shake the American people from their lethargy. History does indeed repeat itself. One need only remember World War II. Hitler was ravaging Europe, toppling governments and capturing countries, killing the Jews and enslaving whole peoples for the war effort, and still the Americans refused to involve themselves until the Japanese attacked Pearl Harbor. It has been said that Churchill, Stalin and Roosevelt were informed of the Japanese attack the day before it took place. Yet no warning was issued. Perhaps Roosevelt understood it was the only way to get the Americans to commit themselves. Must it come to that again before we face Communism head-on? Must we tolerate a dozen Vietnams before...

Dorothy flipped several pages; then the word *children* caught her eye.

It was brought to my attention today that there is a group of children ranging in age from eight to eighteen who have banded together to protest the threat of nuclear war. I find these children astounding. It chills me to realize they fear nuclear attack and death as my generation feared the mythical bogeyman. It makes one reflect on young people's approach to the future. Why should they learn? they must be thinking. Why should they improve when they feel their future is so uncertain? They must feel betrayed by their parents, must wonder why adults appear not to comprehend the danger. I wonder if Chad suffered from such fears when he was younger. I must raise the topic with him the next time I see him.

Dorothy soon realized it would take hours, perhaps days to read the three journals. She picked up the most recent volume, held it to the light and ran her index finger down the entries, searching for one word. *Delta.*

Her scanning stopped when she noticed a discernible change in handwriting. The penmanship was more of a scrawl, the shapes of the letters less defined, and she realized the admiral had written these entries soon after his stroke.

Admiral Addison will assume command of my division. He is a longtime friend and a good officer. Still, I worry that power will change him. He's an extremely secretive man. Even after so many years of friendship, I cannot truthfully say I really know the inner workings of the man. I must warn the committee to keep a wary eye on him. Better men than Addison, better men than myself, have been corrupted by excessive power.

Because of the necessary secretiveness of the organization, it's difficult for any member to be totally aware of a leader's activities. That is a serious flaw I overlooked in reorganizing...

Involuntarily, Dorothy cried out. Here it was!

...flaw I overlooked in reorganizing Delta. It was the individual power and lack of control of the leaders that proved the downfall of the original organization.

Dorothy continued to scan the entry, but the single word *Delta* kept flashing before her eyes. The mere fact that she had discovered the name in the admiral's journal proved the organization existed, that he had reorganized it. The revival of Delta was no myth, no paranoid fantasy of Quinn and Jonathan McKinney. The admiral's self-incrimination brought tears to her eyes. Frantically she turned the pages, searching for yet another name. For Chad's name. She found it, and she began to moan even before she had read the paragraph.

God help me! Addison has recruited Chad as a Delta operative! My grandson a trained assassin! What motive lies behind Addison's action? Does he intend to use my grandson for D day? He tells me he hasn't informed the boy of my involvement in Delta, hasn't even told him I'm aware of its existence, yet there was a strange inflection in his voice when he told me this. A threat? Since my illness, the bastard has my power. What more does he want from me? He may take everything—everything *except* my grandson, except Chad, the last of my bloodline!

The entry continued, but Dorothy could read no further. She closed the journal and sat staring into space. Tears flowed freely down her cheeks. Her lips trembled, and there was a ringing in her ears. The ringing slowly registered on her brain, and she identified it as the doorbell. She forced herself to her feet, clutching the admiral's journals, and went to the open panel. She heard Mati answer the door, heard Jonathan's voice, and Ginny's. Suddenly she felt too weak to climb down the folding steps; she just sank to the floor beside the opening, holding the journals to her chest and crying soundlessly. She heard Mati telling Jonathan where to find her, heard his and Ginny's footsteps on the stairs.

They stood at the foot of the steps, staring up at her. Jonathan's eyes were magnified by his eyeglasses, and his expression was one of concern. He gave Ginny a gentle push toward the bedroom door. "Go take your bath," he told her.

He didn't speak again until Ginny had gone hesitantly into the bedroom and closed the door. Then he said to Dorothy, "You found the proof, didn't you?"

Unable to speak, she nodded.

"Is it conclusive?"

Then Dorothy found her voice. "They were both members of Delta! My son and my father! Oh, God, Jonathan! I have to talk to Quinn!"

"Yes, you should do that," Jonathan said with a calm that was belied by the excitement in his eyes. He climbed the folding steps, unconscious of the threatening creaks beneath his weight, and pulled himself through the opening, then sat beside Dorothy, his legs dangling through the panel. "May I read the journals?" he asked quietly, and extended his hand.

Dorothy clutched them tighter to her bosom. "Only Quinn!" she cried. "I'll show them only to Quinn!" She saw the surprise on Jonathan's face, saw it mingle with distress caused by her admission of mistrust. "I'm—I'm sorry, Jonathan," she said, weeping. "Do you realize what these journals say about two people I loved?"

"I realize what you must be feeling," he said patiently.

"Why the admiral? Why Chad?" she cried.

"Perhaps we can find the answers to those questions in the journals," he told her. Again he reached for the leather-bound volumes.

Dorothy slid back, away from him. "Not *we*," she said defiantly. "Quinn only! He'll know what to do. He'll protect Chad's name, even the admiral's." Her tears blurred her vision.

"We're beyond merely protecting names," Jonathan told her. "If our suspicions about Delta are correct, its efforts go far beyond reputations—even your son's and your father's. We have no idea what Delta's objectives may be, but your father's journals may save many lives. They obviously made a serious mistake when they murdered Chad and the admiral. Too many questions have been raised. The foundation of the organization is threatened, and they're going to be forced to clean up loose ends before a full-fledged investigation begins. There may be enough in the admiral's journals to convince the Pentagon to launch—"

Dorothy interrupted in a voice that was scarcely audible, saying, "Get me Quinn on the telephone. I'll do whatever he tells me."

Jonathan stared at her silently for a moment. He managed to restrain his urge to force the journals from her. The pipes that ran through the attic vibrated as the shower below was turned on; he heard Ginny singing, her voice muffled.

"Quinn's telephone number in California is on the pad in the study," Dorothy told him stiffly. "If he says to give you the journals, I will."

"Yes, all right, I'll call Quinn," Jonathan assured her. "It would be better if I could tell him exactly what the journals contain, but if you insist . . ."

"I'm sorry, Jonathan. I do insist," Dorothy said.

Sighing in frustration, Jonathan descended the folding steps. He had just planted his feet in the hallway when the doorbell rang. "Are you expecting anyone?"

"No, no one," Dorothy said.

Jonathan heard Mati's footsteps approaching from the kitchen. Because he was around the corner from the second-floor landing, he couldn't see the maid, but he knew instinctively she intended to answer the bell, perhaps even turn off the alarm system and open the door before she peered through the viewer.

"No!" he shouted. "Mati, don't—"

A burst of gunfire cut off his warning. There was the sound of splintering wood, and then the door crashed inward as the alarm sounded.

"Stay up there!" Jonathan shouted at Dorothy. He snapped the folding steps against the panel and flung it closed in her pale and frightened face.

Mati had been halfway across the entryway when the gunfire had torn through the door and the door had come crashing inward. She froze in shock and confusion. Then, as she turned to flee, there was more shooting. The bullets smashed into her back and propelled her body across the highly polished floor to land at the base of the staircase.

On the second-floor landing, Jonathan made a dash for the nearest door. He caught a fleeting glance of the maid's body sliding across the floor, leaving a trail of blood behind. At least the alarm system had gone off, he thought. The police would be summoned. If only he and Ginny could hide long enough—

"Up there!" a man shouted.

He heard the reports of the automatic weapons at the same instant the bullets tore into his flesh. The impact slammed him into the door frame. He slid down the wall and rolled onto his back, his head propped against the molding, his chin forced down over his chest. His entire body was strangely numb. A bullet in my spine, he thought. He knew he was dying, perhaps just moments from death, but oddly, there was no pain. Instead of being engulfed in darkness as he would have expected, his vision, even without his glasses, was acute. Blood was oozing out from under him and puddling on the black-and-white tiles.

He watched detachedly as men rushed up the circular staircase. There were four of them, all young, all wearing designer jeans and polo shirts. They were clean-cut, nice-looking young men who, except for the automatic weapons in their hands, could have been on their way to a dance or a fraternity meeting. One stood out from the others because of the bandages across the bridge of his nose. Jonathan recognized him immediately as Admiral Burke's Key West bodyguard. The four men moved with such precision that they appeared to have been choreographed. Almost, he thought, actors in an elaborate television commercial, because the entire scene seemed unreal.

One of the men approached him, poked him in the side with the toe of his highly polished boot.

Between the man's spread legs, Jonathan saw Dorothy's bedroom door open. Ginny, her face a mask of fright and puzzlement, stood in the open frame, wearing one of Dorothy's dressing gowns and with a towel wrapped around her head like a turban. Her face literally dissolved as the bullets struck her.

The operative beside Jonathan said, "This one's still alive!"

"Then finish the bastard!" came the order. "The bitch has had it. She won't be giving any more interviews!"

Jonathan sensed rather than saw the weapon aimed at the top of his head. Before he heard the explosion the blackness engulfed him.

DOROTHY COULDN'T have disobeyed Jonathan's command to remain in the attic even if she'd wanted to. The sound of gunfire, along with the burglar alarm, at first paralyzed her with fear. Still clutching the admiral's journals, she remained sitting beside the floor panel. When the gunfire grew louder, the intruders having obviously climbed to the second floor, she dropped the books and clamped her hands over her ears. The journals landed on the panel with a heavy thud, and she caught her breath in terror, expecting the sound to draw attention to her hiding place.

She heard a man shout, "The bitch has had it. She won't be giving any more interviews!" and she understood that they had killed Ginny, thinking she was Dorothy.

Time stretched to unimaginable length, moments becoming an eternity.

"Shall we search the house?" she heard someone ask.

"No time! Let's get the hell out of here!"

Dorothy heard footsteps pounding down the stairs and crossing the entryway. Then there was no sound except the uninterrupted shrieking of the alarm system. Knees trembling, she got up and pressed one foot against the panel. It slid open. The sound of the alarm was so loud she thought it would shatter her eardrums. She bent, and pushed at the steps until they unfolded.

Before she had descended the steps, she saw Jonathan, his body at a crazy angle, his head against the wall, blood spattered on the plaster around it like an aura. There was a puddle of blood on the tiles, blood on his clothes, a trickle of blood oozing from his temple to collect and drip from the broken frame of his glasses. She forced her gaze away from him. At the foot of the steps she remembered the journals and returned to the attic to collect them. The second time she descended she deliberately avoided glancing in the direction of Jonathan's body.

When Dorothy dashed into her bedroom, she almost tripped over Ginny's body. The young woman was sprawled on her back at the foot of the bed, her arms thrown out at her sides. There was only a mass of bloody flesh where her face had been. Dorothy's intended scream was nothing more than a whimper; she still hadn't overcome the numbness brought on by terror. *That should have been me,* she thought, and turned away from Ginny. She found her handbag and hurried from the room.

Downstairs the entryway was a shambles of shattered wood from the door, broken porcelain and shattered crystal. Dorothy stepped over Mati's body. Again she whimpered, then choked on a sob as she fled the house and ran down the walk to the car. She threw her handbag and the journals in the back, fumbled with the keys and finally managed to start the engine.

The sound of approaching sirens mingled with that of the house alarm system as she drove quickly away.

42

Mountain View, California

QUINN HAD FALLEN into a fitful sleep across the bed with his clothes on, waiting for Jonathan McKinney to call.

The telephone awakened him, and when he answered, Alex Mayfield's immediate statement brought him out of his grogginess. "Chief Loomis just called me, Commander, and he wants me on the base immediately."

"Did he explain why he wants to see you at this ungodly hour?" Quinn asked, alerted by the nervousness in the yeoman's voice.

"No, only that it was important and couldn't wait until morning. He sounded strange, Commander."

"Can you clarify?"

"No, Commander. Just strange," Alex answered. "He didn't sound like himself." Uncertainly he added, "It was . . . fear, perhaps."

Fear before the kill, Quinn thought, often expressed merely by a quiver in the voice, a tic at the corner of the mouth, a parched throat or a dilation of the pupils. The bravest of men suffered from it, usually unaware of the chemical changes in their bodies, their minds fully occupied by their objective. Was that what Chief Loomis planned for the yeoman? To eliminate him? Quinn sat up and switched on the lamp. His travel clock read 3:00 a.m. It would be 6:00 a.m. in Washington; Jonathan should have called long ago.

"I have no choice but to meet with him," Alex said, cutting into his thoughts. "If I don't keep the appointment, I'll be suspect. Provided I'm not already," he added.

"Yes, you'll meet with the chief," Quinn agreed, "only not alone. Come by and pick me up. Do you think you can get me onto the base without difficulty?"

"It's possible, Commander, at this hour," Alex said. "I won't be able to drive my Corvette. No room for you to curl up on the floor. But no problem. I have a second car. I'll be there in half an hour."

Quickly Quinn showered under a cold spray, shaved and dressed in Levi's and a dark shirt. The entire process took less than twenty minutes. He returned to the telephone and dialed Dorothy's Washington number. The phone rang several times before a man answered with a gruff "Hello."

Quinn felt a shiver along his spine. "Who is this?" he demanded.

"Who are you calling, mister?" the voice countered. There was a clicking sound, as if someone in another part of the house had picked up an extension.

"Dorothy Bannen," Quinn said tightly.

"Who's calling?"

"Commander Quinn Bannen, her ex-husband. I'm calling from California. Who the hell is this? Where's Dorothy? Put her on the line."

The voice lost its gruffiness. "I'm sorry, Commander, that's impossible. May I have the number you're calling from?"

Quinn hesitated.

"My name is Hartmann, Commander. Washington P.D. Please give me your number so I can verify your location. There's been some difficulty here."

"What sort of difficulty?" Quinn mumbled, feeling the muscles of his chest and abdomen suddenly tighten with dread. "Please! What's happened to Dorothy?"

"Give me your number and I'll call you back immediately, Commander."

Quinn gave the number of the motel and his room extension. After being assured that his call would be returned without delay, he hung up and waited, grabbing the receiver on the first ring.

"Commander Bannen?"

"Yes, damn it! What's happened to my wife?" Quinn shouted.

"I'm sorry, Commander." The voice took on a professional tone of sympathy. "Your wife and a gentleman we haven't yet identified have been murdered. There are some questions you may be able to—"

Quinn dropped the receiver back into its cradle.

Shaken, he sank onto the edge of the bed and sat rocking his upper body back and forth in an unconscious expression of agony. *When this is over we'll get the pieces of our lives back together,* he had told Dorothy.

The phone began to ring again, but he didn't answer.

Quinn was still sitting on the edge of the bed and the telephone was still ringing when Alex knocked on his door. He rose, walked stiffly to the door and let the yeoman in without speaking. Going to his suitcase, he removed a revolver and shoved it into the waistband of his Levi's, then put on a lightweight summer jacket to conceal it. "Let's go," he said tonelessly.

Alex glanced at the unanswered telephone, then at the commander.

The expression in Quinn's eyes told him not to question, not even to speak. He followed the commander out into the rainy night.

43

Dulles Airport, Washington, D.C.
DOROTHY SAW her reflection in the automatic doors of the terminal and realized she looked like a derelict. Her white summer dress was covered with dust from the attic. There was a heavy smudge on her right cheek. Her hair was in disarray. Although she couldn't see her eyes from that distance, she knew her expression was bordering on madness. No wonder people were staring at her, she thought. She knew she should go to the rest room and attempt to put her appearance in order, but she dared not leave her position near the bank of pay telephones.

She had placed a call to Quinn's California number, but the motel operator had told her the room didn't answer. She had emphasized how important it was to reach her husband. Not former husband or ex-husband—she now thought of Quinn as *her husband*. She had pleaded with the motel operator to place a note on Quinn's door so that he'd return her call the moment he got back to his room. The operator had had a sleepy, impatient voice, but after she'd promised him a sizable tip from Quinn if he complied with her request he'd promised to do as she asked. She had then taken an Out of Order sign from a nearby phone and placed it on the phone she had used.

She had a wait of almost two hours before her flight to San Francisco was scheduled to depart. She sank into a chair, her ticket resting on her lap atop the admiral's three heavy journals.

She took a tissue from her handbag, moistened it with her tongue and wiped at the smudge on her cheek. It was then that she noticed the blood on the side of one of her white shoes, near the sole. Ginny's blood, from when she had almost tripped over the young woman's body. I mustn't think about that now, she warned herself, and drew her feet back under her seat so that the shoes were no longer visible. She carefully applied lipstick and ran a comb through her hair, actions she normally would have performed without thought but now concentrated upon in order to keep from thinking about Jonathan and Ginny and Mati.

After fleeing the house, she had driven around aimlessly for almost an hour before deciding on the airport. She knew she should have stopped and telephoned the police. No doubt the police would think she was the faceless victim sprawled at the foot of her bed, just as the murderers had. But if she notified them, they would demand she come in, might possibly even locate her and prevent her from catching her plane. She had to reach Quinn, had to get the admiral's journals to him. Besides, what could she tell the police about the men who had invaded her house? Only that there had been more than two of them—four, she thought— that they had used automatic weapons, that she had heard the rapid gunfire above the sound of the security alarm, that scattered bits of conversation had convinced her that the men belonged to an illegal organization known as Delta. *Delta.* Would the admiral's journals convince the police that Delta existed? Or would they consider it the ramblings of a madman?

Dorothy opened one of the journals at random.

Even with all I learned about the evil evolution of Delta during my investigation, I still regretted the necessity of disbanding the organization. I understood the original concepts of its creators, its potential. An organization unlimited by political control, untethered by military policy, beyond criticism by foreign and domestic leaders because there was no known government funding—in short, an organization that did not exist. A vigilante organization shrouded in utmost secrecy, a myth that could not have been proved if individual leaders had not gone beyond the authority of its controller. Even while the evidence of Delta's existence was being destroyed or buried in archives unobtainable for decades, it occurred to me that the organization could be reformed. Delta's potential for achievement outweighed its adverse possibilities. The flaws, though serious, were the product of ill-chosen leaders, power-hungry men who could have been controlled.

"Oh, Admiral," Dorothy mumbled aloud. With an effort she held back the tears that threatened when she thought of her father's mistaken belief that an organization like Delta could be controlled.

The major fault of Delta was that its leaders were chosen not from the military but from the country's wealthiest businessmen, men who attempted to control the world's political spectrums more for their own financial gain than to defeat Communism. In their greed they even threatened our own government with chaos on more than one occasion.

Dorothy glanced at the clock, then looked hopefully at the telephone with the Out of Order sign. Why didn't it ring? Why? Where could Quinn be at such an early hour in California?

The Washington sun was bright and hot. Heat rose from the concrete in shimmering waves. Each time the automatic doors slid open to admit someone the hot, humid air rushed inside like a thief trying to snatch away the air-conditioned coolness. A commuter flight to New York's La Guardia

Airport was announced on the loudspeaker; three men sitting near Dorothy rose and hurried toward the gates.

She returned her attention to the journal, absently turning the pages, realizing they would have to be carefully studied by Quinn, then by the proper authorities. Jonathan had been right; it was no longer a mere question of reputations.

The new committee will consist of seven men, six of whom will be carefully selected officers from all branches of the military. The seventh should be well placed in government, as should the controller. The six officers will control a "division" of operatives ranging in number from fifty to one hundred. No individual division leader should undertake a project without the controller's approval and the knowledge of the committee. This provision eliminates the cause of the original Delta's downfall.

The weakest link in each division will be its operatives. These men—and women—should be carefully screened, then informed only on a need-to-know basis. They should be handpicked from the abundant rosters of social misfits, plucked from military prisons if need be, and trained to follow orders without question. They must display no compunction in the taking of human life. With the hostility now prevalent in today's youth, there should be an abundance of potential operatives. Recruiters should establish further requirements and create infallible guidelines. After operatives have been meticulously screened, they should be monitored until their devotion to the organization is proved beyond a shadow of a doubt. Operatives working in pairs should be instructed to consider their partners with suspicion. Operatives are expendable. If doubts arise regarding their loyalty, they should be eliminated without hesitation.

"Chad!" Dorothy cried aloud in a voice full of pain.

People seated near her in the terminal turned and studied her curiously.

She closed the admiral's journal, not daring to read further for fear she would be reduced to hysterics.

Her mouth was dry. She glanced at the coffee shop, then decided that if anything went into her stomach she would be incapable of keeping it down. As the minutes dragged by, she continued to sit near the bank of telephones, thinking of Chad, of the admiral—and praying Quinn would call soon.

44

Moffett Field, California

ALEX TOOK the Moffett Field exit off 101 and looped back over the freeway. As always when he drove his Plymouth Horizon, he missed the power of the Corvette's 454 engine; the second car was for economy and to use while he restored the vintage Corvette. Of course, Commander Bannen couldn't have concealed himself inside the Corvette; as it was, he'd been forced to curl his six-foot-plus frame into a fetal position to fit on the floor behind the driver's seat, where he now lay covered by a blanket.

"We're approaching the gate, Commander," Alex announced. His hands were damp as he gripped the steering wheel. "I don't anticipate any problem. Just stay still."

"Understood," Quinn murmured.

During the busy daylight hours, the commander could have sat in the front seat as a passenger and Alex wouldn't have been challenged by the marine guards. Security was more lax during the day. Alex wondered how much Delta relied on this laxity for its operations. Better security would have prevented the fake Red Cross emergency leave for Commander Sontag; checked out through the proper channels, Sontag's father's death would have been proved false, and the commander brought up on charges.

Alex slowed the car and came to a halt just behind the line marked Stop. Because he was known to be assigned to the admiral's staff and because he frequently arrived in the early-morning hours to complete his work load, the marine guards were familiar with him, even joked among themselves about his zealousness, thinking he was bucking for a stripe. The marine on duty glanced at the windshield sticker and at the badge Alex held up and motioned the car through with a stiff salute.

"We're inside, Commander," Alex said, and Quinn shifted on the rear floor to ease his cramped muscles.

Alex parked in the lot facing Chief Loomis's building. He climbed from behind the wheel, then stooped and spoke through the open window. "There's a light on in the chief's office. No one else around that I can see." He straightened as Quinn threw the covering blanket aside. "Damn it! Hold on, Commander!" He had glanced up at the chief's window and had seen the man's giant frame silhouetted against the brightly lit interior of his office. "The chief's looking down," he murmured.

Quinn peered over the front seat and spotted the figure in the window. "Cross to the entrance and go inside," he instructed Alex. "That should take him away from the window. Take your time. Once you're inside, don't rush to his office. I'll need a chance to catch up with you. You don't want to be alone with that bastard any longer than necessary. We don't know what he has in mind." Quinn kicked the blanket from his legs. "I hope we're not underestimating the man."

"Do you think he's on to me, Commander?"

"It's possible," Quinn said. "If so, and if it's his intention to take you out immediately, can you take care of yourself, Alex?"

For the chief's benefit, Alex pretended to lock the car door. "I keep myself in shape," he said quietly. "The chief's a big man, but he's not very fit. I'm going now, Commander.'' Alex walked to the entrance of the building with a slow, deliberate stride. Just before moving out of sight of Loomis's window, he looked up and waved.

Quinn saw the chief move away from the window without acknowledging Alex's wave. Quinn climbed from the back seat, waited a moment to make certain Loomis didn't return to his vigil at the window and then made a dash for the building entrance.

Alex knew Quinn would be forced to take the stairs because using the elevator would alert the chief that he and Alex were not alone in the building. Not only would the stairs take Quinn longer, but also, the fire door might have been locked by the cleaning crew. Alex would have taken the stairs himself, but the elevator door stood open, apparently sent to the main floor for his convenience by Loomis. He stepped inside and pressed the button for the chief's floor. As the doors slid closed, he saw Quinn rush into the building and head for the stairs.

Tension had stiffened the muscles of Alex's neck and made painful knots in his stomach. Despite his claim to be in good shape, he hadn't been involved in a fight since he'd been stationed on Eniwetok. Chief Loomis was a big bastard. Despite his age and bloated form, he was an expert at hand-to-hand combat. Alex told himself that his nervousness was unfounded, that the strange undertones to the chief's voice on the phone hinted at nothing out of the ordinary. The hour of the meeting was peculiar, true—but then, he reasoned, perhaps meetings in the middle of the night were routine for a clandestine organization such as Delta. Again he thought of the fire door and hoped the cleaning crew had failed to secure it.

The elevator came to an abrupt stop, and the doors snapped open. The hallway was dark, lighted only by a Fire Exit sign over the stairwell door. He stepped out of the elevator, and the doors banged closed behind him.

"Mayfield?" Chief Loomis had thrown open his office door, his giant frame filling the opening. "Down here. You've been here before. Come on, let's get this over with!" The odd inflection that had been in his voice on the phone still remained.

"Yes, Chief. I just got confused in the darkness," Alex called.

Chief Loomis moved back into his office, mumbling something under his breath.

Alex moved forward quickly, pausing briefly beside the stairwell door but not daring to test the handle. Although he listened, he couldn't hear Quinn's footsteps on the stairs.

The chief's outer office was also dark, the inner door with its semiopaque glass panel half-closed. Alex broke his stride only for a second, to draw a deep breath of air into his lungs; then he crossed the outer room and stepped into the chief's office.

Chief Loomis was sitting behind his desk, his swivel chair tilted back, his hands locked behind his head. He had removed his uniform jacket. There were large, dark sweat stains circling the armpits of his shirt. Despite the heat, the air conditioner was not on, and the window was closed. The venetian blinds had now been drawn. The chief's piercing gaze never left the yeoman's face as he motioned him to the chair in front of his desk.

Alex sat, his back held straight, and placed his elbows on the chair arms, hoping he appeared more casual about the meeting than he felt.

The chief continued to stare at him, his eyes probing Alex's.

He's doing it deliberately to make me nervous, Alex thought. He tried to keep his voice modulated as he asked, "What's so important you needed to see me at this hour, Chief?" When Chief Loomis didn't answer immediately, he added, "Another case like Commander Sontag's?"

Loomis dropped his eyes. He glanced at his wristwatch and registered mock surprise at the hour. "To dedicated men like myself, the military is a twenty-four-hour-a-day job," he said evenly. "Tell me, Mayfield, are you a dedicated military man?"

"Yes, Chief," Alex answered without hesitation.

"Yes, well, that was my first impression of you," Chief Loomis said. "But then, first impressions are often erroneous, aren't they?" He let his swivel chair snap back into an upright position, and he rose. "That was a clever bit of business you pulled off, getting Commander Sontag's emergency leave. You're a skillful yeoman, a credit to your rate. I'm only sorry our organization can't give you an accommodation. However, that's the way of it when you operate as we do. Everything highly classified. No glory for our loyal members."

"I wasn't expecting an accommodation, chief," Alex said. "The success of an assignment is glory enough."

Clasping his hands together behind his back, the chief moved around the desk and began to pace. "Is it?" he murmured. "I wonder if that's entirely true." His pacing brought him closer to Alex's chair, and he noticed the yeoman pull back slightly. "You seem nervous, Mayfield."

"No, Chief. Just tired," Alex said.

"Yes, well, I forgot you young men need more sleep than men my age," the chief told him. He was behind Alex's chair now. He noted that Mayfield sat with his back ramrod-straight, that he was restraining himself from turning in his chair. There was sweat on his brow. Goddamned traitor! the chief wanted to shout. He'd at least have the satisfaction of telling the young prick why he was being killed before he snapped his fucking neck. Directly behind the yeoman, he stopped his pacing. "Exactly how much have you managed to learn about Delta, Mayfield?" he bellowed.

The instant Alex started to spring from his chair, the chief grabbed him from behind. He locked one powerful arm around Alex's chest and pinned his arms to his sides; the other arm encircled his neck. He crushed the younger man against his body, making movements impossible. "I'm going to kill you, Mayfield," he snarled, "and I'm going to take great pleasure in doing it! You're going to know pain first, excruciating pain. Then I'm going to break your god-damned neck."

Alex could feel the breath being squeezed from his lungs. He opened his mouth to speak, but the arm around his neck kept any sound from coming out. He could feel the chief's breath against his ear, smell its foulness.

"I'm going to stuff your body in the furnace," the chief went on. "It's summer, and you won't be found for months. Not unless the odor of your rotting flesh becomes so loathsome the cleaning crew hunts you out." He tightened the pressure of his arm around Alex's neck until there were explosions of light in front of the yeoman's eyes. Then he slackened his grip expertly to keep Alex from losing consciousness. "But first, my traitorous friend, you're going to give me all the information you've learned about Delta. All of it!"

Alex was gasping for air. Where was Quinn? The fire door to the stairwell must have been locked. If he was forced to use the elevator, the chief would hear it and be alerted. Alex knew Loomis could snap his neck in a matter of seconds.

"What have you told your buddy Commander Bannen?" the chief snarled. "After you, I'll deal with him. Tell me, damn you! What does he know? What do you know, Mayfield?"

"I—I know about Commander Sontag," Alex managed. "That he's a member of Delta."

"Yes, of course. It's my fault you learned about Sontag. He's one of our leaders. You didn't know that, did you, Mayfield?" The chief's grip tightened again, but not enough to cut off Alex's breathing, just enough to painfully restrict the air his lungs were crying out for. "What else?"

In a rush, Alex cried out, "Admiral Addison, Captain Musolf, Captain Ellison, Marshisky, Everett, Sloane..." When he could think of no more names, he continued with "Marshisky kept at Alameda on drugs...an assassin...New York...the thirteenth..."

"Holy Christ!" Chief Loomis shouted.

As Alex had hoped, the shock of learning he had uncovered so much information about Delta caused the chief to slacken his grip. The instant Alex was capable of movement, he made a valiant attempt to tear himself free. He rammed his elbow backward into Loomis's abdomen, then tried to forced his arms upward.

But Loomis had not been taken off guard enough to loose his victim. His viselike grip drew the yeoman back against his body. "I don't know how you learned so much, Mayfield. But now you die!"

Quinn sprang through the door. Before the chief could harm Alex or defend himself, Quinn drove his fist into Loomis's back. The air gushed from the chief's lungs. At the same moment, Alex twisted and flung himself backward, knocking Loomis off balance.

Loomis delivered a hammering blow to the yeoman's back. As Alex pitched forward into the desk, the chief spun to meet his attacker. His eyes widened with surprise when he found himself confronting Quinn Bannen.

Before the chief could recover from his surprise, Quinn struck him just below the rib cage.

Chief Loomis rolled with the punch and came back with a powerful swing of his fist. Quinn sidestepped and was dealt only a glancing blow. The chief pulled a knife from his pocket and clicked the blade open. "I'll cut both your goddamned throats!" he cried. He crouched, his lips curling back over nicotine-stained teeth. "I wanted you, Bannen, even more than this young fucker!"

"Then here I am, Loomis! Come and get me!"

The chief took one cautious step forward, his knife at the ready.

Quinn snatched up the straight-backed chair. Without breaking contact with the chief's eyes, he also snatched up the man's uniform coat and wound it around his left arm for protection. Like the chief, Quinn crouched to make himself a smaller, less vulnerable target.

The two men circled each other.

Dazed, Alex pulled himself off the desk.

"Get back, Alex!" Quinn shouted as the chief edged closer to the yeoman.

Alex's reaction was immediate. He flung himself backward, just barely avoiding the slashing blade as the chief tried to slice his stomach.

Quinn feinted with the chair, and Loomis stepped back.

Alex saw the handle of the revolver protruding from the waistband of Quinn's Levi's and wondered why the commander didn't use it. Then, in the same instant, the answer occurred to him—if the commander pulled the revolver, the chief would force him to use it. Bannen was trying to avoid killing his opponent.

Loomis was circling, trying to get the open door at his back, but Quinn was holding his ground. "Less than an hour ago the order went out to kill you on sight, Bannen," the chief growled. "You and every other bitch and son of a bitch who's put their noses where they don't belong will be taken care of."

Quinn's face was a mask of hatred. "I've heard about my wife," he said between clenched teeth. "And my friend Jonathan McKinney. You'll pay, Loomis! Delta will pay!" He swung the chair at the chief's head.

The chief held up his arm to take the blow, then lurched forward with a jab of the knife. Quinn's arm, padded by the chief's uniform jacket, took the slash; the blade cut through the fabric and, judging by the flicker of pain in his eyes, reached his flesh.

The chief gave a guttural laugh. "Next time your throat, Bannen! Then your balls! You're soft, Bannen! A civilian pussy!"

Quinn displayed no response to the goading. He still clung to the chair. He advanced slowly, driving the chief toward a corner. Then he lunged, in a move that reminded Alex of a lion tamer confronting a dangerous jungle cat. The chief's knife hand became entangled in the rungs of the chair. Quinn's left fist shot forward into the chief's face.

The big man took the blow with a grunt. Blood gushed from his nose. He flung the chair away, still clutching the knife, and made another jab at Quinn.

Quinn proved too swift for the chief. He brought his padded arm up and caught Loomis's knife hand from below, driving the blade up above the chief's shoulder. At the same moment he stepped into the big man and drove his right fist into his abdomen. The chief stumbled backward but regained his balance immediately. Moving like a youthful street fighter, he advanced, jabbing with the knife and driving Quinn back against the wall between the desk and the file cabinet. Alex realized Loomis was trying to limit the commander's space and put him at a disadvantage.

Alex edged around the desk in an attempt to get behind the chief. He knew the man wouldn't allow himself to be trapped between two attackers, but the effort of holding both men at bay might prevent him from zeroing in on Quinn. "You can't take both of us, Chief!"

"I've taken more and better men!" Loomis said with a snarl. But doubt had been planted in his mind; it registered in his eyes. His shirt was now entirely drenched with sweat, and his breathing was coming in loud gasps.

"You were younger then," Quinn told him evenly. "You're an old man now, Chief. A relic. You're only good for training younger men. For hiding behind secret classifications like Delta.''

''I'll show you fucking bastards!'' the chief cried, and lunged forward.

Alex grabbed the telephone, the only item on the desk, and flung it at Loomis. The cord reached its length before the instrument found its mark, but the receiver, continuing from momentum, struck the chief just above the brow. The blow was solid. The big man stumbled in midlunge, lost his balance again and was not so quick in regaining it. Quinn leaped forward, seizing the knife arm and forcing it above the chief's head. He threw his weight against the man's body and sent him teetering backward. Both men crashed into the wall and fell to the floor, still grappling for control of the knife. Each fought for a superior position as they rolled across the floor. Because of his weight advantage, the chief won. He straddled Quinn and struggled to tear his knife arm from Quinn's grasp. His massive paw of a left hand pressed down against the commander's Adam's apple, his fingers digging in to tear at his throat.

Quinn freed one leg and brought his knee up hard between the big man's legs. The chief cried out but maintained his grip on the commander's throat. The weight of him was crushing the air from Quinn's lungs.

Alex stepped forward with a well-aimed kick that caught Loomis in the back of the neck. He grabbed the chief's knife arm by the wrist and gave it a quick backward jerk. There was the unmistakable sound of bone splintering. Quinn, freed, delivered a blow to Loomis's jaw. The chief's body went suddenly limp, and he collapsed on top of Quinn. It took both men to heave him onto the floor.

Alex tore the telephone cord from the wall and used it to bind the chief's hands behind his back. Then both men lifted him into the swivel chair.

Quinn sagged against the wall, murmuring breathlessly. ''I hope to hell all that noise didn't attract attention.''

"The cleaning crew's already gone," Alex told him. "The building will be empty until 0600."

Quinn glanced at his wristwatch and dragged himself away from the wall. "That doesn't give us much time," he said. He stepped up to the chief and slapped him across the face. When the big man didn't respond, he told Alex, "Get some cold water. We have to bring this bastard to if we're going to get some answers from him."

Alex found a bucket in the utility room, filled it in the head and returned to Chief Loomis's office. Quinn gestured for him to douse the unconscious man. It was a task the yeoman enjoyed.

The chief sputtered, choked and opened his already swollen eyes. He pulled at the cord restraining his hands and tried to rise from the chair.

Quinn shoved him down again. "I'm going to ask you questions, Loomis. I want straight answers. Who ordered the execution of my wife?"

The chief spit blood, and it spattered Quinn's shirt.

Quinn backhanded him. "Who murdered my son?"

Chief Loomis clamped his lips together and said nothing.

"Why did Sontag have to get to New York so quickly? What's happening on the thirteenth?"

Quinn's next blow landed on the chief's broken nose. Blood gushed freely, outlining his thin lips and oozing off his chin.

Alex saw that Quinn's face was so altered by hatred that it was scarcely recognizable. "Commander?"

Ignoring the yeoman, Quinn demanded, "What was Admiral Burke's involvement with Delta? Did he recruit my son? What's Delta's objective? Answer me, damn you!"

Chief Loomis's eyes rolled back in his head.

"More water!" Quinn demanded of Alex.

When Alex returned from the utility room with another bucket of water, Quinn had dragged the chief from his chair

and positioned his body on the desktop so that his head
hung over the edge. He watched in horrified fascination a
the commander dug his fingertips just deep enough into the
chief's throat to control his air supply.

"I'm going to tear your throat out, Loomis, unless you
start answering my questions."

"I—I know the kind of man you are, Bannen," Loomi
croaked. "You're—going to kill me anyway." He gasped
wheezed, struggled to draw air into his lungs past the
blockage of Quinn's fingers.

Quinn removed his hand from the chief's throat. "I could
kill you slowly," he said without emotion. "Tear your body
apart a little at a time. Did your training teach you to han
dle pain, Loomis? Did you instruct my son how to ignore
pain? How was he killed?"

"Poison," the chief sputtered, and a gleam of satisfac
tion flickered behind his eyes. "It—ate through his guts
Bannen! It must have taken an hour, maybe two."

Quinn had gone extremely pale. "That's why his organs
weren't returned?" he murmured, more to himself than to
the chief.

"Couldn't have been much left to send back," the chief
told him.

Quinn raised his arm and positioned the edge of his hand
above the chief's throat.

"Commander, he's baiting you!" Alex shouted. "He
wants you to kill him! For Christ's sake, don't!"

Quinn's hand hesitated in midair above the chief's throat.
Then slowly, he lowered it to his side. "If I kill you, Loomis,
it'll be slowly. One, maybe two hours of agony, just like
Chad." He pressed his thumb and index finger against the
chief's left eyeball as if he intended to pluck it from the
socket. "I have nothing to lose by killing you," he said
"Delta's already taken my son and my wife. It's left me
nothing to live for except revenge."

Seeing the expression in the commander's eyes, Loomis suddenly began to shout as loud as his injured throat and nose would allow.

Quinn turned to Alex. "Clamp your hand over the bastard's mouth," he told him. "Go on!" he shouted when Alex hesitated. "He was going to kill you. Don't waste your sympathy on the son of a bitch!"

Alex stepped forward, but before he could comply with the commander's order, the chief stopped shouting.

"All right, Bannen," he said. "I'll answer your goddamned questions. Why not? I'm finished. Delta's finished. What difference does it make if you know the truth?"

Quinn removed his thumb and finger from the chief's eyeball. "Why was it so important Commander Sontag get to New York quickly?"

"First let me up," Loomis muttered. After Quinn had pulled him into a sitting position, he slid his legs off the edge of the desk, then stood on wobbling legs. He glanced from Quinn to Alex, who had backed away to stand beside the window. Because his head had been forced back over the edge of the desk, the blood from his nose had drained into the cavities of his eyes, and it was impossible to tell if he was able to focus.

"Why did Sontag go to New York?" Quinn repeated.

"He's a member of the Delta committee," the chief answered. "The committee is meeting tomorrow night."

"Where?"

"A hotel."

"What hotel?"

"I don't know. Near Central Park."

"How many members on the committee?"

"Seven."

"Why are they meeting? What happens on the thirteenth?"

The chief lowered his head, shaking it rapidly from side to side in an attempt to clear the blood from his eyes.

Without waiting for him to answer his last questions, Quinn demanded, "What are the names of the seven on the committee?"

"I know only Addison and Sontag," the chief said.

"You're lying! Let's see if losing one eye will bring out the truth!" He took a threatening step toward the chief, but the chief stumbled away from him, tucking his head down against his arm as if to protect his face and eyes.

"I swear I only know Addison and Sontag," he cried. "I shouldn't even have known about Sontag. It was set up that way. Only the seven committee members knew one another's identities. The lower-ranking officers only knew their division leader. My division leader was Addison, that bastard! He replaced Admiral Burke when the old man had a stroke."

"Who ordered the execution of my wife and son?"

When Quinn had mentioned his wife earlier it had not struck home with Alex that she had been executed, not until now, when Quinn repeated the question. Only last night he had walked in on the commander in the middle of a conversation with his wife; he had been embarrassed at being present while the commander murmured his expressions of love and affection. "Oh, God, Commander, your wife, too! I'm sorry."

Quinn ignored him. "We know Delta is going to assassinate someone. Who? Where? New York, on the thirteenth?"

Chief Loomis appeared reluctant again to answer questions. Neither Quinn nor Alex had noticed that he had managed to work his wrists free of the binding telephone cord.

"Answer me, damn it!" Quinn shouted.

The chief turned his bloody face slowly to confront his interrogator. His thin smile was made even more sinister by the blood outlining his mouth. "Too late, Bannen," he said matter-of-factly. "There is nothing you can do to stop Delta. Not now. Not ever!"

"I wouldn't count on that, Loomis," Quinn told him. "We'll take what we learned to the Pentagon, and we'll take you, too. With what they get out of you, they'll ferret out every one of your fucking leaders, every operative."

"You'll learn nothing further from me, Bannen," the chief said, his voice taking on an odd quality that Alex recognized from Loomis's call summoning him to Moffett Field. "What you've learned won't be enough to stop Delta."

"What makes you suddenly think you're going to be strong enough to hold back, Loomis?" Quinn asked. "I'd still gladly tear you apart a piece at a time."

The chief's smile broadened. "Not only are you going to learn nothing more from me, Bannen, I'm also going to deny you your revenge." Before either Quinn or Alex could reach him, he lunged forward and flung himself at the window.

Alex instinctively turned away to keep the glass from striking his face and eyes. In an instant he turned back. There was only a gaping hole where the window had been; the venetian blinds and the cross bars in the middle of the frame were gone. He stepped up beside Quinn, and both men stared down to where Chief Loomis's broken body lay on the tarmac, scarcely visible in the darkness.

Alex knew that the sound of the shattering window had to have been heard, but perhaps no one had been able to tell where it had come from yet. "Let's get the hell away from here, Commander," he said.

When they came out onto the sidewalk they saw the flashing light on a shore patrol car as it moved toward the buildings from the gate.

"This way, Commander," Alex cried. Knowing they'd be spotted immediately if they made for his car, he led Quinn around the side of the building.

"Where are we going?"

"To the admiral's offices," Alex told him. "That's where they expect me to be, so that's where they'll find me if they come looking. It's only two buildings over. When it's safe, I'll come back for the car, pick you up, and we'll leave by the back gate."

When they arrived at the staff admiral's offices, Alex sat down behind his desk, picked up the telephone and dialed base security. He identified himself as the admiral's yeoman, said he'd heard a commotion and seen the shore patrol car's flashing lights from his window and asked what was happening.

While Alex was on the telephone, Quinn went to the watercooler and helped himself to several glasses. His throat was dry and constricted. His stomach lurched, and he was forced to make an effort to keep the liquid down. The slash on his forearm was throbbing painfully. His jacket sleeve was soaked with blood, which was dripping down over his hand. He took paper towels and applied pressure to the cut.

Alex hung up the telephone. "They haven't determined if it was foul play or suicide," he told Quinn. He removed a first-aid kit from his desk, pushed back the commander's sleeve and began to clean the wound. "It's not deep, Commander, thank God. I'm not a corpsman." He wrapped the wound with gauze and tore off a strip of tape. "As soon as I finish this we'd better get off the base. If they find you here, it'll raise questions."

Quinn wasn't listening to him. He had slumped to the edge of a desk, his expression thoughtful. "Loomis may have beaten us after all," he murmured. "We learned very little from him. I wonder if all the members of Delta are kamikaze."

"I'd say we learned more than the chief wanted us to know," Alex returned. "We know there are seven division leaders and Admiral Addison and Commander Sontag are two of the seven. We know the full committee is to meet in

New York in a hotel near Central Park." Alex stepped back and examined his handiwork; at least the bandaged forearm had stopped bleeding. "We also know to be more careful of the next Delta member we question in the event they are all suicidal."

"The next one?" Quinn said.

"I was thinking of Captain Musolf," Alex told him. "Perhaps we can use some of his own psychological tricks on him. The only problem is, he divides his time between Moffett and Alameda. I don't know where he's scheduled for today." He snapped the first-aid kit closed. "But I can find out." He returned to his desk and picked up the telephone.

When Alex got through to the Alameda Naval Station hospital, he identified himself as the yeoman attached to the Moffett Field admiral's staff and told the corpsman on duty that he was complying with an urgent request from the admiral to locate Captain Musolf.

Quinn had picked up an extension and was listening.

"I'm afraid Captain Musolf left on leave last night," the corpsman said.

Alex choked back his disappointment. "It's imperative I locate him," he said evenly. "For the admiral. Does anyone on the staff know the captain's destination?"

"I do," the corpsman answered. "New York City. I heard him making the travel arrangements. Where he's staying in New York I can't tell you, but you can check with his commanding officer."

"Thank you. I'll tell the admiral you've been helpful." Alex hesitated, then asked, "The admiral's interested in a patient the captain was treating. His name's Marshisky. I believe he served under the admiral at his last command."

"I remember him," the corpsman said quickly. "He was released yesterday. Between you and me, Petty Officer Mayfield, I don't think Marshisky was ready for release, but the captain okayed it. Scuttlebutt was, Marshisky was a privileged case of Captain Musolf's. Maybe your admiral and the captain already conferred, but then..." Suspicion began to change the corpsman's voice.

"Thank you for your time," Alex said, and broke the connection. "It appears we've lost the captain," he told Quinn.

"Not necessarily," Quinn said. "Not if we go to New York."

ALEX TURNED THE CAR into the motel parking lot and killed the engine.

They hadn't spoken during the drive from Moffett Field; each had been preoccupied with his own thoughts. Now Alex turned and spoke to Quinn. "The chief said the order went out to kill you on sight, Commander. You'd better pack your things and come back with me."

"What makes you think you weren't included in that same order?" Quinn said pointedly. "In case you haven't realized it, Alex, you can't go back to your apartment, and you can't report for duty, not until we've exposed Delta. That's why I said *we* hadn't necessarily lost Captain Musolf if *we* go to New York. We're safer as a team than separated." Quinn opened the car door. "Come up while I pack. Then we'll make plans."

Alex climbed from behind the steering wheel and silently followed Quinn up the flight of steps to the second-floor landing. He saw Quinn pluck a piece of paper from his door and was aware of the sudden change that came over the commander.

Quinn had been jolted by the note. His hand shook as he fumbled with the lock. He flung the door open and dashed for the telephone, then propped the piece of paper against the lamp and began dialing a number.

Your wife called. Urgent you return call immediately.

The message was followed by a number with a Washington, D.C., area code and the signature of the motel manager, with the time of the call jotted below.

The call had been received a good half hour after Quinn had spoken to the policeman who had informed him his wife and an unidentified man had been murdered.

"Please, God, make it so!" he prayed as he dialed the last of the digits.

45

Dulles Airport, Washington, D.C.
FIFTEEN MINUTES before her scheduled flight time, Dorothy gave up hope that Quinn would return her call.

She left her seat finally to go into an airport shop where she purchased cigarettes and a canvas bag in which to carry the admiral's journals. As she waited for the clerk to make change, she heard her name, looked up and saw her photograph flash on the screen of the miniature television set the clerk had been watching at the counter. It was an old photograph, taken ten years previously, but it had been a favorite of the admiral's, and he'd kept a framed copy of it on his desk. The image faded and was replaced by a camera shot scanning the entryway, showing Mati's body crumpled at the foot of the staircase. The next shots were of Jonathan on the upper landing, his head tilted at an odd angle against the baseboard, and of Ginny's body sprawled at the foot of the bed. The camera angles had been carefully chosen to conceal the worst horrors of the victims' deaths. As the image of the newscaster replaced the scenes at her house, Dorothy felt herself begin to tremble out of control; the ringing in her ears prevented her from hearing the words of the news report.

The clerk looked at Dorothy oddly as she handed her her change, then watched as she hurried away.

To reach her flight gate, Dorothy had to pass the bank of pay telephones where she had waited for so long. As she did, she realized the phone with the Out of Order sign was ringing. An elderly man in a gray pin-striped suit was about to answer it. Dorothy dashed ahead of him and snatched up the receiver.

"Quinn? Quinn, darling? Is it you?"

"Dorothy! Thank God!"

She knew by his voice that he had heard the news of the Washington shooting and her supposed death. "It was Ginny," she told him quickly, "Jonathan's friend. The poor woman, she was just an innocent bystander! But Quinn, I found the admiral's journals! It's hard to accept, but my father was responsible for Delta. According to his entries, he was on the committee charged with investigating the existence of the organization in the early sixties, then charged with disbanding it. And later it was he who resurrected it. The proof's all here, Quinn. I've been reading the journals for the past two hours. Oh, God, Quinn! He mentions Chad and Admiral Addison and—"

"Dorothy, calm down," Quinn broke in. "You're speaking so fast I can't—"

Dorothy heard her flight number being announced for departure.

"Quinn, the number you called is Dulles Airport. I'm coming to you, darling. I'm bringing the journals. Together we'll decide what must be done with them. Jonathan said it was too late to worry about reputations—the admiral's or Chad's—and he was right. I have to go now. They're announcing my flight."

"No, Dorothy! Wait! Not here! Don't come here!" Quinn cried.

"I don't understand, Quinn." Her voice quavered as fear began to edge into her chest. Didn't he want her with him? she wondered. "I have my ticket. The flight leaves in less than five minutes. I need you, Quinn. I can't stay here alone when—"

"Take the shuttle to New York," Quinn told her firmly. "Check in at the Plaza Hotel. Use an assumed name. As long as they believe you're dead, you're safe. Use my housekeeper's name—Esther Wade. Do you have that?"

"Yes, but—"

"I'll join you at the Plaza as soon as I can get there."

"Yes, Quinn, yes. The Plaza. Esther Wade. Quinn, my father wrote that Admiral Addison recruited Chad, that he's also responsible for his execution. Chad was trying to emulate you, Quinn. He was trying to gather information to expose Delta as you exposed the military drug experiments."

"I'd surmised as much," Quinn said darkly. "Dorothy, once you've checked into the Plaza, stay put. If you need anything, use room service. Do *not* go out. I don't want you running the risk of being seen and recognized."

"Whatever you say, Quinn. I'll wait for you."

"I love you, Dorothy."

"I love you too, darling. I've always loved you. Always."

When Quinn broke the connection, Dorothy hung up and wiped the tears from her cheeks. I can make it now, she thought. Knowing Quinn loved her, knowing they would be together in New York, she could hold her frayed nerves in check until she felt the protection of his arms around her.

PART FOUR

46

New York, N.Y.

To think I recommended Addison to the committee as my replacement! What a blind old fool I was not to have seen his true character. I thought he was my friend. We even graduated from the same class at the academy. He introduced me to my wife, was my daughter's godfather; he was always welcome in my home; I even covered his ass when he was threatened by Quinn Bannen's exposure of the illegal drug experiments. If ever a man was Judas incarnate, it is Addison!

Chad—if there is a heaven and you're looking down on me now—can you ever forgive me?

I would gladly have sacrificed my life in your place. Forgive me, too, for not having the courage to immediately confess my involvement in Delta when I learned of your recruitment. Perhaps if we had talked then I could have discouraged your foolishness—for I knew without a shadow of a doubt that you were going along with Addison only to expose the organization. You had more than a physical similarity to your father.

In retrospect, I can see that I made a grave error in giving no consideration to Delta's operatives. It didn't seem necessary; they were selected because they were so easily expendable. How could I have known my own grandson would become one of their number?

How Addison must have enjoyed the irony of my situation; how he must have gloated at my suffering!

But I will have my revenge. I swear before God, Addison, you'll be sent to hell for what you've done!

Dorothy came up behind the stool where Quinn sat reading and bent to lean her cheek against his back. He felt her trembling and reached his hand over his shoulder to her, but she pulled away, walked to the bureau and the bottle of brandy ordered from room service. She poured drinks for both of them, added water to hers and carried a glass to Quinn.

Still, it will be a ticklish matter, bringing Addison before the committee. I suddenly don't feel I truly know the men I selected as Delta's leaders. If I didn't know Addison, after all these years, how can I trust my judgment of the others? Perhaps such extreme power had affected them all. Power madness is what destroyed the original Delta. History can't be allowed to repeat itself. The chaos of governments, the manipulations and assassinations—all must be limited to "the Cause," alone.

Quinn took the glass from Dorothy and sipped the strong brandy. She had marked several entries in the admiral's journal, and he had read most of them. Exhaustion was beginning to take its toll; he had not slept in more hours than he cared to remember. The brandy intensified his tiredness. "I need a clear head to read more," he said, and closed the journal.

Dorothy took the journal from him. "Before you sleep, I want to read you the admiral's last entry before we left for Key West," she told him. She opened the journal and read:

"Delta has passed fail-safe! D day cannot be stopped without exposing the organization. I wouldn't want to do this even to destroy Addison. Despite everything, I continue to believe in the concept of Delta. Americans and the American military must be protected at all cost. Our plan will jar people out of their lethargy. Americans don't trust their politicians and yet they allow them to continue manipulating our future by restricting our armed forces. When it comes to nuclear war and its inevitability, they are like ostriches who bury their heads in the sand. If we are not to be conquered, we must strike now, before Russia surpasses us even further in the arms race. D day will send a signal around the world. The day after the assassination, presidents, prime ministers, leaders in all key countries will be attacked and killed. General chaos will be the order of the day—all created by six divisions, less than a thousand operatives. Delta will step in and restore order. Those who oppose us will be eliminated."

Dorothy hesitated. She glanced at Quinn in deep distress.

"Go on," he said.

"Eliminated as Congressman Hackermann was eliminated today."

"Congressman Hackermann and his wife, Amanda, were our friends," she said quietly. "He was killed here in New York the day the admiral and I left Washington for Key West, supposedly by a gang of young muggers." She sank onto the edge of the bed and took a healthy gulp of her brandy and water. "Was my father mad, Quinn? Could he have been insane without my being aware of it?"

Because he didn't know how to answer her or even how to comfort her, Quinn said nothing.

Dorothy still had the admiral's journal open on her lap. She glanced back at her father's final entry and read:

"I had the satisfaction before my stroke of selecting the operative who will be our assassin on D day. He is Russian, with papers that have been authenticated. There was no difficulty in forging additional papers identifying him as a member of the KGB, nor in planting this information with Interpol and the CIA. He has a drug addiction and mental disorders, but not so severe as to be beyond our control. He is obsessed with the idea of assassinating a high-ranking American political figure. In the event he should survive elimination by our backup operative, he has been convinced the assassination is by direct order of the KGB.

"I must close this entry. My daughter and I must leave Washington for Key West because of the untenable position Quinn Bannen has placed us in, stirring up questions, shouting conspiracy...."

Dorothy fell silent and closed the journal.

Quinn had moved from the stool to a comfortable chair. He sat with his eyes closed, his head against the chair back. "In President Eisenhower's farewell address he said we had to guard against the acquisition of unwarranted influence, whether sought or unsought, by the military-industrial complex," he said quietly. "He could have had the admiral and an organization like Delta in mind. We now know what Delta plans. We know an important political figure is to be assassinated day after tomorrow in New York City. But who? That's the question. And even if we find the answer in time, who do we get to listen to—"

Quinn broke off speaking when he heard a knock on the door. He was immediately out of his chair, alert. Moving to the door, he removed the revolver from the waistband of his trousers.

The knock came again, then, "Commander? It's Alex."

When Quinn let the yeoman into the room he noticed that his nose and forehead were brightly sunburned; when Alex removed his sunglasses, his dark eyes were ringed by paler flesh. He looked as exhausted as Quinn felt. He nodded at Dorothy, then handed a slip of paper to Quinn. "I've covered a two-block radius to the east, west and south of Central Park, Commander," he said. "Those are the hotels. Neither Admiral Addison, Commander Sontag nor Captain Musolf are registered at any of them." He slid into a chair as he spoke and bent to massage the soreness in his calves. "What do we do now, Commander?"

Dorothy had risen from the bed. "You should have told me what you were doing," she said to Quinn. "I could have told you where to look."

Both men stared at her.

"Admiral Addison always stays in the same hotel when he's in New York," she told them. "He always stays here. At the Plaza."

Alex's flush of embarrassment didn't show because of his sunburn. He looked at Quinn apologetically. "And I'm always being told how efficient I am," he said critically. "I didn't check the Plaza, Commander. I checked every hotel except the one we're staying in. Jesus! I'm sorry."

Quinn moved to the telephone. "I'll check now," he said. He dialed the desk, said he was expecting three friends to register, gave the names of the three officers and waited for the desk clerk to check his records. When Quinn hung up, he said, "None of them is registered, nor have they made reservations."

"I know Admiral Addison wouldn't stay anywhere else," Dorothy said firmly. "I remember discussing it with him. He doesn't think any hotel compares with the Plaza. He's been staying here for years."

"Then they've taken a suite under the name of a leader we're not familiar with," Quinn said. "Remember, there are seven on the committee. Six from the military and one with political power. For all we know, the bastards could be next door." He began to pace back and forth across the room. "We have no choice but to take turns stationing ourselves in the lobby," he told Alex. "We can only hope we identify a member of the committee before they identify us." He returned to the bedside table and picked up the telephone.

"Who are you calling?" Dorothy asked.

"Captain McKay at the Pentagon," Quinn said. "He refused to help me before, treated me like a leper, but I've got to try again. I have to make someone listen. We can't stop Delta on our own. Perhaps the admiral's journals will force them to take me seriously."

"Quinn, they must!" Dorothy said. "Even if they won't believe you about Delta, they'll be forced to investigate an assassination threat."

"But whose assassination? I'm going to sound as vague as I feel. McKay's going to think I'm just a man crying wolf again." Quinn's brow was furrowed, beaded with anxious perspiration. "We can't allow a single member of Delta's committee to escape," he murmured. "If they do, Delta will undoubtedly be resurrected again and again now that the admiral's given them the guidelines."

Dorothy stepped up beside Quinn as he dialed the Washington number. "Let me talk to Simon McKay," she suggested. "We were all friends in the old days. Even if we hadn't been, he'd want to talk to me now. Who wouldn't accept a call from a woman he believed was murdered the day before?"

47

New York City

QUINN RAN HIS HAND nervously through his blond hair, folded the newspaper he had been pretending to read and got to his feet. He had been sitting for more than an hour.

His legs were cramped and his hopeful outlook was turning to frustration. Glancing quickly around, he strode across the Plaza lobby to where Alex sat partially concealed by a potted plant.

The young man glanced up from a magazine, his eyes meeting Quinn's. The sunburn on his nose and forehead had begun to darken and the skin was showing evidence of peeling. His dark sunglasses rested on the top of his head. Perceiving Quinn's frustration, Alex said, "If they have a room in the hotel, Commander, we'll eventually spot one of them."

"*If* they have a room," Quinn repeated. "Eventually may be too late. Seven men could meet anywhere—a restaurant, a bar, even benches in Central Park. If most of them are in the age group of Admiral Burke and Addison, they'd just appear to be innocent old men sunning themselves in the park. Who'd suspect them of plotting an assassination, let alone the manipulation of the government, of the world?" The anxiety in his blue eyes intensified. He glanced at his wristwatch. "And where is McKay? His flight was scheduled to land more than an hour ago."

Alex knew there was nothing he could say to calm the commander. Both of them were exhausted to the point of being ready to collapse. The yeoman let his gaze travel beyond Quinn, checking out the faces of everyone visible in the lobby in search of Admiral Addison, Commander Sonag or Captain Musolf. The Plaza Hotel was extremely busy. The commander's ex-wife had been right when she'd said earlier, "The tourists flock to New York in the summer, while the New Yorkers escape to the Hamptons, Fire Island or Florida."

It was nearing five o'clock. Beyond the glass doors, Alex could see that the automobile and pedestrian traffic had almost doubled in the past fifteen minutes. A group of guests who had checked out were waiting near the door for limousine service to the airport. Another group was arriving;

the bellmen were scurrying for their luggage. There was a steady stream of people to and from the nearby elevators.

A small girl with blond braids stood beside her mother's chair, bouncing a large rubber ball with rainbow stripes. The mother kept admonishing her, but the girl continued slapping the ball down against the carpet and catching it as it bounced above her head. When the ball slipped from the girl's hands and bounced into the milling stream of guests, Alex watched without interest. The girl cried and complained to her mother as the ball was inadvertently kicked farther and farther away from her by the feet of the guests.

Then Alex felt a jolt of recognition. His gaze had picked up a pair of highly polished black shoes—navy issue. His eyes lifted. "Commander Bannen!" He indicated the crowd crossing the lobby toward the elevators.

Commander Sontag was wearing a beige suit with a black-and-tan-striped tie. Except to a trained eye or to another military man, there was nothing about Sontag to distinguish him from a thousand other businessman staying at the hotel. His deep-set eyes were fixed directly ahead of him, and his pinched face showed signs of stress from the heat and humidity. He carried a brown paper bag tucked under one arm; its shape told Quinn it was a carton of cigarettes. Perhaps the brown Sherman's from the shop located on Broadway, Quinn thought, remembering that Sontag liked them and always stocked up before a deployment.

As the girl dashed in front of him, chasing her ball, Sontag glared down at her. He said something to her, then to her mother, who was chasing her across the stream of traffic. The woman glared at him in return.

Quinn turned his back when he saw that Sontag was going to pass almost directly in front of them. Alex had picked up his magazine and was holding it so that it concealed the lower part of his face. Quinn brought a hand to his forehead as if to soothe away a sudden pain above his eyes and watched Sontag through spread fingers.

Commander Sontag approached the desk and spoke to the clerk.

He was handed two messages.

He glanced briefly at both pieces of paper, then folded them and shoved them into his coat pocket. Then, instead of going to the elevators, he turned in the opposite direction with a slow, deliberate stride. At the corner where the restaurant was situated he turned right and disappeared behind the columns.

"He's apparently meeting someone in the Oyster Bar," Alex said. He dropped his magazine and rose. "I'll stick with him, Commander. You'd better stay here in case your friend from Washington arrives. We wouldn't want him paging you, would we?"

"But Sontag knows you, Alex," Quinn said.

"He knows us both, Commander. It's cocktail hour in Manhattan. The bar's probably crowded." He forced a weak smile. "Besides, I have my disguise." He pushed the sunglasses down onto the bridge of his nose and walked quickly away.

The Oyster Bar was even more crowded than Alex had anticipated, with more men and women coming in from the street entrance. He gave up the idea of ordering a drink and wedged himself against the wall near the service area. The noise of chatter and laughter was deafening. He let his gaze sweep the faces at the bar itself until he was satisfied Commander Sontag wasn't among them. Then he pushed away from the wall to mingle with the standing customers. When he still didn't see Commander Sontag it occurred to him that the man might have entered the bar to walk through and exit to the street. Although he had given no indication of it, he might have spotted either Quinn or Alex in the lobby and fled. Just as the yeoman was about to return to the lobby and inform Quinn that Sontag had evaded them, he spotted Sontag. He was seated at a corner table, his back to the bar; he had turned to signal a waitress, and his profile had been unmistakable. He blocked Alex's view of his companion.

Alex carefully edged his way forward, keeping himself inside the ring of customers huddled near the bar. When he had almost reached the end of the bar parallel to the corner table there was a jostling of customers as two men who had been seated on stools rose and began pushing their way through the crowd to the exit. The customers around Alex parted, leaving him suddenly exposed to full view of the corner table. It was then that he recognized Commander Sontag's drinking companion. His heart skipped a beat. He'd never forget the ashen face of Admiral Addison— "The Gray Hawk," one of the officers had called him.

The admiral was lifting a glass to his mouth. His eyes suddenly turned in Alex's direction. Too late to turn away, Alex thought. If he recognizes me— But a man suddenly pushed past Alex and weaved his way between the tables to the corner. He slipped into a vacant chair, and the three men put their heads together to be heard above the den of noise. Alex didn't recognize the newcomer.

He edged his way back through the crowd and made for the lobby, where he reported what he had seen to Quinn.

"So the bastards are gathering," Quinn said tightly. "I was afraid we'd missed them." He had taken the chair Alex had vacated because it afforded him a clear view of the main entrance. His hands, resting on the chair arms, had closed into fists. "Now we have to learn what room they're in," he said, "and then we can—" Quinn stopped speaking and got to his feet. "That damned son of a bitch!" he hissed. "Don't acknowledge me in front of these bastards, Alex. If I'm delayed, stick with Addison or Sontag and find out what room they're using." He walked quickly away.

Alex turned to see a captain in full dress uniform and a man in civvies crossing the lobby, heading for the reception desk. Quinn, his face flushed with anger, was rushing to meet them.

Quinn grabbed Simon McKay's arm and directed him, none too gently, to the far corner of the lobby, stopping behind the guests waiting for the airport limousine so that they were partially concealed. "Why the hell didn't you come in sounding a cavalry charge?" Quinn snapped.

Captain McKay's only reaction was a slight lifting of the eyebrows. He was a man of fifty, with salt-and-pepper hair and hazel eyes. Since Quinn had known him he had put on weight from his posh Pentagon duty station; he had a sallow complexion and a puffiness beneath his eyes that testified to late-night socializing. McKay turned to the man at his side. "Bannen, this is Captain Montalvo. I felt it necessary to contact him after you phoned."

Captain Montalvo was a tall man, ten years younger than McKay, with black hair, dark eyes and a swarthy complexion. He wore a dark blue business suit, a pale blue dress shirt and a paisley tie. His shoulders were broad, and his suit coat was nipped in at the waist attesting to the fact that he had not allowed himself to go to seed as McKay had. His smile showed even, white teeth but was belied by the coldness in his dark eyes. "Commander Bannen, a pleasure," he said.

Quinn ignored the hand the captain extended to him. "Simon, what the hell are you—"

"Captain Montalvo's with Pentagon Intelligence," Captain McKay announced. "It's only fair to tell you I've told him everything you and Dorothy told me on the phone."

Quinn turned away from McKay to confront Captain Montalvo's steady gaze. "And did you believe him, Captain?" he asked. "Do you believe an illegal organization named Delta exists? An organization that's responsible for my son's death and the death of Admiral Burke, to name just two?"

Captain Montalvo looked nervously at the surrounding crowd, obviously trying to determine whether their conversation was being overheard. When he turned back to Quinn, the smile had faded from his handsome face. When he spoke, his voice was carefully modulated. "What I believe, Commander, is that you're under considerable stress. I accompanied Captain McKay to this rendezvous to persuade you to return to Washington with us. Both you and your ex-wife. After all, Commander, you're retired navy. We take care of our own."

Quinn's laugh was hollow. "What you'd like is to prevent an embarrassment to the military," he said. "What's it going to be, Captain? A news flash that I'm demented? That my wife is deranged? That she rigged her own death by killing our friends? No, Captain. Delta does exist! Neither of us is insane."

"I'd appreciate it, Commander, if you'd lower your voice," Captain Montalvo told him. "We are investigating rumors of an unauthorized organization within the military, but frankly, Commander Bannen, we believe it's a myth, a vicious piece of propaganda started by those who oppose the growing power of the military."

"And if I told you I have unquestionable proof that Delta exists?" Quinn demanded.

Captain Montalvo's dark eyes shifted, dropped. "I would, of course, be interested in such proof," he said. "I'd like you to show it to me."

"I'll bet you would!"

"You seem to be looking on me as an enemy, Commander. I assure you Pentagon Intelligence will keep an open mind. We'll carefully weigh whatever information you turn over to us. If such an organization as Delta exists, we'll—"

"You'll disband it a second time," Quinn cut in. "Destroy all evidence, or bury it in secret archives."

The muscles in the captain's face were tightening. "A second time?" he said, plainly struggling to maintain control.

"Don't play uninformed with me!" Quinn snapped. "You know as well as I do that Delta was investigated by a committee headed by Admiral Burke over two decades ago. The admiral found that Delta truly did exist. It was no myth. He was charged with disbanding the organization."

"I know nothing of this," Captain Montalvo said flatly.

"I put it to you that you're lying, Captain," Quinn said challengingly. "The Pentagon is also probably aware that Admiral Burke resurrected Delta."

"I personally knew Admiral Burke," Captain Montalvo said, "and I find it hard to believe he'd act against the military. Since the man is dead of a heart attack and can't defend himself—"

"Not a heart attack, Montalvo. The admiral was executed, just as my son was executed. And the admiral can still speak for himself—or against himself, as the case may be— through his journals. Fortunately, he was a man who liked to put everything down in black and white. Not necessarily wise for a man involved in resurrecting Delta. He's even recorded guidelines for the organization's leaders and operatives. He listed very few of their covert activities, but he did make reference to the elimination of Congressman Hackermann and to an assassination of a political figure, planned for the thirteenth. Tomorrow, Captain."

"I'm aware of the date, Commander," Captain Montalvo said stiffly. He turned to Captain McKay, who had been listening intently. "Simon, would you excuse us?" He waited until McKay had moved aside, out of earshot, before saying, "Commander, as a representative of the Pentagon, I insist you turn the admiral's journals over to me. That, Commander, is an order."

"So the controller and seven leaders of Delta can either go free or have their wrists slapped?" Quinn said. "Sorry, Montalvo, I'm forced to disobey your order. If I have anything to say about it, those men will face court-martial, and their activities will become public knowledge. It's time the shroud of secrecy was lifted and the American people were given a glimpse of what goes on. One secret act breeds another. Who's to say how many Deltas exist in our system?"

"Be reasonable, Bannen," Montalvo said. "You can't go public. You don't have a scrap of concrete evidence. Nothing except the scribblings of a sick old man. Who's going to believe you? Some radical newspapers? A few communist-controlled countries that already hate us? You'll get a minimum of press coverage; then the whole story will be dismissed as a paranoid delusion. You'll not only have embarrassed the military, you'll harm yourself, as well. You'll be labeled a traitor, Bannen."

"In some circles I'm already considered a traitor, Captain, because I embarrassed the military once before."

"I'm aware of that. Be assured it'll be turned against you. You can't win, Bannen. Turn over Admiral Burke's journals to me. I assure you the matter will be looked into. If such an organization as Delta does exist, it and the men involved will be dealt with internally." Montalvo motioned for Captain McKay to rejoin them.

Beyond the two captains' shoulders, Quinn saw Alex suddenly rise from his chair.

Admiral Addison, Commander Sontag and a man Quinn recognized as Brigadier General Clayton were rounding the corner, coming from the direction of the Oyster Bar. Quinn's gaze settled on the admiral's pale face; he had never liked Addison, but the emotion that consumed him now was hatred. The three officers, dressed as civilians were moving toward the elevators. Alex, his dark glasses covering his eyes, moved ahead of the trio. When he saw which elevator they were going to take he stepped in ahead of them, wedging himself in at the back with his head lowered. The elevator doors closed.

"I assure you the matter will be looked into," Captain Montalvo repeated. "Now, Commander, if you'd come along with us?"

"A confidential investigation isn't good enough," Quinn told the captain. "I'm sorry, but—" He saw Captain Montalvo's hand move to the lapel of his coat. He'd already observed that the man wore a shoulder holster. He wondered how many men had accompanied the two captains. His gaze darted around the crowd, settling on a man of about twenty-five, dressed in jeans and a knit shirt; he was lounging on the fringes of the group of guests waiting for the airport limousine, but it was apparent he was not one of them.

"If you'd come along peacefully, Commander..." Captain Montalvo said, his hand still resting on his lapel.

Quinn's revolver was pressing into the small of his back, but he knew he would never reach it if Montalvo suspected his intent. He assumed an expression he hoped passed for one of defeat. "I did what I could," he murmured. "You win, gentlemen."

Montalvo glanced at McKay and said, "I told you he'd be reasonable." His hand came away from his lapel. He reached for Quinn's arm and started to guide him toward the doors. He was caught completely by surprise when Quinn's fist slammed hard into his abdomen. Even before Montalvo doubled over from the pain, Quinn sent McKay rocketing backward into the group of hotel guests.

As he darted through the doors, Quinn had a fleeting glimpse of the young man pushing his way through the crowd to pursue him.

Quinn ran between the taxis and limousines waiting at the hotel entrance. Knowing he would stand little chance of outdistancing the younger man in Central Park, he turned right, reached Fifth Avenue and weaved his way quickly around the pedestrians, not daring to look back for fear of colliding with someone. When he reached the entrance to Bergdorf-Goodman, he stepped quickly inside, pressed back behind a counter and peered through the glass door.

It was only moments before he saw the young man from the hotel lobby darting among the pedestrians, his head

turning quickly as his eyes searched for Quinn. Quinn
stepped back through the doors and pressed himself close to
the building until he saw that the young man had proceeded to the next corner and stopped and was looking in all
directions in confusion. When his eyes turned in Quinn's
direction, Quinn stooped, pretending to tie his shoe. When
he looked again the man was no longer in sight. Doubling
back to Fifty-eighth Street, Quinn walked rapidly past
Bergdorf's, a theater and some small shops, crossed the
street and slipped into the Oyster Bar, looking for a telephone.

Dorothy answered on the first ring. "Quinn! What's
happened? Where are you?"

"In the hotel," he told her. "Dorothy, I want you—"

"Alex called," Dorothy said, interrupting him. "He has
the room number where the committee is meeting." She
gave him the number, then said, "He's waiting for you in
the corridor. Quinn, what are you going to do? What happened with Simon McKay?"

"I should never have trusted the bastard," Quinn said
hotly. "Listen, Dorothy, there's something I want you to
do." He hesitated before saying, "It's asking a lot of you,
but it's something that occurred to me when you said you'd
have no difficulty getting McKay to accept a call from you."

"Quinn, I'll do anything," she assured him.

"All right, then listen carefully," he said.

48

New York City

WHEN QUINN LEFT the elevator on the twelfth floor, the
corridor was empty.

"Here Commander!"

Alex had opened a door halfway along the corridor, and
he gestured Quinn forward. The room was a maid's service
station. Just as Quinn ducked inside and closed the door, the

elevator gong sounded; the doors slid open, and two men emerged. As they walked past the utility room, Quinn heard, "...a lot to answer for, damn him."

"He's jeopardized the entire operation, but still you have to hand it to the old bastard..."

The voices faded away. A door opened and closed.

"I heard in the elevator that two officers are delayed," Alex said. "Something to do with storm conditions in Florida. Thank God Commander Sontag didn't take a good look at me. I felt like a trapped animal in that elevator with them, but I couldn't think of any other way of finding out what room they were using."

"You did well," Quinn told him. "Better than I did with McKay or that bastard from Pentagon Intelligence." The bitterness in his voice was evident to the yeoman. He listened at the door but heard nothing; he opened the door and stepped into the corridor. "How are you at picking locks, Alex?"

Alex smiled. "I picked a few in the days before I became a respected member of the navy, Commander," he admitted.

"Well, let's hope it's something you don't forget, like swimming or riding a bike. I want you to get us into the room next to the committee's. And quickly. Think you can do it?"

"I'll try, Commander." Alex moved down the corridor and stopped in front of a door at the end. "They're in there," he said in a whisper, indicating the next room. Then he bent to examine the lock.

Quinn watched the corridor and the indicator lights above the elevators.

"I don't know, Commander," Alex murmured. "It doesn't look as if I've retained my touch for—" The lock clicked. Alex shoved the door open and they both stepped inside.

There was an open valise on the suitcase rack, and a makeup case lay on the dresser. A nightgown was thrown over the back of a chair, and a pair of shoes was placed neatly at the foot of the bed. The bed had been made, but someone had lain on the spread, leaving the indentation of a lightweight body that had been curled into a fetal position.

"Let's hope the lady doesn't return soon," Quinn mumbled. He moved into the bathroom and returned with a drinking glass. He positioned the rim against the wall beyond which the committee was meeting and pressed his ear to the bottom. "Old-fashioned but effective," he told Alex.

"I MAY HAVE ACTED without proper authority," Admiral Addison said, "but I was only protecting Delta. As I told you, Admiral Burke's grief over his grandson had affected his reason."

Five members of Delta's committee sprawled in chairs in the outer room of the hotel suite, resembling, Admiral Addison thought, patients waiting in a doctor's reception room. As always when they met, the atmosphere was charged with tension. Since their involvement with Delta was not recorded in any file or computer, they were at their most vulnerable during committee meetings. Except for Senator Lawton, who had been recruited because of his political connections and his financial contributions to the organization, the Delta committee members were all military. Commander Sontag was the youngest; the others were all over sixty. Another common denominator was their involvement with American industries that fed the military machine. Admiral Addison considered himself the only member whose motives were pure.

"Then you confess to ordering Burke's elimination?" Brigadier General Clayton asked.

"I confess," Admiral Addison said with a wary sigh, "on the grounds of the protection of Delta. There wasn't time for discussion and authorization."

"Most irregular, just the same," the brigadier general mumbled.

A murmur of ayes and nays filled the room.

Admiral Addison turned from the window where he had been standing staring down at Central Park. "I had no choice," he said.

"But it was Burke who came to me with the suggestion of resurrecting Delta," Clayton reminded the other men. "No man could have been more devoted to his country or to the organization than Burke. We have to credit him with being our founder. I can't believe that grief over his grandson would drive him to expose Delta."

"He was ill and knew his time was limited," Admiral Addison said. "Don't ask me why, but I assure you his intentions were clear. He intended to expose us. You, me, the entire operation. I couldn't allow that to happen."

"No, of course not," Brigadier General Clayton said. "Still, Addison, you stretched your authority again by ordering the execution of his daughter and that damned reporter. It's the major news in Washington, crowding even the Capitol Hill scandals off the front pages. You may have gone too far. The Pentagon had already initiated a confidential investigation into the rumors concerning Delta, but it was low-key. These murders may instigate a full-fledged investigation. Christ! What we don't need more of in Washington is investigations. Certainly not of Delta."

Senator Lawton leaned forward in his chair and reached for the scotch and soda on the cocktail table. "The controller's concerned, also," he told them. "With the headlines and television screaming about murders that might be connected to political intrigues, he refused to attend this meeting. Call me paranoid, if you will, but I feel we should call off tomorrow's operation."

"That's absurd!" Admiral Addison shouted. "We can't turn weak-kneed now! It's less than fifteen hours away!"

"I agree with Addison," Commander Sontag said. "Do you realize the months of planning that have gone into this operation? Everything's been worked out in minute detail. All that's waiting to be done is the words *Kill One* spoken into that telephone. Then there'll be no further contact with our operatives. Even we can't stop it then."

"But the danger..." the senator said.

"The danger will be greater if we delay," Addison cut in. "If D day goes ahead as scheduled, can't you imagine the chaos the country's going to be thrown into tomorrow? And the entire world the day after? We've operatives in every military installation in the free world. When Kill One is announced as a success, a chain of events will be unleashed that even we will have no power to stop. Presidents, prime ministers, cabinet members...if only half the assassination attempts are successful..." The admiral let his words hang in the smoke-filled room. Then after a moment, he said quietly, "Delta will restore order, gentlemen. Our safety will be assured. Who will question the saviors of law and order?"

Senator Lawton, his face white, leaned back in his chair and gulped at his drink. Half a dozen military minds had gone mad, he thought. Even when he'd been recruited as a member of the Delta committee he hadn't believed the project would come to fruition. He'd taken it as a political game, a path to securing even more political power. Now he was facing D day—he thought of it as Armageddon—and he was terrified. "We still must vote," he mumbled. "It must be unanimous." Despite the air conditioner, he felt as if his body were encased in a steam cabinet.

"Yes, we'll vote," Brigadier General Clayton confirmed. "If Sax and Marshall ever get here. These damned summer storms."

Admiral Addison smiled down at the senator. "And after we've voted, we'll place the Kill One call," he said
pointedly.

49

New York City

QUINN MOVED AWAY from the wall and began pacing the
hotel room.

He had heard only a few words from the committee's
suite.

Alex, who had stationed himself beside the door, suddenly turned and motioned to Quinn. "The last two committee members are arriving," he whispered.

Quinn heard a knock on the door of the committee's
suite. Then Admiral Addison's voice: "At last. Come in,
come in. We're anxious to get this..." The door closed,
cutting off his voice.

Quinn glanced at his watch. They'd been hiding in the
hotel room for more than an hour and a half. Time enough,
he hoped, for Dorothy to have put their plan into action. He
moved to the phone and dialed her room number.

The extension rang several times before Dorothy answered. Quinn knew immediately by the din in the background that she had succeeded in attracting the news media.

"Quinn, I've got two major television network newscas-
ters here, plus reporters from the *Times* and *Daily News*.
Thanks to Amanda Hackermann, we also have two Secret
Service men and three of New York's finest. I told the reporters what happened to Jonathan and Ginny. Amanda's
now discussing her husband's murder. She believed me
without question when I showed her the entry in the admiral's journal saying Congressman Hackermann was eliminated by Delta. Quinn, can you hear me? It's havoc here!"

"I hear you, darling," Quinn said, as loud as he dared.
"Can you hear me?"

"Yes, barely, but I can hear you," Dorothy answered "Quinn, Simon McKay is also here. So is a captain from the Pentagon. They tried to stop the interview, but Amanda and I wouldn't let them."

"Dorothy," Quinn cut in. "We're ready! Can you bring them now?"

"Yes, darling. Immediately."

No sooner had Quinn hung up than Alex stepped quickly away from the door. A key was turning in the lock. Quinn sprang for the light switch and, with the room in darkness pulled Alex into the bathroom.

A small woman in her mid-thirties stepped into the room Laden with several bundles, she had difficulty flicking the light switch, and she dropped her purse as she made for the bed to deposit her packages. Her back to the open bathroom door, she removed her blouse, then stepped out of her skirt. Moving to the thermostat, she turned up the air conditioner. She undid the pens holding her French twist in place, and her auburn hair spilled around her naked shoulders. She retrieved her purse from the floor, removed a cigarette, lit it and then settled down on the bed to smoke and wait for the air conditioner to cool her body.

Quinn and Alex stood behind the open bathroom door watching through the narrow crack afforded by the hinges When Quinn saw that the woman had settled down for at least as long as it would take her to smoke the cigarette, he allowed himself to relax. If the woman had come into the bathroom, he would have had to silence her. Her scream might have alerted the men in the suite next door. Although he hadn't heard much that was spoken in normal voices in the next room, the men there would certainly hear a woman's scream.

The telephone rang, and the woman reached for it with weary "Hello."

Alex, shifting his position wedged behind Quinn, bumped the commode with his leg. The wooden lid was loose and

craped across the porcelain in what both men took as a
leafening alarm, but the woman only glanced toward the
pen door, then went back to her conversation. "I simply
an't, Suzanne. I'm too beat to sit through another play. I'm
oing to take a long bath and get some sleep. Yes, I adore
ondheim, but . . ."

Quinn heard a sound from the corridor. Shutting out the
woman's voice, he listened intently. Then he turned to Alex.
"Come on," he said in a normal voice. He stepped through
he bathroom door, Alex at his heels, and with a nod to the
woman he made for the outer door.

They had reached the corridor before she overcame her
hock enough to scream.

The elevator doors stood open, and people were stream-
ng into the corridor, Dorothy and a woman Quinn thought
ust be Amanda Hackermann in the lead. Dorothy looked
a the opposite direction, then turned and saw him and
aved. She started forward, pursued by several reporters
nd a television cameraman with a Minicam balanced on his
noulder. Behind the reporters, the tall Captain Montalvo
nd the uniformed Captain McKay followed with grim
xpressions.

The cameraman dashed past Dorothy and Amanda,
urned and began filming them as they proceeded down the
orridor.

The woman inside the room Quinn and Alex had used
ontinued to scream.

Quinn spun around as the door to the committee's room
pened.

Drawn by the woman's screams, Admiral Addison and
ommander Sontag stood in the opening, the other offi-
rs of Delta behind them. Admiral Addison's ashen face
ll when he saw Quinn Bannen, and behind Quinn, Ad-
iral Burke's daughter—his goddaughter—trailed by re-
orters and cameramen. A spark of recognition flamed
hind his gray eyes as he recognized Captain Montalvo

from Pentagon Intelligence. The admiral attempted to push
back those behind him so he could close the door, but Quinn
stepped forward to prevent him.

Dorothy and those behind her came to a stop six feet away
from the door. Her eyes bored into Admiral Addison's for
a long moment before she lifted her hand and pointed.
"They are the murderers of my son and father," she said
evenly. "Of Congressman Hackermann and Jonathan
McKinney and God knows how many others. Those,
gentlemen, are the leaders of Delta."

Quinn observed the shock and defeat in the men gathered in the doorway. How unimpressive they were in their
civilian clothes, he thought. Without their gold braid and
their brass and their chests covered with metals they appeared exactly what they were—old men. Dangerous and
criminal, but old men, nevertheless, who could lose themselves in a crowd.

Then Quinn's eyes settled on Admiral Addison.

Admiral Addison was staring directly at him.

The expression in the admiral's cold gray eyes destroyed
his sense of triumph.

And those eyes continued to haunt him, long after he had
returned to Dorothy's room.

He undressed, showered and came in to sit on the edge of
the bed as Dorothy opened and poured the champagne she
had ordered from room service.

She handed him a glass, then touched hers to his. "We did
it," she said dully, "but I feel curiously hollow."

Quinn agreed. "It's not over," he said. "The seven committee members have been arrested, but somehow I feel it
isn't over. We're missing something." He set the glass of
champagne aside untouched. "The key's with Addison," he
said thoughtfully. "Something in his expression. But what?
What?" He rose from the bed, the towel around his middle, and began to pace.

"Whatever it is, they'll get it out of them, darling," Dorothy told him. "There's nothing more we can do. The shame of Delta is going to be unraveling for months, maybe longer, but—"

A knock at the door cut into her thoughts. She looked to Quinn with an expression that asked if she should answer.

He nodded.

Captain Montalvo stood there. He looked past Dorothy to Quinn. "May I have a word with you?" The captain no longer had the attitude of assurance he had displayed earlier in the hotel lobby. "It's important, Commander," he said when Quinn hesitated.

"Then make it quick," Quinn told him.

Dorothy closed the door behind the intelligence man. "A glass of champagne, Captain? We don't seem to be in the mood to celebrate."

"Nor I," Montalvo said flatly. He moved to a chair and asked permission to sit.

Quinn nodded. "What have you learned from the unholy seven?" he asked.

"The senator is in such a state of shock and fear he has had to be sedated," Montalvo answered. "As for the six officers, they'll give only their names, ranks and serial numbers. They're tough old birds."

"You sound almost complimentary, Captain," Dorothy said darkly. "The stark reality is they're murderers, and should be looked on as such."

"Yes, ma'am," the captain said. He ran a hand through his black hair and turned his dark eyes on Quinn. "I'll tell you straight out, Commander, we've clamped a security freeze on the news release."

Dorothy looked from the captain to Quinn. "What does that mean?" she demanded.

"It means we failed," Quinn said tensely. "It means Delta can be swept under the military carpet. Again."

"No, it doesn't mean that at all, Commander," Montalvo said. "The security freeze is for twenty-four hours only."

"So the Pentagon can come up with an acceptable explanation why an organization such as Delta can exist?" Quinn said.

"So we can attempt to unravel the extent Delta's gone to before the evidence is buried even deeper," Montalvo countered. "You'll get your public airing, Commander. Thanks to your wife and Amanda Hackermann, we can't prevent that. We've given ourselves twenty-four hours to learn all we can. After the news release there may be those who go underground. The one Admiral Burke refers to in his journals as "the controller," just to name one. We're convinced he holds a high government position, but unless the senator or one of those six officers decides to open up the man could die of old age before we discover his identity."

"What about the operatives?" Quinn asked. "There could be more than five hundred of them. Trained assassins, terrorists. They're not suddenly going to become model citizens because they're no longer under the direction of Delta leaders."

"We think we can deal with that problem through the computers," Montalvo told him. "Even without Delta's access codes, we have experts who can pull every individual flagged by the symbol of the bisected triangle."

"They're undoubtedly scattered all over the world. In every military installation."

"We're aware of that. It'll take time, but we'll gather them up."

Quinn moved to the bedside table where he had set his glass of champagne, picked it up and drained it. "The admiral wrote that the operatives were their weakest link," he said. "As it turned out, it was the leaders themselves."

"But the operatives are the clear and present danger at his point," Captain Montalvo said.

"Explain that, please."

"We believe the six officers are taking the attitude of POWs—name, rank and serial number only—because they're stalling for time," the captain said. "Some operation was put into effect before their apprehension. If they keep silent, the operation will continue on schedule."

Quinn felt a surge of adrenaline. "Of course! That's explains Addison's expression! It's been haunting me. Those cold gray eyes...it was a...a look of victory! Those bastards put what they're calling D day into effect from their hotel suite! They were arrested with the satisfaction of knowing the wheels were already in motion."

"But what is D day?" Captain Montalvo said. "We can't stop it unless we discover what it is."

"An assassination," Quinn said. "Who, I can't tell you. But the targeted victim has to be damned important. From the information Alex Mayfield and I have gathered, it's to be—" he glanced at the travel clock on the bedside table "—today, the thirteenth. Possibly at Parke-Bernet Galleries."

"Parke-Bernet!" Dorothy cried. "You didn't mention that."

Both men turned their attention to her.

"Then it's obvious who they intend to assassinate," she told them. "Amanda Hackermann and I were talking about it earlier. There's a special summer auction at Parke-Bernet tomorrow. Their catalog lists an André Derain painting. The First Lady has been trying to acquire a Derain for the past four years. Delta's intended victim is truly damned important. It's the president!"

50

New York City

THE LIMOUSINE WAS PARKED across the street and half a block away from the famous New York auction gallery.

Inside, concealed by the dark windows, Alex and Captain Montalvo sat facing Quinn and Dorothy. It was five-fifteen on a Saturday afternoon. The heat inside the limousine was oppressive. Dorothy had gone shopping for a new outfit on Fifth Avenue and had had her hair done at Elizabeth Arden, but the humidity had already taken the curl out of her hair, and the lightweight summer fabric of her dress clung to her body. Taking an envelope from her purse, she fanned herself as she stared pensively from the window.

The auction was scheduled to begin at six o'clock. Customers were already arriving for a preview of the art to be auctioned. The police had put up a barricade along the sidewalk; as always where the famous and near-famous were expected to gather, curious spectators were gathering. Two patrolmen were pacing back and forth in front of the building, and another on horseback was keeping the traffic flowing. As arranged by Captain Montalvo, there were also two burly men in business suits, obviously Secret Service agents, lounging near the auction house's entrance.

"We thought the senator would be the first to break," Captain Montalvo was saying to Quinn. "Now we've lost him. The guards found him early this morning. He'd used his necktie to hang himself. The poor bastard. It must have taken him a long while to die. His face was—"

"Please, Captain," Dorothy said. "Spare us the details."

"Yes, certainly. I'm sorry." The captain stretched his long legs and ran a finger beneath the collar of his shirt. Despite the heat, he had not removed his suit coat. His swarthy complexion was covered in perspiration. "The president and the First Lady arrived in New York last night,'' he said. ''We reached him at his son's apartment on Park Avenue. Since his visit is unofficial, only those in the inner circle knew about it. That means either the controller is among them, or he has the ear of someone who is. The Secret Service is compiling a list of possibles.''

''And the operatives?'' Quinn asked. ''How is your computer expert doing on breaking the organization's code?''

''He's already succeeded,'' Captain Montalvo said with a measure of pride. ''We have a list of 572 individuals whose records were flagged by the symbol of the bisected triangle, their ranks ranging from seaman and private to captain and colonel. Then, of course, there are the leaders.''

''Who are still giving only name, rank and serial number?'' Quinn said.

''They'll break, Commander,'' the captain said confidently. ''Eventually.''

''Or take the senator's way out. Or die of old age. Or plea-bargain. End up with their wrists slapped, maybe stripped of their ranks. You see, I still have no faith in the system, Montalvo. I didn't a decade ago, and I don't now. Those bastards are responsible for the deaths of my son, my friend Jonathan McKinney, my father-in-law and God knows how many other people. Those officers should be tried publicly, then executed. That would not only give me satisfaction, it would discourage some future madmen from forming another organization like Delta. I know you think I'm a vengeful bastard. You're damned right I am. We both are.'' He reached across and took Dorothy's hand. ''But we've done all we can,'' he said, more to Dorothy than to the captain. ''We'll testify, of course, for whatever good it'll do. Then we're done with it. We have to put all that's happened behind us and get our lives back in order.''

Dorothy looked at him without speaking, her expression signifying agreement.

Alex had been staring out the window, his gaze traveling from face to face in the crowd gathering around the gallery entrance. He regretted he hadn't had a glimpse of Marshisky when he'd overheard the conversation between Captain Musolf and the assassin. Unless he happened to overhear the man's voice, he had no hope of recognizing him.

The patrolman on horseback moved close to the limousine, the flanks of the horse almost brushing the glass as he rode past. A taxi had stalled and was blocking traffic.

The small radio transmitter-receiver on the seat beside the captain made a squawking sound. He picked it up and pressed a button, and a voice said, "The presidential limo's crossing Park Avenue now, Captain. Estimated arrival time sixteen to seventeen minutes."

"Do you think this is going to work?" Quinn asked doubtfully.

"It'll work, Commander," Captain Montalvo assured him. "We'll catch the would-be assassin. If you're to have the justice you seek, we need his testimony against the Delta officers." He pointed toward the crowd at the gallery entrance. "You see two policemen and two obvious Secret Service men. That's what you and the assassin are meant to see. There's another dozen agents among that crowd, more inside the gallery. Then there are those riding with the stand-ins for the president and First Lady. When he makes his move, we'll apprehend him."

"What if he doesn't make a move?" Quinn said. "What if he recognizes your stand-ins for what they are?"

"He won't," Captain Montalvo said. The radio sputtered again and claimed his attention.

Dorothy leaned against Quinn's shoulder. In a whisper, she said, "We'll get our lives together, Quinn. We will. I love you, darling."

"And I love you, Dorothy," he whispered in return. "I only hope you'll be happy on a horse ranch."

"With you, I will," she assured him.

Alex straightened in his seat, leaned closer to the window. "There's something strange about that patrolman on horseback," he commented to Quinn.

The radio squawked, "Five minutes, Captain. The limo's turning into the block."

As Quinn turned to follow the direction of Alex's stare, he saw the two Secret Service agents in front of the gallery move forward to the curb. Both held radios similar to Captain Montalvo's and were speaking into them. The crowd had pressed closer to the barricade in anticipation of the president's arrival. Quinn saw the patrolman on horseback. "What's strange about him?"

"He's supposed to be directing traffic," Alex said, "but he didn't stop to say anything to the driver who's double-parked or to the cabdriver who stopped to discharge a fare in the middle of the street."

"Just damned ineffective, I'd say," Quinn murmured. He saw the presidential limousine approaching from the far end of the block. He turned back to the captain as he held the radio to his mouth and said, "This is it. Look lively!"

Alex watched the patrolman on horseback turn his horse between two cars and rein to a halt at the curb. A man in khaki slacks and a bright-colored sport shirt pushed through the crowd. He was wearing sunglasses and carried a large canvas tote bag over his left shoulder. As the patrolman leaned down to speak to the man, Alex felt a sudden jolt of recognition.

"Captain Musolf!" Alex cried. "Speaking to the patrolman on horseback! The patrolman must be Marshisky!"

Captain Montalvo responded immediately by shouting into the radio, "Suspect patrolman on horseback! Repeat, suspect patrolman on horseback! Don't apprehend! Repeat, don't apprehend! Wait until he makes his move!" He turned his dark eyes toward Alex. "Are you certain?"

"He's talking to Captain Musolf," Alex replied. "And what better disguise to get close to the president?" His voice faltered. "But I've never seen Marshisky. I've just heard his voice." He turned to Quinn.

But Quinn had slid forward in his seat, his face pale, the muscles in his jaw rigid. As he had turned to look at the patrolman on horseback, his gaze had been caught by another man moving hurriedly through the crowd. The man jumped the barricade and made for the entrance to the office building across from the gallery. He was dressed in jeans and a blue polo shirt and was carrying a large briefcase. There were bandages across the bridge of his nose.

"Everett!" Quinn cried. He opened the limousine door and leaped out, Alex behind him, before Captain Montalvo had time to respond.

Everett disappeared inside the lobby of the office building.

"Damn it, Commander!" Captain Montalvo called after them. "Come back before—"

His voice was cut off as Quinn and Alex raced for the building entrance.

At almost six o'clock on a Saturday, the lobby of the office building was almost empty. An old man was closing his magazine stall; a woman was using the single pay telephone in the far corner. As Quinn and Alex dashed into the lobby, the doors of one of the two elevator opened and two men in business suits got out. The indicator for the second elevator was moving upward. Quinn held the doors of the empty elevator until the indicator on the other stopped at the fifth and top floor.

As they moved upward at what seemed a snail's pace, Quinn took the revolver from the waistband at the back of his trousers. He flipped off the safety catch, then shoved the revolver into the pocket of his summer jacket, which was still clutched in his hand.

Alex saw the frozen expression on Quinn's face and read
t correctly as raging hatred. His own voice cracked as he
aid, "Everett, Commander... he's one of the men I heard
Chief Loomis say was a backup for Marshisky."

"A backup for the operation would be more accurate,"
Quinn said tightly. "Not for Marshisky. If my guess is right,
Everett's to kill Marshisky as soon as he assassinates the
president. It's an old strategy, one that's been used success-
ully in the past. Hire an assassin, then hire a second to take
out the first. It leaves less evidence, or, if you plant it on the
first assassin, it leaves the evidence you want to be found.
'd place odds Marshisky's carrying documents that connect him directly to some government or intelligence network Delta wants charged with the president's death."

"But Chief Loomis mentioned two backups, Commander," Alex reminded Quinn. "Everett and Sloane. If
what you suspect is true, then Delta's taken double precau-
ions. Even if we stop Everett, Sloane will undoubtedly be
positioned at another location to take out Marshisky
whether he assassinates the president or is apprehended. The
bastard doesn't have a chance."

"It's Montalvo's show," Quinn said. "Let him direct it.
only want Everett. I'm sure he killed my son!"

When Raymond Everett reached the fifth floor, he walked
directly to the last office in the corridor.

The sign on the door read Walter Cole, Rare Coins
Bought and Sold.

A buzzer sounded as he opened the door and went in.

The office was one long rectangular room with a counter
unning down the middle. The upper section of the counter
was encased in glass, with coins displayed on dark blue vel-
et. Behind the counter were two desks, both piled high with
atalogs, newspapers and small coin folders; behind the
lesks were several windows looking out onto the street.

An old man with white hair and bifocals was busy gath-
ring up the coins from the display case to be locked in his

safe for the weekend. His hearing was impaired, and he failed to hear the buzzer. He only became aware of Everett when the young man set his briefcase on the counter with enough force to cause the glass case to vibrate. He straightened and looked down the counter in irritation. "I'm sorry, sir. I thought I'd locked that door. We're closed until Monday."

Everett unsnapped the lock on the briefcase and partially lifted the lid. "That's unfortunate," he said, "because I've inherited some rare coins I need to sell." He started to close the lid. "Napoleons."

The old man's eyes responded behind their magnified lenses. "Napoleons? They're very rare indeed." He moved a short distance toward Everett, to where a display tray had been set up under a high-intensity light. "I'll take a look at those. Mind you, there are a lot of counterfeit napoleons."

The proprietor of the store obviously expected Everett to bring the coins to the tray under the light, but Everett had no intention of altering his position. He knew from reports that the alarm bell was on the edge of the counter, directly beneath the lamp. "I can wait until Monday," he said flatly, and began to close the lid of his case.

"No, no," the old man protested. "For a napoleon I can keep my dinner waiting." He moved farther along the counter until he was directly in front of Everett. "If you'll give me a look, I'll tell you immediately if they're genuine or—"

Everett had whipped the knife from the briefcase and slashed the old man's throat before he'd finished the sentence. The man was dead before he hit the floor behind the counter. Everett opened the case and quickly began to assemble the rifle it contained.

Even though he worked with concentration, he heard the elevator doors open in the corridor; then he heard the footsteps of more than one person—he guessed two—on the ceramic tiles as they moved along the corridor. He stepped quickly to the door of the coin shop, opened it and pressed his eye to the slit. He was right—two men. They were moving in opposite directions from the middle of the corridor, where the elevators were located, trying doors as they went. The younger man was moving toward the coin shop. Everett immediately recognized the man going in the opposite direction as Commander Bannen. He closed the door soundlessly and stepped back so that it would conceal him when it was opened.

Sloane, he thought, would have to take care of Marshisky.

As for him, he'd have the satisfaction of taking care of Commander Bannen and his friend.

A smile spread across his thin lips.

The son, the grandfather and now the father—all three his!

EVERYTHING WAS HAPPENING so quickly, Dorothy was in a state of confusion. First Quinn had cried, "Everett!" and he and Alex had leaped from the limousine and dashed into an office building. Then Captain Montalvo, cursing, had stepped out into the street and slammed the door on her. She had watched him disappear into the crowd, the radio pressed against his mouth and concealed by his turning his body away from the equestrian patrolman.

She turned and stared through the rear window and saw the presidential limousine pull almost even with the patrolman, whose mount began to pace alongside the limousine as they made for the gallery entrance. He leaned down from his horse and spoke to the driver of the limousine, gesturing toward the taxi that blocked the painted curb meant for discharging passengers. The presidential limousine pulled over behind the taxi, several feet short of the red carpet that had been rolled out across the sidewalk. The curbside door of the limousine opened, and two men who looked like Secret Service climbed out. The two Secret Service men out-

side the gallery moved forward. Men dispersed in the crowd
also began to edge forward, among them Captain Montalvo. The patrolman's hand was resting casually on top of
the holster of his revolver. The traffic was now at a complete standstill, but he made no pretense of directing it. Instead, he kept his horse close to the limousine.

The Secret Service agents surrounded the presidential
limousine and appeared to be deliberately ignoring the patrolman. The rear door opened again, and a man with a remarkable resemblance to the president emerged, turned and
bent with his hand extended as if to help out the First Lady.

It was then the patrolman pulled his revolver.

As if the scene had been carefully choreographed, everyone responded immediately. A Secret Service man pushed
the president's stand-in back into the limousine. A second
agent leaped for the patrolman, grabbed the arm that held
the revolver and tried to yank him down from the horse.
Another sprang from his other side and wrapped his arms
around the patrolman's waist. The patrolman lost his revolver in the struggle but managed to retain his seat on the
horse. He hammered one Secret Service agent in the face
with his fist, tried to kick the other away and spurred the
excited horse into action.

At that moment a shot rang out. The patrolman lurched
forward in the saddle, clutching at the side of his neck.
Screams rose from the crowd as people began fleeing in all
directions. The patrolman managed to jam his fist into the
face of the Secret Service man still clinging to his waist.
Blood spurted from the man's nose, and he went down.

The horse was now moving at a gallop along the narrow
passageway left between the jammed up traffic and the
parked cars. Dorothy saw that the horse would pass directly by the limousine. She slid across the seat and quickly
threw open the door to block its path.

The horse reared with a panicked neigh.

The patrolman, weakened by the bullet that had lodged
in his throat, lost control and slid from the saddle to the
pavement.

The Secret Service agents were on him in an instant.

Captain Montalvo pushed through the crowd. "Is the son
of a bitch still alive?" he demanded.

"He's still alive, captain," one of the men assured him.
"And ours, thanks to this lady's quick thinking."

Captain Montalvo's dark eyes fixed on Dorothy for a
moment, then turned quickly away.

ALEX HAD the small-caliber revolver the commander's wife
had taken from her purse and given him the day before. He
held it tightly in his right hand as he tried the office doors
with his left. He had tried all but one door, and every one
had been locked. The last door had lettering that read Walter Cole, Rare Coins Bought and Sold. He glanced over his
shoulder at Quinn and saw that the commander was trying
the last door at his end of the corridor. Perhaps, he thought,
Everett had gone on up to the roof.

He reached for the handle of the door and was surprised
to discover that it turned in his hand. Crouching, he pushed
the door open with his foot, the revolver held in both hands.
His gaze took in the open briefcase on the counter with the
partially assembled rifle, and also the blood that was spattered across the glass display case.

"Here, Commander!" he shouted.

At that moment a shot was fired in the street, followed by
terrified screams.

As Alex took one step into the room, Quinn screamed,
"No, Alex!"

But the warning came too late.

Everett stepped around the edge of the door and grabbed
the hands clutching the revolver. He jerked Alex into the
room, kicked the door closed and slashed at him with a
knife.

Alex instinctively twisted his head to one side to avoid the blade. The point cut a thin line along his jaw. Both his hands, though still clutching the revolver, were held firmly in Everett's viselike grip. The operative drove them downward, and at the same time lifted his knee. There was a crunch of bone. Alex felt an explosion of pain. The revolver discharged, and one of the glass display cases shattered. Alex threw his shoulder against his opponent and at the same time tore his hands free and upward. The revolver dangled momentarily with his broken finger through the trigger, then sailed out of his hand and across the counter.

Everett had been caught off guard when he'd tried to knock the revolver from the yeoman's hand. His foot wasn't planted firmly when he was struck by Alex's shoulder, and he staggered backward, dragging Alex with him. A good six inches taller than Alex and more muscular and better trained at combat, Everett literally lifted him from his feet, then slashed out again with the knife. The yeoman grabbed his wrist, but not before the point of the blade cut into his side. Everett saw pain and fear in the yeoman's eyes and felt a flood of pleasure. Then his pleasure turned to surprise as the yeoman managed to force his knife hand back and away from his body and drive his knee upward into Everett's groin. He swung out, caught Alex at the side of the head and sent him into and over the counter. He leaped over the counter himself, not to finish off the yeoman but to reach the revolver.

Everett hadn't anticipated so much difficulty in killing Commander Bannen's young friend; he'd expected it to be easy, something to be performed with quick precision. It was the gun in the younger man's hand that he had wanted, because he hadn't had time to assemble his rifle. Alex's struggle had cost Everett precious time. He knew the commander would come charging through the door at any moment. As soon as he landed on the opposite side of the counter, Everett's eyes began their search for the revolver.

Stunned, Alex had landed on top of the body of the old opin dealer. The cuts in his side and along his jaw were creaming with pain. Bile rose in his throat at the sight of the old man with the slit throat. His vision was blurred, and his heart was racing. Clutching the counter, he struggled to his feet. He had heard Everett come over the counter behind him and expected at any moment to feel the knife drawn across his throat, leaving him like the old man. But when he turned he saw Everett rummaging through the debris on top of one of the desks.

Just as Everett located the gun, grabbed it and turned, Quinn burst through the door.

Everett had intended to shoot Alex first, but he spun now toward the commander.

Quinn's first shot caught the operative in the collarbone. Splintered bone and blood splattered across Everett's neck and over his shirtfront. The force sent him reeling backward. His responding shot went high, striking the wall above Quinn's head.

"Give it up, Everett!" Quinn shouted. "You've failed! Delta's failed!"

Everett was slumped against the window. His hands had fallen to his sides, but he continued to hold the revolver. He tried to move, teetered. His eyes sought Quinn's, his pupils dilating, unable to focus properly. "Can't fail!" he cried. "Can't!" Tears of pain and frustration were spilling down his cheeks. "What's it ... all been for if Delta fails? Chad, Iona, Emily, the admiral! Those people in Washington! Can't fail ... can't!"

Alex, too weak to stand, had slumped across the count-

Everett raised the revolver again.

Quinn's second bullet caught him in the chest.

Everett was thrown back against the windowpane. The glass shattered, and he pitched through.

AS QUINN HELPED ALEX out onto the sidewalk, Dorothy ran up to them.

"Oh, God, Quinn! When that man's body came crashing through the window I thought it was you!"

"I'm fine," he said evenly, "but we have to get Alex to a hospital."

"There's an ambulance on the way," she told them. Indeed, it had just turned into the block with its siren blaring.

Captain Montalvo disengaged himself from a group of men and approached them.

"Did they catch the others?" Quinn asked Dorothy.

"Yes, all of them," she told him. "And alive. Marshisk was shot, but he'll survive. They caught another man named Sloane and Captain Musolf."

Alex, who was supported by Quinn, said, "Then Delta truly failed, Commander? It's over?"

"It's truly over, son," Quinn assured him.

EPILOGUE

California

QUINN AND DOROTHY SAT on the ridge overlooking the valley.

It was nearing sunset, and the distant horizon was streaked with a palette of colors. The weather had turned cooler, and the first fires since summer were evidenced by the smoking chimneys of the houses in the valley.

Dorothy, who had worn only a sweater, huddled against Quinn for warmth. She felt totally at peace. "I love your valley," she said quietly.

"I'm glad," he told her. "I was afraid you'd find it boring after the excitement of Washington."

"I'm never bored with you," she assured him. "I never want to see Washington again. Or New York. Or Key West. I'm content here with you. If that's letting the world pass me oy, then let it." Since they had come to the ranch she had even refused to watch television or read a newspaper.

"I had a letter from Alex today," Quinn told her.

"How is he?"

"I invited him to spend his next leave with us," Quinn old her. "He accepted."

"Good. I like him. He reminds me of . . . of Chad," she said.

"Yes, me, too. He enclosed some newspaper clippings. Do you want to know about them?"

"Are they concerning Delta?"

"Yes. Of the six officers of Delta's leadership committee, Admiral Addison seemed the least likely to violate their vow of secrecy, yet he's been the first one to break. He identified the controller as—"

"Quinn, I don't want to know," Dorothy said, interrupting him. "I'm glad Admiral Addison broke. I'm glad hat ends Delta once and for all, but I don't want to know about it, or talk about it again. I want to put it all behind me and concentrate on us. Do you understand, darling?"

"I understand," he answered quietly. He put his arm around her and drew her into the protective curve of his body.

As he stared out over the peaceful valley, Quinn prayed hat it had truly ended. Still, he was realist enough to suspect that Delta might once again be resurrected by madmen determined to manipulate governments and rule the world.

Under God's heaven, nothing was permanent.

Dan Fortune is back—neck-deep in murder

MINNESOTA
Strip

Private investigator Dan Fortune is up against one of his grisliest cases ever! Hired to locate a missing boy who is determined to avenge the brutal murder of a Vietnamese refugee, Fortune finds himself deep in a nasty network of white slavery, narcotics, prostitution and...hired killers.

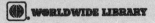

A gripping thriller
by the author of The Linz Testament

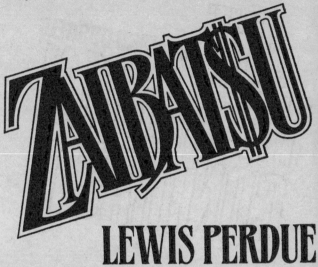

ZAIBATSU

LEWIS PERDUE

The world's most powerful bankers conspire to gain control of
the world's financial future. Only one man is prepared to stop
them, but he needs every ounce of cunning to stay alive...